BY CAMILLE BORDAS

The Material

How to Behave in a Crowd

Partie Commune

Les Treize Desserts

THE MATERIAL

THE MATERIAL

A NOVEL

CAMILLE BORDAS

RANDOM HOUSE

New York

Published in the United States by Random House, an imprint and division of Penguin Random House LLC, New York.

RANDOM HOUSE and the HOUSE colophon are registered trademarks of Penguin Random House LLC.

LIBRARY OF CONGRESS CATALOGING-IN-PUBLICATION DATA

NAMES: Bordas, Camille, author.
TITLE: The material: a novel / Camille Bordas.
DESCRIPTION: First Edition. | New York: Random House, 2024.
IDENTIFIERS: LCCN 2023038554 (print) | LCCN 2023038555 (ebook) | ISBN 9780593729847 (hardback) | ISBN 9780593729854 (ebook)
SUBJECTS: LCGFT: Humorous fiction. | Novels.
CLASSIFICATION: LCC PS3602.O678 M38 2024 (print) | LCC PS3602.O678 (ebook) | DDC 813/.6—dc23/eng/20231011
LC record available at lccn.loc.gov/2023038554
LC ebook record available at lccn.loc.gov/2023038555

Printed in the United States of America on acid-free paper

randomhousebooks.com

2 4 6 8 9 7 5 3 1

FIRST EDITION

Book design by Barbara M. Bachman

For
Adam Levin

THE
ENEMY OF
COMEDY

—

1

ON WEDNESDAYS, THREE OF THEM HAD TO PERFORM, IN TURN, A
four-to-six-minute routine that the whole class then proceeded to
rip apart, joke by joke, beat by beat, until there wasn't anything left
and the budding comedians went home to consider other possible
career paths. After searching the internet for what other jobs existed, though, after twenty minutes of this, they already had a joke
about it begging to come out, a joke they thought would kill next time
they went up for critique, one that played on how unfunny they'd
been that last time, how they'd considered retraining, going into
plumbing or whatever, counseling, but then realized how bad they
would be at that, too (joke-joke-joke), and it would all be so meta, so
self-deprecating, no one would have a choice but to laugh and laugh,
and just like that, they were at it again—writing.

Except, of course, next workshop, they realized everyone else had
gone for it as well, the modest bit, the apology, and their own critique
of it was merciless: "It's been a bit overdone," they said, "this 'I'm
only good at telling jokes' stuff."

School was supposed to widen your horizons, leave you with the
feeling that everything was yet to be invented, or reinvented, but
after a semester in the comedy program most of the students felt the
opposite, that jokes were in limited supply, and that they weren't
finding the ones that were left fast enough.

Their teachers could sympathize. Or at least Dorothy could. She
remembered her fear at their age, whenever she wrote a joke, that
somebody else was writing the exact same one (or the same one but
better, or the same one but worse—all options equally bad) and would

tell it to an audience before hers was stage-ready. She had pictured a race back then: comedians, scribbled-on napkins and Xerox-warm paper sheets in hand, rushing to deliver their lines to a faceless man who collected all jokes and would soon whistle the end of the hunt. On good days, that fear of the whistle had kept Dorothy up and writing. On bad ones, it had turned into fantasy—if only that whistle existed, she'd thought, if only someone could blow it now, what a relief it would be, to hear that it was all over, that she could stop trying.

"Were they funny in their application tapes?" Ben Kruger asked her, about their current students.

Kruger had only started teaching in the Stand-Up MFA three months earlier. He wasn't buying the students' despair. He believed they were hazing him, that they were being deliberately unfunny to test his commitment as a mentor. It was an egotistical view—no young comedian would ever risk looking bad in front of another, especially one as famous as Kruger—but Kruger had spent more time talking to Hollywood people than comedians lately, and his paranoia was reaching new levels.

"Of course they were funny," Dorothy said, trying to ignore the question's subtext, Kruger's implication that perhaps she and Ashbee were unable to recognize a good bit, raw talent, promising young people.

"So, what," Kruger said, "they just start sucking when we admit them? They just come here and suck for a year?"

"They don't suck. Dan is good. Olivia."

"They don't suck for *a year*," Ashbee said. He'd just joined them in the conference room.

"When do they become good again?"

"End of their first semester," Ashbee explained, like it was science. "Right around now, in fact. Soon they'll start doing their impressions of us, and that will be rock bottom for them. You'll see. They get good again after that."

"Impressions?"

"It's pretty embarrassing."

"But you have to laugh a little," Dorothy said. "Even when it's not funny, you have to laugh at at least *one* thing when someone does an impression of you."

"I don't laugh," Ashbee said. "You can't start laughing when it's not funny. That's the worst thing you can do to a young comedian."

The job of teaching comedy, Ashbee often said, consisted almost exclusively in sitting there, not laughing, while your students tried something. It could be painful, for all parties involved, but that was how they learned—it was in your silence that they eventually heard something click.

"Well, I always laugh a little when they do me," Dorothy said. "Maybe it's a woman thing."

The room was filling up, a particularly well-attended faculty meeting, Ashbee noted. He remembered that pre-winter-break meetings tended to be, because of the cookies. The Victorianists always made cookies before Christmas.

The Stand-Up MFA was attached to the English Department, which many English professors resented (comedians belonged in Performing Arts, if they belonged anywhere at all in academia, was the thought), but the resentment was civil. Ashbee liked that about academics, that it never went beyond whispers in the hallways, or petitions no one read.

"Should we make an announcement about the show tonight?" Kruger asked.

Their students were performing that evening in a traditional end-of-year battle against the Second City improv troupe.

"No one wants to go to that," Dorothy said.

Theodore Sword, the current English Department chair, took his seat at the conference table and thanked everyone for coming.

"I know we're all tired," he said, "and some of you have class in an hour, so I will keep this brief."

Kruger, on his notepad, jotted down the words "I'll be brief: Part One, Section A, Subsection 1." He was toying with the idea of a bit about academics, how convoluted they could make the simplest proposition. He crossed out the whole thing. "I'll be brief," he wrote on the next line. "I'll be brief for three reasons—" and felt more satisfied with that structure.

"I have news to share," Sword said, for real this time, not under Kruger's pen.

No one had expected news. It was the last week of the semester. Last-week meetings were for self-congratulation and snacks.

"I have news to share regarding Manny Reinhardt."

Kruger stopped doodling. He looked at Dorothy, who looked at Ashbee. They hadn't been warned that the meeting would be about Manny. For weeks, Manny had been scheduled to be their visiting professor of comedy in the spring, but a student association had raised concerns about the hire, and last Ashbee had heard from Sword, it was time to find a replacement.

"What about him?" someone asked, from Rhetoric. "Did he break anyone else's nose?"

"There's borderline behavior with women now, too," said someone from Theory. "I read about it last night."

The distinguished professor of medieval studies said she wasn't at all surprised.

"You could always hear it in his jokes," she said. "The guy hates women."

The comedians remained silent. It bothered Dorothy, though, that "just listen to his jokes" comment. As if Manny had only ever written about women. To reduce Manny's all-encompassing misanthropy to simple misogyny was dishonest, Dorothy thought, or proof that even an overeducated English scholar could fall victim to partial readings, scanning someone's work for the lines that fed their theory while ignoring those that questioned it. And how had the papers come to discuss Manny's treatment of women? It had all started with Manny punching a guy at the Comic Strip, Thanksgiving weekend. The guy—an up-and-coming comedian—hadn't pressed charges, but he'd posted photos online of his broken nose and swollen eye, gaining tens of thousands of followers in the process. He'd been honest, too, about having looked for it (he'd called Manny many names), and for a few days, it had seemed like the internet would sort it out, dividing itself between "boys will be boys" and "nothing ever justifies violence" factions until everyone got tired. But in the last week, bizarre stories had started to emerge. Three women had come forward with accusations of emotional misconduct. It appeared that Manny had slept with each of them at some point, once and only once, proposed marriage that same night, and never called again.

"I'm glad he won't be coming here," the person from Theory said. "My kids come do their homework in the teachers' lounge sometimes."

"Wait, what? Reinhardt's a pedophile now?" Vivian Reeve said, from Creative Writing.

Though Ashbee and Dorothy were relieved to hear someone speak up for Manny, they wished it hadn't come from Creative Writing. Everyone on the Fiction faculty was trying a little too hard to befriend them, probably hoping for some TV connections. Vivian Reeve had cornered Kruger at his first department party back in September, to flatter him, to share with him her idea that comedians were to the twenty-first century what novelists had been to the twentieth, the artists that the public turned to for enlightenment, for comfort and understanding. They were the new social critics. More Americans had streamed Kruger's special the week it had come out on Netflix than would read a novel that year, she'd told him, numbers that Kruger had been flattered by, but unable to verify.

"The man is fifty-four," the distinguished professor said. "All these women he slept with were, like, twenty-five. Sound like children to me."

"He's not on trial for being *gross*," Vivian Reeve said.

"He's not on trial at all," Sword reminded everyone. "So let's go back to the question of his hire."

"What hire?" one of the Victorianists asked. "There's no hire. We can't hire a visiting creep."

Sword informed her and everyone else in attendance that in spite of undergraduate agitation, in spite of the Comedy Strip altercation and the . . . persistent marriage proposals, the university had confirmed Manny Reinhardt's hire.

"The paperwork is in. Mr. Reinhardt signed it this morning."

Kruger glanced at Ashbee and Dorothy. They were beaming. He tried to force a smile. Kruger hadn't shared this with them, but he'd been pleased with Manny's fall from grace. Not that he disliked the guy (the guy was hilarious), but the idea of Reinhardt's forced retirement didn't sound half-bad. More room for Kruger, Kruger thought. He believed it worked that way, that getting the status and respect you deserved was only a matter of room being made for them by people who'd recently lost both. Also, maybe he *did* dislike Manny a little. He was pretty sure Manny disliked *him*. Years ago, when asked in an interview who the most interesting young comedians were, Manny hadn't named Kruger, an omission Kruger had interpreted as intentional, a direct insult.

Sword wasn't able to say anything for a while. Whose decision was this? his colleagues asked. What kind of PR nightmare was the administration devising for itself? Hiring a man with a history of violence? Of emotional misconduct? Even just for a semester? This would be national news, the professors said, and they seemed to understand what that meant as they said it, their names possibly printed in *The New York Times,* potential email invitations to write an op-ed, and not just for *The Chronicle of Higher Education.*

"Look, I don't like this any more than you do," Sword managed to say once the room had started recycling arguments (except he did, he did like it, he was a big fan of Manny Reinhardt's and couldn't wait to meet him). "But my hands are tied. The decision is coming from way up."

"Whose decision is it exactly?"

"It's coming from way up," Sword repeated. "And the dean signed on already. It's a done deal."

These were thuggish methods, half of the room agreed. Unacceptable. What next? What next if the department gave in to upper administration thugs? Should they simply let them decide whom to hire from now on? Let them handle the curricula, the committees? Place their own friends in teaching positions to give them honorable front jobs? This notion of a professor mafia gave Ashbee the ghost of an idea for a bit: wise guys given front jobs in academia rather than on construction sites, what that would look like. The cast of *The Sopranos* teaching linguistics. Paulie Walnuts misunderstanding Virginia Woolf. Or better yet, actually, funnier, Paulie Walnuts *relating* to Virginia Woolf, feeling her struggles deeply. Ashbee waved away the image as quickly as it came. He'd vowed never to let his teaching life encroach upon his comedian life, to not turn into one of those people in Creative Writing who could only write campus novels once they became teachers. It wasn't easy, but he'd held himself to it. As the founder of Stand-Up as an academic discipline (the Chicago MFA had been the first of its kind), Ashbee could've been first on many jokes to be made about the job, but he'd refrained. Now that comedy programs had opened all over the country, teaching comedians went for it, used their students as material, and used their colleagues, too—the campus setting in general. They made fun of the concept onstage, the concept of teaching comedy, teaching people how to be funny. They all presented it as an impossible task and threw their own students under the bus as proof, quoting their worst jokes, all the while cashing the university's biweekly checks. Ashbee believed that using your students as comedy fodder was an abuse of power, but he'd come to understand that the kids actually sought it, the onstage nod. Better to be made fun of by a famous comedian than never mentioned at all. He looked forward to retirement.

Sword glanced at his watch and then through the window, down all nine floors to the L train platform he would later stand on himself, when it was time to go home. Everything was gray, the platform, the rails, the buildings and the air around them, everything appeared crusted in salt post-blizzard, as if salt itself had fallen from the clouds, and not snow. This was Chicago to him, this texture. He was relieved whenever the city went back to it. First signs of winter made Lydia melancholy, though, more than usual, and he felt like a bad husband for finding beauty in the sky's color, that finger-blended pencil. He'd just taught his last class of the semester. After weeks of sad stories and black-and-white films, he'd wanted to end his Epiphany seminar on a light note, discuss romantic comedies, make fun of all the running involved in romantic epiphanies. The students hadn't gotten it. When they realized they loved someone, they'd said (and they'd said this as if it happened to them once a month), they could just text them.

Sword heard a colleague say the word "unbearable" and remembered at once where he was—not on the L platform yet, not yet home, not only in a department meeting but running it. He made accidental eye contact with Dorothy as he turned his gaze back to the room, and wondered if he should hold it (at the risk of coming off as predatory) or break it immediately (at the risk of coming off as the scared-of-women type). Dorothy broke it first to look down at her nails. She'd been thinking about painting them lately. Something she'd never done before. Would it be weird to start in her late forties? she wondered. Would it look desperate? She hadn't been onstage in years, but she had a new special in preproduction, and she wondered about presentation, how she should present herself now, whether to stick to what she'd done her whole career (her appearance and her sex an afterthought, things that, in an ideal world, would go unnoticed, so focused would the audience be on the strength of her writing) or change it up to better fit the times, hop onstage all made up and bare-legged. She hated her legs. Not that there was anything wrong with them, really, but who needed to see them?

The meeting ended and she stayed behind in the conference room with Kruger and Ashbee. One of them should contact Manny, they decided, make him feel welcome.

"When's the last time you heard from him?" Dorothy asked Ashbee.

Ashbee had been the one to send Manny the invitation to teach with them for a semester. He hadn't expected him to agree—this was an invitation Manny had declined every fall since the program had started. Ashbee usually dealt with Manny's agent, but Manny had responded directly this time. He'd just taped a new special, and he wouldn't be touring during the months Ashbee mentioned: the stars were aligning, for once, and he'd be delighted to give teaching a try. "These kids are my son's age," Manny had also written. "Maybe this will help me understand his generation better." He'd written to Ashbee as if Ashbee had been part of his life the last thirty years. Ashbee barely even knew Manny had a son. Hadn't really spent any time with Manny since the nineties, and even then, it had been somewhat forced, circumstantial, only brought about by the sudden shrinking of New York's comedy scene, all those clubs closing one after the other, Ashbee and Manny two of a handful of guys to hold on for dear life, to fight for time on the remaining stages. They were often the last ones to leave a club back then—Manny because he loved drinking, Ashbee because he needed to tell himself he'd squeezed out the night's every possibility, met everyone there was to meet. They hadn't liked each other much.

"We exchanged a few emails back in September," Ashbee told Dorothy. "Practical stuff about the program."

"And since the . . . accusations?" Dorothy said.

She wasn't sure what to call what was happening to Manny. She thought punching someone was worse than asking women to marry you, but no one seemed to care about the punching anymore. What people seemed to find important was whether Manny had offered marriage before or after he'd had sex with the women. Dorothy couldn't quite see what difference that made.

"Since the accusations, we haven't spoken," Ashbee said.

Dorothy looked at Kruger.

"You?" she said. "You talked to him lately?"

Kruger had vastly exaggerated his connection to Manny. They shared an agent, and had done a charity event in Los Angeles together the previous year, but that was about it. The only words they'd exchanged that night had concerned the food in the greenroom. Three months ago, he'd heard Manny on a podcast poking fun at comedians who tried to make it as serious actors, and because the movie Kruger had shot with Meryl Streep was about to come out, he'd taken it as another jab at him specifically.

"We haven't been in touch," Kruger said. "I don't think I should be the one to call him anyway."

"Why not?"

Kruger thought of his father then, who hadn't answered or returned his calls the last couple of days. He was probably just tired, Kruger thought. The nursing home would've told him by now if something had happened.

"I don't think he likes me very much," he said, about Manny. "Plus, I'm new to the program. It's probably better if one of you walks him through everything."

It was enough of an excuse, but Kruger added more, for extra protection. He was teaching in just a bit. He had a phone call scheduled with his agent after that, and then the battle against Second City tonight.

"Nothing says we have to call him *today,*" Ashbee said.

"Really, I think it's better if Dorothy calls him," Kruger said.

"Why's that?" Dorothy asked.

Kruger wondered which she would be least offended by: if he called her a woman, or if he called her a girl.

"Because you're a girl," he said.

Dorothy raised an eyebrow. She knew what he meant, of course.

"Ben's right," Ashbee said. "It's stronger if it comes from you. He'll know you're not one of the crazy ones, always siding with the women no matter what. And you can reassure him that our female students aren't either."

"I don't know what our female students think," Dorothy said.

She'd heard Olivia talking about it with Artie, though, before their improv class on Monday. How the accusations against Manny were counterproductive because they made women look weak, and calculating, and whiny. Who cared whether Manny proposed or not? Olivia had asked Artie. What did it matter whether he'd talked about marriage before or after sex? People said that if he'd mentioned it *before,* then he'd purposely misled the girl. But then what did it say about the girl? That she'd only fucked a celebrity she wasn't attracted to because she pictured financial security on the other side of it? Was *that* a good reason to sleep with someone? This hadn't been Dorothy's conversation to step into, and so she hadn't, but she'd thought that Olivia was forgetting to consider the small possibility that all these women had been in love with Manny (people did that sometimes, fall in love instantly), that they'd believed it was mutual and had been hurt when they'd realized Manny would never call. Not that being heartbroken gave you any right to talk to the press, but it did make Dorothy feel for the women. When Manny had told her, almost thirty years earlier (*after* they'd had sex), that maybe they should get married, she'd known to laugh in his face, but still. There'd been a part of her that hoped he wasn't kidding.

"I guess I'll give him a call," she told Kruger and Ashbee, not looking at either.

2

ARTIE WAS UP FOR WORKSHOP TODAY, AND CLASS WAS IN AN HOUR. HE rehearsed his bit one more time in front of the mirror, something his roommates made fun of him for. Rehearsing in front of the mirror was for actors, according to them, not comedians. It was for vain people. A good comedian was the opposite of vain, they said (though none of them seemed to know what the word for that was). Artie argued that the best comedians were those who had total control over their slightest expressions, complete self-awareness, and how did one get to complete self-awareness without observing oneself a little bit too closely for a while, without a touch of vanity?

"That's the whole trick," his roommates had said. "To have one and not the other."

"I know what you're thinking," Artie said to his own face in the mirror. He thought it was a great way to open, acknowledging the audience's doubts. "You're thinking, *This guy is too good-looking to be funny*."

Which was something he'd heard countless times.

"It wasn't always like this."

Part of Artie's four minutes today involved showing his classmates a blown-up photo of his teenage face (not the worst photo of him that existed, but a close contender) and pointing at different "problematic" areas with a laser pen. The problematic areas were zits and crooked teeth, that kind of thing. Nothing crazy, nothing out of the ordinary. An unfortunate haircut. He'd been a bit fat, too, at the time, which wasn't something anyone could believe when they saw him today, at twenty-four years old. He thought it would be funny, adopting a cold professor persona, presenting on his own face as if it were the map of an old battlefield, going over the forces at work, the opposing factions.

One of his roommates knocked on the bathroom door.

"Your mom's on the phone," he said.

"I'm busy."

"She says it's important."

He pushed the door open and handed Artie the phone. Why did they even have a landline? Who was paying for this? On his way out, his roommate glanced at Artie's teenage photo, the blown-up face printed on cardboard, and didn't even smile at it.

"Mom," Artie said into the phone. "It's Wednesday. I'm rehearsing."

"I know, sweetheart, but Mickey's missing."

"He's not missing. He's probably at Ethel's."

"Have you heard from him?"

Wouldn't he have told her first thing if he'd heard from his brother? Was there a joke to be made about this? Either to his mom, right now, or in general, later and for an audience, about how people didn't think before they spoke?

"Mickey's a grown man," Artie said. "He'll show up in a couple of days."

"That's not the definition of a grown man," his mother said. " 'Shows up eventually.' "

Wasn't it, though? As opposed to "runs away from responsibility and severs all ties to start over elsewhere, never to be heard from again"? Didn't being an adult mean pushing away that fantasy eighty times a day and judging those who gave in to it?

"How's Dad doing?" Artie said.

"Why are you asking about Dad now?"

Artie heard his father clear his throat in the background. You always thought he was going to say something, he cleared his throat so much, but Artie couldn't remember him speaking the last few times he'd visited.

"Well, his son is missing," Artie said. "I thought I'd ask how he's taking it."

"Your father is fine. And even if he wasn't, you think I would know? You think he would *tell* me? Have you met the man? You think that today, at fifty-six years old, your father is going to start expressing complex emotions?"

"Not everything needs to be said," Artie said. "You can get a sense of how people are doing by just looking at them."

"He looks the same as always."

Artie heard his father clear his throat again.

"Is he wearing the black suit or the gray?"

"Exactly," his mother said, but then caught herself right away. "You're one to make fun. You always wear the same hoodie yourself. And pants, and shoes. I bet your underwear is all the same, too."

"Mom."

"You and your father, from the same cloth. A single outfit for all occasions, and incapable of expressing your feelings."

"I'm in the *trade* of expressing my feelings," Artie said.

"You only tell jokes."

"I tell stories."

"You *interrupt* stories, is what you do. You stop when you get to the good punch line."

"That's the concept," Artie said. "That's the concept of comedy."

"I know, sweetheart. I like it. I like laughing. I'm just saying, the things you say onstage, they're not stories. They're the funny bits from larger stories. You cut your stories in a way that you never go into what's moving about them, so I'd argue you actually do the *opposite* of expressing your feelings. You *run away* from feelings."

"That's very insightful, Mom. Thank you for your critique."

"It's not a critique. If you dove into your feelings onstage, you wouldn't be funny. Feelings aren't funny."

"Okay. I need to get ready now."

"Offstage, of course, you can tell me anything."

"I know."

Artie also knew that he couldn't end the conversation on an *I know,* how dismissive *I knows* were.

"Mickey's fine, Mom," he said. "Probably at Ethel's."

"I don't like that he still sees her. She's too old for him."

"That's a very retrograde thing to say."

"Do you think it's my fault?"

"What? That Mickey's attracted to older women?"

"That he's an addict? I drank so much when I was pregnant with him. I was still bleeding like usual, I didn't know I was pregnant before month four."

Artie'd heard the whole guilt shtick before, its various built-in excuses. It wasn't the first time Mickey had gone missing. Their mother using the word "addict," however, was a recent development. He didn't like it. Maybe it was the word itself, though, not her saying it. "Addict" made his brother sound weak, or like he was in a perfume commercial—eyes half-closed in some supermodel's wake, unable to resist the smell coming off her dramatic neck. That's what the word was for now. Ads. The world of commerce wanted you addicted to snacks, to apps, to some new show on TV. "Your New Addiction Is Here!"—that's how commercials went now. People in high places wanted you addicted at all times, addicted and obsessed—another word they'd managed to make the public believe had positive connotations. The product didn't matter—in fact, the need for it disappeared the minute there was no supply left, proof that no one had ever been addicted to it in the first place. What had to be kept constant was the flow of trash to be passively ingested. But Mickey needed heroin. Not just any substance. When heroin was gone, heroin had to be found. It could not be replaced by a spin-off, or the new fragrance by Yves Saint Laurent.

Artie thought it was like rape—the word "rape." How "rape" used to mean someone being dragged into an alley by a stranger, gagged, beaten up, savagely penetrated, and left for dead behind a trash can. How "rape" had now come to encompass any sexual act performed without obtaining verbal consent. He was okay with that, in principle: words taking on larger meanings, larger responsibilities over time—language was a living entity, it adapted to its speakers. But then it seemed to him that when that happened, other words had to step in to fill the vacuum left by the bigger word's promotion. He felt there should be a word for what "rape" used to mean. He wondered how women who had been left for dead in alleys felt about it. The new meaning.

"Hello? Am I boring you?"

"No, Mom, of course not. I was just thinking."

"Thinking about what?"

"Thinking about rape."

"Jesus, what is wrong with you?"

"About the *word* 'rape.'"

"Don't even think about using that word onstage. You can't make fun of rape."

"Who said I wanted to?"

"You don't think about anything unless it's for a bit."

"I think about Mickey pretty often, and I've never mentioned him onstage."

Artie's mother thought about it for a second.

"That's because addiction isn't funny," she said. "It isn't funny at all."

"Neither is rape," Artie said.

"Forget about it. Just don't ever say the word. Only women comedians can use it onstage. Women comedians who have been raped themselves."

"Make me a list, okay?" Artie said. "A list of what I can and cannot talk about onstage. That way we don't have to keep having these conversations."

"That's a great idea. I'll put it in an email."

About three more minutes were devoted to saying goodbye. Artie promised his mother he'd call Ethel, see if she'd heard from Mickey, and after hanging up with her, he took his cellphone out of his pocket, thinking he would do so right away. Olivia had tried to call him, though, while his phone was on silent, and his priorities were instantly rearranged.

3

ARTIE COULDN'T HAVE KNOWN IT, BUT THERE WAS NOTHING PERSONAL there: Olivia had tried to call everybody. Everybody she knew in the area who owned a car. Her own car was in the shop, and she needed someone to take her to O'Hare later to pick up her sister. Her sister (her twin) didn't get into cabs or onto subway trains. She'd had bad experiences in both. Olivia had told her that Chicago was different, because the trains there were mostly aboveground, but Sally had asked how much time she'd have to be underground, total, between O'Hare and Jackson, where Olivia could meet her after workshop, and the truth was, more than half the trip. Sally wouldn't do it. She would just wait at the airport for an extra hour for Olivia to be done with workshop and come pick her up.

"Your sister sounds complicated," Johanna said. "What's her favorite movie?"

"You'll ask her yourself. She's coming to the show tonight."

"I can't wait to meet her. Are you, like, *identical* identical?"

"She's a bit taller and fatter," Olivia said. "Never took up smoking is why."

"Same voice?"

"Similar. We laugh the same."

"Same taste in men?"

"We laugh at the same ones."

"First period on the same day?"

"Quit it, Jo. I just want to have a nice old coffee time with my friend before workshop. You think you can do that?"

"What else am I doing? Aren't I drinking coffee across from you? In this beautiful diner we patronize every Wednesday?"

"You're digging for jokes. I don't want to be funny right now. I'm exhausted. Making arrangements for Sally is exhausting."

"Do you think she feels the same about you?"

Jo never quit. The more frustrated you got with her, the longer she went. Her role model was Andy Kaufman—who she was convinced was still alive. In the diner, between loud sips of her coffee, she asked Olivia all the questions about twins that came to mind. She asked some of them twice. Olivia humored her in the end, because Jo was up for workshop in an hour, and you had to respect the way performers warmed up. Neither of them was a huge fan of Kruger's work, but they respected his opinion, how he never sugarcoated anything in class. They wanted their act to be undeniable, sure, but perhaps more important than that was being told when it wasn't. They could tell that Kruger wasn't impressed with their group overall. He'd smiled a few times so far, but mostly he winced during workshop, and the goal had almost become not to make him laugh so much as to get him, as you told your jokes, to a relaxed and neutral position, face-wise. "If he could just look bored and not *in pain,*" Artie had said a few weeks back. "If he could only yawn."

"I hope Artie goes up before me," Jo said when she ran out of questions to ask about twins.

"He's not that bad," Olivia said.

"He tries too hard. Anyone who means so well . . . the world spits them out first."

"Give him some time. It takes a while to stop giving a fuck and really be yourself."

Jo raised an eyebrow. She decided to let the "be yourself" thing fly.

"Did you guys sleep together or what?" she asked.

"I still haven't fucked anyone in the city of Chicago," Olivia said. "Chicago virgin."

"You haven't fucked in four months?"

"I went home for Thanksgiving."

"Ah," Jo remembered. "Right. I was sick that whole weekend. I forgot to even miss you."

"There's a guy there."

"Well, *ob*viously there's a guy there. A guy you sleep with."

"On occasion."

"On national holidays."

It was curious what Jo and Olivia knew and didn't know about each other yet. They'd met four months before (orientation day) and had quickly become inseparable, but still, it was impossible to go over everything that had made you who you were in just a few weeks, and there was a lot of ground left to cover (previous boyfriends, relationship to hometown), whole territories they had been reluctant to visit so far. For instance: Sally. You'd think Olivia would've been talking about her sister nonstop (as some twins tended to do, as a way to talk about themselves without seeming like they were), but she'd only just mentioned that she and Sally were identical twins, and she'd only done so because Sally was visiting and the truth was going to come out anyway. Before that, when Jo or others had asked about siblings, Olivia had merely said, "Yes, one sister, younger"—even though Sally was only younger by a pop-song length.

"Thanksgiving was like two minutes ago," Jo said. "Why does your sister want to visit again so soon?"

"She wasn't home for Thanksgiving," Olivia explained. "She and my mother don't speak."

"Why not?"

"Because our stepfather molested Sally when she was a kid and my mother took a little too long to believe her."

"Is this a joke?" Jo asked, though she knew that wasn't the kind of thing Olivia went for. "Shit," she said. "That's intense."

Olivia regretted mentioning it. With both hands, she pulled her coffee mug closer to the edge of the table and leaned forward, staring directly over it for a minute, at her own reflection in the black liquid. Then she poured in a thimble of creamer and watched her face dissolve on the surface, after which she took on a project, through creamer addition, of turning her black coffee the exact diner-beige color of the cup it was in.

"It's fine," she told Jo. "I just need to pick her up at the airport, is all. She doesn't do cabs and subways."

"Of course."

Of course? Olivia thought, adding two drops of creamer and stirring. Why "of course"? Did having been molested as a child mean you couldn't do anything on your own in adulthood? That you would forever be afraid of everything and everyone? It was horrible of her, she knew that, but Olivia often thought that Sally should've gotten over it by now—not forgiven or forgotten, but set the events aside somewhere deep in her brain, behind a bolted door to be opened only in case of absolute emergency.

"Maybe you could rent a car," Jo said.

"I'm kind of broke these days."

"Maybe she could pay for it?"

"She's visiting. You're supposed to pay for everything when someone visits."

"I think it's the other way around. I think the visitor's supposed to pay for things, because you're putting them up."

"No, you're supposed to pay. Because they're making the effort."

And Sally was making a big effort, leaving her routine for three days, her safe little house with all the alarms and her safe little town with the country's lowest number of assaults per capita. To spend two whole nights in Chicago. Where Olivia had seen a homeless guy's dick just this morning, and where the only friends she'd made so far were the kind who got a kick out of making people uncomfortable. It was Sally who'd insisted, though. She'd only ever seen Olivia perform twice, at high school talent shows, and was under the impression that getting into the Stand-Up MFA meant that Olivia's career had accelerated, when really the program felt more like a pause so far, time to stare at your material one last time before you threw it all away to start over from scratch. They'd all lost confidence by now. Their whole class. They were halfway through their degree and hated everything they'd ever written. Yet they were supposed to go onstage tonight, get humiliated by Second City.

"Is your sister cool with molestation jokes?" Jo asked.

"You don't have any molestation jokes."

"Dan loves that kind of shit. Maybe one will slip out tonight. Maybe we should warn him."

"If it's funny, she'll laugh. She has a good sense of humor."

"Dan's funny. It's a shame it's the only thing to say about him, really, but he's funny."

"Then she'll laugh."

Olivia's phone rang—Artie, calling her back. He would be happy to drive her to the airport, he said. He would drive to school instead of taking the L, and they could leave right after workshop. Olivia said he was the best, and that she owed him one.

"You don't owe him shit," Jo said after Olivia hung up. "You're giving his whole life meaning right now. I'm not even sure he *has* a car. He might be buying a car this very minute, just so he can be of service to you."

"Artie's crush on me has been vastly exaggerated," Olivia said.

"Does he know you guys are picking up your identical twin? His head is going to explode."

"I think I just said my sister. Didn't I?"

"His head's going to explode."

Jo said she shouldn't say anything and film Artie's reaction at O'Hare. Olivia agreed, but only so they would stop talking about Artie. She made the mistake after that of drinking from the coffee whose color she'd been adjusting this whole time, and the pain in her stomach was immediate.

"Why do we keep coming here?" she said. "Why do we do this to ourselves?"

"Because everyone is already making fun of the Starbucks crowd, and the Dunkin' crowd, and the high-end coffee shops crowd. We need to find new kinds of people."

"We never talk to anyone here."

"We're soaking in the atmosphere."

"We're soaking in stale, warmed-up water. We're ruining our digestive systems."

"I feel like Andy would like this place," Jo said. "I'm sure he's in a diner right now. Not having coffee, but maybe ice cream. Or just a glass of milk."

Jo had a clear idea what Andy Kaufman would look like now, in his seventies. She paid a lot of attention to men in that age group. She'd watched a hundred times the clip in which Andy brings his parents to be interviewed with him on Letterman, and she'd analyzed his father's features closely. She was aware that some people took her conviction that Andy Kaufman was alive as an act in itself, assumed that she was faking her certainty, but she truly wasn't, and her biggest fears were (1) failing to recognize Andy Kaufman if she ever met him on the street, and (2) dying before Andy Kaufman came out of his faked-death bit and missing the punch line.

She was annoyed by people who believed Andy was alive and tried to track him down, though, who, if they found him, would destroy Andy's bit before it was ready to land. If she ever met him by chance, Jo often fantasized, if Andy worked at a roadside diner she ended up at, she wouldn't say anything to break the spell, stupid things like "I love your work" or "Tank you vedy much" when he brought her apple pie. She'd just play along, ask Andy if he liked the area, what his favorite item on the menu was. Maybe, when he'd say, "I'll refill your coffee right away," she'd answer, "Please take your time, I am very patient," but that would be it, that would be the only hint she gave that she recognized him and respected the long joke he was setting up.

"Andy Kaufman is dead," Olivia said. "And if he isn't, then he's an asshole for letting his parents believe that he died."

"Maybe his parents were in on it. They seemed pretty cool. Like, very encouraging and loving. They went along with his stuff."

"No mother would go along with *that*."

Jo knew that Olivia was right, that Andy hadn't told his parents. She tried not to think about it, to keep her focus on the joke he was playing.

"And what if he *is* a dick?" she said. "Who cares? Dicks are every-where. You're the first to defend people like Reinhardt."

"All Reinhardt did was sleep with young women who kind of re-gretted it afterward," Olivia said. "That's ninety percent of my sex life. Regret."

"He broke Lipschitz's nose, too," Jo said.

"No one cares about Lipschitz. The guy deserved it. If no woman had said anything about fucking Reinhardt and having their feelings hurt, the Lipschitz incident would be closed already."

"Why would he propose *marriage,* though?"

"I guess he's a sap?" Olivia said. "Last I checked, it wasn't a crime."

"You shouldn't have a problem with Andy hurting his parents' feelings then. That's not a crime either."

Olivia said that if Andy Kaufman had faked his own death, he'd done more than hurt his parents' feelings.

"He ruined their *lives,*" she said.

"I thought that what mattered to you was the work."

"It is. I'm able to laugh at misogynist jokes even though I'm sitting on a tampon right now. It's the writing of the joke that matters. I have yet to hear Kaufman's comeback."

"So, you're defending the rights of artists to be dicks, but only if you like their work."

"I'm saying the bigger a dick an artist is, the more I have to like his work. If I am to overlook the dick part."

"You're saying there's a scale. A graph: x-axis, y-axis."

"Artists have a right to be dicks, but not bigger dicks than you would allow people in other professions to be. You're a sleazeball? Fine, my dermatologist is a sleazeball. I still go to him. He's good with skin. Sleazeball gets a pass in this context. But you fake your own death? That's extreme. I wouldn't trust that person with anything."

"Artists have to experiment," Jo said. "They have to go further than regular people."

Olivia hated this kind of talk.

"See, I hate this kind of talk," she said. "Artists *are* regular people.

There's no separate penal code for sculptors or whatever. They shouldn't have to be examples, but they shouldn't get to play the artist card to get off the hook either. Like, if our neighbor drives drunk, he's the scum of the earth for endangering our children, but we think it's normal for movie stars to get a DUI once in a while because, what, their lives are so hard?"

"I see your point."

"We accept that writers leave their families because little kids ruin their focus . . . but how is it that truckers manage? Brain surgeons? They don't need as much space for their thoughts?"

"What did your stepfather do for a living, by the way?" Jo knew Olivia had never met her real father. "Is he in jail now? How long was he with your mother?"

"And all this stuff about comedians killing themselves in such high numbers because they're so *sensitive*, because they *feel everything so strongly* . . . last I checked, dentists were still killing themselves more than us, and construction workers had the leading suicide rate by profession. Does that mean they're the better artists? That they should be the ones onstage instead of us?"

"Seriously. What did your stepfather do?"

"Who cares what he does?"

"He still works?"

"Yes. He's a forester."

"He molested a child and he's still allowed around people?"

"It's not the kind of forest where people go," Olivia said. "And Sally never pressed charges."

"Can't you press charges for her?"

"Can we go back to talking about Andy?"

They didn't go back to Andy. Workshop was upon them. It was a ten-minute walk to the classroom building, and Olivia would want to be early to smoke one in front. They left the diner and walked in silence for a block. Jo wasn't quite sure how to deal with the information that Olivia's sister had been molested. It seemed Olivia didn't want to talk about it, but still. It was a big thing to blurt out and then run away from. The question was, of course, had the stepfather molested Olivia too? Was Jo supposed to ask?

"It really sucks about your sister," she ended up saying, in between two screeches of the L.

Olivia regretted telling Jo anything about it. She'd had to, though. She knew that Sally would bring it up, her childhood trauma (she always did), and be shocked that her twin hadn't mentioned it to her new best friend.

"It does suck," she said. "It sucks for me, too."

"Of course," Jo said. "You have to take care of her."

Olivia stopped walking then and stared at Jo. She would do her best Valley girl voice, she decided.

"No, I mean, it, like, sucks for *me*?" she said. "It's always 'Sally Sally Sally' and 'How's Sally doing?' but no one ever asks how *I'm* doing, you know?"

Her vocal fry was on point, and Jo started playing along.

"That bitch has been getting all the attention," she said.

"Exactly!" Olivia said. "I mean, right? No one ever asks about *me*. We're *iden*tical, but my stepfather molested *her* and not *me*. How do you think that makes *me* feel?"

Jo laughed and broke character.

"That's dark," she said. "I love it."

She decided to believe it was true, too, the "not me" part.

4

PARKING DOWNTOWN: THREE HOURS, THIRTY-FIVE DOLLARS. A WEEK'S worth of groceries. Artie couldn't let Olivia know this. It would make him look desperate, like he'd do anything for her. Though he guessed agreeing to pick up her sister at O'Hare in rush-hour traffic was already a big step in that direction. But no, he thought, doing her this favor, that was just *nice* of him. Being nice was good. It was never the thing that swept her off her feet and got you the girl, but if it was down to you and another guy later on, all other things being equal (were they ever?), if a pros-and-cons list was drawn to determine who was the better party . . . He tried to think up ways for Olivia not to find out that he'd parked there, right under Millennium Park. Maybe he could tell her he'd parked too far? To just wait for him in the lobby while he went to get the car? Olivia loved walking, though. She'd want to walk with him, even in the cold. And then she'd see that he'd lied, that he hadn't parked that far, just expensively, and she'd know what kind of man he was—not only the kind of man who lied about small things but, worse, the kind of man who couldn't find good street parking, the kind of man who was either too unlucky or too impatient to be given, or wait for, a small, good thing.

He was supposed to make his classmates laugh at some point in the next two hours, but it was okay to be focused on something else. Maybe he'd find that not thinking about his act so close to showtime would make him a better comedian. It was counterintuitive, but intuition was overrated, he thought. Intuition was for lazy people, it was for people who didn't want to think too hard.

His phone lit up in his hand. He hadn't let it out of his sight much since his call with Olivia, in case she called again. He thought it was a text, and in a way, it was, only it was one from the phone itself. "You have a new memory," the message said, and Artie took the bait, tapped his screen to see it. "On this day 5 years ago," the screen said, right above a picture of Mickey, Artie, and their grandfather eating ice cream in the snow. None of them were smiling in the photo, but they'd been happy, Artie remembered, celebrating the first big snowfall of the season the way they'd always done: two scoops each in a sugar cone. Artie's grandfather only ever ate ice cream when it was freezing outside. He maintained that he couldn't digest it otherwise. He was dead now. And who knew where Mickey was.

"Wow, thanks a lot, dude," Artie said to his phone, and his words echoed in the parking garage.

It was the third or fourth time the phone had forced him, un-prompted, to look at an old picture, but Artie only now realized the absurdity of the phrasing: "You have a new memory." What did that even mean? That he hadn't had it before? Also, the screen wasn't showing him a *memory*, only a stupid selfie. More of that impreci-sion, he thought, more of that turning words into more or less than they actually were—manicures into "self-care," meat into "protein." A photo wasn't a memory. A photo was a photo. The memories Artie had of that day weren't at that angle, the light was different. They might end up reduced to that angle and that light, though, if he looked at the photo long enough. He deleted it. He decided to never take a photo again.

He tried to imagine the idiot at Apple who'd come up with the idea. He pictured a big conference table, a dozen ugly men brain-storming, one of them having a eureka moment, another completing his colleague's inspired hunch by saying "We'll call them . . . *memo-ries,*" everyone else in the room getting chills, crying genius. Had no one at that meeting thought, *Maybe we'll cause people to think of dead loved ones at completely inopportune moments*? Had no one in that room ever suffered at all? That's what you were left with when you let human stupidity program artificial intelligence, Artie thought: arti-ficial stupidity.

He was out walking on Columbus Drive now, making a right on Monroe. Turning his back to the lake, he thought this had to be one of the best views of downtown, how beautiful Chicago was when the sky was gray. He reminded himself not to take a photo.

He imagined other things "smarter" smartphones would alert you to in the future. Maybe your contact list would soon be synced with hospital records so that no one would have to make the tough phone calls anymore—"You have a new death in the family."

He saw Olivia and Jo in the distance, smoking by the classroom building. Kruger was approaching from the south, coming to class, as always, holding his Dunkin' coffee. If Artie kept up the same pace, he would have to walk alone with him for about a block, he calculated, and so he slowed down, pretended, in case someone saw, to have received an important text. Artie was under the impression that Kruger hated him, which of course Kruger didn't, he also told himself. Couldn't famous people only hate other famous people? Still. Artie should've said something about Kruger's first movie appearance when his classmates had. They'd all gone to see *The Widow's Comedy Club* back in September and come up with compliments to serve Kruger, about his scenes, about pacing. Artie had stayed silent, which Kruger must have noticed. The movie, in which Meryl Streep discovers in herself a vocation for stand-up after the death of her husband, wasn't bad. Artie had even been moved by the speech Paul Rudd (playing her son) gave Streep near the end. He simply hadn't found anything to say about Kruger's performance specifically. He wasn't even sure what he'd thought of it, whether Kruger's acting had been great or terrible. It was hard to tell the difference sometimes.

"Shit, fuck," Artie said to himself. Kruger had seen him across Michigan Avenue. Kruger was now raising his Dunkin' cup in Artie's direction. He was going to wait for Artie to cross the street. They *would* walk that last block to class together. It was all happening. And right away, a preview of the discomfort to come: the awkwardness of having to wait for the light to change while someone else was watching from the opposite sidewalk. What was the etiquette there? Did you have to look at the other person? Mind the traffic? Gaze in the distance, pretend to be deep in thought?

Artie opted to look at his phone again.

Kruger stared at him the whole time. *I'll make fun of him,* he thought, because that's what comedians did when they felt discomfort oozing out of other people, and Artie's discomfort was palpable across six lanes of traffic.

Also: *of course* Kruger had noticed that Artie hadn't commented on his movie. It was his job to notice things. He'd also noticed that he'd noticed, had already berated himself for noticing, for caring about such petty things.

The light changed. Artie didn't look Kruger's way as he crossed the street, but Kruger continued staring, to ensure maximum unease on Artie's part, and that their eyes would meet the second Artie stopped pretending to have anything on his mind other than the upcoming torture of having to walk to school with his teacher. There were many ways to make people uncomfortable, Kruger knew, but he favored a solid stare. A stare was simple, efficient. Worked every time. Had on Kruger, at least, who'd endured it all as a kid—the words and the fists and the looks. The looks had always been the worst.

The more he looked at Artie, though, the less Kruger wanted to toy with him. Artie made him sad, really. The boy had no future in comedy. He was just too pretty. Kruger knew that pretty boys could be funny, and that they had feelings, too, but no audience would ever give them a chance. People didn't want more doors open to the beautiful. *Fuck you, Artie* was what the world was telling Artie. *You're white and you're handsome, and now you want a career? Did you think this was the sixties?* And yet there was Artie, trying, hopeful. He was even coming to workshop with . . . what? What could there be in that cardboard tube in his armpit? Props for his bit? Jesus. You had to feel sorry for the kid. Kruger decided not to make fun, not to ask what was in the tube. He didn't want to know unless and until he absolutely had to. He could do small talk instead. Small talk was good. People expected comedians to always be on, to be funny even offstage, *jocu-*

lar, at the very least, but Artie wasn't *people,* Kruger thought, Artie was a comedy student, *his* student, and it was part of his job as a teacher to show him that real-life comedians were nothing more than real-life people, some of them high energy and a joy to be around, some of them mean and biting nonstop, most of them mildly depressed and misanthropic.

"You didn't have to wait for me," Artie said when he reached Kruger. "I would've understood. It's too fucking cold out here."

"It's going to get a lot worse, you know that?"

Artie didn't. He'd seen it in movies, but this was his first Chicago winter. Not that New Jersey was much better.

"How much worse?" he asked Kruger, and neither of them could believe they were still talking about the weather.

Kruger had grown up in Naperville, just thirty miles west. He had a few stories about the cold. For the past ten years, in L.A., he'd told exaggerated versions of them to waitresses and barbacks who'd never seen snow. He told Artie about a girl he went to school with whose eyes had frozen shut one winter morning before first period. The girl had teared up from the cold, blinked, and been unable to open her eyes back up. Kruger's father, who'd been a teacher at the school, had brought her inside, and her eyelids had thawed immediately, but the way Kruger told the story now, she'd been blinded for hours and the rest of the kids had tried to get their own eyes to freeze shut all day so that classes would be canceled.

"Your father was a teacher at your school?" Artie asked.

They were walking fast at least. Jo and Olivia were getting closer.

"He taught history, yes," Kruger said.

"Were you ever in his class?"

"I had other teachers than him, but the way I remember junior high, I was never *not* in his class," Kruger said. "And my mother was my fourth-grade teacher. Can you imagine?"

Artie couldn't. A parent, to his mind, was someone whose day had to remain a mystery. You had to be able, as a child, to imagine that Mom and Dad became something amazing when you weren't looking—otherwise, what hope was there left for you?

"At least it made it so you weren't bullied, I guess. Being the teacher's kid."

"That's funny," Kruger said. "You should write that down."

Kruger didn't want to talk about his father. Why had he brought him up? Louis, like Artie, hadn't said anything about his movie. Kruger had sent him a link. He had to have watched it by now. What else was there to do at the old folks' home?

When they reached the building, Jo immediately pointed at the tube under Artie's arm.

"What the fuck is this?"

"You'll see," Artie said.

"Prop comedy is the worst," Jo said.

"Andy Kaufman did props."

"Don't even say his name."

Olivia thanked Artie again for agreeing to drive her to O'Hare later.

"No sweat," Artie said, but why? He hated the phrase. Calling attention to bodily fluids. "I parked like a loser, though," he added.

Honesty was his best option. Preemptive self-criticism, too, using a word like "loser" to describe himself—this would keep Olivia from having to come up with it herself, and if she didn't say the word herself, then she wouldn't quite internalize it.

"What do you mean, like a *loser*?" Olivia said, blowing cigarette smoke in Artie's face. Smoking was a habit Artie would want her to get rid of if they were ever to be together, but one he pretended to have no issue with at the moment.

"Millennium Garage," he said.

Olivia was still exhaling.

"I'll give you some cash," she said.

"That's not what—"

"Very classy, Artie," Jo said. "Asking the girl for parking money."

Kruger watched the kids give one another shit for a minute. It was always nice when he realized he liked them, that it was only teaching he wasn't fond of. More than nice, it was a relief. He'd been worried, at first, to think that his dislike of teaching could mean he was jealous of his students, their youth and energy. He didn't want to be jealous, or bitter. Bitterness was bad for comedy. Bitter comedians tried to convince themselves they weren't bitter, just another shade of angry (and anger was good, all performers agreed on that, anger was funny), but people recognized a bitter man when they saw one. If Kruger liked his students, if he liked them as people, then it meant he wasn't there yet.

Artie mentioned something he'd seen on Twitter, and Jo said to get off Twitter, Twitter was for squares.

"Oh, but wait," she added. "You *are* square. Never mind. By all means, keep reading about every idiot's opinion on what category of people gets kicked out of inclusivity today. That way you'll know exactly what jokes you can and cannot make, and everybody will laugh."

"Isn't that the goal?" Artie asked. "To make people laugh?"

Jo stared at him and shaped a square in the air with her finger.

The wind blew Au Bon Pain's sidewalk sign toward them, slowly. They'd all seen similar signs knocked by wind gusts before—A-frames fold onto themselves and fall flat on the pavement—but never one dragged like that, solid on its four feet. The sign moved like a reluctant child pushed by his mother on the first day of school, or a bad spy. It looked so human Artie almost expected it to stop for a chat when it reached them. But the sign passed them by and went on its way, and though they all looked at it in awe, no one mentioned it. Artie breathed in air so cold it burned and said that, as a square, it was perhaps his role to remind everyone that it was time for class.

5

Dear Manny,

An email was better, Dorothy had decided minutes after Ashbee and Kruger left the conference room. Less intrusive.

Long time no see!

She deleted the line. Then resolved not to delete anything further, to treat the Gmail window as a live recording of her thoughts. She wrote the following:

I understand you've had some PR issues lately. Remember when people used to say there's no such thing as bad pub-licity? Well, I haven't heard that in a while.

Anyway, I'm told we're going to be colleagues next month and I want you to know that we're all thrilled about it here, and that you can see our little department as a refuge and a beacon in the shitstorm. It's a weird fucking place. Maybe the best thing I can do to prove our (or at least my) loyalty to you in this moment, to prove that I'm not bullshitting about being your friend in all this while actually getting ready to stab you in the back, is to give you, in writing, all the dirt about the place. Which would get me fired, probably. So you have ammunition if I ever fuck you over.

First off, everyone's ugly here. I'm talking about faculty, of course, and I very much include myself in the lot. Some of the students look good though. NOT IN A WAY THAT WOULD MAKE ME WANT TO SLEEP WITH THEM, however, let's make that very clear. I don't very much sleep with anyone anymore anyway. Also, I don't think I've ever in my whole life slept with someone younger than me. Isn't that sad? But yeah, maybe you've been in L.A. long enough that you forgot what real people look like. It will all rush back to you when you come to Chicago.

Ashbee has become less of a climber with age. He almost looks content now, once in a while. Kruger is nicer than I thought he would be, which I guess isn't saying much. I only dislike him a little. I couldn't understand why he came here at first (he definitely doesn't need the gig), but I think his father lives around here? Maybe the old man is sick. There's probably guilt involved. Not a big sharer, Kruger.

The rest of the department is mildly entertaining. I get a kick out of reading the signature quotes they choose to put at the bottom of their emails. The quotes take longer to read than the actual emails, and they all say the same thing about justice and freedom, but if James Baldwin said it it's better than if Einstein did etc., and so the authors change all the time according to a trading board academics pay attention to and is I think updated every second on social media. Anyway. I guess that's not really dirt I'm giving you. Everywhere's the same.

What else? A colleague told me the other day about his theory that stand-up was like porn. He said going to a comedy club in order to laugh was like jizzing watching porn. That it was all planned-out amusement that, in the moment of completion, brutally sent us back to the meaninglessness of our lives. He called laughter a "discharge."

You'll like Chicago, I think. I mean, I know you've been here before, but the school will put you up nicely, a big-ass apartment in Wicker Park, next to a good Costa Rican place.

Though maybe you don't eat out much these days, I realize. How is it, by the way, when you go out? Is it more like everyone actively HATES you, or more like everyone pretends they don't know you anymore?

We just had a faculty meeting about you, and no one here is indifferent, I can tell you that much. I'm still in the conference room as I write this. It's all windows here, very nice view of downtown. The classrooms have the same kind of views, you'll see. It's gorgeous and all, very dramatic, but not really conducive to comedy, in my opinion. It's like we're lawyers in a movie. I pull the shades down when I teach.

My favorite student here is Olivia. It's a cliché thing to say, but she reminds me of me at her age, and I guess I wasn't that bad, even though of course I hated myself at the time. Which you might remember from all those nights we spent together. Not that only a self-hating woman would spend the night with you. That's not what I meant. I meant you might remember me complaining about being myself a lot, about how horrible it was to wake up as myself every day, and to go to bed in my own body, ay, how unbearable. Maybe you thought I was joking, I was being so dramatic and whiny. I remember you laughed a lot. And I WAS trying to make the whole thing funny, but the sentiment was real. I really thought about killing myself all the time back then. Now I only think about it once or twice a month.

Should she mention she had a new show? Her email was already longer than she wanted it to be. Email always made you sound crazier than you did on the phone, she thought, because you were talking alone.

I finished writing something a couple months back. If all goes well, I'll tour it next summer. Not sure who'll want to see me onstage at this point. It's been nine years since I've toured anything. My audience has either died off or forgot-

ten me. My mother says I've waited too long, but it must've
felt shorter to her because she thinks Obama is still presi-
dent. She's forgotten half the people in her life, but for
some reason, your name stuck, and she asks about you
every time we talk. She gives me shit for not marrying
you back in the day. She thinks we were made for each
other because we both had the same job (she still calls it
"standing-up," by the way, in case you're wondering)
("Manny does standing-up, you do standing-up, it would've
been perfect!"). She thought you could understand me and
be patient with me in a way that other people couldn't. Of
course, when I dated a comedian for real and brought him
to dinner, she hated everything about him, and her whole
theory fell apart.

Would Manny wonder who the comedian was?

When I dumped the guy, I told her, "Mom, you see, it's not
just standing-up that I need in a man, I need other positions
too," which of course wasn't funny at all, but I refuse to be
judged for the jokes I don't take to the stage. It was just
reflex snark, excess air somewhere, no more than a burp to
me, but she took it to heart. She said, "Why do you always
have to make everything everyone says sound so stupid?"
and I have to tell you, Manny, that made me feel like shit.
I could've cried right there and then, because she meant it.
She was upset. I'd upset my mother. It's like she'd been
meaning to tell me this for years, and for some reason,
this had been the last straw. The silence in the room after
this . . . I remember it better than most conversations
I've had.

Maybe that was enough about her mother, Dorothy thought. She
looked up from her iPad and through the window, at the view she'd

mentioned, the buildings and the small people in them. The people were usually hard to see during the day, but the clouds were so dense now that early afternoon looked like night, and lamps were already on here and there, outlining human shapes at their desks. In the wine-colored building Dorothy liked, a lone man's silhouette was facing a big TV, and she rolled her chair closer to the window to try to figure out what he was watching. Sword came into the conference room about a minute into her investigation.

"It's always disappointing, isn't it?" he said.

"Watching people?" Dorothy said.

"At this distance, yes."

Sword said that in the movies, whenever someone looked at neighbors in buildings across the street, it only took a few seconds before they witnessed a murder, or couples having sex. He regretted saying "sex" immediately. He didn't know Dorothy well enough.

"In real life, though," Sword went on, so that he wouldn't end his thought on the word "sex," "people are actually working."

Dorothy said she'd seen a couple fucking once, through her window, back when she lived in New York.

"You just need to be more patient," she said. "You need to truly have nothing better to do all day."

Sword lived in a house now, in Oak Park. The only stranger's windows he could see from his own were Mrs. Gruber's, one of the old ladies his wife was helping regain motion after her hip surgery. Sometimes, he saw Mrs. Gruber do her rehab exercises in her living room and assumed she hoped Lydia was watching, would congratulate her at their next session.

"Sorry if I'm interrupting," he said to Dorothy, pointing at her iPad. "I was heading home and realized I'd left my phone behind."

He couldn't leave it at that.

"Any plans for winter break?"

"The usual," Dorothy said. "Watch snuff movies, snort cocaine."

"Kind of your standard weekend, but on a larger scale," Sword said. It was the most words he'd ever exchanged with Dorothy Michaels one on one. Was he riffing with her? Was he riffing with a well-known comedian? He couldn't wait to tell Lydia about this.

Dorothy broke the spell when she asked Sword how he spent his own weekends.

What could he say? That unless he found a movie sad enough for her to want to stick around, Lydia was in bed by eight most nights, their son was at Stanford, and he missed them both?

"To be honest," Sword said, "it hasn't been much fun lately. My wife . . . she's not doing so great."

"I'm sorry to hear that. Does she have cancer?"

"What? No. Nothing like that. She's a bit depressed, is all."

"Well, that's good," Dorothy said. "That's better. Though I wouldn't say depression is *nothing* like cancer."

"Just a bit depressed. Not a full-blown depression."

He regretted saying anything. What had he expected? Pity, perhaps. Comfort. Not Dorothy jumping to cancer.

"I'm sorry," he said. "I shouldn't have said anything. I'm oversharing here. What do the kids say? TMI?"

"Is this the first time your wife's been depressed?"

Both Dorothy's and Sword's phones rang at the same time then, an alarm sound, like for a tornado warning, or Amber Alerts. They looked down at their screens. "Active Shooter on Campus," the screens said. "Seek Shelter Immediately."

"Is this a joke?" Dorothy asked. "I mean, an exercise?"

"I'm not aware of any exercise taking place today," Sword said. "But they don't always warn the chairs."

He wasn't sure that was true.

"What are we supposed to do?"

It was the first time in her five years of teaching that Dorothy was seeing the active shooter message.

"Protocol in this case is to lock the door and wait."

Sword went to the door and gave the pea-size knob lock a turn.

"Well, *that* should keep death at bay," Dorothy said.

She was laughing but terrified. What kind of lock was that? What had happened to bar locks and hardwood beams? What had happened to portcullises?

"We can prop some tables against the door," Sword said. "If that would make you feel safer."

Dorothy had only thought, not mentioned, the portcullis thing. She must've looked more scared than she realized.

"That's fine," she said. "Probably just an exercise anyway."

The words "active shooter" kept flashing through her head. Sword turned off the lights.

"I think it's in bad taste, though," Dorothy said. "Those active shooter exercises."

"How is an active shooter exercise different from a fire drill?"

"What do you mean? It's way scarier! I'm scared someone's going to come in and shoot me in the head right now."

"And you're not scared when you hear a fire alarm?"

"No one fears they're going to die in a fire. That's not a fear normal people have. Whereas guns . . . it's kind of always in the background. It's the white noise of American life."

Sword's support for Americans' right to bear arms, he knew, made him an oddity in academia. He'd told very few people about it, and figured now probably wasn't the time to discuss it with Dorothy. All he said was that perhaps a good person had a gun now, too.

"That's such an American thing to say," Dorothy said. "You're so American."

"I thought you were from Texas," Sword said.

"Yes, but my mother is Italian. I share the Italian views on gun control."

"You mean that we should only arm the Mafia?"

"Very funny," Dorothy said. "Not at all cliché."

Sword apologized for the Mafia comment.

"Did I offend you?" he asked. "Did I manage to offend Dorothy Michaels?"

"I'm unoffendable," Dorothy said.

Sword understood that she might believe this. Offended people were so easy to come by these days, he understood why someone would want to stand out and pretend they were unfamiliar with the notion. But certainly she was lying, he said. There had to be a politician that offended her, at least, an idea. Another comedian's success, perhaps?

"Things *annoy* me," Dorothy said. "Most of what I hear I think is ludicrous, but offensive? Taking offense? There's a form of delusion in it, of egomania. It's for people who can't accept that not everyone thinks exactly like them. Being offended is for children."

"You wouldn't be offended if I said something very sexist right now?" Sword asked.

"I'd be a little sorry for your wife, maybe, but why should it bother me? As long as you don't screw me over—at which point I would be angry, not offended—I see no reason to care all that much."

Sword said perhaps they should look up the exact definition of "offensive" in the dictionary.

"It seems we might have a different understanding of it."

He typed in the word on his phone, and Dorothy remembered that she'd been writing to Manny. She went back to her iPad and started a new paragraph.

> There's actually an active shooter in the building right now and so we had to shelter in place and i'm now stuck in the conference room with my department chair. Maybe the active shooter thing is not great advertising for our school, but I think you wouldn't hate the situation if you were here with us right now because the guy (my chair, not the shooter) just interrupted our conversation because he felt the need to look up a word's definition on his OED app before we could go on talking. we're alone in a room together and we might die in a minute but I'm finishing up an email to you and he's looking at his OED app! We might be spending our last minute of life on the internet.
> you don't meet these kinds of people every day.
> come work with us!

Dorothy debated whether she should sign or not, then opted for no signature. More dramatic this way. She hit send and went to the *New York Times* website to see if there were any "Breaking: Downtown Chicago Active Shooter" headlines. Nothing. Sword was probably right anyway. Probably an exercise. That's why it was okay for him to be looking up "offensive" in the dictionary at this moment.

She glanced at him and saw that he wasn't reading the *OED* anymore but scrolling through pictures of his family. When she looked back at her own screen, she thought Manny had responded already, but it was a "System Delivery Failure" notification.

6

IN WORKSHOP, A COUPLE OF BUILDINGS NORTH, JO WAS WRAPPING UP.
Her bit was called "The Year After, at Marienbad" (she insisted on
titling her work, though Kruger kept saying it wasn't necessary), and
no one got it. Instead of listening quietly to the critique that followed,
like she was supposed to, Jo tried to explain herself by showing the
class long clips of the movie *Last Year at Marienbad,* which she'd
drawn inspiration from. For a minute, it wasn't clear whether this
was still part of the bit, so Kruger let her do it.

"The movie itself is hilarious because it's so pretentious," Jo said.
"All the characters are so stiff and self-important, and the plot makes
zero sense because we never know if they're lying or telling the truth
or dreaming or remembering."

"Sounds like shit," Dan said.

"And so, since the mystery at the center of the movie is never explained," Jo went on, "I thought I could run with the idea that every
year something weird and unexplained happens in Marienbad, and I
imagined that the weirdest thing that could happen to that specific
cast of characters would be for them to suddenly acquire a sense of
humor."

"Okay," Phil said encouragingly. "I see. That wasn't super clear in
your bit."

"Of course it wasn't," Kruger said, ready to assume now that Jo's
performance was over. "You can't rely on your audience having seen
a French movie from the sixties in order for your jokes to land."

"Even *Breathless*?" Jo asked.

"Let's see," Kruger said. "Who in this room has seen *Breathless*?"

Of all six students, only Marianne raised her hand, but Marianne didn't count, because she was—like Godard himself, she reminded everyone—Swiss.

"I see your point," Jo said, and she went back to her seat.

Artie was up next. He clipped the blown-up picture of himself to a paperboard easel he'd never seen anyone use.

"I know what you're thinking," he started. "You're thinking, *This guy is too good-looking to be funny.*"

Kruger stopped him right away.

"Don't tell the audience something they already noticed."

Kruger usually let the students go uninterrupted, even when they were bombing hard, but his father was on his mind, and his father always said that teaching was adapting to the class you were given: if something wasn't working, if your students weren't learning, you had to change things up.

Artie was confused.

"Should I go on anyway?" he asked. "Or should I try to find a better opening line?"

"Don't tell the audience something they already noticed," Kruger repeated, and Artie said he thought it was kind of the principle of comedy, actually, to find common ground with the audience, to point out stuff they'd already noticed but hadn't perhaps quite realized yet that they'd noticed.

"No one cares that you're pretty," Kruger insisted. "No one wants to *think* about pretty at a comedy club. If they're thinking about your looks too much, then they'll start thinking about *their* looks, and they'll be self-conscious, and they won't laugh, because everyone's ugly when they laugh."

Artie wasn't sure he agreed with that, but the whole class nodded, and he let it go.

"Okay," he said. "But the entirety of the bit is kind of about my looks, so what should I do?"

"Do something else," Kruger said. "Improvise. Crowd work. Anything."

Artie had never done well in improv. They had improv with Dorothy once a week, and he'd skipped two of those classes already, made up fevers. He'd faked hoarseness once, too, thinking this would allow him to sit in class and quietly watch the others perform—a way to be absent while still showing up—but it had backfired when Dorothy said improv was finding ways around your weaknesses and spent the better part of two hours trying to squeeze a bit of decent physical comedy out of him.

"I don't know," Artie said to Kruger. "I've got nothing."

"You're not allowed those words in our line of work," Kruger said.

Which Artie knew, of course. The way around writer's block was to write about writer's block until something interesting came up. It was one of the first lessons imparted on them here. Take note of everything you see that gives you the slightest brain jolt. No need to form a full thought about it right away, much less a joke, but to take note was important. If it was anything worth pursuing, it would keep working within you. You could never be empty if you took notes all the time.

Artie had been keeping a notebook since he was a teenager, but he'd always been ashamed about it. Part of him believed you were a bad writer if you needed one, laborious. His parents had never seen it, for example. Not that they knew much about writing, but the notebook would've made them self-conscious, Artie thought, and wonder what their son was seeing at the dinner table that they weren't. It felt particularly wrong showing up with a pen anyplace his father was. The man was so intent on making little out of things, on never riffing, on noticing only the bare minimum for survival (where the water pitcher was, the emergency exits), that he might not have even seen the notebook if Artie had set it on the table, but his wife would've brought it to his attention, and he would've said something like "What's there to write about us, son? We're not interesting," after which Artie would've been forced to agree, or worse, to listen to his mother's follow-up, her attempts at convincing her husband and children that that was nonsense, that there was in fact a lot to say about their family, and then after that serve them, as illustration, one of the two anecdotes she liked reliving (the time they'd been robbed by highway police in Mexico on their honeymoon, the time Mickey had won first place in the regional chess tournament and met the governor—two anecdotes in which Artie didn't appear).

Artie thought back on the notes he'd taken so far today. At breakfast, he'd written something about ex-girlfriends showing up in dreams as if you'd never broken up with them (the big talk still to be had), and the relief it was after a dream like that to wake up alone in bed in the morning. He wondered if that was a universal dream, a universal feeling. After his phone call with his mother, he'd noted: "addicted = positive." Right before the start of class, he'd written down that scene he'd imagined with the tech company idiots. It might not be the most promising bit to pursue, but in this moment, it was the clearest in his mind.

"My phone wants to bond with me," Artie started. "It really wants us to be friends."

Olivia was smiling already. Because he was funny? Because she could tell he was driving into a concrete wall? Artie wondered if he should take his phone out of his pocket for illustrative purposes, elected not to.

"I was walking around earlier," he went on, "minding my own business, and it just *texted* me. It used to be *people* texted you, now it's your own phone checking in."

Mild chuckles—not from Olivia, not from Kruger.

Artie mimed the act of holding a phone, not to his ear (no one did that anymore) but at chest level, eyes looking down into it.

"I thought, you know, if my phone wants to tell me something, it has to be important, right? Like there's a terrorist attack in the neighborhood, or some kid is being raped nearby."

He shouldn't have said "raped," he thought.

"But you know what the dumb phone wanted? It wanted to see if I remembered a *fish*ing trip I took five years ago, with my grandfather."

Why say a fishing trip? He'd never been fishing in his life.

" 'On this day five years ago,' it said, with a big stupid selfie of my grandpa and me. What a weirdo. The phone, I mean, not my grandpa. Why remind me of that day, of all the days we've had together since I bought it? Was it a particularly meaningful fishing trip for my phone? And I didn't realize it? Why is it so important that I remember the fishing trip *now*, right this moment?"

No laughter.

"This phone, it's like having a girlfriend, really. I feel like there's more coming, like I can get quizzed about our life together at any point. Do I remember our first night? When I plugged it in by the bed, protective plastic still unpeeled?"

The phone-as-girlfriend shtick wasn't working, wouldn't work. Artie needed to change course.

"Worst part is," he said, "my grandpa died a couple years back."

God. Why? What was he doing? Why wasn't Kruger stopping him *now*? Quick, come up with a funny death.

"Nothing extraordinary. He just 'had a fall,' as they say, and he died. I didn't take a photo of it, though, of my grandfather falling, so I guess my phone just doesn't know it happened."

Marianne laughed at this, and Artie wondered what had been funny, what was worth digging into more. The idea of taking a photo of a loved one's falling to his death? Or that your phone could actually become a better friend to you if you recorded your whole life on it, not just the good parts?

"Maybe that's why people do crying selfies now," Artie said. "Post photos and videos of themselves crying. Have you seen those?"

No encouragement from the room, but a nod from Olivia.

"At first, I thought it was pure narcissism, or actresses audition-ing for a part, because it was only pretty girls filming themselves in the beginning, remember? Big eyes, mascara drips, cute sniffles. But then ugly people started doing it too, they started filming their ugly crying faces, and I thought there had to be more to it. So I started reading the captions. Have you guys ever read the captions?"

Still no answer from his classmates, but he had to make the pauses, look up to his audience, pretend they were in this together.

"You get all kinds of stuff in the captions: 'I may look bubbly and fun, but this is also me, hashtag also me, hashtag real life, hashtag me, hashtag dealing with past traumas.' Or things like 'Look what you did to me, Chad!' All kinds of stuff. One that comes back a lot, though, is this: 'So I remember how bad I felt.'"

This was something to let sit for a second, and so Artie paused again.

"What does that mean, 'So I remember how bad I felt'? Won't they be able to remember how they felt if they don't post it on social media? If other people don't see it? If they don't store it in the cloud?"

There hadn't been a laugh since Marianne's, a century ago.

"I complain that my phone sends me stuff, but when it sends me a fishing trip memory, what do other people get? A picture of their crying face, which reminds them of that time Chad slept with Lucy? Does anyone want this? Isn't that already what our brains are for? Shooting bad memories at us at random?"

The number of questions you're asking, Artie told himself. *That's desperation, pure and simple.*

"Not that good memories are much better. I mean, who wants to remember joyful moments? They're gone forever. You'll never re-create the exact conditions. Might as well make actual photo albums and look at them. The best times of your life, gathered all together in one place for you to browse and remember how much better things used to be."

How had he gotten here? Could he even wrap up at this point? What threads were there to bring back together?

"Anyway," he said, a word they'd been told to avoid. "I don't need a smartphone to remind me how big of a loser I am. A regular phone is good enough technology. As long as it's a number my mother can reach, I get to feel bad about my life a satisfactory amount."

Artie thought it would be clear this was his last line, that improv was over, but after a few seconds of silence, he had to add: "I want to stop now."

The class started their critique right away.

"He said 'anyway,'" Phil noted.

"That was painful," said Jo. "Not just him saying 'anyway.' The whole thing."

"Why did you think it was painful?" Kruger asked.

"Because it wasn't funny."

When asked to be more specific, Jo explained that Artie was trying too hard to say something.

"Instead of just talking, I mean."

"I agree," Phil said.

Olivia was more encouraging, but Artie assumed it was only because he was giving her a ride later and she didn't want it to be too awkward.

"It was very raw," she said, "but I think there's some good stuff to keep digging at. Like, with the randomness of memories. There could be some physical comedy there, maybe, like, when the memories hit him. Or more description of the memories themselves, and how they clash with the photos. Maybe you could show actual slides? From your actual life?"

"If he puts actual slides in, it becomes the *Mad Men* episode where Draper pitches the Kodak carousel," Dan said.

Artie hadn't seen *Mad Men,* but he nodded anyway.

"Unless he also puts *jokes* in," Jo said. "I think the key here is something *funny* should happen."

"The *Mad Men* thing is interesting," Marianne said. "Artie's bit could be a parody. Parodies of famous scenes can be great."

"It's not that famous a scene," Phil said. "I haven't seen it."

"You haven't seen *Last Year at Marienbad* either."

The rest of the class agreed, over Phil's objection, that the carousel scene in *Mad Men* was famous enough that a parody could work, was in fact maybe a great idea, after which everyone started talking about Artie's improv as if Artie's intention had been to riff on *Mad Men* all along. It was too late for Artie to admit that he'd never watched *Mad Men,* that episode or any other. It didn't really matter anyway. The world was too full, he thought, and nothing you said would ever be considered original thinking, even when it felt pretty original to you. Submitting your work for critique meant sticking around after a performance in order to hear people talk about other things your performance had reminded them of.

He felt extremely depressed for a minute. He was only ever depressed for minutes at a time, but they were intense minutes, thinking-about-ways-to-kill-himself minutes. His brother had told him once that what Artie felt wasn't depression, because depression lasted longer than a few minutes. "Then what do I have?" Artie had asked. "What's my problem?" To which Mickey had said that Artie's problem was he wanted too much attention. Coming from any other drug addict who went missing every few months, it could've been a pot/kettle moment, but Mickey's goal had never been attention. Artie actually believed that what his brother wanted was the opposite of attention, that the reason behind the drugs was he actually wanted to be forgotten, didn't even want to have to think about Mickey Kessler himself. Artie sometimes believed that his brother's hope in disappearing repeatedly was for his disappearances to become so routine he'd reach a point where people would stop wondering where he was, or noticing he was gone at all.

Everyone in the room was still giving their opinion on the *Mad Men* scene. They'd spent more time discussing it than Artie's performance by now. Olivia admitted to having been moved to tears by Jon Hamm's monologue the first time she'd seen the episode, and then even more so the second. Kruger thought that was interesting. He asked the class why they thought it was that a great scene could affect us more deeply the second time we saw it.

"I wouldn't call the *Mad Men* scene a *great* scene," Jo said.

"It's about anticipation," Marianne said. "You know something amazing is going to happen, and so you're already wide open when it comes. You take it in full force."

"It should be the opposite, though," said Phil. "Full force is when it takes you by surprise. If you know in advance what's going to happen, it should all come to you diminished."

"That's true if the scene is just *all right,*" Marianne said. "If a scene is just all right, you dissect it the second time you see it. You look for the tricks and the ropes and understand how it works so well. But if it's *great,* you don't even *think* to look for the ropes. You're blinded to the ropes. You end up thinking maybe there aren't any. That's why it becomes even more powerful."

"You don't see the ropes in the *Mad Men* scene?" Jo asked.

"We're not talking about *Mad Men* anymore. Ben's question was about great scenes in general."

"I'd be happy with people just laughing the first time," Artie said, and it was his most successful joke of the day. Even the corner of Kruger's mouth moved up a little.

"Do you have questions for the class?" he asked Artie, a ritual query that marked a student's exit from under the microscope and reentry into society.

You weren't supposed to have questions at the end of workshop. You were supposed to thank everyone for being so thorough ("What a tremendous help!"), leave the stage humbly, and try to wait until class ended to have your breakdown.

"I don't think so," Artie said. "I think you guys were pretty thorough."

He was still standing next to the gigantic photo of himself.

"I'm sorry you had to see this," he added. "I don't know why I talked about my dead grandfather there. That was lame."

"It wasn't the worst part," Dan said.

Artie swore he hadn't been fishing for sympathy. "I know emotion is the enemy of comedy," he said.

"Says who?" Phil said.

"Well, it's not like your bit was particularly *moving*," Marianne said.

"I think our Artie here has been reading Henri Bergson," Kruger said.

"I don't know who that is," Artie admitted, and explained it was just something his mother had told him earlier on the phone. That comedy couldn't be moving, or else it stopped being funny.

"Well then, I guess your *mother*'s been reading Henri Bergson," Kruger said.

"Do you listen to everything your mother has to say about comedy?" Jo asked.

Only Marianne had ever read Bergson's book about laughter. She said it was very interesting, but written before Charlie Chaplin or anything truly funny, so maybe it was outdated.

"Chaplin is moving *and* funny," she said. "I wonder where he would have fit in Bergson's theory."

"Can you guys think of other comics that move you and make you laugh at the same time?" Kruger asked. "Specific bits?"

He didn't like asking for names, but sometimes you had to. He assumed it made his students uncomfortable to be asked for favorites, because they knew comedy was a small world, and anyone they named had the potential to be their teacher's nemesis.

"Andy Kaufman," Jo said. "On Letterman. When he calls his grandmother on the phone."

"Louis C.K., the old Chinese lady," Dan said. "Bill Burr and the ape."

"Dave Chappelle, the Bourdain suicide," Marianne said.

"Manny Reinhardt," Olivia said. "The bit about his blind neighbor."

"I don't hear a lot of female names," Phil complained. You could always count on him to say something like that.

"Well, why don't you give us one?" Marianne said.

Olivia said that it was easier for a man to be funny and moving at the same time, because all a man had to do to move an audience was let it know that he was not entirely oblivious to his surroundings, and sometimes even capable of emotion, and that was enough to break people's hearts.

"Whereas women," she went on, "you *expect* them to be full of doubts and feelings. You *expect* them to notice how sad everything is all the time. So it doesn't have the same impact when they let you see their humanity. It's never poignant. It's almost just annoying."

Phil thought that was sad and unfair. He wasn't sure he agreed with Olivia, but in order to repair centuries of injustice toward women, he'd pretty much decided to never contradict one again, even though it seemed to make every girl he knew uninterested in having any kind of conversation with him.

The room was silent for almost a minute after Olivia spoke. Not that she'd said anything deep. It wasn't the silence a group made while thinking. It was the silence of collective low blood sugar, of class break due imminently.

"You know what?" Jo said, bringing everyone out of their torpor. "The more I look at Artie next to that big photo of himself, the funnier it gets. Maybe it's even moving, too. Maybe I'm moved by it."

They all looked at Artie again, and then at the photo of younger, pimply Artie beside him.

"You're right," Marianne said. "I feel something."

Artie stood straighter and prouder by the paperboard.

"No no no no no," said Jo. "Don't do anything stupid. I think it's stronger if you just sit there and look a little lost."

Artie grabbed a stool and sat on it. Everyone stared some more. Jo gave a couple of directions ("Maybe sit *in front* of the photo rather than next to it," "Try to forget about the photo altogether," "Forget about us"), and Artie followed them. He started thinking about other things, about how he should call Ethel, and how he should try to befriend his brother when he showed up again. It wasn't the first time he'd formulated this project. Two years earlier, he'd started reading more novels so he and Mickey would have something to talk about. Conversations about books had been a little stilted, though, Artie remembered, a little forced. They'd ended up putting distance between them rather than bringing them closer. Artie thought back on how it felt like they hadn't been reading the same novel sometimes, like he'd bought a counterfeit edition, or the librarian, after taking a quick look at him, had decided to lend him a simplified one, the for-morons version, with just the biggest plot points and none of the secondary actions and main undercurrents that Mickey—who'd read the full version, for smart people—spoke of. He'd had to explain to Artie that it wasn't so much that Jake Barnes was doing the decent thing by not sleeping with his friend's ex in *The Sun Also Rises* as that his dick had been shot off in the war. Artie hadn't caught that part about the dick. Which seemed pretty instrumental to the plot. Talking about books with Mickey had been like attempting conversation from two sides of a precipice—Mickey on one, Artie on the other, Mickey trying to get him closer to the edge, Artie trying not to fall in.

Perhaps he should get into heroin, Artie thought, his classmates still staring, some directly at him, some at his old photo. Perhaps he could share a heroin addiction with his brother. He'd tried heroin, a handful of times, to see what the fuss was about. Heroin was pretty great, but not quite to the point that he'd want to devote his life to it. *You can't even get addicted to heroin,* he'd berated himself more than once. He was under the impression that addictive personalities lived life more fully, that by being a restrained, solid kind of guy, he was missing out not only on the intricacies of world literature's best storylines but on a much bigger secret. He had this idea that a person's existence was like a big Renaissance oil painting, full of details and nuances and reflections, and that his had been painted over by that lady who'd butchered her local church's fresco by wanting to be useful. All blobby brushstrokes and flat tints. Almost blurry. When he'd first seen the meme, the portrait of Christ next to the old woman's restoration of it, he'd thought: *Mickey on the left, Artie on the right.*

He thought about how empty his life would be if Mickey disappeared for good this time, and when he remembered that people were watching, Olivia, his classmates, his teacher, it was because they were all laughing.

7

THIS WAS GETTING TOO LONG FOR AN EXERCISE, BUT DOROTHY WAS intent on keeping the mood light. She tried to guess who the shooter was. She listed a couple of undergrads whose names she remembered from group emails—kids who sent letters to the entire department whenever injustice occurred somewhere in America, demanding a statement be made in solidarity with the victims.

"Though I guess that's exactly the type of kid we have nothing to fear from," she said to Sword. "If what you demand at their age are statements, odds are you'll live a pretty uneventful life."

She was biting her nails. Sword hadn't said much the whole thirty minutes they'd been stuck together in the conference room, and she was starting to get annoyed with him. It was just like her, she thought, in a life-and-death situation, to direct all ill thoughts not at the shooter lurking around but at the poor guy who failed to entertain her while it happened. If she survived today, she'd have to write about it. The thought made her a little sad.

"It's probably a kid no one has really noticed before," she said. "The perfectly average student."

"Why are you so sure it's a student?" Sword asked.

"No one over twenty-two has the energy."

"So, not even a *grad* student."

"Definitely not one of mine," Dorothy said. "The MFAs are too lazy for that kind of . . . effusion. And comedians don't deal with anger that way."

"Right," Sword said. "You guys kill people with words."

His earnestness gave her chills. Did people really say things like that? On some level, Dorothy knew that they did, but she'd never quite believed it. *You guys kill people with words.* Jesus. Maybe it was better when he didn't talk. No wonder his wife was suicidal, she thought, even though she wouldn't have called it a thought—word combinations of this kind appeared in her head like well-placed commas in a sentence: she barely noticed them.

Sword understood he'd said something wrong. "I think I just found out what offends you," he said.

"I told you," Dorothy said. "I don't get offended."

"Metaphors. I offended you with my metaphor about killing people with words."

"You didn't offend me. I just found it ridiculous, is all."

"I should've known comedians don't like metaphors. Metaphors are just one more thing to make fun of."

"*Bad* ones are. But some metaphors are fine. They can even be useful sometimes, in a medical context."

"What's so wrong about 'killing with words'?"

"Well, it's cheesy, for one," Dorothy said. "It's grandiloquent. It's vague."

Vagueness was, to her mind, the biggest crime of them all. There was a class of people, though, who thought there was power in vagueness, who mistook imprecise writing for a reflection of life's deepest ambiguities. She realized Sword might be part of that group.

"Vague isn't necessarily bad," he said. "It mirrors the human experience."

How was this guy allowed to teach English? Dorothy wondered. She'd had respect for him before.

"Good writing is supposed to transcend human experience," she said, "not just mirror it. Otherwise, all I would have to do for critics to call my next show a masterpiece would be to write an hour's worth of random words, and I would get blurbs like 'Astounding! Just like life! Makes no sense at all!' That's some bullshit. Good writing has to be clear at all times, controlled, even when it describes ambiguous situations."

"Some people like to get lost," Sword said, a sentiment Dorothy chose to ignore.

She went back to biting her nails. She and Sword were sitting next to each other on the floor, along the wall that the door was on, at an angle they assumed the shooter wouldn't be able to see them from if he peeked through the narrow window above the knob. They were starting to get cramps from keeping their knees folded so close against their chests, but they didn't dare stretch their legs. There was still enough daylight filtering through the windows that any movement could drag along its own shadow and reveal their position.

"I think what I don't like about a vague metaphor is when everyone pretends they see exactly what the author meant and I'm the only one to not get it," Dorothy said. She hated to find this out about herself, that she apparently was the kind of person who, faced with the threat of imminent death, couldn't stand silence. When imagining her last moments (something she'd done countless times since childhood), she'd always pictured herself as a wise, Buddha-like figure, someone who would look inward and make peace with herself. Her father had been that way. But it wasn't happening for Dorothy. In what could be her last moments, it turned out what she needed was to yap about bad writing, to keep doing exactly what she'd been doing her entire life.

"I still don't see what's vague about killing someone with words," Sword said.

Dorothy explained it was the exaggeration around artists in general that pissed her off. Like she could kill anyone with her work, she said. She couldn't even flick anyone with a joke.

"Manny Reinhardt punched someone in the face," Sword said.

"Exactly," Dorothy said. "He used his fists."

Where did this idea come from, anyway, that art had to inflict pain on its audience? That that was the goal—to kill it, slay it, break its heart, punch it in the gut?

"I think it's because we know that artists suffer for their art," Sword said. "So we think art that is successful is art in which that pain gets transferred to the audience somehow. Shared."

"Why does everyone have to imagine artists *bleeding* on the page? Consumed, going *men*tal?"

Writing her shows had always been painful for Dorothy, but she'd decided long ago that she'd have all her molars pulled before she admitted it. She thought only great comedians were allowed to admit to suffering, that admitting to it herself would only get people wondering who the hell she thought she was, and why she believed her work was so important that they cared if it got written or not, performed or not. "If it hurts so bad, why don't you quit?" was what she was afraid to hear. No one would miss Dorothy Michaels's next hour of comedy, no one would sit in contemplation of what could've been.

"You say you hate exaggeration around artists," Sword said, "but comedians are the ones who came up with all the death metaphors. *Dying* onstage when they suck, *killing* when they succeed."

He had a point, but Dorothy didn't feel like giving it to him. She looked at her phone, where she hoped to see news that the shooter had been apprehended. The "situation" they were in still showed as "unfolding."

"What about we stop talking about death and killing for a minute?" she said. "Can we do that?"

They talked about their mothers.

Sword's had been dead five years, so he only had nice things to say. He wanted to hear about Dorothy's mother's immigration story, though, how she wound up in Texas, and why Dorothy never talked about being half-Italian in her comedy.

"I never found the fact funny," she said. "Americans only know about Italian Americans anyway, not Italian Italians. It wouldn't work."

"You speak Italian with your mother?"

"She never taught me. At the time, people thought bilingualism made children stupid."

"She must regret it now," Sword said.

"I learned it later. It's just I have a terrible accent. I sound like Brad Pitt in *Inglourious Basterds:* 'Aweeva-durtchi.'"

"I love that movie," Sword said. "Brad Pitt. What an interesting trajectory."

"He's got range," Dorothy said. "He's a great comic actor."

Of all of Brad Pitt's career, the scene that came to Dorothy's mind in that moment was the one where he gets shot in a closet in *Burn After Reading*. She'd laughed so hard at it in the theater. The work his face did in that half second between being discovered and being shot dead—there was a whole story there. As in: someone could've written a novel about that half second. Terrified idiot foresees way out of potential violent death by telling his killer a funny story about how he ended up hiding in his closet. That the audience never gets to hear the funny story in question, that George Clooney is so shocked to find Brad Pitt between his shirts that he shoots him on sight, is of course the perfect move. It surprises and makes sense all at once. Yet the beauty of the scene lies in our belief that Brad Pitt's character has a story to tell. That if Clooney doesn't shoot, we'll get to hear it.

But Clooney shoots.

Dorothy image-searched "brad pitt closet scene" on her phone and only realized as she showed Sword the results how unsavory that was.

"Are you giving me options of faces to make when the shooter gets here?" Sword said.

Dorothy apologized and pulled her phone back.

"I wasn't thinking," she said.

Sword imitated one of Brad Pitt's closet faces (the first one, with the double chin) to let Dorothy know she was forgiven.

Dorothy hadn't thought about her own face so far. Only the shooter's. She'd been so focused on trying to guess who the shooter was that she'd forgotten to think about what her last words should be if he got to them, or the last face she'd make. Sword said he already knew what his last words would be, that that was something he'd decided upon years ago. Dorothy thought that was the first interesting thing he'd said. She asked him what the words were.

"I'm not telling you my last words," Sword said. "We're not dying yet." They still hadn't heard a single gunshot.

"But how did they come to you? Did it sort of hit you, or is it something you took days to think about?"

"It took about an afternoon," Sword said.

Dorothy couldn't decide whether that was long or short.

"Is it a sort of all-encompassing statement about your life?" she asked. "Is it a whole sentence?"

"I'm not telling you anything. It's between my wife and me."

"Your wife knows what your last words will be?"

"Of course she does. She's the one who wanted me to pick them. She told me hers, too."

"But that's the ultimate mystery," Dorothy said. "Why would she stay with you now that she knows what you'll say last?"

"She said it was in case I die and she's not around. So she doesn't have to spend the rest of her life wondering what my last words were."

"What a fun home life you have," Dorothy said.

"Or vice versa," Sword went on. "If she dies first."

"So you can't even change them if she dies first and you remarry?"

Sword looked through the window and thought of Baudelaire: "Quand le ciel bas et lourd pèse comme un couvercle"—the sky as a pot lid, weighing on everything. He'd considered Baudelaire for his last words, and other French poets, but it had felt a bit solemn in the end, a bit too self-important.

Dorothy asked again what the words were. She didn't want silence to take hold.

"Just look at it as a silver lining," Sword said. "If the shooter makes it to this room, you'll get to hear them."

"Only if he shoots you first," Dorothy said.

"True."

"If I go first, I have to warn you, I have no good last words to offer. I'd rather focus on last expressions, I guess. The last face I'll make. When he shoots me, if there is indeed a shooter in the building, I don't want to make a stupid face, like the deaths you're not supposed to care about in the movies."

"Why does it matter? Are you afraid the shooter will be *filming* you?"

Dorothy hadn't even considered the possibility.

"I don't want to give him the satisfaction, is all," she said. "That's why I'd like to guess who it is before he gets here. So at least I'm not taken by surprise when I see what he looks like. A surprised face would be the worst."

She wanted defiant, a defiant expression. She wanted dignity.

They heard footsteps in the hallway.

Sword inched closer to her and took her hand. The footsteps got closer, too. Dorothy held her breath. She wanted to block her ears, but also to leave her hand in Sword's (when was the last time someone had held her hand?), and so she just started humming, which she thought would cover the sound of the shooter's steps.

"What are you doing?" Sword whispered. "He's going to hear you."

The footsteps in the hallway stopped a split second after Dorothy went quiet. Had the shooter heard her *quit* humming? Weren't the walls supposed to be soundproof anyway? Hadn't Sword himself told her this? That you could hear what happened in the hallways, but couldn't, from the hallways, hear what happened in a classroom? The shooter couldn't have heard her, Dorothy thought. She'd hummed the kind of hum that only echoed in the hummer's skull.

They heard clicking sounds. The sounds came from right behind the door. They were familiar clicks, quick, bubbly, unnerving. Sword mouthed the words *Is he texting?* and Dorothy tasted tears coming up her throat. She wasn't going to cry now, was she? She wasn't a crier. More clicking. A couple of seconds of silence, then a swishing sound. The sound of a text being sent. The shooter had sent a text. Dorothy oddly expected to be the recipient of that text, but her screen remained dark. The shooter sighed behind the door and started typing again. One click sound per key hit. She never understood people who kept those sounds on. Did they do it to prove to everyone around them that they had people to talk to? Important messages to pass along? And what about those guys who walked the streets with their phones in front of their mouths, Dorothy wondered, who held their phones like tartines, like they were about to eat them? They clearly wanted strangers to witness their conversations, but why? And why was she thinking about different categories of people she despised right before dying? She squeezed Sword's hand.

Behind the door, the shooter finished typing another message, but the sound that followed wasn't that of a text sailing off, or an email. It was a sound Dorothy didn't recognize, that made her think of a mother shushing a child. Maybe it was a tweet? Maybe the shooter was tweeting about this? She'd never written a tweet, didn't know the sounds Twitter made when you . . . *sent* one? They heard the shooter sigh again. Dorothy thought she recognized Artie's way of sighing, the characteristic uptick at the end.

I think it's Artie, she mouthed to Sword.

Arthur Kessler? Sword mouthed back.

Artie was probably looking for her specifically, Dorothy thought. She'd been hard on him in improv class two days ago. Not as hard as she could've been, but she'd said things—that he was closed off like bad shellfish, that you couldn't get anything unrehearsed out of him, that he had to be more generous with his stage mates, and give them something to play with, and try stuff, and shift the pace, take more initiative—and now he was going to kill her for it. Was it better to be killed by someone you knew or by a total stranger? Artie's footsteps resumed. They took him three doors down, to the bathroom at the end of the hallway. Sword's office was just across from that bathroom, and he was familiar with the double squeak the bathroom doors made.

"He's taking a bathroom break," he told Dorothy.

"Are you sure?"

"A hundred percent. The door closed behind him."

Dorothy said this was their chance to escape, but Sword wasn't convinced.

"Maybe that wasn't the shooter," he said. "Maybe that was just someone who didn't get the alert on his phone."

"He was *using* his phone," Dorothy said.

"Maybe he didn't get the message."

"I don't understand . . . do you want to die here? Do you want to be killed by a Ryan Gosling look-alike?"

"Artie Kessler doesn't look like Ryan Gosling. He looks more like a young Paul Newman."

"All good-looking people look the same to me," Dorothy said.

She'd only ever fallen for ugly guys. Ugliness was superior to beauty in that it lasted much longer, she liked to say, paraphrasing Serge Gainsbourg. No one she'd ever said this to had known Gainsbourg to be the author of the quote, and so she'd claimed it as her own more than once, something she felt guilty about right now, something she wished she could correct before she died.

Sword was still holding her hand.

The expectation was they should sleep together, she thought. Maybe that was why he refused to leave when they had an out—maybe he felt they hadn't taken advantage of their being locked in a room together, all that electric, fear-generated energy.

"We need to leave now," Dorothy said. "We'll reminisce about our near-death experience at a later juncture. We'll get drunk over it, I'll buy you any scotch you like. I'll even sleep with you if you want. But we need to get the fuck out of here right now."

Sword said there would be no sleeping together. "I love my wife," he said, and the simplicity of the sentence touched even him.

Dorothy was annoyed that he could think she hadn't figured that out.

They left the room.

8

IT WAS A FIRST FOR ARTIE: BADLY NEEDING TO TAKE A SHIT *AFTER A* performance. He darted out of the classroom the second Kruger called the break. He ran a block to the administration building, where he knew the bathrooms would be empty. He'd received no active shooter message. There was no special security protocol laid out downstairs. All he had to do to get in the lobby was scan his university ID. The usual.

In the elevator, he faced two options: go up to the ninth floor, the one he was familiar with, where the English Department administration was, or try any of the other floors, where other departments had their quarters, and look for a bathroom where he would be less likely to run into someone he knew. He pressed 9 and felt like a loser. He had no spirit of adventure, he thought. It was what Dorothy had said to him in class on Monday: he never tried anything new. He was twenty-four years old and set in his ways. Taking a shit on the ninth floor. Walking in his father's footsteps.

The need to shit had arisen when his classmates had started laughing at his "bit." He'd always thought that a room erupting in laughter at something he did onstage would be glorious, would allow him immediate access to a new stratum of life, one for better people, that he would perhaps stop feeling his body for a minute. When he'd imagined that moment, he'd pictured the world suddenly acquiring a warmer tint, a new glow, and inspiration being unlocked—which meant, to him, not that jokes would pour out of his mouth easily and forever from then on but that he would see a way forward, if only briefly, through a life as a comedian. But everything around him still looked pasty, and all that his cohorts' laughter had unlocked was his bowels. What was so funny about what he'd done? He'd simply stayed silent for five minutes next to a photo of himself as a kid. Was it just better when he didn't talk?

His mother texted him to ask how workshop had gone, and whether he'd called Ethel yet. Artie was surprised to get reception in the elevator. Maybe only a mother's message could make it through all the layers of steel. He tried texting back, but his answer wouldn't send.

The words "better not to try at all than risk failing" crossed his mind. He knew that wasn't the actual phrase, but for years, he'd heard Mickey say it like that, words in the wrong order, in relation to their father—"better not to try at all than risk failing" being, to Mickey, a good summary of their old man's mindset. ("God forbid I should *try* something new," Mickey had once yelled at their father after getting grounded for some adventurous behavior—back when he'd still engaged in adventurous behavior, before heroin. "You'd rather be burned alive than see someone have a little fun and get out of their fucking lane for a second." To which their father had responded that lanes were there for a reason, that they kept life running smooth, and that true freedom was not in switching lanes but in finding a way to have fun in your own, words that Artie had found extremely wise in the moment but that Mickey had convinced him minutes later were all wrong: freedom was in crossing the lines.) Artie wasn't sure why he was thinking about the phrase now, exiting the elevator. He *had* tried something. It was unclear whether he'd failed or not, but he had *tried*. In that way, he was already more accomplished than his father. His father had a good job, though. He made money. Artie couldn't quite see money in the cards for himself. And his father had found love, too (his parents did love each other, it seemed). Which reminded him: text Mom. He stopped in the middle of the hallway, by the conference room, to write to her that he hadn't been able to reach Ethel, but that she should try not to worry. "Mickey always comes back," he typed, then erased, then typed, then erased again, the whole process causing him to sigh the first sigh Sword and Dorothy heard from behind the door.

The bathroom was only a few steps away now, but Artie's need to shit had receded. He hoped for a temporary recession rather than a full-on disappearance. He knew, though, that on occasion, a shit that had felt impossible to ignore, a shit that had demanded his whole attention and constant little physical adjustments on his part not to come out when it wasn't supposed to, could just vanish into the ether, never to be heard from again. Like a tornado. That's the image that crossed Artie's mind. This had happened to him countless times since childhood, usually around presentation days at school. It had happened to him at his grandfather's funeral, too. The need to shit had been so intense that day, during the service, and the impossibility of leaving the room to attend to the need so very obvious, that Artie had almost made peace with the idea that he would shit himself in front of everyone on his way to the lectern (he, unlike Mickey, or their father, had wanted to say a few words). But the pain in his stomach had ceased the second he'd made it to the stand. He'd been able to focus entirely on his speech, to return to his seat walking normally (though still with the heaviness that a funeral required), and he hadn't felt the need to shit again for a whole twenty-four hours. Where had that pre-eulogy shit gone? he'd wondered at the time. Where did vanishing stress shits go, in general? There had to have been studies about it, Artie thought. He wondered if certain needs to shit weren't just mirages your brain whipped together for you when it felt you were sinking, to lure you away from sad thoughts. Smoke and mirrors.

Still standing in the hallway, Artie wrote down some of these ideas in the new note-taking app he'd downloaded. He typed:

- phantom shit=put together by brain to short-circuit fear and sadness (lure, crutch)
- a eulogy is a kind of presentation

In the process of saving this to his phone, Artie saw the first line of the last few notes he'd consulted. The last note he'd opened was the bit he should've done in workshop today, the one Kruger had discarded right out of the gate. They'd been told by Kruger himself that it was wise to keep everything they wrote, that one never knew when a bit would unlock, that it took years, sometimes, for a joke to reveal where it was it'd always intended to go, but Artie still deleted the note. He heard for the first time the sound that the app made when it deleted something, the sound that Dorothy, on the other side of the door, heard as "mother shushing child." To Artie, it sounded more like a wind gust in the desert. It was only when he heard it that he realized the sound on his phone was still on. He thought of his imminent one-on-one car trip with Olivia and sighed. The pressure in his stomach came back. He walked to the bathroom.

There, he doused a wad of toilet paper with Purell and wiped the toilet seat before he pulled down his pants. He sat on the clean, still-humid ring, took his phone out, and watched on YouTube the *Mad Men* scene everyone had talked about in workshop, the one in which Don Draper/Jon Hamm pitches Kodak a way to sell their brand-new slide projector. Solid stuff, he thought. Easy to write a comedic parody of because every line in the original was sharp and clear. It would only be a matter of mirroring the beats. The *Mad Men* scene played on the idea of nostalgia. The slide projector had the power to take you back to "a place where [you] ache[d] to go again," it said. The mirroring parodic line could go something like "takes you back to a place you wish you'd never been," Artie thought. The parody would work around the idea that the slide projector Artie presented onstage only held your most shameful memories, for you to watch and browse and relive in the dark. He would have to show embarrassing photos of himself. The one he'd brought today would work, but there would need to be a lot more, like in Don Draper's pitch. In his pitch for Kodak, Draper showed company executives photos of his own pregnant wife, beaming, photos of their wedding, of friends dancing, photos of children playing and children sleeping. Artie would have to show his audience at least ten embarrassing pictures, to stay on the same pattern, the same kind of rhythm. Maybe he could take a selfie on the toilet right now? He still hadn't managed to shit. The need seemed to have evaporated once more. He watched the *Mad Men* scene again. Kruger had told them before that specificity was tantamount to good writing, but in the case of the *Mad Men* scene, Artie thought, it was the genericness of Don Draper's family photos that made his presentation work. We all had a place we ached to go again. Time passed for everybody. If Draper had been too specific in his choice of photos, his nostalgia wouldn't have been contagious. Whereas shame, Artie thought, shame relied on detail. If he wrote a parody of the scene in which he replaced nostalgia with shame, the embarrassing photos he showed would have to be hyperspecific. He gave out a long fart and wondered if shame wasn't, in fact, the opposite of nostalgia. Maybe his bit would be smarter than he'd realized. He played the scene once more. In it, Don Draper said, "Teddy told me that, in Greek, 'nostalgia' literally means 'the pain from an old wound.'" It could be funny to open on it. "Teddy told me that, in Greek, 'shame' literally means 'the pain from an old wound.'"

Did you need permission to write a parody of something? You probably did. Should he use background music onstage? The music in the scene was so pretty, but that was probably another permission to get. Artie was a sucker for film scores. He got goosebumps every time he heard the theme from *Jurassic Park*, for example. Just the thought of it now . . . He played the *Jurassic Park* theme on YouTube at full volume. When the music ended, he heard crying in the next stall.

"Is everything all right?" Artie asked through the partition.

"Please don't kill me," a woman responded. "I have a son."

"Professor Reeve?"

Artie had met with Vivian Reeve in her office once—his aunt Sophie was a big fan, he'd had to ask Reeve to sign copies of her novels for her.

"What are you doing in the men's room?" Artie asked. "Why would I kill you?"

Reeve said the men's bathroom was the nearest door when she received the active shooter/take shelter message.

"What message?"

"There's a shooter in the building."

"I didn't get any message."

It took Artie a minute to convince Vivian that he wasn't the shooter. Once she decided to trust he wouldn't kill her, they both exited their stalls, and Vivian showed him the message.

"Did you call the cops?" Artie asked.

"The police get pinged automatically when there's an alert like that."

"How long has it been since you got it? I didn't see any police outside."

"Almost an hour."

"They should be here by now."

Artie had always assumed he would be a coward in such circumstances. It surprised him not to be afraid, to be taking matters into his own hands. Maybe it was because Vivian Reeve had heard him fart and listen to the *Jurassic Park* theme while on the toilet. He understood that she had other things on her mind right now and wouldn't bring it up, but he knew she would remember all of it later and think strange thoughts about him. He had to present her with another Artie right away. A dependable Artie. An Artie who reassured and took charge. He called 911. They hadn't received any calls or information about an active shooter on campus. They were on their way.

"Stay where you are," the operator said. "Someone will come for you."

9

OLIVIA WAS ON HER SECOND CIGARETTE. CLASS BREAKS COULD GET FAIRLY
long. Kruger, a former smoker, always came down to the sidewalk
with his students to get whiffs of tobacco. He often encouraged Marianne and Olivia to light a second cigarette, sometimes even a third.
He never seemed to want to go back into the building.

Marianne was smoking in his face, a few yards away from Olivia,
telling Kruger everything she knew about Henri Bergson. Olivia was
jealous of Marianne's confidence, her skin, all the things she knew—
her European education. At least she wasn't jealous of her work. She
had to constantly remind herself that this was the most important
thing.

"Look at me, I'm so French," Jo whispered in Olivia's ear, impersonating Marianne. "I need to read a book about laughter in order to
understand the concept."

"She's not French," Olivia said. "She's Swiss."

"Same difference."

Phil came to them and apologized to Olivia for not answering her
call earlier.

"I'm sorry I missed it," he said. "I was writing."

Her classmates, as far as Olivia could tell, used the term loosely.
To them, "writing" could mean thinking, it could mean getting high
and staring at the wall, it could mean taking a walk alone at night.

"I'm working on this bit," Phil said, "where I'm impersonating
Aristotle. So the writing has to be extra good."

"Right," Olivia said.

She overheard Marianne say "Henri Bergson" again, pronouncing "Henry" the French way, like *ennui*. So pretentious, Olivia thought. She didn't know Bergson had in fact been French.

"Do you guys know where Artie went?" she asked Phil and Jo.

They didn't. No one knew anything, Olivia thought. She certainly didn't. She hadn't learned one thing so far, in this Master's of Stand-Up Comedy, and taking breaks in the middle of classes where you weren't learning anything made the fact even more obvious. It was exhausting, actually. They'd been on break for almost half an hour. She decided to look up Henri Bergson's *Laughter* on Wikipedia, and was offered the following page:

> *Laughter* is an audible expression
> of merriment or amusement.
> *Laughter* may also refer to:
>
> - *Laughter* (Ian Dury & The Blockheads album)
> - *Laughter* (The Mighty Lemon Drops album)
> - "Laughter," a 1994 song by James from the album *Wah Wah*
> - *Laughter* (1930 film), a 1930 film starring Fredric March
> - *Laughter* (2020 film), a Canadian film directed by Martin Laroche
> - *Laughter* (book), a 1900 collection of three essays by Henri Bergson
> - *Laughter* (novel), an Arabic novel by Ghalib Halasa
> - *Laughter* EP, a 2017 release by Tiny Vipers

Instead of clicking the link to Bergson's book, Olivia visited the page on laughter itself. For all that she'd tried to cause it in people, she realized, she'd never been curious about the physiological phenomenon. She learned that you started to laugh around your fourth month of life. That you laughed twelve times more, on average, when with another person than when alone. That a certain Chrysippus (a Greek Stoic philosopher from the third century B.C.) had died of

laughter after seeing a donkey eat his figs. She read about kuru, a dis-
order also known as "the laughing sickness"—one of its symptoms
was you kept shaking with uncontrollable, pathological bursts of
laughter. You could die from it. She read that on some old battlefield,
a soldier's head had been chopped off and catapulted back to his
men, and one of them picked it up to find the head was still laughing.
(*Still* laughing? Olivia thought. Why had it been laughing in the first
place?) She learned that rats laughed when you tickled them. They
had to know the tickler, though. If they didn't know the tickler, they
didn't laugh. Which made perfect sense to Olivia. She felt close to the
rat in that moment.

　　She tried paying attention to the description of what happened in
your body when you laughed, which muscles contracted, what the
larynx did, but it didn't speak to her much. She hated thinking about
the body anyway, about the whole thing being a mere reactionary machine, pretty much the same for everyone. She focused on the photos
that Wikipedia contributors had chosen for the page, and was happy
to see one of a "crowd laughing at Manny Reinhardt's HBO special
Figure It Out." But the other two images were puzzling to her. Of all
the faces, famous and anonymous, that they could've picked to illustrate laughter, the authors had gone with politicians. Theodore Roosevelt ("Theodore Roosevelt laughing"), Bill Clinton, and Boris
Yeltsin ("Boris Yeltsin and Bill Clinton having a fit of laughter, Octo-
ber 24, 1995"). She wondered why politicians laughing would be
considered a perfect illustration of the phenomenon. Was it another
case of what she'd said herself in workshop? That because you expected men to be strong and keep all types of emotion at bay, you
couldn't help but empathize with them whenever they showed one?
All the more if they were supposed to be solid and composed at all
times? Because yes, just watching these photos of powerful men
laughing made her smile. Their laughter, even frozen in time, had
something contagious, whereas she wasn't sure a picture of Angela
Merkel laughing would've had the same effect. Was she a misogynist?
She showed Jo the photos.

"What the fuck?" Jo said. "What did they choose for the ice cream entry? The picture of Putin and Erdogan eating some together?"

They looked up the Wikipedia page for ice cream. It was longer than the one about laughter.

They didn't pay attention to the first two police cars, and when all Michigan Avenue traffic split to make way for the third, the fourth, and the fifth, they plugged their ears, assuming it was but a temporary disturbance—those sirens, to their minds, only ever passed by you on their way to other places. When it became obvious that the cars' last stop was the admin building, Olivia, again, wondered where Artie was.

"They're setting up a perimeter!" Phil said.

Kruger and Marianne stopped talking about Bergson and moved closer to the rest of the group. Traffic was already being redirected, cars U-turning on Michigan.

"Should we go see what's happening?" Marianne asked.

Sword and Dorothy were walk-running toward them, having exited the administration building just before the police arrived. They explained to everyone that there was a shooter in there, and that the shooter was Artie.

"Artie was just in class with us," Olivia said.

"Did you hear gunfire?" Phil asked.

Kruger thought of his father again. The image of Artie holding a gun made no sense to him, but it hadn't made sense either, a few months back, when the Naperville Police Department had called to inform him that his father was in custody after shooting someone at the bar.

Olivia and the others established that Artie couldn't be the shooter, given the time at which Sword and Dorothy had received the first active shooter alert.

"We didn't get any alert," Marianne said. "Shouldn't the message that there was a shooter on campus have been sent to the whole community?"

"Absolutely," Sword said. He remembered this from safety train-

ing. He hated what he felt in that moment, that every university mis-
hap was somehow his responsibility. "We'll have to look into it," he
said.

Could he go home now, though? He should probably let Lydia
know he'd be late. He'd refrained from calling or texting this whole
time, not wanting to worry her, but now that he'd made it out alive, he
could tell her what was happening. Maybe the day's events could even
work as a wake-up call for his wife, he thought, propel her back into
the world. She could've lost him! Maybe this was a blessing in dis-
guise.

Marianne said something European about gun violence. People
tried not to pay attention, but she insisted. This would never happen
where she was from, she said. How many more deaths would it take,
etc. Some might've waited to know more before they started joking,
but for Dan and Jo, it was never too soon.

"We *need* gun violence," Dan said. "Just like we need unaffordable
healthcare. It's what makes us who we are."

"It keeps us angry," Jo said. "It keeps us on edge."

"That's why no one's funny in France," Dan said. "Because you
French people have it too easy."

"I'm not fucking French," Marianne said.

"I wouldn't boast about being Swiss. Switzerland is even worse.
You guys don't even have *homeless* people. What do you even get angry
about?"

"There are *lots* of amazing French and Swiss comedians," Marianne insisted.

She named names, but no one had heard of them.

Sword couldn't believe what he was seeing. The kids had just been
told about a shooter on campus, that perhaps one of their friends was
in the building he targeted, and they'd already changed the subject.
They'd discussed it for a second as something that was happening far
away, then moved on to teasing the one foreign student in the group.
His eyes searched for Dorothy's, for Kruger's. Were they finding this
normal? Was this normal comedian behavior? He knew comedians

were wired to find levity in horrible situations, but this? Dorothy looked about ready for bed, like she could fall asleep any minute. Kruger was nowhere to be seen. Kruger had left.

TV crews were trickling in. WGN, ABC-7, NBC-5. Bystanders were starting to press against police barriers. Phil asked if anyone else thought they should get closer to the perimeter.

"You just want to be on camera," Jo said.

"I want to see what's up."

"You want to skip your own workshop."

"I don't think we're going back to class," Phil said, and he looked around for Kruger to confirm. "Where did Kruger go?"

While they all debated where Kruger might've disappeared to, Olivia approached Sword to ask, simply, how he was doing.

"You must've been so scared," she told him.

"I kept it together for Ms. Michaels," Sword said, winking at Dorothy.

Why the wink? Wasn't winking illegal now? Dorothy didn't notice anyway. She was in her own world, typing fast on her phone. Texts to loved ones, Sword thought. Notes for a future bit, Olivia assumed.

"Did you think you were going to die?" she asked him.

Olivia'd been about to die once herself, back in high school, but she never talked about it. The cause of death would've been suicide, and she knew people wouldn't consider it as close an encounter with death as they would a hostage situation, or a car crash. To her, though, it was all the same. She'd looked at death head-on, she'd felt it seconds away. An acceleration.

"I don't believe I did," Sword said.

Olivia gave him time to think about it and elaborate, but he didn't add anything. He was like those people who answered, "Can't complain" when you asked how they were doing, Olivia thought. She'd always felt there was something aggressive about that. How could anyone not have anything to complain about? They didn't want to share it with *you,* was what it was, they didn't think *you* were worth sharing it with. She considered telling Sword about the day she'd almost killed herself, see if that helped him say something interesting. He would probably have to call some kind of university counseling service, though, if she told him.

"Are you worried about your friend?" Sword asked her, and it took Olivia a second to understand that he was talking about Artie.

"Not really," she said. "Artie can charm his way out of any situation."

The charm thing was an exaggeration, of course, but she did believe Artie's life was in no danger at all. No one had heard gunshots. No one was running out of the building covered in blood. She and Artie would have something to talk about in the car now, at least, on their way to O'Hare. Though once they picked up Sally, it would probably be best not to mention the shooter incident.

Sally hadn't been home that day, years ago, when Olivia had thought so seriously about killing herself. "Seriously" wasn't the word, really. "Seriously" implied a certain length of time. More like "vividly." The thought had been *vivid* that day, for the first time. Before, there had always been a buffer between any suicidal thought Olivia had had and the idea that she could act upon it—the two had never quite aligned and faced each other. If she thought, *I want to die,* something within her immediately shrugged its shoulders and said, *Tough shit.* Or, depending on its energy level, just hung there all sorry and dumb, like a bad salesman. That "something within her" was her sadness, Olivia thought, its own character in her life. An annoying presence, but also comforting, like a mother, not anything that would ever want to cause her harm. Or so she believed, until that day. Because that day, Olivia had thought, *I want to jump out the window,* and her sadness's answer had been *Do it.* In a split second, it had all appeared clearly to her—that suicide wasn't just for other people, that she could do it, too, that she could do it anytime, in fact, and most of all do it now. Until then, her suicidal thoughts had been like bird-watching through broken binoculars—she'd been looking at shapes so far, splashes of color, quick movements, the *possibility* of a bird (the possibility of suicide)—but now it was as if someone had, on a whim, decided to fix the focus wheel, and not only was the bird all of a sudden high-def and undeniable in the collecting lens, it was staring right back at her. Death was staring right at her. She wanted to ask Sword if he'd felt the same thing she had, in the face of death, a sort of grand-scale hypnic jerk—that falling sensation, right after going to sleep, your body trying to catch itself on the sheets. That impression of at once falling inside of yourself and through a narrow tunnel straight to the center of the earth. She'd thought that day that perhaps that was all that death was, a big hypnic jerk, except instead of waking yourself up, you got to see what was at the bottom of the tunnel. And she was almost there. She could already picture her body on the sidewalk, eight floors below. Her aunts gathering around Sally, *poor Sally,* to have to see her twin do this to herself, to have to see and bury her own dead body, in a way. And also, wasn't Sally the one who'd suffered the most? Why would *Olivia* do such a thing?

Sword was looking elsewhere now. They were done talking. No one wanted to talk about death with her. Death was only something to joke about.

"I have to make a phone call," Sword said. "I have to call my wife."

"Of course."

"She has depression."

Was he just going to tell everybody now? He'd said nothing for months, and now, what, it was time to cash in on some sympathy? Sympathy from comedians? He'd just witnessed how cold their breed was.

"She must be worried sick," Olivia said.

She tried to eavesdrop on Sword's phone conversation with his wife, but only heard a few words about ordering in and calling a neighbor for company. She considered going up to Dorothy to ask about *her* brush with death, but Dorothy scared her. Women scared her, in general. Accomplished women like Dorothy, but even just regular women like her mother, and her mother's friends. They all seemed to know something she didn't, to be both annoyed that she didn't know it and reluctant to share it with her. Maybe it was something to do with love, she thought, with being in love. That was something Olivia had never experienced. She wondered sometimes whether that was because she'd never met the right person or because she was incapable of the feeling. She'd tried everything to experience it. She'd dated the boys everyone wanted to date, the boys no one wanted to date, and a few in the middle. She'd had fun (especially with the middle category), but not much more. Six boys had told her they loved her so far, and she'd felt embarrassed for all of them. She'd broken off contact with each immediately.

Artie's name appeared on her phone. Olivia thought that meant he was about to die. *The shooter must be closing in on him,* she thought, *maybe he hears him approaching, and he wants me to be the last person he writes to.* In a split second, she pictured her whole life after this point, the tragic story she would tell herself and others about her aborted love story with a young comic talent, bright future ahead, a promise cut short by senseless violence. Could you fall in love with someone *after* he was dead? Maybe that was the key. You felt the feeling without having to share it with the person. Then you told your story to whoever asked about your love life, and you got all the sympathy. People understood if you never fell in love again after that. You were excused from the whole charade for the rest of your life.

She was already bracing herself for a declaration of love from Artie, words she could memorize and repeat to herself before bed every night if he died. Maybe she could fall in love with him *right now,* she thought, a few minutes before he died, rather than after the fact— that would be more powerful. The text said:

> Stuck in admin building. Hope to be out in time
> to drive you to o'hare!

A bit disappointing, but still something she could twist a little. *To the very end, Artie was thinking about how he could make my life easier.* She had to text back, didn't she? That's what people did when they were in love. She started typing something, but what if he hadn't muted his phone and her text revealed his position? Precipitated his demise? She held off on sending and rejoined the group, Jo and Phil and Marianne and Dan. They were still wondering where Kruger was, if he'd run away out of fear or what.

"I hope Artie's all right," Olivia said, trying to get into character.

"Relax," Jo said. "I'm sure he's not even in the building. All we know is Dorothy *thought* she heard him sigh."

"He just texted me. He's inside."

That sent a cold wave over them all, colder than the icy air coming from the lake.

"What the fuck is he doing in admin?" Marianne said. She was shivering. Her lips almost blue.

"People take shits there after hours," Dan said. "It's nice and quiet."

They all thought about it. Dying on the toilet. Like Gigi Cestone in *The Sopranos,* and Elvis, and Evelyn Waugh, and King George II, and Lenny Bruce. Even if Artie was shot in a hallway, the story would be that he died on the shitter.

The wind brought down screeching sounds from a train braking on an L line nearby. That sound was all Olivia had known about life in Chicago before moving there. She'd heard it on *ER* reruns as a kid. Not a program suited for children, but one her mother had wanted her and Sally to watch every week, in the hopes that it would both instill medical vocations in her daughters and show them that good men existed.

"Wait, are they leaving?" Phil had been studying every move the police made, and the camera crews. Equipment was being loaded back on vans. "Did they arrest the guy?"

Word came in long minutes later that there had been no shooter. Active shooter message: a prank fomented by an undergraduate student who'd hacked the university system and sent an alert to all phones in a certain perimeter. The kid was going in for questioning. "Probably just wanted to skip class," one of the cops said. He didn't even seem that angry.

What could've been prolonged collective relief (No one was dead! No one would die!) immediately turned into individual frustrations.

Sword's inbox would fill with indignant emails, he thought, each one of his colleagues demanding he take to different deans different and highly specific questions about the failure of the university security system. It was better than having to send condolence emails, *of course,* but no death or injury in the community also meant that there wouldn't be a moment of silence and dignity before the email storm.

Olivia was disappointed. The first quivering signs of romantic interest vanished the second she understood that Artie's life had never been threatened. She wouldn't fall in love today.

For Dorothy, it was mostly annoyance at the afternoon's outcome. This was bad storytelling, she thought. "It was all a prank!"—you couldn't end a story that way. She usually liked giving up on bits. It felt like deep-cleaning her apartment, but without the physical effort. She should've been glad, then, that this prank ending was making the decision for her—it was such a silly punch line, useless to write toward—but something prevented her contentment. It wasn't as simple as "I felt all this fear for nothing," but that was definitely part of it. The idea that everything in her life had the potential to become material had always soothed as much as exasperated her. She was never able to tell whether she was living something or already writing it. But to know that a third party, a bored undergrad, had been pulling the strings of her life and work the last couple of hours . . . that was new. That was infuriating. At least her email to Manny had bounced back, she thought. She wouldn't have to edit the story she'd told him.

IN
LONG SHOT

—

10

MANNY HADN'T OPENED THE BLINDS IN A WEEK. THERE WERE TOO MANY windows in his brownstone, and he feared paparazzi might be hanging around the block. Though, in all honesty, it wasn't just that: natural light depressed him, too. Always had. He only came to life at sunset, when someone (or something, most likely—a sensor, an algorithm) turned the streetlights on.

Maybe he should move to Iceland, Manny thought. More nighttime there. Iceland in the winter, then the South Pole in the summer, whatever city they had near there. This reminded him of something stupid he'd seen on Twitter. Everything did. Someone had tweeted that, in an effort to be more inclusive, Americans should stop using "Northern hemisphere–specific seasonal language," because people had to be aware that what was summer for them wasn't summer for everybody else on the planet. The person suggested we only use month names from now on, or refer to chunks of time by quarter number (Q1, Q2, and so forth). A lot of people had congratulated the person on her idea, but then someone had immediately made fun of her, responded that another tiny inclusive thing we could do as a species was avoid heliocentric temporal language and replace today's date with "Stardate 36992.4.8," for example. This had made Manny both laugh and want to shoot himself in the face. Not because the original tweet confirmed how stupid the world was becoming, but because it had only taken someone else four minutes to come up with and type out the Stardate response. Manny thought people were too fast now. Jokes were coming in too fast. He didn't post to Twitter himself and didn't understand comedians who did. Why would they kill a joke instantly by giving it to the whole world at once? And for free? There was something admirable there, in a way. These people had to believe the well would never go dry, that jokes would just keep on coming and coming. He wished he had that kind of faith in himself. Was the new generation just better? More confident? The Stardate guy wasn't even a comedian, Manny didn't think. Probably just someone bored at work.

Manny'd talked about it with Bill Burr once, why Burr was releasing good material for free all the time on his podcast, but Burr had said Manny was an idiot: of course he wasn't doing it for free. Still. Twitter, a podcast, those were not venues for comedy. Good material was for the stage. Live TV, perhaps. It was for a physical audience, first and foremost. If you couldn't hear a laugh, the joke was wasted. And as long as you could tell it and hear new people laugh, it was still alive. That's why comedians before radio, before TV, had been able to sell their jokes to younger performers when they retired. Not everyone had heard them yet. Not that Manny would ever want to buy a joke from someone else. It was just how it used to be. The business changed all the time.

His ex-wife called. She'd been calling once a day since the first scandal (the beating at the Comedy Strip), twice since the second (the marriage proposals), to check on him. Rachel called in the morning, to make sure Manny wasn't too hungover, and again in the dead of the afternoon (which she knew had always been the worst time of day for him), to try delaying the hour at which he would start drinking.

"I'm not going to quit," Manny told her. "You know that. I don't believe in that."

"You don't believe in sobriety?"

"All the AA bullshit. It's too extreme."

He'd actually started and abandoned a bit about AA years ago. It was based on an actor he'd met at a charity event who'd gone onstage to tell his story and kept repeating he'd been sober a year, a little over, in fact. He'd given the audience the exact number of days, and everyone had applauded. Manny had, too (he wasn't an asshole), but really, as he was clapping, he'd wondered why the number mattered. The way he understood the "One day at a time" motto was that every day of sobriety was so excruciating that it didn't help to think about the future, yet AA gave you color-coded chips to mark the length of your sobriety, certain anniversaries, and there was a contradiction there, to Manny's mind. It seemed greedy to want people to know both the endlessness of your pain and how much of that endlessness you'd gone through already. And what did the chips even mean? If you never recovered but were always recovering, if you could slip at any moment and all there was to do was get to the end of the one day you were in without a drink and in the morning the clock started all over again, then who cared how long you'd been suffering? You don't ask Sisyphus how long he's been doing this, with the stone. Or you *could*, but there isn't much to do with the answer.

"It's not like I beat up women when I'm drunk," he told his ex-wife on the phone.

"I know. It's the timing. It's making people conflate all the stories," Rachel said.

"I just propose *marriage* to them," Manny said. "Apparently."

"Some would argue that's worse."

"Don't give in to this shit, Rach. Words hurting more than physical violence. You're smarter than this."

"I was making a joke."

"Leave the jokes to me."

Why was he being such a dick? It was nice of Rachel to call. Rachel had always been good to him.

"I'm sorry," he said, and he asked about their son. "Has August heard back from Boothe yet?"

August would take the bar exam in February. In the meantime, he was interning at Boothe, Bloom & Boghosian in Chicago. He'd been waiting to hear if they'd let him assist in the courtroom on the Delgado trial, which was starting tomorrow.

"Still waiting," Rachel said. "He's pretty confident they'll say yes, though."

Where did that confidence come from? Manny wondered. Certainly not from him. And Rachel wasn't a glass-half-full type either. None of the role models they'd picked for August had been.

"Did you tell him I was moving to Chicago for a few months?"

Rachel didn't respond right away.

"They still want you to teach there?"

"Of course," Manny said. "They're reasonable people. They understand the situation is absurd."

Rachel took another second.

"I don't want to tell Auggie anything about Chicago unless you're absolutely certain you're going," she said.

Manny thought he shouldn't have mentioned August. When he mentioned August, their conversations started sounding like after-school specials.

"He's twenty-six years old," he said. "He can take it if there's a change of plans."

Manny and his son hadn't talked much the past few years. A handful of emails, birthday calls, a couple strained days around Christmas every year. Rachel was convinced it had to do with the divorce, that August was mad at his father for cheating, but Manny wanted to believe his son simply had a life to live. It was so unusual, someone living his own life, not judging the way other people did it. He told Rachel she should stop protecting him so much.

"How about you *start*?" Rachel said.

Manny knew all the money he'd put into his son's education didn't make him a good father, so he didn't mention it, but the soundproof walls in the basement so August could play drums, the martial arts lessons, the French tutor, all the books he wanted . . . didn't that count as protection, too?

"Your son is blowing big-shot lawyers to be first row on a fucking *murder* trial, and you think he needs some kind of psychological preparation before he sees his *father*?"

"It's a Ponzi scheme trial," Rachel said. "Not murder."

"Didn't the guy's daughter die, too?"

"Suicide. Unrelated. And don't talk about Auggie like that. He's not *blowing* anyone. He works very hard."

Manny knew Rachel would've hung up on him just a few weeks ago for the "blowing" comment.

"All I'm saying is, I'm a fucking cliché," he said. "Not a monster. There's a big difference."

"At least he's on your side in all this," Rachel said.

"Is he?"

"He says these women have no case against you."

That was different from being on his side, Manny thought.

"What about me breaking Shitlip's nose?"

"Auggie says if Lipschitz doesn't sue, there's no reason not to go back to your life."

Manny respected that his son saw the world through a specialized prism. Even if that prism was law. At least it wasn't social media. August didn't claim to know everything, the way other kids his age did. He had one area of expertise, he knew to stick to it, and that was perhaps the best you could hope for—for your child to know enough about one thing that he could recognize the things he didn't know about. It had been hard for Manny, though, to accept his son's career choice. As an artist, you were supposed to say you didn't want your kid to follow in your footsteps, it was such a hard and unfair world, so unpredictable, and you didn't want your baby to suffer and be rejected all the time, the way you had been, etc., but then when your son became a lawyer, you *had* to wonder where you fucked up, what he saw in you that disgusted him so much.

"Still," Manny told Rachel. "I think I'll have to apologize. No way around it."

"I'm sure Auggie would love that," Rachel said.

"I was talking about a *public* apology."

"Right."

"What would I have to apologize to August for? I cheated on *you*, not him."

"Never mind," Rachel said. "I misunderstood you. Public apology, yes, that's a good idea. You'll have to address the drinking thing too, for sure. All three women said you drank a lot. Do you have a draft you want me to look at?"

Of course he didn't have a draft. When his agent had first suggested he apologize about Lipschitz, Manny had asked to think about
it, and in the time it had taken him to think about it, the women had
come forward with their stories of marriage proposals, and now he
didn't know what he was supposed to apologize for. If he wrapped it
all up in the same statement, it would add to the confusion. People
would think he'd been violent to the women, too. His head was ex-
ploding. He'd been worried for a week that he had brain cancer and
these were the symptoms—frequent headaches, punching guys at
comedy clubs. He'd cried a couple of times, too, since the shitstorm
had started. In fact, he'd wanted to cry when Lipschitz had called him
a wash-up at the Strip, a dinosaur ("And not even the good kind,"
Lipschitz had said, "not even one we remember"). It was because
Manny had wanted to cry that he'd punched him. He'd punched him
in order not to cry. Maybe crying was a symptom. He tried to chase
the cancer thoughts away, like he'd been doing for days.

"I don't have a draft," he told Rachel. "Michelle keeps telling me
the agency has apology specialists that can write one for me. I think
she's getting impatient."

"Maybe you should trust her."

"I don't want anyone to ever write anything on my behalf. And I'm
okay apologizing for the punch. It's the marriage proposals that I'm
not apologizing for. That shit's ridiculous. Also, I didn't propose. I
didn't say, 'Will you marry me.' I don't think I said that. I probably
said, 'Maybe we should get married.' That's what I usually say. As you
may recall. 'Maybe we should get married' is very different. You're
the first person I said it to that took it seriously, by the way. Everyone
does now. You were ahead of your time."

"Don't be an asshole," Rachel said. "Don't pretend you were joking when you proposed to me."

"You'll never know."

He promised her he wouldn't drink until he had a draft of an apology, and that he would send it to her.

"I'll show it to Auggie then," Rachel said. "If that's okay."

What could Manny say? August would have to see it anyway.

"Brilliant," he said. "We can work on it as a family. Create new memories."

They hung up. Manny opened Word on his computer. He'd judged all public apologies so harshly before, the same words for everyone. Now it was his turn, and he couldn't find better ones. The problem was, he *had* to keep it bland, he thought. You couldn't be funny in an apology, or try to be clever. Apologies had become mere phatic functions of language, automatic responses no one really paid attention to, or noticed, unless they never came. Dullness was the goal. The reader/witness of the apology had to forget that the apologizer was a real person, and apologizing a hard thing to do. Manny wrote:

I'm an idiot, have always been an idiot.

He wrote about his childhood, how hard it had been, and how he realized that the amount of anger he carried was perhaps a form of disease. He struck the word "disease." Claiming a disease was making excuses, not apologizing. The key was for people to come out of this thinking he had a disease without him having to say the word. Which should be easy to do, he thought. Everyone saw diseases everywhere now. Everyone was sick. He'd almost convinced August, on his law school applications, to check the "disability" box, because August had a very high IQ, and Manny thought hyperintelligence should be considered a mental illness.

He wrote about August and Rachel, how much he loved them, and how sorry he was to have brought shame onto them. He wrote about Lipschitz, of course, though he'd learned from reading other apologies that it was better not to go into much detail when it came to your victim. He stuck to the words "promising" and "talented," even though Lipschitz had never made him laugh, and insisted that there was never any excuse for violence, even though he didn't believe that was true either.

Manny knew the draft was far from clean, but he wanted to start drinking, so he sent it to Rachel. That's when he saw Dorothy's email. Since the Strip, he'd set it up so any email he received triggered a fake

and immediate "System Delivery Failure" response—people would
think he was off the grid, but he could still see everything everyone
wrote to him. He thought it was a joke at first, that Dorothy was joking about being stuck at school with a school shooter, but it wasn't
funny, and Dorothy had always been funny. He hadn't seen her in
years, sure, but funny people didn't just become boring. Especially if
they remained childless, which, to his knowledge, was still Dorothy's
situation. He wanted to call her, but didn't have her number anymore. He called Ashbee, and seemed to wake him from a nap. Ashbee
wasn't aware of any shooters anywhere. He was home, five miles
from campus. He was pretty sure Dorothy was joking, and told Manny
not to worry.

"I just want Dorothy's number," Manny said.

He'd never much liked Ashbee. Ashbee had always struck him as a
try-hard. When he'd heard about Ashbee starting up a graduate comedy program twelve or so years before, Manny had first thought it was
a joke (it would've been Ashbee's best), but then when different
sources had confirmed it wasn't, he'd understood it might've been
Ashbee's true calling, teaching what he couldn't do but had spent his
life attempting.

Ashbee gave him Dorothy's number.

"And we agree that you don't care for Kruger's number," he added.

"Correct," Manny said.

Ashbee wanted to riff. He didn't talk to Manny Reinhardt every
day.

"Only Dorothy's. Dorothy: you'd like to know if she's alive. Kruger: can die a slow and lonely death."

"Correct," Manny repeated.

"Very well."

Manny thought calling Ashbee with such a pressing request would
spare him from lousy jokes and small talk. But Ashbee was going to
be his colleague now. Manny had to give him a little something.

"Does teaching leave you any time to work on your own stuff?" he
asked. "We haven't seen a new Ashbee show in a while."

"Not sure that's what the world needs right now," Ashbee said.

"Another middle-aged man ranting about his experience as a middle-aged man."

"Except you're a *Black* middle-aged man," Manny said. "I don't know about *needs,* but the world definitely wants to hear what you have to say."

"I guess I just don't want to partake," Ashbee said. "I'm not much into all that stuff. I'm selfish at heart. I've never wanted to speak for anyone other than myself."

They exchanged banalities about writing, how speaking for oneself was the only thing one could do in the end, one's best shot at universality, etc. Ashbee said something about animal memes. He had a theory that, soon, comedians would only be able to joke about other species if they wanted to stay clear of scandal. After that, it would only be a question of time before people started getting offended on behalf of the animals in question, but still, there was a window there for now. With animals. People recognized themselves in animals. You just had to look at the most popular memes on the internet. Like the swan meme, the swan at the party. Did Manny know what he was talking about? Manny didn't. He didn't follow the animal memes.

"I'll send you a link," Ashbee said, and a few minutes later, he did.

He sent Manny a link to an essay about memes, too. Manny wasn't a reader of essays. Would he have to read essays now? On comedy? Would that be asked of him now that he was going to teach stand-up classes?

He dialed Dorothy. No response. Hearing her voice on the outgoing message, Manny realized he couldn't quite match a face to it anymore. He'd spent three or so years with her in the nineties closing every cheap bar in the West Village, and they'd slept together, too, a handful of times, he'd seen all her shows, but he couldn't remember anything specific about her features. He didn't pay a lot of attention to faces. He'd even had a hard time distinguishing August from other short, dark-haired boys in kindergarten. He remembered a lot of things Dorothy said, though. One in particular, not long after he'd met Rachel. He must've talked about Rachel a lot back then, he'd fallen so hard. Rachel was writing for *Sex and the City* at the time, and when he'd told this to Dorothy, Dorothy had said that *Sex and the City* was an unrealistic portrayal of women, not because the women on-screen paid too much for shoes and never gained weight in spite of all the food they had between already lavish meals, but because none of them ever talked about their mothers. Manny had used the line a couple of years later, in his first Letterman interview, not mentioning that it was Dorothy's. Letterman had asked him about Rachel, by then his wife, and what he thought of the show she worked on, because Manny's brand of comedy was so far from the *Sex and the City* vibe, and Manny had said, "I actually love the show. I'm a Charlotte through and through," to which the audience had laughed too generously. "The only critique I would have," he'd added while they were still laughing, "the only critique I would have—and I tell my wife this all the time—is the show is a bit unrealistic because the girls never really talk about their mothers." Even louder laughs had ensued. "I would like to hear them talk about their mothers a little, you know? Understand where they're coming from." Women had come to him after the show to tell him it was so true, what he'd said, that they'd never noticed it, but yes, the absence of mother talk in *Sex and the City* was astounding, now that they thought about it. Rachel hadn't appreciated the comment. She'd told Manny that night, when he'd come home, that the show's creators had made a deliberate decision not to have Carrie and the girls talk about their families ("not just their mothers, by the way, their whole *families*"), that the show was about something else, and now they were going to get letters, her bosses, and they would blame her, and Manny should never have undermined her work so publicly. "It was just a joke," Manny had said, and thought, *Someone else's joke, at that.* The whole way home, he'd worried that Dorothy would call him, angry that he'd used her line on Letterman. She hadn't said at the time that it was a line she wanted to use for something, but still. Manny felt like shit for blurting it out. It had presented itself in a moment of stress (the biggest interview of his life so far), and he'd grabbed onto it.

Dorothy never called about the line, never mentioned it, but twenty-some years later, alone in his curtained living room, Manny was still mad at himself for stealing it. He was vulnerable these days. Because he was being attacked left and right in the press, he was afraid that it might surface, that Dorothy would decide to let the world know that Manny Reinhardt had once stolen a joke from her, a less successful female comedian.

The email she'd just sent, though, insisted that she was on his side. And maybe she was dead now. Maybe one of the only people who was on his side had been shot, Manny thought. His phone rang, but it wasn't Dorothy, only Rachel telling him what he already knew, that his apology needed a lot more work. Manny promised he'd draft something else right away and poured himself another bourbon. Contrition came easier this time. Not because of the bourbon, but because he'd just remembered how bad he'd felt that night after Letterman, using a line that wasn't his. He tapped into that old guilt and wrote something decent.

Rachel said that version was better, more heartfelt. That she would send it to Auggie for legal advice. Manny asked his ex-wife if they called their son Auggie at work, or August. She said everyone called him Auggie, even clients.

"It's a shame," Manny said. "We gave him such a good name. August Reinhardt. He could have been a novelist with that name. An astronaut."

"Auggie Reinhardt is nice, too," Rachel said. "It has a nice ring."

"It sounds like he'll only ever defend small-time crooks."

Rachel said small-time crooks needed defending, too.

While he was on the phone with Rachel, Ashbee left a message to let him know that the shooter thing had been a prank. Everyone was safe and sound. "Got to go," the message ended. "I'm at the barber's, I have a date tonight."

The news that Ashbee had a date, the bad music playing at the barber's in the background, all intensified the silence in Manny's own apartment. He hadn't seen anyone in days. Even food deliveries were left on his doorstep. All contact with the outside world was mediated through the phone in his hand, that black rectangle that sud-

denly reminded Manny of the monolith in 2001. It was the same
black, wasn't it? Shiny and opaque. Malevolent. He felt as lonely as
he had in hospitals, when August was sick as a baby. That feeling he'd
had back then that he would never again be anywhere else. That life
would go on for others outside the hospital, but not for him, and not
for August, that hospital time would be their time, the entirety of it,
their lifetime. Remembering this, he felt his heart compress, a
sponge being squeezed. Was he having a heart attack? Was it cancer?
Was it just sadness? Maybe he was lonely, Manny thought. Maybe that
was it. What did lonely people do? They read books. He should read
something.

He read the essay Ashbee sent, about memes. Meme writers were
even less understandable to Manny than comedians on Twitter. At
least comedians on Twitter were trying to get something out of their
posts, expand their following or whatever, generate buzz, while
meme writers . . . these people didn't even want credit. That made no
sense to Manny. No sense at all. Although anonymity was the best way
not to have anyone mess with you if your joke didn't please. That was
unfair, Manny thought. If you had the guts to show your face, you got
in trouble. But if you gave up on putting your name out there, you
could make any joke you wanted, unsavory, downright appalling,
even not funny at all: the joke would find its audience, and no one
would ever wonder whether the person who'd made it had been allowed to make it. No one cared who they were.

> No one knows who makes these memes. Their anonymity
> renders them a kind of pure expression, as if the culture
> dreams them up at night while we're asleep, and we
> awake to puzzle at their meanings.

Manny reread these lines several times. A *pure expression*. Our society's unconscious, the collective dreams we dreamed at night. Of
course. Memes couldn't have authors. Memes were our tea leaves,
our oracles. If we found out who wrote them, the spell would be broken. Maybe one guy wrote them all in New Zealand, or Siberia. All the

memes. Maybe an artificial intelligence did, a web of computers, an alien civilization, a god. Memes were the last bastion of comic freedom, Manny realized. He called Ashbee again, but Ashbee didn't pick up, Ashbee was getting ready for his date. Manny wanted to tell him it wasn't animal memes that were safe, but memes in general, all of them. That you could still say whatever you wanted to say there. That they should teach their students how to write memes, not stand-up, that memes were the future.

About two minutes later, the idea struck Manny for what it was: ridiculous. Anonymity—who wanted that? What comic didn't want the world to know that a good joke was his? Manny never believed people (people like Rachel) who said they didn't want to be famous, that all they needed was for their work to be recognized in the very small circle that mattered. They said they didn't want to lose control over their image, that fame was toxic, and fame *was* toxic, yes, people knew too much about you, Manny thought, people knew too much about *him*, especially, right this minute, but if he was being honest, wasn't it better than them knowing nothing at all? Than them not even knowing his name? Wasn't everyone knowing what a shitty person he was better than having to introduce himself to new people all the time? Introducing yourself sucked. Starting from scratch. Figuring out what to put forth, what lies to tell. Of course he was ashamed that everyone with an internet connection knew he slept with women thirty years younger than him and became an idiot who brought up marriage after too many drinks, but he would be ashamed anyway, famous or not—shame had always been his motor, what kept him writing. He'd always written to erase previous shameful stuff with new material, new material he became ashamed of after he toured it long enough, and so on and so forth. That was the cycle he'd been in for decades, so what if he was ashamed on a grander scale now? Maybe it would get him to a new level, writing-wise. He'd been stuck on the same plateau for years. He'd been stuck at home, too, for over a week now, with the blinds drawn, because he'd been told to lie low, that was what one did in his situation, but really, he couldn't wait to show himself again, and maybe he should get back into the world right this instant, not listen to what others recommended. It was his life, and he didn't want to hide. Manny wanted to be seen. It wasn't purely selfish—he wanted to see others, too, and not just the front they presented to the world but who they really were. He wanted to know their fears, their favorite jokes, what kept them up at night. He wanted to see his son. He looked up flight times to Chicago. He could be there in five hours if he left his apartment in the next few minutes. Arrive at O'Hare at 10:02 P.M. August worked late. They'd have a drink together. They'd talk. Manny booked his ticket.

11

DOROTHY SAID THEY COULDN'T JUST GO HOME AS IF NOTHING HAD happened, that they needed a drink. They all ended up at the Gage. Sword pretended to think about options other than alcohol, but Dorothy ordered vodka, which started a chain of requests for spirits. Olivia went with mezcal, Dan scotch, Marianne cognac, Artie tequila, and Phil (as Sword did in the end, too) ordered bourbon. Jo asked for a glass of milk, but that was only to be weird—she didn't touch it.

Phil had never had bourbon before. It was the only American liquor he could think of. He didn't think it was cultural appropriation to drink a margarita (his favorite drink), but he also imagined that he would get teased for having one. Olivia would say something about Mexican identity, how he was stealing from her ancestors (her maternal grandmother was from Jalisco). Or maybe no one would notice, given that all the attention was on Artie. Artie, the hero, who'd called the police.

"We all assumed they'd been warned by the system," Sword said.

Artie wasn't too comfortable with the "good job" looks. He was glad that Vivian Reeve hadn't joined them for a drink, but soon she would start talking. People would find out he'd been listening to *Jurassic Park*'s theme while on the toilet. Artie knew it didn't matter what he said now, what bravery points he managed to garner preemptively: no amount of preliminary work would ever make up for the image of him people would have once Vivian talked.

"Vivian was crying," he said. "I didn't know what else to do."

"You call the cops every time a woman cries?" Marianne asked.

"Isn't that what you're supposed to do now?" Artie said. "Turn yourself in? On behalf of all men?"

Dan and Olivia laughed. Jo said Artie's response would have been funnier if he'd stopped after "Isn't that what you're supposed to do now?"

"I didn't realize we were still workshopping me," Artie said.

"We're always workshopping you."

Phil wasn't liking his bourbon much. He envied Artie's tequila. Artie was barely drinking it.

"Vivian thought *I* was the shooter," Artie said.

"So did I!" Dorothy's vodka was making everything interesting to her. The vodka, and the fact that Manny had left her a message. She felt like a teenage girl—not the one she'd been herself, but a cliché version from the sitcoms, the girl a boy's attention turned to goo in the high school hallways. Dorothy wasn't in love with Manny (she wasn't sure she'd ever been), but that such a famous man had inquired about her safety and well-being made her feel important. That didn't happen often.

"I thought you were coming after me specifically," she told Artie.

"Why would I come after you?"

"Because I was mean to you in class the other day."

Dorothy wasn't supposed to say things like that. Never question your teaching methods in front of your students was the rule. If you were not proud of how a class had gone, you either forgot about it or found a way to tell yourself the kids had learned something from the fiasco. In that way, teaching was different from performing. The audience shared part of the responsibility.

"I sucked," Artie said. "I deserved every bit of what I got."

He made a solemn promise to never shoot Dorothy. He said he would probably never shoot anyone, honestly. He didn't see that in the cards for himself.

Olivia was the first to order a second drink. She went outside to smoke before it arrived, and it hurt Artie a bit that she couldn't help it, even as they were talking about him. He saw her, through the bay window, struggle to light a cigarette in the wind, and kept watching as a young man immediately stopped to help her out. She hadn't put a coat on, and the man opened the sides of his own in front of her, in a flasher-like posture, to create a windless pocket of air. Artie thought the man would leave once the cigarette was lit, but even though he didn't smoke one himself, he stuck around to chat with Olivia in the cold. Perhaps Olivia's whole life was like this, Artie thought. Good-looking men stopping by to solve her problems. Was he not going to be one of them himself in thirty minutes? Driving her to O'Hare?

Phil saw him look. Phil had decided not to date or fall in love again for a while. When people asked about his love life, he joked that it didn't make sense for him to start a serious relationship before he was famous, because his fame would ruin it, create an asymmetry impossible for the couple to ignore. The official line was he didn't want a woman he loved to see the change in him—there *would* be a change—but in truth, Phil simply hadn't had the courage to go up to a girl and introduce himself lately, wait to see if she was interested. He didn't know what made him interesting anymore.

The fact that he wasn't on any dating apps had led his classmates to accuse him of asexuality, and even once, after Jo had read out loud from an LGBTQ+ glossary that was circulating on campus, of demisexuality (a demisexual being someone, they'd all learned that night, who could only sleep with people they were in love with). Phil had said that he wasn't demi-, or a-, just your run-of-the-mill cisgender white male, a phrase he'd seen Dan and Artie wince at. Phil understood why cisgender white males didn't like hearing the words "cisgender white male." He'd been like them not so long ago. He'd hated being reduced to his skin color, gender, and sexual orientation. He was so much more than that! A redhead! An epileptic! A volunteer at a homeless shelter! A gifted pianist! But then he'd heard someone say that gays and lesbians had been reduced to their sexuality since forever, and people of color to their color, so why should he have a problem with it? That had gotten him thinking. He'd never heard it put so simply. Why shouldn't he suffer the same indignities as people he was no better than? His parents hadn't agreed. They'd argued that what white people were getting wasn't "privilege" but the basic decent treatment everyone should receive, that white people were experiencing the baseline that society should strive to have minorities experience as well, and that what people like Phil were doing was going to get everyone treated equally shitty rather than equally well. It was certainly a nice idea, raising minorities' treatment up to the level of straight white people's, but Phil didn't think it could work, or not quickly enough, and anyway, he believed that in order for true equality to be achieved, cis white men and women needed to understand what it was like to be narrowed down to broad traits that they didn't think said much about them. That's why when someone called him a white male, he didn't mind cringing a little bit: it was part of his education.

As interested as he was in thoughts of fairness and equality, though, he still found them hard to make funny. His poor timing in becoming socially aware right before he was accepted into stand-up school was funny in itself, he knew that, but he was growing wary of self-deprecation. You had to be careful not to go too far with it. Phil knew it was possible to hurt other people by talking shit about yourself.

"How's your tequila?" he asked Artie, still jealous of it.

"Do you want it?" Artie said. "I'm only having a sip or two. I have to drive Olivia to O'Hare."

He was still staring at her through the restaurant window, smoking and chatting with the kind stranger.

"What's your plan here?" Phil said.

"My plan?"

"With Olivia."

"We're going to pick up her sister," Artie said.

"And?"

"And then we'll bring her to the Empty Bottle for the show tonight."

"Don't be thick," Phil said. "You're going to be alone in your car with her for like an hour. What are you going to *say*?"

"Don't encourage him to prepare lines," Jo said. "That's lame."

"Professor Sword here has lines prepared for when he *dies,*" Dorothy said. "He and his wife, they've picked their last words together. Isn't that sweet?"

Was she drunk already? She shouldn't have said that. Sword had told her about the last words in a moment of vulnerability, when he thought he might have to use them. Why was she ridiculing him now? It was the Manny effect, Dorothy thought. It was Manny's voicemail, contact with Manny, even indirect contact with Manny. It made you cocky. It made you stop thinking before you spoke, because you were confident that you would find a way to make what you said hilarious midway through saying it. But she had nothing.

Sword was staring into his bourbon. He just wanted to be home, watching a movie. It was Dorothy who'd insisted he join them at the Gage.

"How can you already know what you'll want to say about your whole life?" Artie asked Sword. "I don't even know how I'll feel about *today* when I go to bed."

"That's because you're still young," Sword said, and for a moment, it seemed he wouldn't say more than that. "You don't know yet which of your choices will pay off, so everything is high stakes. It's all high highs and low lows." Another pause, a sip of bourbon. "With me, it's different. I've gone through the main steps already, career, marriage, kid . . . I expect things to roughly remain on the same plane from now on. Perhaps a slight incline toward the end."

"That is so sad," Jo said.

"I understand how you could see it that way," Sword said. "But really, after the constant stress of your twenties, the self-doubt of your thirties, and the anguish of your forties, it's nice to relax a little bit. It's like biking down a hill now."

"You're making me want to kill myself," Jo insisted.

Another student telling Sword that he made her want to die would've had him apologizing for minutes. But the comedy students never complained about anything to the hierarchy. It wouldn't cross their minds to write to the dean about Sword making them feel this way or that. It was like they didn't know deans existed.

Phil asked Dorothy if she felt the same, that the stakes became lower as she aged, or if what Sword was talking about was rooted in male privilege.

"Well, I'm not married," Dorothy told Phil. "I'm not even dating anyone. I have no children. And I'm trying to teach *you* guys something for a living. How fulfilled do you think I am?"

Dorothy was being pretty anti-feminist, Phil thought, linking personal fulfillment to marriage and children, but he wasn't going to touch that. Some things only women were allowed to say.

"I might be barren, for all I know," Dorothy added. "I've never even had an abortion."

"I don't think it's a male thing," Sword said. "That life gets easier in your fifties. Look at Manny Reinhardt."

"You're using Reinhardt as an example of *non*–male privilege?" Phil said.

"I'm just saying, here's a man who could've just taken his leisurely ride through fame and glory, but then, boom: violence, accusations of emotional misconduct."

"I'm not sure where you're going with this," Jo said.

"He's trying to make you feel better," Dorothy said, "by showing you that life can be eventful and suck at any age."

"Manny *Rein*hardt's life sucks?" Phil said. "Excuse me? What about the women he abused?"

"*Ab*used?" Dan said.

"You really drank the Kool-Aid," Jo said.

Which was something Phil's parents told him all the time: "You drank the Kool-Aid, son." But they'd drank some kind of Kool-Aid too, in their day, hadn't they? Wasn't that what being alive was, to some extent, participating in society, drinking whatever it gave you? Otherwise, you were on the sidelines your whole life? Otherwise, you were a misfit? "But I don't understand," Phil's father would say to that. "Don't you *want* to be a misfit? Isn't that what you went into comedy for?"

"And you," Phil told Jo. "You've internalized male domination to the point that you're siding with it. You're okay with turning your back on your whole gender."

"You don't even *know* my gender," Jo said. "I just made it up in my head."

"All right, kids," Dorothy said. "That's enough. Keep some anger bottled up for tonight."

Phil obliged, and kept to himself what he wanted to tell Jo, that she was a conservative, and that there was no problem with being a conservative as long as she realized how unoriginal a position that was for a comedian to occupy. Comedians were always looking to ridicule the new thing, the new vocabulary, the new phrases. That was expected. But wasn't there a way to incorporate the new without the latency period of calling it stupid? His fellow students all blamed the times for declaring certain topics off-limits, but wasn't that exactly the kind of challenge a great comedian should want to tackle? Taking his or her or their intelligence for a spin along the new edges, the new limits? Except he couldn't find a way through it all yet. He'd been thinking about Aristotle a lot since Sword had had them read his *Poetics* in class, a text in which the Greek philosopher promised that after speaking of tragedy, he would offer his thoughts on comedy and an explanation of what was funny, only to never mention it again. The world had agreed to assume that Aristotle's thoughts on comedy had been lost, but the more Phil thought about it, the more he believed the man had never written them. He thought it would make a good bit, too: Aristotle persuading his friends and colleagues that, yes, he'd written the comedy part, but couldn't quite remember where he'd put it—"dog ate my homework" type stuff. Phil liked to imagine that Aristotle could've been like him in some way, struggling over comedy, ultimately not knowing what to say.

Olivia came back from her cigarette break and asked what she'd missed.

"Phil isn't too happy that Reinhardt is coming here to teach," Dorothy said, and as everyone's eyes turned to her, she understood that she had delivered news.

"Reinhardt is coming here?" Olivia said. She was beaming. "I thought undergrad protests had canceled his class?"

"Kruger didn't tell you?" Dorothy said. "He was supposed to make the announcement in workshop."

She was slightly worried about Kruger. When they'd gone back to the classroom for their bags, the kids had noticed he'd left his phone behind. The oversight had disturbed them more than his leaving without a word (who willingly went anywhere without his phone?). It had bothered them so much that Dorothy had had no option but to make fun of the kids. They wouldn't have made it for a day in the eighties, she'd said, but the truth was, she didn't know how long she'd make it there herself, if someone decided to send her back without her phone. She would probably try to smuggle it on the trip.

"I can't believe we're going to meet Manny Reinhardt!" Olivia said.

Artie had never seen her so happy.

"I don't know how comfortable I am with this," Phil said. He turned to Sword. "Is the whole department behind Reinhardt's hire?"

Jo, who'd been making tight little balls of her paper napkin, threw one of them in Phil's face. It bounced off his nose and landed in his bourbon.

"What the fuck is wrong with you?" she said. "Why did you apply to this program at all?"

Jo threw another paper napkin marble, which again ended up in Phil's glass.

Dorothy's phone rang.

"Speak of the devil," she said, flashing her screen to the table so everyone could see it was Manny calling her again. She'd saved his number right away. *What's wrong with you?* she berated herself as she made her way to the bathroom to take the call. *Why so proud?*

Her "hello" echoed against the bathroom's marble counters. Manny was on a plane to Chicago, he said, calling from the first-class cabin. On a plane to *Chicago?* Dorothy's heart did the opposite of skipping a beat. Two quick ones bubbled up when there should've only been one. Had her email worried him that much? Did he like her more than she thought? Would he want to turn the plane around when she told him the active shooter situation had been a prank?

He knew the active shooter situation had been a prank. He was coming to see his son.

"Of course," Dorothy said.

"It's really last minute," Manny said. "I haven't told him yet that I'm coming."

He said perhaps Dorothy could see where he was going with this. He didn't want to impose on his son. He was wondering if Dorothy had a place where he could stay tonight, for a few nights, even, maybe. Like a guest room?

"I would go to a hotel," he said, "but I'm trying to lie low these days."

Dorothy didn't immediately have an answer for him. She couldn't readily picture the layout of her apartment. It was her old place that came to mind instead, the one in New York City. No guest room there. Barely room for herself.

"Whatever you need," she said after a few seconds, after it all came back to her—her walk-up in Ukrainian Village. "I have a guest room. I even have two bathrooms! You won't have to see me at all!"

"Well, I *want* to see you," Manny said. "I wouldn't be asking if I didn't want to see you."

"Right."

Dorothy looked at herself in the bathroom mirror. Who would want to see *that*?

They exchanged practical information. Dorothy would be out when Manny landed. She had to go to the students' show.

"You should meet me there," she said.

Manny wasn't sure it was a good idea.

"You're going to have to show your face eventually," Dorothy said. "Maybe this is the perfect occasion. Friendly room. Young comedians and friends of young comedians. Could make you look good."

"Could make me look like a creep," Manny said. "Showing up in a club full of twentysomethings."

"These are going to be your students next month. You're going to *have* to be around them. If you come see them perform tonight, it'll show that you're taking teaching seriously. It's a good look. Just don't flirt with them, okay? Don't ask anyone to marry you."

"Wait, what? I can't even ask you?"

Dorothy tried not to think too hard of the way he'd meant "even," not *even* her.

"Not even me," she said.

12

SOMEWHERE OVER PENNSYLVANIA, THE WI-FI STOPPED WORKING. THE flight attendants apologized for the inconvenience, but they didn't mean it. They were the parents on the flight, Manny thought, treating all passengers like children whose problems were irrelevant but whom you still had to comfort when their toys broke. How many times had Manny, as a young dad, had to tell August that he was sorry about something he wasn't responsible for? "I'm so sorry Cassie doesn't want to be your friend, kiddo." "I'm sorry you forgot your book on the bus." "I'm sorry your sweater itches." How was any of it his fault? Though, well, in the grand scheme of things, yes: all his fault. For making August in the first place. Every single one of August's bad days would be on him and Rachel, in a way. Perhaps August had gone through most of the bad days he would ever have, though, perhaps he'd piled up the bulk of his allotted share in infancy. Just a few days old, he'd been diagnosed with Hirschsprung's disease. Curable, but tricky. Baby August couldn't shit on his own. The latter part of his intestine wouldn't contract, wouldn't spasm the shit along and propel it forward (downward?), so it all remained stuck up there and you had to go get it with a tube and a pump. For a year, they'd done that, Rachel and Manny, in turns, manually pulled the shit out of their infant son, until he was big and strong enough for surgery. Rachel was worried that this year of enemas would scar August forever, psychologically, and the many months of colostomy bags after that, but the boy had grown up well adjusted.

Manny had called him after Dorothy, but he'd gone straight to voicemail. He'd left a message. He would be in Chicago for a few days, but a friend was putting him up, no pressure on him to pull out the couch or anything. He'd invited him to meet for a beer at the Empty Bottle, too. He was trying to convince himself of what Dorothy had said, that showing up at the club would make him look good. It could make him look good to August, in any case. A teacher caring for his students. Manny tried to picture it, but it didn't make much sense. Him, a teacher? He hadn't thought this thing through when Ashbee had offered. What was expected of him exactly? Was he just supposed to sit through the students' bad jokes and give them feedback? Was that the idea? Or was it more of a lecture type thing? He took out his notebook and decided to write down everything he'd learned in almost forty years of stand-up. He thought it would take a while, but after ten minutes, he only had this, and not much more to add:

NOTES FOR CLASS

- There are two kinds of jokes: ready and not.
- In comedy, good memory is your best asset.

Maybe they could watch old comedians, Manny thought, study old comedies. Or he could simply show the students how a comedy routine got written, bring to class different drafts of what he was working on at the moment, let them see how long it took to put something decent together. But then they would leak some of his new jokes online, wouldn't they? Manny didn't even know if he should keep working on the new show. Now that he was himself an aggressor, a predator, a part of the problem, going onstage with it would only amount to provocation.

His next show was about half-written and its working title was "Not All Adults Here"—which was, as far as Manny was concerned, what trigger warnings and safe spaces translated to: people refusing to grow up and understand that life sucked. Everyone wanting to remain in a bubble, a child, so they could keep reading YA novels on their commute without being made to feel bad about it.

Manny asked the flight attendant for another beer, which she brought over without a smile. He'd thought at first that the lack of smiling was due to her recognizing and disapproving of him, but she treated everyone the same. There were jokes to be made about flight attendants, he thought, how they'd ceased to be nice in the last few years, or pretty, same as nurses (before World War II, flight attendants *had* been nurses, he'd read somewhere), how those once sexually charged professions had evolved to become regular jobs, held by women who looked like your mother. Such jokes could never be made, however, in the current climate. And that was a good thing, Manny thought. As dreary as political correctness was for comedy, with all the new fences built around forbidden topics, it went both ways: people were deprived of potentially great jokes, but also spared terrible ones, sexist or otherwise. Sexist jokes still existed, of course, but comedians had to put extra thought into them now. They had to be worth the trouble their authors would get into, and so they tended to be funnier.

Not that it mattered, in Manny's case. Sexist jokes, even good ones, would not be welcome from him ever again. No matter how the rest of his days unfolded, there would always be a vague aura of scandal around him. People would remember hearing something about Manny Reinhardt and younger women—harassment, perhaps, something sexual, certainly. Manny didn't have sexist jokes so far in "Not All Adults Here," and he hadn't *planned* to write any, but the realization that he could never make one again bothered him. What if he found the model joke, the sexist joke to kill all other sexist jokes? What would he do with it? There was nothing personal when he made a sexist joke, nothing against his wife, his sister, his nieces, or his mother. To Manny's mind, all the jokes existed in the form of embryonic blobs in the air, they were the thoughts people exuded and rejected all day, and his job as a comedian was to grab onto the most horrible of these thoughts and shape them right in order to serve them back to those who'd run away from them. He was in the business of finishing people's horrible thoughts so they didn't have to go there themselves. A dirty job, but as long as people thought horrible thoughts (and they would never stop thinking them, no matter how hard they pretended), someone would have to do it.

He didn't always enjoy it. Sometimes, he didn't want to go where he went. Often, he disgusted himself for going there. But if he didn't say things that shocked even himself, then he was failing, then he wasn't doing his job right. Right? He needed to be a little uncomfortable, the audience needed to be a little uncomfortable. If they never were, if they were always in agreement with what Manny said, then it meant Manny hadn't gone far enough, hadn't handed them a clean enough mirror. He didn't understand people who went to a comedy club, or to a movie, or to the theater, to feel good about themselves. Most people weren't good. Didn't they want to hear from someone else who wasn't?

Maybe he could sell his future sexist jokes, Manny thought, if future sexist jokes came along. He'd never sold a joke before, but he knew people who did. He could sell his sexist jokes to female comedians, to Dorothy, for example. Dorothy would be allowed to make them. He could sell racist jokes to Black comedians.

What would be left for him, though? If he sold all his offensive jokes to people who were allowed to make them? He could still joke about alcoholics, Manny thought, his father having been part of that community, he himself verging on membership. He could keep anti-semitic jokes. Jokes about rich people. About Hollywood. Ugh. He crushed his empty beer can and gestured to the stewardess for a third. He couldn't tell if anyone recognized him on the plane. He'd jumped from the cab to the airport's express security line to the Admirals Club lounge to the plane's first-class cabin without anyone bothering him. Rich people tended not to bother celebrities, though. Rich people didn't even *look* at celebrities, whereas Manny knew that if he just walked across coach now, two or three guys would stop him to chat, ten would stare, twenty others would badly pretend not to stare. He'd wondered what it was with rich people, if they went through rich-people training once they'd amassed a certain amount

of money, an intensive course in which they were taught how to properly eat an ortolan, and to leave celebrities alone because it was
déclassé to care about fame. Although such a course couldn't exist, or
else he would've been offered it. He had to be richer than most people on the plane.

He wondered if Ben Kruger was richer than him. That bastard had
to have made a lot of money with the Meryl Streep movie. Manny
didn't think he was jealous. He'd been offered movie roles before,
had always turned them down. There was something about Kruger
that annoyed him. At first, he'd thought it was the way Kruger looked—
his eyes, in particular, which seemed to never fully open or close—
but maybe it was bigger than that, the eyes a mere symptom of a larger
condition. The neither/nor condition. Neither a bad comedian nor a
good one, neither a good actor nor a bad one. Yet people seemed to
love it, Kruger's mediocrity, his in-betweenness. It was *real,* or whatever they called it. But now what was it with the teaching? Why had
Kruger taken a teaching job? A serious one, too, not just a visiting
position, like Manny was accepting. They were probably paying him
a lot, but still. Was it a status thing? Could it be that Kruger *believed* in
teaching?

His son was the main reason Manny was giving teaching a shot.
August had never admired anyone more than his professors at the
University of Chicago. Manny had heard him on the phone with his
favorite teacher once, when August was home for Christmas after his
first semester of law school. He'd heard him laugh harder than he'd
ever heard him laugh before. That had hurt a bit. What could a law
professor have said that was so funny? He'd wanted to take the phone
from August and tell the guy, "*I'm* the father, *I'm* the one who didn't
sleep for years thinking the kid might die, who the fuck are *you*?"

He didn't think about August's childhood illness that much, to be
honest, but hearing him laugh with his professor that day on the
phone had brought it all back at once. It had surprised him to remember it so clearly, the anguish, the smell of the soap they used in
the hospital. It had surprised him because the only parts of his life he

remembered so vividly tended to be those he'd written about, and he'd never written about August's condition. He'd promised Rachel back then, when August was a few weeks old, to never use his illness for work, for laughs, to never talk about August onstage, in fact, and he'd kept his word. He'd talked to strangers about the most private and embarrassing things (hemorrhoid treatments, taking his mother off life support), but never August. That was a long time ago, though, Manny thought. That he'd made that promise. August was healthy now, everything had turned out great. Maybe it was time to really put it behind them. Manny immediately made fun of himself for thinking that writing about something equated to "putting it behind them," how cocky it was to believe that, to decide for the whole family what they were done with. And yet . . . maybe now was the perfect time to write about August, about having been August's father, a parent to a sick child. Yes, forget movies! Manny thought. Movies were boring. They moved like warships. You controlled nothing. What Manny had to do was write an hour of comedy about August's first years of life, when he and Rachel constantly feared he would die. A comedy special about sick babies! That was the new frontier. That would surprise everyone. Everyone would be expecting a contrite performance from him next, tepid jokes about male-female relationships, jokes about how horrible men were, and so on. No one would see the sick-child thing coming! And it would be his story, too, Manny thought. He could never be accused of having no right to tell it. Well, August could accuse him of that, he guessed. Or Rachel. If August was okay with it, though, Rachel would be, too.

Big ideas didn't usually come to Manny like this. His shows tended to build one beat at a time, until he figured out patterns, what the whole thing, unbeknownst to him, had been about. But this, what he was going through now, this was what people referred to as "inspiration," he thought. He could see the whole show. Rachel's pregnancy, the baby's first days, the terrifying wait for a diagnosis, the horrible jokes that had come to his mind, and that he'd kept to himself. He'd look like a terrible father at times, but also like a great one in the end, he'd taken such good care of August! The show would be hilarious and moving. He could almost see it write itself.

Manny looked around the first-class cabin. He had the odd feeling of being the one in charge, and the only one to know it, responsible for getting everyone where they needed to be.

13

AS THEY GOT TO HIS CAR, ARTIE RECEIVED THE EMAIL HIS MOTHER had promised him earlier, containing the list of topics he could and couldn't joke about. Artie opened the passenger door for Olivia and debated reading the email aloud to her. He couldn't tell how much was okay to talk about your mother with a girl. His most recent girlfriend had thought it funny, the one before that creepy, and Olivia was hard to read. She didn't say much about her own family. Not onstage, not when she was drunk, and certainly not when she was sober. By the time he'd walked around the car to his door, Artie had decided to keep the mom talk to a minimum. Let this trip be about Olivia, he thought. Let her talk about whatever she wanted.

Olivia wasn't talking, though. On the way from the bar to the parking lot, she'd only broken her silence once, to reiterate how much she appreciated Artie's driving her to O'Hare. Silence while walking to the car was okay, Artie had told himself, especially in this cold, but now that they'd made it to the comfort of his Golf, now that the engine was running and heat slowly bringing blood back to the tips of their fingers, he couldn't let it take hold. He had to talk before they left the garage. Set the pace.

"Are you excited to see your sister?"

Olivia lit a cigarette.

"I'm Larry David," she said, cracking the window, letting all the heat out. "I don't get excited."

Artie didn't mention that she'd looked pretty excited to hear that Manny Reinhardt would be their teacher next semester. He didn't say anything about opening the window either, opening the window while the heat was on, something his parents would've crucified him for.

"Where is Sally coming from anyway?" he said instead. "I never asked."

"Maine."

He really had nothing to say about Maine.

"Isn't that where Jo thinks Andy Kaufman is hiding?" he tried.

"No," Olivia said. "Jo thinks Andy Kaufman is in Vermont."

"Right."

Olivia knew she wasn't making it easy for Artie, but she had other things on her mind. Since Dorothy had told them that Manny *might* come to the Empty Bottle tonight, she was going over everything she had, her strongest material, what would impress him the most (she'd previously thought about bringing second-tier bits to the show, always worried that some other aspiring comedian in the room might steal her best stuff). She was cursing Sally in her head, too, for coming tonight. She'd have to take care of her. She wouldn't be free to be herself, whatever that meant. She didn't know exactly who she was, deep down, but she knew it wasn't the Olivia she was around Sally.

"Do you have other siblings?" Artie asked.

"Just Sally," Olivia said. "But twins count double."

"Sally's your twin?"

"Did I not mention it?"

"Identical?"

"I take issue with that qualification. But yes."

"That's so cool."

Maybe Artie could take care of Sally for her, Olivia thought. Maybe he could get a crush on Sally instead of her.

"I have a brother," Artie said, determined to get a conversation going. "We're not twins, but I like him a lot."

"Liking someone is hard," Olivia said. "Loving's easier."

"You think so? Do you love a lot of people?"

"I mean, not really, but I love Jo, for example. I just met her a few months ago, and I loved her instantly. I'm not sure I like her, though. She can get pretty annoying with the Andy stuff."

Olivia dragged deeply on her cigarette, angry at herself for launching this thing about love vs. like. She neither loved nor liked her twin (which had to be some sort of crime, she thought, for which there had to be a special place in hell), so why say anything at all?

"What bit are you gonna do tonight?" she asked.

Artie said he wasn't sure. He'd hoped that what he'd prepared for workshop would've been deemed ready, but since Kruger hadn't let him go past the first line . . .

"Maybe I should just go for it anyway," he said. "Prove Kruger wrong."

"If he comes," Olivia said. "Guy just fucking ghosted us midworkshop."

The air looked liquid around them, the cars up front and in all three mirrors like their tail- and headlights were melting. Staring at them, Artie felt one of his heavy pangs of sadness. This wasn't going like he'd imagined. He'd imagined depressing weather, sure, but that the inside of his car would act as a rampart against the dissolving sky, a few cubic feet of warmth in which he and Olivia would joke and share personal stories. Instead, Olivia was letting the outside leak in through the window, he was freezing, and they were talking about work. Maybe silence was better than this, he thought. Olivia noticed his mood switch. Perhaps she wasn't that uninterested in him. She asked what was wrong.

"Nothing," Artie said. He couldn't tell her what was wrong, that the world looked ugly and that no one liked him. Or loved him, or whatever. That he felt alone, violently so. "I was just thinking about my brother," he said. It wasn't exactly a lie. In a way, Mickey was always on his mind. "He goes missing sometimes. He's missing right now. I was just wondering what he could be doing."

"What do you mean, he goes missing?"

"I mean he doesn't answer his phone, his friends don't know where he is, and my mother freaks out."

"Like, for how long?"

"He always comes back," Artie said.

Olivia had a lot more questions. She wanted to know where Mickey usually went, where they usually found him, and why Artie never talked about him onstage.

"Funny you should mention it," Artie said. "I just received an email from my mother in which she lists all the topics she feels I should and shouldn't joke about. I didn't have time to read and see if my brother being a flaky junkie was in any of the categories."

"You didn't say he was a junkie."

"Do you want to see the list?"

"You know, you talk about your mother a lot."

"I don't."

"You kind of always slip her into your bits," Olivia insisted.

"It makes her happy," Artie said.

"It's not like she's in *workshop* with us."

"It's normal to talk about your family onstage. Every comedian does it."

"I don't do it," Olivia said. "Jo never does it."

She was right, of course. There was no reason for Artie to bring up his mother this much.

"Want to see my mom's list?" he repeated, and he handed Olivia his phone.

There was such trust in that gesture, Artie thought. He hoped Olivia could feel it. His phone in her hands looked like any other phone—it in fact looked like Olivia's own phone—but Artie knew it was his, that the way the apps were organized on the screen would take her a second to figure out, that at any moment, an image might pop up, another "memory," or an ex's text, divulging something extremely personal about him. He wondered what would be better: a text from an ex who missed him, or one from his brother. He could tell that talking about Mickey had earned him some points. Girls liked stories about mysterious men, unfit for the world. Few could think of those men as boyfriend material, though, and that's when the "concerned brother" character came in. Artie knew he owed a good portion of his sex life to Mickey. Mickey was the fascinating one: he painted, he made music, he suffered, and, occasionally, he disappeared. When you waited for him at the bar, you never knew what he would come in looking like. Skinny and translucent, pink and bloated, fit as a boxer, wearing bum clothes, good clothes, or even once, unexplained to this day, emerald surgical scrubs. But Mickey was a moving target, an impossible catch. It didn't matter how interested in him you got: he had to pick *you* (and in his whole life, he'd only ever picked Ethel). Whereas Artie was always available as the next best thing. The good brother. The safer bet. Girls could stay in proximity to Mickey's aura of excitement and danger, hear all the stories about him and feel Artie's pain, without risking anything more than a boring date night once in a while. They could have both the tragic story and the decent guy.

Olivia was opening his email now. For the next however many minutes, she would be in control of his life. Maybe she was right now deleting an important email he'd just received and would never see. Maybe Mickey was calling and she was sending him to voicemail.

"Here we go," Olivia said. " 'From: Leora Kessler.' The subject line is 'Ideas for Material.' "

"I'm all ears," Artie said.

" 'Part One: What You Can Joke About.' "

Artie, according to his mother, could joke about the following:

- himself
- Aunt Sophie's fiasco at the matchmaker's
- politicians (but not female ones, unless far right)
- popular books (if not by women)
- food
- Hitler and other dictators (but Artie had to "be careful around genocide")
- herself and Artie's father ("as long as you talk about things that happened before you were seven and that we'll be able to deny if too embarrassing")
- car trouble
- girl trouble (just nothing sexist)

"Who wants to hear about car trouble?" Olivia said after getting to the bottom of the list.

"My father is always interested," Artie said.

"What's his name?"

"Leonard."

"Leonard and Leora," Olivia said. "That's very nice."

"Leora means 'light' in Hebrew," Artie said, and wondered why he said it. Olivia hadn't asked about the meaning of Leora, and he'd decided not to talk about his mother more than necessary. What was so hard about that?

"You're Jewish?" Olivia asked.

"Well, yeah."

Artie always thought it was obvious, what he was. He'd grown up convinced it was written on his forehead. He hadn't believed it when he'd heard that 40 percent of Americans didn't personally know any Jews.

"You never talk about that in your comedy either," Olivia said.

"About being Jewish? It's not that funny."

"I like it when Reinhardt does it."

"You like everything he does."

"He's a genius."

Artie said that Jews were basically seen as white people nowadays, so no one thought it was interesting.

"People fucking hate you, though," Olivia said. "White people *and* Black people hate you. Arabs, Mexicans . . . everyone hates you. I guess maybe Asians are okay with Jews, but I might be wrong about that."

"Do *you* hate Jews?"

"I don't discriminate," Olivia said. "Default setting: I hate everyone equally. I hate myself. I hate people for being people, though, mostly, not for looking a certain way or believing in this or that bullshit."

"That's fair," Artie said. "People are horrible."

Except he didn't believe that. He liked people. He liked meeting new ones at parties. What was he thinking, agreeing with Olivia on everything? Did he think women liked that?

"I mean, some people are fine," he corrected himself. "Like you, for example. Even though you're an antisemite."

Olivia enjoyed being called an antisemite. She laughed a little. She insisted he should hone his Jewish material.

"Especially since joking about Hitler is allowed," she added. "Your mom's pretty open minded, by the way."

"Are you kidding? I don't know what we would talk about at home if we didn't talk about Hitler. Her favorite books are about Nazis. Her favorite work of art is a statue of Hitler kneeling."

"Oh, I know what you're talking about!" Olivia said.

She'd heard about the Hitler sculpture in college art history. Artie had actually seen it in Warsaw ten or so years earlier with his parents—his only trip to Europe. He and Olivia were bonding, Artie thought. Bonding over *Him* (the title of the Hitler sculpture). His sadness was gone. Olivia had finished her cigarette and closed the window. He was getting warmer, and the traffic ahead was starting to look like a seventies movie more than the depressing present, the lights in the windshield sharp clusters of grains rather than droopy blobs of red. Olivia was making suggestions about what he should work on, Artie thought. She was interested. And he did have one idea for a bit about Holocaust survivors. She might like that. She might like to hear about it. It wasn't ready at all, but it could be good one day. He started giving her the beats.

About two years earlier, he said, his great-uncle, a Holocaust survivor, had been approached by a museum in Seattle to have his inter-active hologram made. A handful of museums had started doing this, filming and recording the few remaining Holocaust survivors for hours in a special 360-degree studio while asking them hundreds upon hundreds of questions about their experience and their life before and after the war. Certainly Olivia had heard of this? She hadn't. From that footage, Artie explained, nerds in California made three-dimensional holograms of each Holocaust survivor, holograms who would be capable of answering any question future generations might have about the Shoah. The survivor would, through technology, become a new kind of survivor, Artie explained, a supersurvivor, a survivor of his own death. His great-uncle had agreed to do it, and the whole family had gotten to see a preview of his hologram before it went up for a temporary exhibition. Even Mickey had come to see it. Mickey and Artie had gotten a little drunk beforehand, to better deal with their great-uncle's hologram. They'd laughed when they'd first seen it appear, but then they'd quickly started crying. They'd told themselves it was the alcohol, but Artie wasn't so sure about that. He'd actually been moved by the hologram, and the other three he'd seen. His parents and cousins had remained in the room with their relative's hologram, but Artie and Mickey had paid a visit to the others, in other rooms. They wouldn't have dared ask their great-uncle's hologram anything, but alone with the 3D ghost of a certain Ezra Gluck, Artie had loosened up. He'd asked the stranger's hologram if he felt like a badass for surviving the war, and the hologram had replied that he didn't really think in those terms, that if he really thought about it, the way he saw it was he'd been selfish, that all those who hadn't survived had probably been less selfish than him. "Jesus," Mickey had said. "Do you have more uplifting questions for Ezra?" and Artie had responded, "What uplifting question can one ask a Holocaust survivor in a Holocaust museum?" after which Mickey had taken the microphone and asked Ezra's hologram what his favorite Holocaust movie was.

"What did the hologram say?" Olivia asked, ready to light another cigarette.

"He said that it was hard for him to watch reconstitutions of the camps. But as far as World War II movies went, everyone should see *Au Revoir les Enfants*."

"Interesting," Olivia said. "It's like an oracle you can discuss pop culture with."

"I wouldn't call *Au Revoir les Enfants* pop culture," Artie said.

"You go there to ask a ghost deep questions about the past, you can ask him *anything*, and you end up talking about movies."

"Well, that's essentially what the bit will be," Artie said. "Idiot me talking to a Holocaust survivor's hologram about World War II movies."

"It's kind of Pythonesque in spirit," Olivia said.

A big compliment for Artie. The bit wasn't yet written, but it already had a spirit! And it was Pythonesque!

"It's just a framework for now," he said.

Olivia was about to open the window again, for the smoke, but Artie said to keep it closed, he could stand it. They were silent for a minute after that, but it wasn't uncomfortable—Artie could tell that Olivia was thinking about what they'd just been saying, and that was good, because Olivia loved thinking, and she might love someone who made her think about new things. She still had his phone in her hand, her hand in her lap. The phone had locked and gone black.

"It's really cool that you'll get to ask your great-uncle anything once he's dead," she ended up saying. "I think they should make holograms of everyone's parents so you can ask them whatever you want without them having to know. That would be a major hit."

"Maybe it will happen in our lifetime," Artie said. "They're made by Spielberg in California, the Holocaust survivor holograms. It won't be long before someone uses the technology for profit."

"They're made by *Spiel*berg?"

"I mean, his foundation," Artie said.

"Did you ask the hologram what he thought of *Schindler's List*?"

"I did, actually. He said, 'No comment.'"

They were about halfway to O'Hare now, and Olivia was laughing. She went on about how the hologram could become the perfect gift for old people in a few decades. Kids and grandkids, instead of giving their parents and grandparents genealogy kits for Christmas, or a few sessions with the ghostwriter who'd put together the shitty memoir of their lives, would buy them an appointment to be made into a talking hologram.

"It will be a win-win situation," she said. "Like, the grandparent becoming a hologram will think, *They love me! They're making me immortal!* And the grandchildren will feel like they don't need to visit so often."

"I loved visiting my grandfather," Artie said.

"I dislike my whole family," Olivia said.

"Even your twin?"

"Especially Sally."

Artie didn't believe her. Everything he knew about twins had come to him mediated by Hollywood, little girls finishing each other's sentences and so on. In sixth grade, he'd been in class with a pair, too, he remembered now. Jean and Louise. The way the teachers told them apart was Louise had a stutter and Jean didn't, but according to Jean, Louise never stuttered when they were alone together.

While Artie silently went over his twin knowledge, Olivia was regretting telling him she disliked Sally, but also hating herself for regretting it, and regretting always having to hate herself for saying things. This was how the inside of her head was at all times: layers upon layers of self-hatred, mixed in with a lot of pride, ideas for bits, and attempts to solve whatever else was going on that day. She was always working on three or four issues simultaneously. Right now, for instance, while talking to Artie, she was thinking about how she'd have to change her tampon at the airport (she'd forgotten to do it at the bar), but also trying to think up what she would say to Manny Reinhardt if she met him in a few hours. Because she was more focused on that than on her conversation with Artie, she was answering his questions way too fast and honestly. She had to switch priorities. She had to pay attention to Artie. She remembered she might want to make Sally his burden tonight. She had to find nice things to say about her.

"I mean, she's my twin," she said. "Of course I love her. But inasmuch as I hate myself, it's hard to be fully indulgent with my spitting image." *Great work,* Olivia thought. *You're making Sally sound so lovely.* "You'll like her, for sure," she added. "She's me, but nicer. Which isn't such an impressive feat, but whatever. She cares about people."

"Is she funny?" Artie asked.

Honesty was probably best.

"She can appreciate dark humor," Olivia said. "But not mine so much. She's always analyzing what comes out of my mouth."

Sally was convinced, for example, because of some of the low-self-esteem jokes she'd heard her make, that Olivia had been abused by their stepfather, too, and that she was repressing the memory. She'd suggested many times that Olivia go see a hypnotist to retrieve the trauma.

And of course Olivia had been abused by their stepfather. If she thought back on those years (she tried not to, but when she did), she assumed the man hadn't even always known which sister was which when he grabbed a hand to put on his lap (it always started that way). She and Sally had looked much more alike back then.

"Are you all right?" Artie asked. Olivia had been quiet for a minute.

"I was just thinking," she said. "Maybe your brother is having a crisis."

"No shit," Artie said.

"Maybe he's having a crisis, and he went to ask the Holocaust survivor hologram more questions about the meaning of life."

Artie took a second to imagine it. Mickey, alone with an old man's ghost, a man-made ghost—laser beams and mirrors—looking for answers.

"You should write for TV," he said to Olivia. "That's pretty good."

"Right? The Holocaust hologram as a shrink for millennials."

They riffed on that for a minute. The millennial asking stupid questions, the hologram answering with pragmatic advice.

"Ezra, why do I feel so empty?"

"You should read more books."

"Ezra, when is my life going to start?"

"You should read the book *Who Moved My Cheese?*"

"Ezra, have you ever had that feeling? That you couldn't spend one more fucking minute in your own body?"

"There should be temporary suicide, for sure." (Here, it wasn't clear whether Olivia was answering as the hologram or as herself.) "I hope someone's working on it."

They went back to their own voices after that, and Olivia said maybe Mickey was actually going to surprise Artie tonight, that maybe he was on his way to Chicago to see him perform.

"Now *that*'s even cheesier than your previous scenario," Artie said. "If you don't make it as a comedian, definitely try to get staffed on *Togetherness*."

"I think that show was canceled."

"You know what I mean. There's always something like it on TV."

He hadn't even watched *Togetherness*. Just the title—he'd assumed it was the kind of show where brothers showed up, supported each other no matter what.

Olivia didn't take Artie's suggestion as an insult. In college, she'd written spec episodes for all kinds of shows, even shows that'd been off the air for years, like *Cheers* and *Studio 60 on the Sunset Strip,* sending them straight to networks in hopes of getting noticed and called to Los Angeles right away for a lifetime of bottled beer and bad puns in musty writers' rooms. That had been her dream. She'd loved writing specs, getting inside the heads of characters who were already established, whose flaws the audience already knew, who didn't need to go through fundamental changes, only new situations, problems that would be solved by the end of the episode.

"I'd love to write for TV," she admitted to Artie. "I wrote a spec episode of *Mad Men* once, for fun." She left out the other twenty-six specs she'd written, she left out the fact that "for fun" meant she'd sent them all Priority Mail Express to Hollywood.

"I didn't know you wrote dramatic stuff," Artie said.

"It's an episode where Don Draper has to find a pitch for Paper Mate, for their felt-tip pens," she went on. "He gives a pen to everyone in his family to see how they react to it, how they use it and all."

"Sounds very intense," Artie said.

Olivia punched him in the shoulder, but it was playful, Artie thought. They were flirting.

"I'm serious," he said. "The suspense is killing me. What do his children do with their felt-tip pens? Does the family ever recover from it?"

"Shut up," Olivia said. "You don't deserve to hear it."

They were approaching the airport, cars were jerking at the last second to be in the proper terminal lane.

"I've actually never seen *Mad Men,*" Artie confessed. "I did watch the scene you were all talking about in workshop, though. It's pretty great."

Olivia tried to gauge the level of sincerity in Artie's voice. She didn't think he could possibly have caught all the nuances of the scene if he hadn't seen the twelve episodes that came before it. He was probably making fun of her.

"For those of us who had to look for father figures in works of fiction," she said, "that scene was a big moment."

"Did you not know your father?" Artie asked.

"Just had a stepfather," Olivia said. "Pretty shitty guy. The worst, really."

A "pretty shitty guy" could mean a lot of different things, Artie thought. So could "the worst." He decided not to press. They were at the terminal anyway. He stayed in the car while Olivia went in to get Sally. She'd asked her to wait by the McDonald's, and there she was, good old Sally, always doing as she was told. She was sitting next to a family of four, all sleeping in positions that looked painful, necks at weird angles, feet near faces. On the other side of her, a young woman was watching videos on her phone, eating chips, looking all cozy. It always made Olivia uneasy, seeing how quickly some people could make a public space their own. Since she'd moved to Chicago, she hadn't even magnetized a take-out menu to the fridge, or taped a photo to a wall. At least Sally looked out of place, she thought, at least Sally looked uncomfortable. They would always have that in common.

14

KRUGER WAS ON THE METRA UNION PACIFIC NORTH LINE NOW, THE ONE that ran along Lake Michigan. He didn't know yet that there hadn't been a shooter on campus. In his rush to leave, he hadn't gone back to the classroom for his phone. He'd heard all the police sirens and felt an irrepressible urge to go see his father at the old folks' home. He knew it was foolish, both to have fled and to be headed where he was, but while on the train, he could act as if neither had happened, or would happen.

He wasn't sure his father would want to see him. He'd moved Louis into Sunset Hill the previous summer, shortly after *The Widow's Comedy Club* premiere, and though he spoke to him on the phone often, they hadn't seen each other since. Every time they talked and Kruger offered to visit, Louis found excuses to be left alone. Kruger had mentioned this to a nurse a while back, the excuses, and the nurse had advised him to give his father some time. She'd said that men, when they first got to Sunset Hill, needed more time than women to come to terms with their new situation. They didn't like to be seen as diminished, she'd said, and the phone gave them a sense of power because they could just hang up whenever they felt they weren't performing as well as they wanted. Kruger had thought the nurse's wisdom a tad misogynistic. Why would men have more trouble adjusting to the facts of old age and decline? Did women have no pride? Had falling apart been easy for Kruger's mother, to the nurse's mind? He hadn't liked her choice of the word "performing," either.

Louis had Parkinson's. He had trouble swallowing his food and

couldn't take long walks anymore. Even bird-watching hurt. Kruger
had wanted to move him to a home for a while, but the tremendous
fighting energy his father had been able to muster whenever the idea
came up had kept buying him time. All that work had come undone a
few months back, however, the day Louis had gone for a beer at the
Glass Eye and shot his gun at another customer—a single bullet,
through the man's hand and the pint of beer it had been holding.
"The guy talked shit about your mother" had been Louis's excuse.

Kruger felt smarter without his phone, more alert. He could've
been a businessman from the eighties, he thought, commuting back
from work to the suburb where his wife and kids awaited him for
dinner. He wouldn't have wanted to be a businessman from the
eighties, not really, or to have children, but feeling, even for a few
seconds, like he could've been anything other than Benjamin Kruger
was always a thrill. He knew that some people were convinced they'd
been born in the right place at the right time, that they couldn't have
been anyone else, or survived long without the internet, or daily hot
showers, but Kruger believed he could've adjusted to any living conditions thrown his way. He was an adapter, malleable, and some girlfriends had praised him for it (before they invariably got tired of the
quality—his easygoingness laudable until it wasn't, until it started
feeling like it was all the same to Kruger, whatever they did, wherever
they ate, that perhaps even a different girlfriend would be fine by
him, too). But Kruger himself often thought his flexibility was a sign
of weakness, that perhaps it meant he wasn't whole. His own life
choices could feel artificial, in retrospect. He admired artists who
said, "I had no choice but to become what I am—[acting/writing/
painting], that's all I'm good at," but they made him feel lazy. Kruger
had become a comic almost by default, and only because it had been
easy for him. Not writing, but the road to fame. The road to fame had
been easy. He'd more or less become famous after his first joke,
hadn't struggled the way Dorothy had, or Ashbee, or Manny, and if he
was honest with himself, had things not worked out right away,
he didn't think he would've had it in him to keep trying for long. He
would've done something else, the next easy thing.

He stared through the train window for a while, at other windows in fast-moving buildings, windows already lit up against the winter's early dusk. Shadows of people moving shadows of things. In the train car, a woman was walking back and forth, lulling her baby to sleep. Kruger kept seeing her reflection in his window, and how she glanced at him whenever she passed his seat. He assumed she would say something at some point, ask for a selfie, or berate him for a joke he'd made in the past.

Kruger tried not to think about what the guy might've said about his mother at the Glass Eye. Louis wouldn't repeat it, and Kruger had to respect that. He'd felt bad enough buying the injured customer's silence behind his father's back. He'd offered to pay the man for his medical expenses, of course, and a fair amount of money not to press charges. He believed that part of Louis was humiliated that the man hadn't pressed charges. Not pressing charges was sending the message that Louis wasn't dangerous, that society didn't have anything to fear from him, and when someone said that about you—"He doesn't need punishment, he needs help"—well, how much lower could you get?

The pacing woman kept looking at Kruger sideways. Kruger thought uncharitable thoughts about her and her baby. She didn't like his work, so what? At least he'd never created anything more than jokes, while she'd made a whole new person, a person from scratch, who would grow up to say stupid things of her own, who would have the potential to ruin other people's lives. Young parents couldn't be trusted to formulate reasonable critiques, Kruger thought.

He tried to be in the moment, to not think about the shooting (Artie in possible danger), to not think about his audition next week (for Paramount), to not think about what his father would say shortly when he saw him. There was a chance his arrival would frighten him—no one showed up unannounced unless they had bad news. Though, Kruger thought, failing at his attempt not to think, what bad news could he have brought to his father? Everyone Louis cared about had died already. No, it would be the opposite, Kruger realized: his surprise visit would raise Louis's hopes in vain. Louis would think that Kruger was coming with *good* news, and the only good news Louis wanted to hear was that his son had gotten his gun back, the M1917 that had been seized by law enforcement after the Glass Eye incident. Louis complained about the gun's confiscation constantly. If he wasn't being charged with a crime, then how could there be a smoking gun to take away from him? Kruger had to step up and apply as the gun's rightful owner, according to Louis. The gun (which had belonged to Louis's own father) had to find its way back to the family.

To get the gun back, Kruger had to find evidence of his family's ownership—photographs of his grandfather holding the gun, military correspondence. He had to learn how to shoot, too, in order for the gun to be properly registered. To shut his father up, he'd booked a session at Lyons Guns and Range a few weeks back, but he kept pushing it whenever the date neared. Their website terrified him. Once a month, they had a "Kids' Night on the range," which they called a "service they provide[d] the community," and Kruger couldn't help but picturing children running for shelter as grown-ups shot at them in the dark. He'd get material out of the experience, if he learned to shoot among children, but he wasn't sure it would be material he'd want to share. If he talked to an audience about needing to get a FOID card and learn how to shoot, he'd have to explain himself, how he'd gotten there, and Kruger wasn't a confessional comic. Though maybe he was reaching a point in his life where he wanted to be, when the idea of talking about himself onstage wasn't as repulsive as it previously had been. Was it just something that happened when you aged? This need to go over your life in public? Maybe it was time. Maybe it was time to tell an audience of strangers that his father hadn't been the same since his wife died, that the old man had shot someone at a bar. That his parents had had him late in life, and that his mother had so many times called her pregnancy a miracle that Kruger could almost touch and feel the parallel life in which she hadn't had him.

The train filled up in Evanston. A teenage girl sat next to him, and Kruger watched as the porter punched holes in her ticket. It looked like a satisfying job, and the porter, happy to have it. Kruger worried on his behalf that they would replace him with an app soon. He was surprised at how little he missed his phone. He was surprised, too, by how few people in the train car seemed to be using theirs. He almost expected the teenage girl to take out a book from her bag and start reading.

He started panicking that his father would ask what he'd been reading lately. Anything good? No matter what Kruger recommended, Louis would deem it shallow, or lacking in rigor. Though his dad hadn't asked about books in a while, Kruger remembered. He mainly just asked about the gun now, when Kruger was planning on getting it back, in a tone that seemed to imply that it was Kruger's fault the gun had been confiscated to begin with. When had the gun become so important to him? Kruger had only seen it once, when he was first learning about World War II and Louis had taken it out from a safe. He'd explained that his own father, Kruger's grandfather, had killed two Germans with it in Normandy, but only because he'd had to, only because if he hadn't killed them, there would've been no future—there would've been no Louis, no little Ben, no more Krugers at all.

The teenage girl next to him did open a book. Joan Didion, *The Year of Magical Thinking*. Maybe she'd just lost someone, Kruger thought. He almost asked her. His own mother had died the year the book had come out, and an aunt had given it to him. He assumed only the recently bereaved had the stomach for it.

Louis must have taken good care of the gun over the years, he thought, if it was still working. Or maybe he'd had it repaired mere days before the Glass Eye. How long had he been walking around town with the gun on him? What had prompted the decision to, from then on, always leave his house armed? Kruger imagined that scene often, that moment in his father's life when he'd realized it would be wise. He imagined it, staring out the train window.

The woman from earlier, the one pacing the train car with her baby, was still throwing him looks.

"I'm sorry to interrupt," she ended up saying. "But are you Ben Kruger?"

Kruger sat up straight. What did she think she was interrupting?

"My sister went to school with you," the woman said. "Emily. Tuft. I'm Veronica. We both had your father in history."

"Yes," Kruger said. "I remember Emily."

They shook hands over the teenage girl in the aisle seat. The teenage girl pretended not to notice, or was perhaps so immersed in Didion's grief that she really didn't. Kruger suddenly felt jealous of her. He wanted to be where she was. He yearned for that kind of focus on a book. How long had it been since one had spoken to him so directly?

"How *is* your dad?" Veronica asked, and her inflection made it clear that she knew about the Glass Eye incident. Her sister probably still lived in Naperville, heard the gossip and all the rumors. She might even know what exactly the man had said about his mother.

"My dad's all right," Kruger said. "As long as no one near him speaks ill of my mom, he's able to behave."

Veronica made a face, tilted her head. Kruger understood immediately that she hadn't heard the same story he had.

"I'm actually on my way to visit him in Lake Bluff," he rushed to add. It was instinct. He didn't want to know her version.

"Oh," Veronica said. "Is that where you ended up putting him?"

Like a plant, Kruger thought, an appliance.

"It seemed far enough from the Glass Eye," he said.

The words "Glass Eye" caught the teenage girl's attention. She looked up from her book and at Kruger for a split second. Her pupils were huge.

"And you moved back to the area for good?" Veronica asked.

She kept glancing at her baby. Was he supposed to say it was cute?

"I wanted to be closer to him, yes," Kruger said.

"That's nice. He must be very happy."

The way she said this, Kruger thought, she knew exactly what had set off his father at the Glass Eye, and that it had to do with him, not his mother.

"I loved your movie, by the way," Veronica said.

Kruger thanked her and prepared to answer the questions everyone had been asking him for months now, how it was working with

Meryl Streep and how she was in real life, but Veronica asked about Paul Rudd instead. Was he as nice as he seemed? Kruger said yes, very nice, and "Cute baby."

Veronica got off in Highland Park. When the doors closed and the train started moving again, the teenage girl next to Kruger said it wasn't such a cute baby, and for the rest of the ride, she kept on reading her book about death.

At Sunset Hill, a nurse told Kruger to make himself comfortable in the lounge, his father would be right with him. It felt like he was auditioning for a part, Kruger thought, or meeting with a TV executive. Except the lounge he was sent to wait in was full of old men watching their show (not a woman in sight), about a watchmaker who traveled through time. The volume had to be near its highest setting, yet closed captions were on for backup. Kruger had a thing for captions. He'd recently started turning them on at home for himself. His hearing was fine, but he liked to see written confirmation of what went on, and perhaps even more than that, he liked the small discrepancies that often appeared between what was said onscreen and the way it was transcribed. He liked hearing a line and having his eyes read something slightly different. It felt like having company.

The captions under the show in the lounge, though, weren't the kind he was used to. They were multicolored and confusing. Lines of dialogue and audio description were assigned to different boxes. There were emojis and numbers on the sides of the boxes. The scene Kruger walked in on, for instance, presented a handsome man in contemporary clothes who, in a saloon, circa 1870, was urging a young prostitute to follow him to the future, where he promised more opportunities existed for her. His line was "Come with me . . . Come with me to the future," and the way the captions rendered it was something like:

 | Come with me . . . Come with me to the future |

123 | (whispering)

Indications not only of what the character said but of how he said it: at what volume and with which emotion dominating at what intensity.

"It's called emotive captioning," one of the old men in the room explained to Kruger.

Kruger said he found it a bit condescending, the emojis, the colors, telling everyone what they were supposed to feel.

"I don't pay attention to the little drawings," the old man said. "They're for the children."

Kruger expressed doubt that many children were watching this show, but understood after a minute that what the old man meant by "children" were people under forty.

"The children are confused," the man said. "They're on the computer all day. They don't have real contact with other people, so it helps them to have the drawings. They're all autistic."

There was no judgment in his voice. He seemed to believe that what he was saying was both true and unavoidable—humanity's fate.

"I'm not autistic," Kruger said.

"You *think* you're not autistic."

The captions on the screen were now color-coded green and enjoining the audience to laugh, but no one in the room was laughing, no one looked like the emoji that captioners had chosen for the scene—the face that laughed so hard it spurted horizontal tears. Kruger had a passing thought about his own movie. Were emotive translators working on it right now? Had someone (a machine?) rated the intensity in his lines?

"I don't see how the emojis are helping," Kruger said. "They don't allow for nuance, which is the whole deal with art, don't you think?"

"I wouldn't call this shit art," the old man said.

"Well, it aspires to be," Kruger said. "The actors are doing what they can."

Reducing an actor's performance to a single emotional nugget couldn't be right, Kruger said. This was the road to one-dimensional portrayals of the human experience. It was encouraging bad acting. It was perhaps even laying the groundwork for no acting at all. Perhaps people would soon go to the movies to watch emojis occupy the whole screen. No actors needed. No dialogue or story, either. Just a few minutes of Smiley Face, to set the mood, one minute of Laugh-Cry, six minutes of Stress, one minute of Bawling, two minutes of Fear, three minutes of Wink and Blushing, a screen that spelled out the word "Resolution," a final Smiley Face to confirm it was a happy ending, and that would be it. "The End."

"Who are you visiting?" the old man asked.

"I'm Louis Kruger's son," Kruger said. He was annoyed that no one in the room had recognized him.

"Kruger Junior," the old man said. "This is starting to make sense."

Other old men started shifting their attention from the TV to Kruger.

"You don't like the subtitles?" one of them said. "You're just like your dad."

"Louis doesn't like *anything,*" another said.

"Can you think of one thing your father doesn't hate?"

"We have this plan, if we find one thing he even just kind of likes, we'll throw a party. We'll have a dance. Can you think of something? Maybe CNN will want to cover the event."

"I like silence," Kruger's father said from the TV room's threshold. "I like it when you guys shut up."

Louis was wearing a three-piece suit. No tie, but still—his elegance clashed with the beiges and tartan patterns of everyone else's robes and slippers.

"Fuck you, Louis," the initial old man said.

"Hi, Dad," Kruger said. "I see you're making friends."

They left the lounge for the privacy of Louis's room.

"Did you get our gun back?" Louis asked before they even made it there.

He hadn't worn suits before, Kruger thought. The suits were a new development. He'd always been well dressed (ironed shirts and cashmere sweaters), but with the suits, Louis was sending a message. *I don't belong here* was the message.

"I just wanted to check on you," Kruger said. "You didn't pick up yesterday."

"Someone would've called you if I'd croaked."

There was only one chair in Louis's quarters, by his desk. Kruger sat on the edge of the bed, assuming his father would take the chair, but Louis remained standing by the door, as if already eager to escort him out. His eyes were sunken deep into their sockets.

"Are you taking all your vitamins?"

Kruger berated himself for the cliché question, the small talk.

"*Vitamins?*" Louis said. "It's all those cripples who should take theirs. It takes everyone here *minutes* to shape the most basic thought."

"They seemed all right," Kruger said.

"I'd have more stimulating conversations in a mental institution. Maybe I can put in for a transfer."

"Do you feel you're slipping out of reality?"

"I fucking wish," Louis said. "It's the constant slipping in that's the problem."

Kruger wanted to tell him about the shooting at school, but the event felt about as distant as his childhood. About as real, too. He almost doubted it had happened.

"I saw one of your former students on the train," he said. "Veronica Tuft."

"The Tuft sisters," Louis said. He'd never in his life forgotten a student. "Nice girls. They should never grow older."

"Girls?"

"Kids." Louis's hand was trembling in his pocket. "People. In general."

This included him, Kruger knew. He'd wondered many times over the years whether he'd disappointed his father more as a son or as a former student.

"There was a shooting at school," he said.

Louis thought he meant Naperville High.

"No, Dad," Kruger said. "A shooting at *my* school."

Louis took a step to his desk, where the day's paper lay. Did he not believe him?

"Well, there's not going to be anything about it in the *Tribune*," Kruger said. "It just happened. The police were just arriving when I left."

"Wait, you were on campus? And you fled?"

The tremor in Louis's hand intensified.

"Another father would've said 'I'm glad you're okay,'" Kruger said. "'Thank you for coming all this way to tell me.'"

"What about your students?"

"'By showing up, you spared me hours of worry had I first learned about the shooting on the news.'"

"Enough with this. What about your students?"

"I don't know," Kruger said.

"What do you mean, you don't know? You don't leave an emergency situation until all your students are accounted for."

Kruger remembered fire drills at school, Louis organizing his students in single file, he and Kruger the last to exit, always, Louis counting the kids once outside, double-checking, triple-checking, how embarrassing his intensity had been, when everyone knew it had just been a test.

"What kind of gun was it?"

"I don't know that either," Kruger said. "Where's your computer?"

"It's been dead for months."

"That's why you haven't seen my movie?"

"Are you serious? You're asking me about your movie now?"

"I was making a joke."

"No, you weren't," Louis said, and after an awkward silence, he resumed. "Did you hear gunshots? What kind of sound did the gun make?"

Kruger grabbed the newspaper from his father's hands.

"I didn't realize you'd want a full report," he said. "Sorry for coming to you so uninformed. I just wanted to see you."

He wasn't sure why he'd taken the paper away from Louis, but now that he had it, it made sense to bury his face in it and pretend to read the headlines. He was hurt and frustrated. He would never "have a moment" with his father, he understood, like everyone did in the movies. One of them would die before it happened. Kruger could feel his heart beat against the notebook in his shirt pocket. He would never understand his father. Perhaps all fathers were unknowable, he told himself, trying to calm down. Fathers never explained themselves. You never knew if they were angry or if that was just the face they made while eating ribs. And you couldn't ask that kind of question, "Are you angry?"—you didn't ask your father that. He'd never asked Louis if he regretted what had happened at the Glass Eye. If his mother were still alive, he would've asked *her*. Though she would probably have said, "Your father had his reasons." Perhaps mothers were unknowable, too, Kruger thought. You only thought you knew them because they talked to you more, but they hid behind all the talk, in the end, they were smarter about the hiding, they did it in plain sight. He'd never had a real conversation with her either.

After a while, Kruger actually started paying attention to what the paper said, the advance write-ups on the Delgado trial, which was scheduled to start the following day. He hadn't followed the affair much, only knew the basics, that a famous Chicago businessman had scammed hundreds in an elaborate Ponzi scheme, that he'd taken from his own parents and children, that his daughter had killed herself right before the whole scandal came to light. The paper was calling the Delgado trial "the Trial of the Decade." Kruger estimated the number of trials of the decade at three per year on average. It was like midterm elections, off-year elections, and presidential elections: Every time, they were the most crucial elections of our lifetime. Voting was always more important than ever. Everything always either the best or the worst it had ever been. America couldn't keep it low-key.

Kruger wondered sometimes what would've happened if the man his father had shot had pressed charges. How much media attention it would've gotten, whether it would've gone to court. If there'd been a trial, Kruger would know by now what the man had said to Louis. If it had really been about his mother, or about someone else. About him. It had to be about him, Kruger thought. That's what Veronica's face had meant, on the train. Though it would've been unlike his father to stand up for Kruger. As a kid, he'd received prank calls, a lot of them, from his school bullies ("Your *father* doesn't even like you, you're the last person he'd save in a fire!"). Both his parents had known about the calls. Whenever she was the one to pick up, Kruger's mother would say Ben wasn't home and could she take a message, but Louis would just hand Kruger the phone and give him a frustrated look, like he couldn't believe this was still happening and it was about time Kruger manned up and found a way to respond.

"You need to learn how to shoot," Louis told Kruger now, in his bedroom, breaking five minutes of silence. "You need to get our gun back. I won't always be here to protect you."

"Protect me?" Kruger said.

"Some people hate you, you know that? They really do."

The way Louis said it, it felt like he was perhaps one of them.

"I know people hate me," Kruger said. "I'm famous. I'm successful. I'm on TV. That's what happens."

"And you think it's worth it?"

"I don't see how learning to shoot would solve anything."

"It would help me sleep at night," Louis said, before repeating: "I won't always be here to protect you."

This time, Kruger laughed.

"You think that's funny?" Louis said. "You think I'm not protecting you? I'm always protecting you, and you know it. Why else would you come here? You think you came here to check on *me*? Let me tell you what happened: you got scared and you ran for your father. That's what happened."

Kruger couldn't tell if his father was joking or not. He smiled at the thought of someone trying to caption the man's emotions for TV. Or his own. What fucking hell.

"What now?" Louis asked, "Would you stop laughing for a second?"

At least now his emotion was clear: Louis was angry. Angry emoji.

Old Angry emoji? Kruger knew old-people emojis existed, but did old and angry ones? Deflation was needed.

"I'll make an appointment at the gun range," Kruger said. "If it makes you feel better."

"If it makes *me* feel better?" Louis said. "Me? Who cares about *me*? It's your life, son. *You're* in charge."

"Yes, sir," Kruger said.

"You need to take this shit seriously."

"My life?"

Louis looked his son in the eye and took back the paper from him. Perhaps he'd meant the gesture as a random display of power and authority (*I can take what you have at any moment, what you have was mine to begin with*), but he didn't do it with enough strength, and a few pages remained in Kruger's hands. Louis tried to grab those, too, but Kruger resisted, and the old man lost his balance as the pages tore. He knocked his hip against the desk and caught himself on the chair, bending his left wrist at a wrong angle. The pain had to have been immediate, Kruger thought, but Louis pretended to be fine. When Kruger rose from the bed to check on him, he rejected his help.

"Just learn how to shoot," Louis said. "That's all I need you to do."

As he watched his father one-handedly rearrange the pieces of the day's paper on his desk, Kruger wished to never get old, or at least not like this. Not with anyone to watch.

"I'll make an appointment," he repeated. "I'll go after winter break."

Kruger pictured himself at the gun range, with all the happy kids who would've just gotten their first gun for Christmas. Yes, maybe he'd get some good comedy out of it.

"You know what?" Louis said. It looked like he'd hurt his wrist, the way his hand hung limply from it, but the shock seemed to have stopped the tremor. "I'll fucking teach you. I'll teach you right now."

"To shoot?"

"Tony has a gun," Louis said.

"Someone here has a gun?"

"Tony."

Kruger tried to remember his father mentioning a Tony before, and then to conjure any past Tony he might've known. No one came to mind. All the Tonys he'd known were fictional characters.

"I thought nobody liked you here," he ended up telling his father.

"Tony has children," Louis said. "He'll understand."

15

DOROTHY GAVE HERSELF AN HOUR TO DOLL UP BEFORE THE SHOW, but an hour was too much. She knew women who set aside three to four to get ready for a date or a party. She'd once witnessed her own mother starting preparations at eight in the morning for an appearance at a fundraiser in the evening. What could she possibly have been doing for ten hours? What was there to do that Dorothy didn't know about? So far, she'd showered, washed and dried her hair, applied body lotion where her skin was dry, put on a nice dress, a bit of lipstick, and mascara. It had all taken her under twenty minutes. What did other women do after that? Dorothy remembered that her mother played records, back in the day, when she was getting ready for a night out. Perhaps she actually spent more time dancing and singing in front of the mirror than she did working on her appearance. Or perhaps *that* was the work, Dorothy thought: looking at yourself so much in the mirror that it didn't feel so odd anymore that other people should see you, too. Perhaps that was the real prep. Getting used to your face, your body, the way it all came together and looked to everyone else. Dorothy had never quite gotten used to any of it. At her agent's request, she'd had to look at herself on camera before her first TV appearance, twenty-some years earlier, so that she could "correct course" on certain physical tics she wasn't aware she'd had. She was touching the microphone stand a lot, for example, in the beginning. Sliding her hands up and down it, petting it like a security blanket. That was weird, her agent had said. Dorothy had been mortified—by the comment and the images. "Like I'm jerking off the mic stand," she'd said, to brush her shame under her agent's laughter. She still touched the mic stand on occasion, but there was a sort of electrical shock now when she did, immediate retraction. And she judged comedians with stage tics, of course, now that she'd gotten rid of hers. Comedians who started laughing at their own jokes before they told them. Or that one who always put her hand on her chest, like she was giving a toast at a wedding.

She had forty minutes to kill before the official start of her students' show. She could have cleaned the apartment, set up the guest room for Manny, but her apartment was pretty clean, the guest room always ready. Maybe the apartment was too clean, in fact, Dorothy thought. It almost looked like no one lived there, like the place had simply been propped with enough books and furniture to give the impression that someone did. All set up for a photo shoot before the place went on the market, the owners already long gone. Dorothy sat on her couch and tried to instill some life in the living room. She emptied her purse like a bucket of water. She'd been meaning to organize this mess for months. Now it was all on the coffee table. She threw away most of the bag's contents, receipts and tissues, half-used Carmex covered in lint where the glued-on label had peeled off, a CVS hairbrush her mother had given her the last time she'd visited, saying that every woman should have one in her purse. Dorothy had never used it. She never used most of what was in her purse, she realized. She did use the iPad, but why? She didn't need to. She had a phone. She had a computer in her bedroom. Why did she need an in-between? Would someone manage to convince the world in a few months that they also needed a screen that would be halfway between the iPhone and the iPad, and then another one after that, slightly bigger than one and smaller than the other? Maybe she didn't need a purse, either, now that she thought about it. A purse was only trouble, an invitation for other people to ask you to carry their stuff. When her cousin and his boyfriend had visited from Italy the previous summer, she'd not only had to show them around the city but also had to hold on to their city guide and sunscreen while she did. She "had the room for it," after all. If she hadn't had a purse, it wouldn't have fallen on her to hold on to Kruger's phone, either. Although maybe it would've—they were neighbors, sort of. Kruger lived a few blocks away. Dorothy had stopped by his place on her way back from school to give him back his phone, but he hadn't been home. She'd heard his parrot through the door, though, eagerly saying, "Who's there? Who's there?" after each knock. Kruger had mentioned the parrot once or twice. He'd talked about the pain in the ass it had been to move an African gray from L.A. to Chicago, but she hadn't paid a lot of attention. She remembered now that he'd said the bird was ten years old, and could go on to live forty or even fifty years more, if Kruger took good care of him. There was something sad about an adult who took on a pet that could live so long, Dorothy had thought then, and was thinking again now. It was opening the door wide to the possibility that your relationship to them might be the defining relationship of your life. *You're one to talk,* Dorothy thought now, staring at her coffee table, even though she hadn't said anything out loud.

A phone lit up on the table. Kruger's phone. It was his agent calling, the best in the business. Manny's agent, too. Michelle Welles. Dorothy let it go to voicemail.

She wondered when she'd heard from *her* agent last. Her agent was still the one who'd told her about her touching-the-mic-stand tic twenty years earlier. Still Kiki. She'd been so happy to have Kiki believe in her back then. Kiki would go to every one of her shows in the beginning. Now Kiki was seventy-two and knew Dorothy so well that they barely needed to talk. She knew which days Dorothy taught, she knew to book small venues, request mineral water in the greenroom, a bottle of red wine, a pack of gum. In a few weeks, Dorothy would receive an email with her tour dates, and all would be in order. Kiki never fucked up. Her friends and colleagues admired Dorothy for sticking with Kiki, they praised her kindness and loyalty, but the truth was, no other agent had ever tried to poach her.

Michelle Welles called Kruger's phone again. Maybe it was urgent, Dorothy thought, maybe Michelle knew something she didn't about Kruger and she *had* to answer. She answered.

"You're not Ben," Michelle Welles said. "May I talk to Ben?"

"Ben left his phone at work," Dorothy said. "This is Dorothy. Dorothy Michaels."

"Dorothy! Oh my God! Is this the first time we've talked in person?"

Dorothy didn't understand what people meant by "in person" anymore.

"Hold on," Michelle said. "Are you and Ben dating? He didn't tell me you were dating!"

"We're not dating," Dorothy said. "We're just colleagues. He forgot his phone in the classroom."

"Right."

Dorothy heard Michelle type something on her keyboard back in L.A. A lot of keys being hit. Two medium-length sentences at least. Was she taking notes on their phone call, or multitasking, answering another client's email while on the phone with her? Kiki would never do that, Dorothy thought. Kiki used pens and paper pads, for starters. Kiki always made Dorothy feel like the only worthy comedian in the world.

"Well, I'll tell Ben you called," Dorothy said, remembering that Michelle wasn't her agent, that perhaps she didn't type while on the phone with actual clients. "I might see him tonight."

"Are you sure you're not dating?" Michelle said. "I won't tell a soul."

"Pretty sure I'm single, yes."

The suggestion reminded Dorothy of being younger, of a time when people were always trying to place her with someone. It seemed they'd needed to know what man she was dating before they could make up their mind about what kind of girl she was. It had been a while since anyone had made assumptions in that area, though, and Dorothy found it didn't annoy her as much as it used to.

"Now that you mention it, I think Ben is single too," she joked to Michelle. "Maybe we can work something out."

"That would be pretty great," Michelle said. It was unclear if she'd picked up on Dorothy's tone. "In this context, I mean. If Ben started dating an older female comedian. Less successful, by Hollywood standards, but edgier, you know? With more cred."

"I'll present him with your arguments when next I see him," Dorothy said.

"And it would be good for you, too," Michelle added.

Was she riffing with her?

"What would be in it for me?" Dorothy asked.

"A *lot* of new fans," Michelle said. "In a heartbeat. Crazy visibility. You're planning a new tour, right? Bigger venues, extra dates. And also, you know, it's nice to have a boyfriend. Ben is a great guy."

"And what if I start dating another client of yours?" Dorothy asked. "What if I start dating Manny Reinhardt? What does my career look like if I do that?"

"I wouldn't recommend it," Michelle said. "Manny's going to be a bit toxic for a while. Let's stick to Ben. *Kruger and Michaels: comedy power couple.* If you start dating him, I'll take you on as a client. Not even joking."

"Not even joking" meant that Michelle had been joking before, Dorothy thought. Except the thing she was now not joking about (taking Dorothy on as a client) depended on everything she'd said before to have been said in earnest.

"That's fucked up," Dorothy said.

"Ah, come on, sweetheart. It's a business. Don't be like the new girls."

Michelle started typing again, perhaps a new email, or perhaps gibberish, a random assortment of letters, just because she'd heard another successful agent once say that you had to let prospective clients believe they needed you more than you needed them, or some such idiocy. Dorothy started feeling sad for Michelle. That's what usually happened when someone irritated her—quickly, she pictured them alone at home on a winter night, heating up instant ramen. It was always the same kind of people who annoyed her: people who seemed comfortable, people who seemed to have found their spot in the world and to think that they deserved a medal for it, people who thought themselves better than those who were still looking, or had given up on ever finding. Dorothy liked to imagine the moment in their future when their confidence would shatter for the first time.

"Plus," Michelle added, "Kiki's bound to retire at some point. You'll need representation."

Kiki would be thrilled to know that Michelle Welles even knew her name, Dorothy thought.

"I'm not clear on the rules now," she said. "Should I give you a call when my agent retires, or when I start dating Ben Kruger?"

"When you start dating Ben," Michelle said. "That's the deal."

"If he gets rid of the parrot, I'll consider it," Dorothy said.

"He'll never get rid of the parrot, honey. We have to be realistic about this."

When she hung up, Dorothy faced the parrot's photo on Kruger's lock screen. The parrot eating corn off the cob. She remembered the way he'd asked, "Who's there?" when she'd knocked on Kruger's door earlier, the level of alarm.

She went to her bedroom to change. What was she thinking, wearing a dress? She put her jeans back on, two thermal shirts, her favorite sweater. She kept the makeup—it was light enough that no one would notice. "Don't be like the new girls." Was that what Michelle had said? Yes. *Don't be like the new girls.* What the fuck did that mean? Don't break everyone's balls? Don't pretend to believe your work is what really matters? What people are truly interested in? Don't look desperate to be young again? Dorothy didn't want to be young again, she didn't think—if anything, being a teacher had cured her of the fantasy. She wasn't jealous of her students. She didn't envy them what lay ahead. She felt sorry for them, in fact, that they had to contend with social media, with the internet, everything archived and available for easy perusal. How could one write anything decent in these conditions? She put her coat on, her hat, her boots (it had started to snow). And there was no such thing as "new girls," she thought. The only ones who believed there were new girls were those who didn't hang out with young people and relied on the media to tell them what the next generations were like. It was always the same girls. Different vocabulary, different clothes, different set of pretensions, but still the same girls in the end: those who didn't mind being girls and those who did. Those who wanted to play with it and those who didn't, those who got along with their mothers and those who didn't, and so on and so forth. All the types repeating themselves, generation after generation, nothing new under the sun. That's how Dorothy was able to recognize herself in someone like Olivia, for example. Though Olivia's reaction when Dorothy had said that Manny might come to the Empty Bottle had annoyed her. She'd seen calculation in Olivia's eyes, an immediate shift from *I can't believe I'm going to meet this guy!* to *How should I play my hand for maximum returns?* That had been disappointing. How silly, though, Dorothy thought, to be disappointed. Olivia didn't owe her anything. It wasn't Olivia's fault that Dorothy saw herself in her. Was that what happened when you didn't have children of your own, by the way? You picked a random young person to place all your hopes in? A substitute child? Except not at all like a child, Dorothy thought, since Olivia (or whomever else she might pick in the future) would never worry about her the way she, Dorothy, worried about her mother, or the way her mother had worried about her own mother, who'd worried about her own mother, etc. It was a cycle of worry that Dorothy was breaking, not having children. No one would ever think about her as much as she'd thought about her mother, or in that way. This idea was a comfort, at times. It was comforting to know that she'd never have that kind of importance in anyone's life. Refusing to have power over someone else's life was still an exertion of power, she believed, a dizzying one. She was exerting power by doing nothing, by not creating more life.

In all honesty, thinking about this could make her a little sad, too, but what didn't.

And speaking of power and mothers, Dorothy thought, she had done it! She'd gone out without a purse. She'd fit everything that needed fitting in her coat pockets, zipped Kruger's phone in an inner one she'd never used. Her satisfaction at leaving the purse behind was similar to the elation she felt whenever she revised a bit and identified a perfect cut, the cut that suddenly made the bit two-legged and life worth living. She never felt better than when she managed to make things take less room. And she still had a whole extra pocket!

She could even have taken a book. Maybe she should have. She was going to be a little early to the Empty Bottle, it was right around the corner. Whatever, she'd talk to the bartender. Sitting at the bar was her favorite, but she'd stopped doing it as much the last few years, assuming that bartenders wanted younger women there, or people like Sword, perhaps, men who were comfortable in their own skin and could talk about sports.

Sword. He had to be home now, with his depressive wife, going over his planned last words with her, perhaps wondering if he should tweak them, perhaps reasserting his belief that they were the right ones and encompassed everything he had to say. What sad sacks people were, Dorothy thought. She didn't believe in famous last words. She didn't believe they were ever the ones that the wife, the sister, or the deathbed friend reported at funerals. She didn't believe in all the *I love you*s. She'd never been near dying herself, granted, but she'd been sick as hell a few times—painful ovarian cysts, couple of bad flus, a severe kidney infection once—and she hadn't felt like telling anyone that she loved them. Even less like making pronouncements on life and its meaning, which was another option you could go with on your deathbed, according to witnesses—the third option being to tell a joke, or at least go lightly, if you couldn't talk very much (a lot of people died calling "Dibs!" apparently, or whispering "You're it!" to a sibling). All awful possibilities. The worst part about last words was, of course, that you couldn't revise them. Dorothy's father had done the right thing, she thought, not uttering any. He'd died long ago after a week of silence and without leaving a note, either, even though he'd been told by his doctors that it was time to put his affairs in order. It had hurt at first, to get no wisdom from her father, or a single "I love you" (he'd never said it), but now she admired him for it. He'd shown his daughter respect by not forcing her to obsess over a last line, a last piece of advice. Though silence was something to parse, too. Oh well. She realized it hadn't occurred to her all afternoon to call her mother.

She made her right turn on Western Avenue and saw Artie looking lost on the sidewalk, searching left and right for a meter.

"It's free parking on Western," Dorothy told him when she got closer.

"Really?"

Artie couldn't believe his luck. A block away from the venue, free parking. Maybe the gods had had a quick meeting over his case and decided to throw him a little something after the ride he'd just had.

"Where's Olivia?" Dorothy asked. "Did you get her sister?"

"We got her, all right," Artie said. "I dropped them off at the door. I thought I'd be looking for parking for a while."

"What a gentleman."

"I was mostly trying to save myself, to be honest."

"Is the sister very boring?"

Artie explained. "Boring" was definitely not the word. The sister was angry.

"Angry is fun," Dorothy said.

Artie explained some more. There had been traumas, he said, in childhood. The sister had been repeatedly abused by a stepfather, while Olivia barely even remembered the guy's face.

"Okay," Dorothy said. "Not fun angry."

And now the sister, Sally, who was Olivia's *twin*, by the way, had done some thinking, and also mushrooms (in a very controlled mushroom-taking environment), and she'd decided it was time to sue the guy.

"Good for her," Dorothy said. "Sue him for everything he's got."

Except Olivia freaked out when Sally told her, Artie said. Big fight in the car. Olivia up front, Sally in the back seat, all the tension bouncing off the rearview mirror. Artie longing for the time (just a half hour earlier) when he hadn't known anything about Olivia's family.

"What do you think?" he asked Dorothy. "Do you think Olivia is a terrible person for not supporting her sister? Or do you think maybe she was molested by the guy too and she's just trying not to think about it anymore?"

Dorothy was usually happy when people told her things they shouldn't have. The reason she had a career, she sometimes thought, was that so many strangers had done that when she was a kid. Back then—often at bus stops, sometimes on the bus itself—a handful of adults had looked at her and confessed to various disappointments, adultery, suicidal ideation. Dorothy had thought this to be a normal thing for strangers to do, because you couldn't really tell your family anything (she knew that), and so you had to find someone who had no stake in the game. She'd thought that was why people went places at night, to find the nobodies they could talk to. When she'd finally understood that most kids her age had never been used as spillways for bitter rants, she'd already accumulated a vast catalog of possible setbacks and ways people had to talk about them, she had a good grasp on facial expressions, accents, faraway looks. Later on, in her professional life, she'd met a lot of actors and comedians who'd had the same experience, in their youth, of being talked to, picked as sounding boards for no reason. For *seemingly* no reason, though, since years after the fact, they all explained it one way or another— actors by saying that they must have exuded a superior capacity for empathy, comedians by suggesting it was because they were stoned and looked like they wouldn't judge anyone that they attracted so many intimate disclosures. In any case, while many of her colleagues had shut themselves away from chatty strangers with time, Dorothy still welcomed unrequested confessions, from fans, from the lady who sold pierogi at Kasia's. Students, however, were not strangers. Students, you almost had to treat like family. You had to be careful what you said around them.

"I think maybe we shouldn't be talking about this," she said to Artie, regarding Olivia's possible childhood trauma. "These are private matters."

"They didn't have a problem sharing all this in front of me," Artie said.

"You're their friend," Dorothy said. "Olivia feels comfortable around you."

"Maybe," Artie said. He didn't believe it for a second. "I just met the sister, though. She didn't seem to care that I was hearing all about it."

He realized as he said this that the reason the girls hadn't cared was probably the opposite of what Dorothy was suggesting, that he was such a nobody in their lives, and would so obviously remain one, that it didn't matter what he knew. It reminded him of being around Mickey's friends as a kid. Them talking about sex and drugs and wanting to kill someone. They were always wanting to kill someone. "I want to kill this fucking guy!"—how many times had Artie heard these words? It was a different guy every time. More often than not, a guy Artie had never heard of, and he would make a note of the name, in case he saw it on the news the next day, the man behind the name found murdered in a ditch, Artie having to keep quiet about what he'd heard the night before. He'd almost hoped for his loyalty to be tested in this way, but he'd never had to cover for any of Mickey's friends. No one ever died. None of the men Mickey and his friends had wanted dead, anyway.

"Forget I said anything," Artie told Dorothy. "You're right. It's none of our business."

Dorothy hated to be the cause of Artie's present face. She'd been teaching a few years now, she'd made peace with the idea that students might be disappointed when they got to know her, because she wasn't funny all the time, but still. She didn't want to be a bummer.

"Let's see if Olivia brings it up onstage," she said. "If she brings it up onstage, then it's open season."

16

OLIVIA WASN'T SURE YET WHAT SHE'D GO WITH ONSTAGE. FOR NOW, SHE was focused on getting Sally drunk, on changing Sally's mind about pressing charges.

"We have to do this the Persian way," she told her twin, trying to catch the bartender's attention. "The Persians believed that any important decision made while sober had to be reconsidered when drunk."

"I didn't make the decision sober," Sally said. "I made it while tripping on mushrooms."

"Mushrooms don't count. It's 'in *vino* veritas,' not *fungi*."

"I don't really drink anymore."

"Tonight, you're drinking," Olivia said.

She ordered beers and tequila shots.

"I thought you said *vino*," Sally remarked. "I'll have a glass of wine, please."

The bartender said he wouldn't recommend it, the bottle had been open awhile, but Sally took her chances.

The place was still mostly empty, Phil in a corner, talking to a group of Second City guys: a handful of undergraduate students Olivia had seen before, standing by the tiny stage.

"You're twins," the bartender noted as he poured from a wine called Jared.

"I was abused in childhood by a man named Jared," Sally said.

"Don't listen to her," Olivia told the bartender.

"Yes. I'm lying," Sally said. "His name was Jarrett."

That was true. That had been their stepfather's name. The bartender didn't care either way. He thought the girls were joking, and had another customer to attend to.

Olivia raised her pint, clinked it to Sally's glass, and drank half.

"I thought *I* was supposed to get drunk," Sally said. "How will you convince me not to sue Jarrett if you get wasted?"

"I have a speech ready," Olivia said. "You just focus on drinking."

Sally drank. Olivia didn't have a speech ready. She just thought she could convince a drunk person of anything. She gulped the second half of her beer and tried not to roll her eyes at the way Sally sipped her wine, or held her glass, as if the glass were only there to display her perfect manicure. Olivia couldn't help it. She was always recording Sally's every move and storing it for later, in her library of stereotypical people's tics and intonations. Sally had been, the last ten years, a peephole through which to look at their stupid generation. Not that Olivia thought Sally was stupid (she wasn't), but Sally wanted to *fit in,* which was somehow worse. Sally did buy houseplants and subscribe to the Ezra Klein podcast, she did organize her books by spine color. She had once gone to a used bookstore just to buy the twelve most appealing green spines she could find, to bulk up that middle portion of her rainbow shelf, which hadn't been growing at the same rate as the others.

"I can tell you're judging," Sally told Olivia. "You have that look of when you're scraping me for parts."

Olivia neither denied nor confirmed.

"I know it's your job," Sally went on. "I know it's your job to look at me and everyone else and point at all that's ridiculous about our behavior and society. I respect it. You know I do. I'm just saying, maybe not right now?"

"I'm sorry," Olivia said, and she meant it. "It's hard to turn it off."

"It's okay," Sally said. "This is how you've been protecting yourself, it's your 'I know everything' carapace, 'I look at everyone and I understand why they do what they do.' It brings you comfort. The distance you keep. You think you're not a player, just an observer. But I need you to be a player right now. I need you to support me."

"Sounds like *you* have a speech prepared."

"I do. I knew you wouldn't like the idea of me suing Jarrett. I *know* you. You don't want to cause ripples. You don't want drama. You despise drama. But this isn't drama. This is my life, Olivia. I need to do this."

Olivia caught herself doing it again, taking note of an intensity she found laughable: "This is my life, Olivia"—a line from a movie.

"Please stop it," Sally said. "I need you to focus. How do you plan on changing my mind if you don't focus? You can't both try to convince me of something and scan me for material at the same time. At some point, you have to make a choice. You're very competent, you're very smart, you can hold many ideas at once in your head, but there are limits to your powers."

"There are limits to your powers!" Olivia repeated, in a superhero movie voice, grabbing Sally by the shoulders.

"Do you ever stop and think about how ironic it is that you spend so much time trying to mimic your *twin*?" Sally said. "It's kind of depressing, really."

"I never pretended it was a happy life," Olivia said.

She drank her tequila. She wanted to be nice to Sally. Why was it so hard?

At some point during Sally's speech, Artie and Dorothy had come in. Olivia wished Artie hadn't witnessed her fight with Sally in the car, that he hadn't heard her reject her sister's announcement that she was ready to sue. She knew it was a bad look.

"I understand it was important for you to come all this way to tell me," she told Sally. "But why did you have to tell me about it in front of Artie? Wasn't that a bit dramatic?"

"I think these conversations should be normalized," Sally said. "I think women should stop having them only among themselves, whispering over tea in each other's kitchens."

"Still," Olivia said. "You don't know him. I don't know him very well either. I'm not super into everyone knowing about our life."

"That's why I brought it up in front of your friend," Sally said. "To get you used to it."

Olivia said that she didn't want to get used to it. She didn't want to be associated with Jarrett any more than she had to, and couldn't understand why Sally would want that either, to put this man again at the center of her life. She told Sally that everything she read on the internet was wrong, that she should fight the urge to share her trauma, that it was stronger to repress it all and let it rot somewhere in your brain than to bring it back to life over and over again, that being alive meant pushing things down deeper and deeper all the time, to make room for new stuff, and that she'd been good at doing this, Sally, she had a nice apartment, a good job, she had a lot of anxiety, sure, but she managed it, she saw a therapist, she took mushrooms, and, of course, she was single now, but she'd had a good boyfriend in college, she'd meet a great guy soon, and why put all this good life on hold for months to relive her horrible childhood, why do this to herself? What did she think suing Jarrett would bring?

Sally stared at Olivia and said "justice." She thought it would bring her justice. "Are you not familiar with the concept?"

Olivia started rolling her eyes again, but Sally was off her stool before rotation's end.

"I need to pee," she said, and disappeared into the small crowd that had gathered by the bar.

Olivia hadn't seen the place fill up. She was now aware of all the men pressing behind her back for the bartender's attention, and she wondered how much they'd heard of her diatribe. One of them took the space Sally had just freed up, and Olivia noticed his hands before she noticed anything else, the stack of dollar bills folded in a money clip, the whole thing casually held between index and middle finger, like the bonus chip you slide the croupier at the end of a lucky night. The bartender came to the man right away.

"Bitters and soda," the man said, extracting a tenner from his money clip.

"You're going to have a lot more fun if you order something stronger," Olivia told him. "We're not very good."

The man looked at her. The man was August Reinhardt, Manny's son, but Olivia couldn't have known it—he looked nothing like his father.

"Are you performing tonight?" he asked. "Second City?"

"MFA."

"I see," August said. "I hear it's a battle between you guys and Second City, but no one can tell me how the winner gets chosen. Is there a jury?"

"It used to be a vote from the audience," Olivia explained. "Like, a show-of-hands type thing. But now I think someone just brings a decibel meter and sees who gets the biggest laughs."

"That doesn't seem very fair," August said. "The loudest laugh for the funniest joke. That's not how it works."

His bitters and soda came. He left the ten-dollar bill on the counter. The bartender didn't quite know what to do with it (bitters and soda were free, ten dollars too big a tip for a free thing), so he left it lying there, went on to take new orders. August didn't notice the confusion he'd caused. Maybe he was someone who was used to paying for water, Olivia thought, someone who asked for bottled and not tap at restaurants. Maybe he thought ten dollars was what bitters and soda cost.

"I think you should go back to an audience vote," he said, "but give people time to think about the show, have them vote the next day, or a week later. Sometimes, the jokes that stay with us are not the ones we laughed loudest at."

The man wasn't flirting, Olivia thought. He wasn't making eye contact, or offering to pay for her next drink. He seemed earnestly interested in finding a solution to the problem of designating a winner, fair and square.

"Are you a comedian too?" she asked him.

"I'm a lawyer," August said.

"Is one of us in trouble?"

She wrote a whole story in her head, about young lawyers haunting comedy clubs and second-tier open mic nights in search of future clients. It wasn't stupid. Comedians did get in trouble. When they did, they counted on their agent to point them to a good lawyer, and young agents would probably come here tonight, too—the guy could leave his card with everyone. Brilliant. Perhaps in a few years,

Olivia thought, there would be a trial in which two or more people in this room would be involved.

Sally came back from the bathroom.

"Where were we?" she asked Olivia.

"Justice," Olivia said. "You said the word 'justice' and then you went away."

"Right."

"Meanwhile, I met a lawyer." Olivia pointed at August, whose name she still didn't know. "Isn't that something?"

"That's rad," Sally said, extending a hand to August. "I'm Sally. Do you do sexual abuse?"

"I don't," August said. He shouldn't have said he was a lawyer. The bar exam wasn't for a couple of months. "I'm Auggie."

"Is that short for August?" Sally said. "That's a great name for a lawyer!"

"Why is that?"

"Doesn't it mean, like, fair and just?"

It didn't, August said.

"And fair and just isn't what you want in a lawyer anyway," Olivia said.

"Do you know someone who does sexual abuse? I'm looking for representation."

August asked a few questions, such as how long ago the abuse occurred, and where Sally lived, and where the abuser lived, and if charges had been filed and in which state. Olivia realized he hadn't said anything about their being twins. At this point, he probably wouldn't. She wondered whether August couldn't see their twinness or simply didn't find it worth mentioning to the two people already most aware of it. Her whole life, she'd been irritated by strangers stating the obvious ("Twins!"), at having to smile at their false assumptions ("I bet you're each other's best friend!") or listen to them talk about some other twins they knew, as if Olivia and Sally would know them, as if all twins went to the Twin Conference in Twinsburg every summer. Now she found August's silence around it more unnerving than the platitudes she'd come to expect. It was like when it rained and you left the bar with someone without having known that it was raining, one of you had to say it, "It's raining," even though the other had noticed it, too. You didn't want to be the one to say something so self-evident, but it was awkward if no one did. It created a tension, or made a preexisting one apparent. Someone had to say it.

The bartender took the ten-dollar bill while no one was looking.

At the other end of the bar, Ashbee, who'd arrived a few minutes earlier, was giving Dorothy the beat-by-beat of his terrible date. The woman he'd bought dinner for had spent the whole evening congratulating herself for only having dated Black men this year.

"Jesus, Ash," Dorothy said. "We've been over this. You have to meet them for a drink first. You can't keep getting stuck for entire dinners."

"I'm an eater," Ashbee said. "I need to eat."

Dorothy found eating in front of people almost more intimate than sleeping with them. Dinner, for her, never came before the sixth or seventh date. Back when she was dating, that is.

"Was the Black thing a New Year's resolution?" she asked. "Is she going back to white men in January?"

"The worst part is that she was right to be proud," Ashbee said. "I mean, not right, but *vindicated*. Everyone in the restaurant looked at us like our union was going to save the world. They looked at us like cute little puppies."

Dorothy found it admirable that Ashbee kept trying to find love, but also hard to care very much about.

"Heard from Kruger?" she asked. "He completely vanished earlier. Left his phone behind in class. I think he might not even know the shooting was a prank."

"Do you think it was a mistake to hire him?" Ashbee said, taking his jacket off. "In this context?"

Dorothy got a whiff of him as he folded the jacket on his knees. He smelled of sex.

"In which context?" she said.

"We shouldn't have hired a white guy."

"White men need jobs, too," Dorothy said.

"Kruger doesn't. Plus, I don't think he likes teaching very much," Ashbee said.

He explained he would've liked to hire Kit Lazarus instead of Kruger, but had spent a lot of energy convincing himself it was a bad idea. Two Black men out of three comedy teachers would've been too much, he told Dorothy. Their colleagues could appreciate one Black man in the teaching lounge, but if they saw two of them come in together, it would make them uncomfortable.

"I saw it when Han was here last semester," Ashbee said. "When other faculty saw us together, shooting the shit or whatever, just laughing, they thought we were laughing at them. Or plotting something."

"You're being paranoid," Dorothy said. "We have like seven or eight Black professors in the department."

"Only one per research group, though," Ashbee said. "One in Theory, one in Victorian Lit, one in Creative Writing, and so on. It's made so there's a Black person every five seats in a department meeting. We're good as long as we're scattered evenly. But put two of us next to each other, it screams communitarianism. People start freaking out."

"You didn't hire Lazarus because you didn't want us to freak out?"

"I know," Ashbee said. "I think I'm the real racist here. I've internalized white fragility. I'm protecting you guys. Or maybe it's even worse. Maybe I got too used to being the token Black guy. I complained about it a lot, on the record, but I guess it's pretty comfortable in the end. I'm alone in my lane, road is wide open, no one can fuck with me. If more Black guys rise up, though, it's a different story. They'll be taking my shit."

"I hear you."

"White people managed to convince me it was *Black* guys who were going to take my shit."

"I hear you, Ash."

"I'm a horrible person."

"I don't think so. I think we're just old, is all. I used to be the same."

"You used to be racist?"

"I used to like being the only girl around at the club," Dorothy said. "If a second girl came in, I got nervous, and I was relieved if she sucked. Part of me thought there was only room for one of us in there."

Dorothy was confident enough in her work now that she knew she was a comedian, not just a female comedian, but back when she'd started (the one-of-each era: one woman, one Black guy, one gay guy), she'd believed that her role as the woman was to make all the woman jokes. She didn't like doing those very much, but she always slid a couple in her sets, to pay her dues, be allowed to stick around, and so whenever a new girl arrived, Dorothy was afraid she would steal her spot by catching the few remaining good jokes there were to make about being a woman (like there could be a shortage of those, Dorothy thought now, like the indignities of being a woman could run scarce—that was a joke in itself).

"Exactly," Ashbee said. "We complained about being the only one of our kind everywhere, but deep down, we wouldn't have shared our spot for the world."

"We thought we were cool."

"We were dicks."

"We were selfish."

"*Were* we, though?" Ashbee asked.

"You just said we were."

"I guess I wanted you to contradict me. What kind of artist would want to hang out with another artist just like him? Same background, same potential jokes? What writer doesn't already live in fear of their stuff getting stolen? What artist is confident enough?"

"So you're saying we were right to hire Kruger. Different enough from you and me."

"Is that what I'm saying? Why are you making me talk about this stuff? This stuff is boring."

"I'm pretty sure you started it," Dorothy said. "You brought up Lazarus. The second-Black-man theory. You brought up your nightmare white date."

"You're right," Ashbee said. "Jesus, I'm boring."

"Did you fuck her, by the way? Your date?"

"Of course I did."

Ashbee sipped his gin and tonic through a candy-striped straw. Dorothy took out her phone to make a note about men and straws, how men loved drinking from straws as boys, then absolutely rejected the notion in young adulthood, until middle age saw them approach it again. There was a joke to be made about this, in which the straw represented confidence, growth. Maybe that's how you knew a man had reached wisdom: when, after decades away, he found the path back to the straw.

"I *want* to talk about something other than being Black," Ashbee said. It didn't bother him that Dorothy was typing. "I really do. Lately, I've been wanting to talk about animals. I want to talk about ducks and stuff, vultures, rhinoceroses. I want to do a whole show about animal behavior, but funny. I'm getting so sick of people."

"Kruger knows a lot about birds," Dorothy said.

She'd never cared much for animals herself, and as Ashbee launched into a description of the bowerbird's mating rituals, she let her mind wander. How nice it was to be out without a purse, she thought, sipping her vodka. Everything zipped in the jacket, everything tucked. She didn't think those words exactly, "everything zipped, everything tucked," but she felt them. She'd read online that some people thought in full sentences, even *heard* themselves think them, but it was rare for her to have definite words appear in her head before she spoke them, or wrote them down, like she'd just done with the straw note. Perhaps that was why she wrote for a living. To know what it was that she was thinking.

"And then the female will mate with the best interior decorator," Ashbee said, about bowerbirds. "Decorating skills are what she looks for in a partner."

Who cared? Dorothy thought/felt. Who cared what the female

bowerbird wanted? Dorothy didn't even know what *she* wanted. In a partner, or in general. She guessed a well-decorated home would be nice. But what else? Would she want to be seductive with Manny tonight, for example? Or would she just be a good friend? Probably she'd be a good friend. Was it sad? That even on a day that she'd truly believed, for a few minutes, to be her last one, she couldn't find it in herself to be horny? That all she wanted was a good friend?

"How much sex do you have?" she asked Ashbee. "Do you fuck like once a month, once a week?"

"Something like that," Ashbee said, taking the change of topic in stride.

"Something like which?"

"I'd say once a week."

"Jesus."

"You think that's a lot?"

Dorothy hadn't had sex in six years.

"I think that's healthy," she said.

"What about you?"

"I haven't fucked anyone in four years," Dorothy said. It was unclear to her why she'd decided four was so much better to admit to than six.

"Is it because you don't want to?" Ashbee asked.

"Shouldn't I want to?" Dorothy said. "After the day I've had?"

She wasn't making a particular effort to keep her voice down. The bar was getting louder anyway, too crowded for easy eavesdropping.

"Do you want us to sleep together?" Ashbee asked. "Is that what you're getting at?"

"Absolutely not," Dorothy said. "I'm just saying, I was stuck in a conference room with Sword for hours, thinking I would die, and now Sword is probably home fucking his wife, as he should, and I'm here drinking like nothing happened."

"Well, nothing did happen," Ashbee said. "There was never a shooter in the building."

"Sword and I *believed* that there was. And now he's home, in bed with his wife."

"It sounds to me like maybe you want to sleep with Sword," Ashbee said.

He was trying to find the humor in all this, Dorothy knew, the funny angle. Since her confinement with Sword, though, she'd been unable to locate it herself, that right distance. She was stuck in the tragedy of the first person—the tragedy of close-up, Chaplin would've said. There weren't that many quotes on comedy that made sense to Dorothy, but what Chaplin had said about life being a tragedy when seen in close-up and a comedy in long-shot, that had brought her much comfort over the years. She was usually able to snap out of self-pity by thinking the words "get in long-shot," but she worried it was taking her too long to get in long-shot today, to get back to the third-person narrator within her that made life bearable.

"You're a terrible listener," she said to Ashbee.

Which he knew and wasn't insulted by. He'd never understood the urge to be a good listener, couldn't relate to those who boasted about the quality. Being a bad listener was to Ashbee more interesting, because then you got people to think differently about their problems, rather than just in the way they'd wanted to think about them all along.

"What about Sword?" he said. "Is Sword a good listener?"

"What I learned today," Dorothy said, "is that when you think death is coming for you, what you really want handy is not a good listener but a good talker."

She said that Sword hadn't impressed her in that area. That he wouldn't even share his planned last words with her.

"Of course he wouldn't," Ashbee said. "You don't say your last words until you're absolutely certain it's time. The potential for embarrassment is too high. It'd be like pulling down your pants after someone asked to see your *cuticles.*"

"Wait, do you know what *your* last words will be?" Dorothy asked.

"Last words in life or last words onstage?"

It hadn't even crossed her mind that someone could be thinking about their last line onstage.

"Last words in life," she said.

"I think so," Ashbee said. "I have some idea. They'd be for my daughters."

"That's nice."

Ashbee thought "mandatory" more than "nice," but didn't say it out loud. He made the mistake of turning to look at the room behind his back, and immediately caught a glimpse of Phil, who understood their eyes crossing as an invitation to come over for a chat.

"Fuck," Ashbee said. "Here he comes. See? I should've hired that second Black man. We could've split the Phil bill—'I gave him Black wisdom last time, it's your turn now.'"

"I split the Phil bill with you," Dorothy said. "He asks about my experience of the world as a woman all the time."

"He expects you to be funny about it, though," Ashbee said. "Me, it's like I have to be *inspiring* or something."

He said this as Dorothy delayed her order of a second drink by crunching between her teeth the vodka-laced ice cubes left from the first one.

"It's so sad when they want that," she said, and the ice biting sent shivers down her neck.

"Inspiration?" Ashbee asked.

Dorothy looked down her glass. Close up. No ice left.

"Yes," she said. "It's sad. When they want that from us."

17

WHAT WAS THE PLAN HERE EXACTLY? KRUGER HAD ASSUMED A NURSE
would stop them from exiting the building, a security guard, but they
were out now, he was, and his father, and that guy Tony, treading
lightly on a fine layer of snow.

Tony didn't look like he belonged in an old folks' home. He was
old, sure, but Kruger had seen vastly more decrepit men just that afternoon, at the English Department meeting. Men who looked like
lifting a teacup would hurt. Men who would complain about it.
Whereas Tony gave you the sense that physical pain was not something worth mentioning, a mere fact of life, about as interesting as
the weather. He looked like someone who'd felt so much of it he might
not notice a fork in his thigh. Perhaps also because he would have
hard muscles there, Kruger thought. When he and Louis had knocked
on his door a few minutes earlier, Tony'd been playing darts, and
Kruger had seen all the muscles in his arms, rolling under the crin-
kled skin. There was something unnerving about a strong man in a
retirement home, he thought. Somewhere on his person, Tony had a
gun.

They were going into the woods now, of course. Maybe Tony had a
makeshift shooting range there, lined-up Mason jars, Hillary Clinton cutouts. Louis had told him, "My son here needs to learn how to
shoot," and Tony had immediately grabbed his utility jacket and
known where to go.

Kruger was walking a few feet behind them, like the reluctant
child that he was at present, but also like someone who would, if

questioned, be able to deny knowing anything about Tony's and his father's intentions. He thought of Artie as he walked, of walking to class with Artie earlier. He was now convinced that Artie was dead, that if the campus shooter had left even just one victim, that victim would be Artie. He should've been nicer to him in workshop, Kruger thought. His father had had three students die on him over the course of his career—two suicides and a drowning—and Kruger had gone to each of their funerals with him. Perhaps Louis would want to go with him to Artie's.

"Here is good," Kruger heard Tony say.

They hadn't made it very deep into the woods, but out of the hundreds of surrounding trees, one had been selected to be shot at, an American beech, perhaps because the whiteness of its trunk almost made it a source of light in the dark, perhaps because two knots on the bark were at such a height that it would seem to Kruger like he was shooting at a man. A man staring at him.

Tony showed him the gun, which he'd been carrying loose in his jacket pocket.

"Ever held one of these before?"

"I've seen my father's up close," Kruger said. "Was never allowed to touch it."

Did that sound bitchy? Tony didn't pick up on it if it did.

"You've seen movies, though, correct? It's just like in a movie. Point and shoot. You right handed?"

"Yes."

"Then that's your trigger finger," Tony said, touching the gun's muzzle to Kruger's right pointer. "Now, if I hand you the gun, you're going to want to slide your trigger finger right there in the trigger hole, but that's verboten. That's not the way to pick up a gun."

Louis was nodding at everything Tony said, but it was for Kruger's benefit—Tony couldn't even see Louis, who stood a step behind him.

"You don't put your finger on the trigger before you're ready to shoot," Tony went on. "You want to avoid all negligent discharge."

Kruger found a place in his head to store the words "negligent discharge." Those would be good words for later, he thought, when he'd either recount this moment or write about it. He watched as Tony presented the right way to hold a gun.

"Fingers around the grip like so, trigger finger along the slide, in a register position."

"No negligent discharge that way," Kruger said.

It turned out, he thought, that the proper way to hold a gun was to make a gun shape with your hand, as if for play, and superimpose it on the real thing.

"Safety first, always," Tony said. "That's why, as you may have noticed, since I took it out, the gun has never been pointed anywhere near my person."

"I noticed," Kruger said. "It's been pointed nearer *my* person."

"Safety first," Tony repeated.

As Tony warned him about recoil and listed the dos and don'ts of grip, stance, and something he called "gun presentation," Kruger felt a surprising calm wash over him. He still hadn't touched the gun himself, but it didn't seem so absurd anymore that he should, that he would, in about a minute, shoot his first bullet at a tree. In fact, he could almost see it having happened already, the moment having slid uneventfully into the past. His first shooting lesson. Why had he been so nervous? Guns were nothing. Tony was holding one. Tony had likely been holding one since childhood, and he'd probably never killed anybody. Most people didn't kill anybody, Kruger thought. No one would die or get hurt right now just because a gun had been taken out of a pocket.

"What are we preparing for?" Tony asked Kruger. "Are you going after someone? Do you plan to have to shoot on the move?"

"What?"

"A moving target?"

"Isn't it always a moving target?" Kruger asked.

Tony didn't respond. He loaded the gun in silence, shaking his head. Kruger wondered if he'd said something stupid or insulting. Perhaps Tony had been a sniper, or a contract killer, someone who'd mostly shot men sitting at restaurants, men waiting at the wheel for the light to change, unaware that there'd been a price on their head.

"I think revenge, though," Kruger said. "In terms of what we're preparing for."

This seemed to surprise his father, who was still looking over Tony's shoulder.

"Revenge from whom?" Louis asked.

"I don't know yet," Kruger said. "I just assume that's what I'll need a gun for. If I ever need a gun."

"Revenge is easier," Tony said, handing Kruger the gun. "Revenge stands pretty still."

Kruger grabbed the gun the way he'd been shown, shaping a gun with his hand, placing it around the real thing, trigger finger along the side, and positioned himself to shoot between the tree's two eyes. It wasn't clear to him why he'd said "revenge." Many people had slighted him over the years, but no one had ever really fucked him over. If Artie had been killed today, would he want to avenge his death? Would that be the thing to shut his father up?

The gun was warm in his hand. Louis and Tony had taken a few steps away from him and out of his line of sight—again, safety first. It was just him and the tree. Him, the tree, and that Andrea Bocelli song that came into his head right then, for no reason he could discern. "Con Te Partirò." A few weeks earlier, out of curiosity, he'd sat in on Dorothy's improvisation class and been made to listen to the song eight or nine times, maybe more. Marianne had played it on her phone while onstage, and Dorothy had deemed it too easy, relying on another artist's earnestness to get your laughs. You couldn't play a Celine Dion song, Dorothy had said, or quote from the movie *The Notebook,* and just stand there to reap the rewards of someone else's labor. If you wanted to use cheesy art as comedy fodder, you had to first recognize what it was that millions saw in it. After saying this, she'd insisted the kids listen to the Andrea Bocelli song until it didn't make them laugh anymore. Until they were moved by it even. She'd played it at top volume through the classroom speakers. She'd wanted them to listen to it once, just once, in its entirety, no laughing, no eye-rolling. Every time one of the students even just smiled, she'd started the song again, from the top. There'd been a moment when it had seemed impossible that they would ever leave the room. That they would ever not be listening to the song. The whole class would start laughing even in the silence before the first note. There'd also been a near success, when they'd all looked solemn and full of feeling for three minutes and fifty seconds of the four-minute song, but the last "Io con teeeeeeeeeeeeee" had triggered a chain of sniggers that had sent everyone back to square one. Dorothy had laughed with them that time, too, but Kruger had remained unshaken for the entire duration of the exercise. He'd looked at the students' faces, mainly. About-to-burst faces. Clenched jaws. Eyes avoiding contact with other eyes. And now, gun in hand, firing his first shot, that's what Kruger's body jumped to, that sense memory of being among other bodies holding off on laughter while being himself nowhere near laughing. He fired six shots, after which Tony declared him a natural.

"Sure you've never done this before?" he asked.

Kruger thought Tony was being condescending. He'd aimed for the spot between the tree's eyes, he said, but all the bullet holes had ended up much higher on the trunk.

"That's not what matters right now," Tony said, approaching the tree. "Look at your grouping."

Kruger followed Tony's finger on the bark, drawing a small circle that encompassed all the bullet holes.

"That's a tight grouping," Tony said. "Tight groupings are a sign of consistency. Consistency is the most important."

"It matters more than aim?"

"You're a natural," Tony repeated.

Kruger had never been called a natural at anything, even in jest. Things could come easy to him (success, women), but never naturally. He'd never suffered much to write jokes, but they'd never *written themselves* either. He'd recently met a comedian who believed that his jokes were prewritten in invisible ink long before he sat at his desk and all he had to do in order for the material to appear, like an image in the developing bath, was to be "present to the whiteness of the page." Was that being a natural? Kruger had felt superior to the other comedian in that moment. He worked harder than *him,* at least. He never carved anything to perfection, like Dorothy did, but still: he spent time with his sentences, and that was honorable. He'd never felt one of his jokes reach its ideal form, however. He stopped working on a joke when it was good enough. And that, at times, could make Kruger think of himself as a fraud. Or maybe not a fraud, but the opposite of a natural—an artificial, maybe. "Good enough" meant it could get a little better, perhaps with another day of work, perhaps another week, another month, so why did Kruger ever decide to stop when he did? It always seemed somewhat arbitrary. How could you tell something was finished? When you worked on a bit, it quickly ceased being funny to you. You had to operate on faith, on a vague memory that the stuff had excited you at some point and was worth pursuing. Tightening a bit could feel right, sharpening it could make you feel smarter, but after a while, what you couldn't count on was knowing whether it was funny at all. You had to rely on others for that. And Kruger was like his father, he didn't much like others, or trust them. Only his own taste was unquestionable. He pretended that people liking his stuff was the right metric, but people had shit taste, everyone knew that, and the truth was, he was haunted by what haunted all artists, the question of whether or not he would respond to his own work, laugh at his own jokes if he were hearing a stranger make them for the first time.

"Well, I think aim is pretty fucking important," Kruger's father said, bringing him back to the gun and the tree. Louis hadn't said anything in a while, but there it came, more disappointment, even though the teacher he'd himself chosen for his son was satisfied. "Tight groupings," Louis insisted. "People don't get killed by *tight groupings*. A single well-placed bullet does it."

"Dad. I'm not planning on killing anyone."

"No one *plans* for it."

An odd thing happened then, which is that Kruger felt at once the full breadth and intensity of his father's life. The feeling went beyond empathy, which was a common enough thing for Kruger. He was used to seeing the world through another person's eyes, experiencing it through their body for a few seconds. That was part of his job. When it happened, though, he never saw *himself* in the person's eyes, the way he did now, in the woods. Kruger saw the scene the way his father was seeing it, Louis's side of the moment they were in. He understood that Louis was in the middle of his own experience, one that involved him, Ben Kruger, his only son, and one that wasn't going as planned. The experience in question could be seen as a nearly four-decade one (raising Kruger) or as this latter half-hour slice (the shooting lesson), a subdivision of the whole—a fractal, in fact, since it had turned out to be more of the same for Louis, a miniature version of what it had been like to raise Kruger from the start. Raising Kruger in a nutshell. Some parents wanted their children to be confident, happy, or maybe just satisfied with what they had, but Louis's goal had always been for his son to be humbled by the world. To know his place. He'd made young Kruger ask his track coach to move up practice an hour so that he could attend both it and his singing lessons on the other side of town. Louis had assumed the coach would humiliate little Ben in front of the team for asking, and for singing at any serious level, too, but the coach had agreed. The whole team had agreed. They'd been encouraging of Kruger's artistic pursuits, while

Louis had been waiting to prove there was simply no time for them in the schedule, no time for singing lessons, that's just how it was. And the comedy thing—how Louis had hoped it would crash before it took off, how ready he'd been to give Kruger the look . . . How were you supposed to teach your child anything? When everything went his way? And now, to top it all off, he turned out to be a decent shot?

Kruger felt all this, but no anger of his own—only his father's anger. He understood it somewhat. He'd been ashamed before, thinking how easy things had turned out for him. Smarter friends from high school were stuck behind desks in Naperville, funnier friends from college in open workspaces. It wasn't fair. On good days, Kruger thought: Who cares? Who past the age of seven still expected the world to be fair? But on others, he felt single-handedly responsible for the rise of the false equation between success and talent. It wasn't as dangerous as the one between success and influence, but it was pretty embarrassing still. Did his father think Kruger didn't know this? That he didn't deserve anything he got?

"Show me," Kruger heard himself tell Louis. He was handing him the gun. "Show me how good *your* aim is."

Kruger had meant for it to be kind, to give his father a chance to shine and, yes, to *show* him, finally, but his request came out threatening. Like a challenge. What if his dad wasn't such a good shot? What if Kruger was about to humiliate *him*?

"I don't need to show you anything," Louis said.

"Of course not," Kruger said, immediately relieved by the answer. "I'm sorry."

Louis was already turning back toward Sunset Hill. Tony, who'd missed all the unspoken words that had just circulated between the Krugers, stopped him in his tracks.

"Come on, Lou!" he said. "Show the kid."

He produced a second gun, from a second pocket, and for a moment, Kruger thought his father would grab it and shoot Tony right there and then. He hated being called Lou.

"I didn't know you had another gun," he said to Tony instead. Kruger saw that his father was calculating something there, forcing a pause. He looked the way he'd looked in class years ago, when a student asked a stupid question and he had to think about how to respond in a noninsulting way. "How much do you want for it?" Louis asked Tony.

Tony said the gun wasn't for sale, but not in any definitive way. There was no mention of an ancestor it had belonged to, or any particular emotional attachment to it.

"My son is rich," Louis said. "He'll give you however much you want for it."

He didn't even look at Kruger for confirmation.

Kruger said he didn't want a gun, but Louis said the gun would be for himself. At his age, you had to have one, he said, which Kruger decided to take the less depressing of the two ways he could think of to take it, as "At my father's age, you need a gun because you have no more strength for close combat," rather than "At my father's age, you need to be able to kill yourself the minute you want to."

"Five hundred?" Tony said.

Kruger had a little less than that in his wallet, cash, and Tony accepted it. He gave Louis his new gun and a box of bullets and said they should be heading back, the soup was going to get cold.

"You should stay for dinner," he said to Kruger. "It's the good kind of soup tonight. Egg-lemon."

Kruger, once again, walked a few steps behind the old men. He liked egg-lemon soup. It was something an ex-girlfriend used to make. Could the nursing home possibly make a decent version of it? It was a five-star nursing home. His father, for all that he complained on the phone, had never said anything against the food. In fact, now that Kruger thought about it, Louis had never said anything against Sunset Hill itself, only the people who lived there, and people, he'd never much liked anyway. Except for his students. He'd liked his students, young people. Kids who humored him by learning his lessons about American history but who, in their heart of hearts, didn't think it mattered much what they knew, because they still couldn't quite truly believe they'd grow up to be adults one day. Once they realized it would happen, though, once they started having hopes and ambitions and talking about them, Louis tended to lose interest. He liked them in suspended animation. In that way, Kruger thought, he should've liked Sunset Hill's residents more. They had to be back to a similar denial—from kids not quite believing they'll soon be grown-ups to old people not quite believing they'll soon be dead. Except, and Kruger realized this had to make a difference, Louis had no authority over them. He wasn't speaking to them with an intimate knowledge of what awaited.

And now I bought him a gun, Kruger thought.

He thought about Artie again, how everyone would lie at his funeral, say that the kid had had a bright future ahead of him. They would lie not only for the parents' benefit, but for theirs as well, Kruger thought, because there was comfort in uttering words that would never be contradicted by facts or the passage of time.

And then Kruger's head went back to soup. He hadn't eaten all day. Could never eat anything before class on class day. Finding this out had surprised him, because eating before a show had never been a problem. He'd eaten unspeakable things minutes before a gig. He was good at swallowing burps onstage, had the timing down to a science—you waited till the audience laughed, you bent your head a certain way. There was a lot you could do onstage while people were laughing. Well, maybe not *a lot,* Kruger thought. You couldn't fully break character and write down your grocery list, for example, but you could check out for a second, take stock. That's what the audience did, after all, when they laughed. They were half there and not. Their eyes were half-closed in that moment, and they retreated to a place within themselves where they let the joke they'd just heard echo. Their brains took a split second to decide whether or not to commit it to memory, how good exactly the joke had been, after which the eyes opened up again fully and the audience was back in the room, ready for more. An audience laughing was a tiny time-out when you were onstage, it allowed for burping, drinking, popping Pepto-Bismol, regrouping. That was why he couldn't eat before class, Kruger realized. His students didn't laugh enough in workshop. They didn't give him those little breaks he needed. He couldn't count on their eyes half closing to make him blurry. Their eyes were always wide open, in fact. Some of the kids even took *notes* on what he said. How could anyone be comfortable in this context? Who could do this on a full stomach?

Hunger made his stomach beat now, in the woods. Sunset Hill was in sight, the wraparound porch, the Christmas lights, some windows glowing orange, others framing fainter sources of light, suggestive of reading presences, a woman by her side lamp, perhaps, so engrossed in her book she hadn't noticed night fall. Smoke was coming out of the chimney, immediately meeting a cloud the exact same shade of gray. This was all very inviting, Kruger thought, it was an inviting nursing home. He wondered what the last thing was that he and his father had laughed about together. Was it on the phone? Was it something to do with politics? They hadn't laughed today, he knew that much. Yet he also knew that the shooting lesson would become a bit. He knew it in his heart. It had made him too sad not to rewrite and try laughing about. He was already thinking about how he could frame it. It could be presented as quirky, "the day I learned to shoot at a nursing home and then ate egg-lemon soup with everyone," or go dark, "the day I bought my sick father a gun." Dark was funnier, especially if his father did end up killing himself with that gun down the line.

He didn't believe this, of course. That his dad killing himself with the gun would be funny. But he *had* to think it. Someone in the audience would think it, and you weren't a good comedian if your audience went darker than you.

Perhaps he would leave the gun-buying thing out of the bit. Have only the shooting lesson with Tony (who would be an easy character to inflate) and his disapproving father ("Well, I think aim is pretty fucking important" was a good line—was that what he'd said?).

But the soup. Would he stick around for the soup? Would the soup be part of the bit? They were on the porch now, Louis was opening the door for Tony, and turning to his son to ask if he was staying for dinner.

Staying for dinner was the professional thing to do. Eating soup with forty-plus seniors had to bring on new levels of sadness and, therefore, new ideas for comedy. But hadn't today been enough? In the sadness department? In the fear department? In the "everything that made you feel small and alone and insignificant" department? He didn't want to go home, either. He didn't want to see all the emails about the shooting. He knew he would read every single one—again, out of a professional obligation to find the funny thing: the perfectly placed typo in the outpouring of thoughts and prayers, the bad meta- phor. There would be terrible timing, too. One of his colleagues, not yet aware of the shooting, would probably have sent an angry email about Manny Reinhardt, how his hire would "forever be the WORST THING THAT EVER HAPPENED TO THIS DEPARTMENT," and that email would be sandwiched between a message providing an updated number of casualties and another giving out details for the vigil downtown. No one would care about Manny's hire after today, Kruger thought. Bastard got away with everything. Though Kruger did, too, in all honesty. He'd paid off a guy out of fear that his father's behavior would reflect poorly on *him*. He'd gotten away with something. His father, not so much.

"So?" Louis asked. "Soup?"

There was trembling in his voice. This was still fairly new. When it happened on the phone, Louis would usually cough and pretend something had gotten stuck in his throat, but this time, he let the shiver make its statement. Tony had gone in and Louis was still hold- ing the door, now for his son. It was the first time since Kruger had arrived that Louis seemed to care what his plans were. He was prob- ably just tired, Kruger thought. Behind his father, he caught a glimpse of the man who'd explained emotional subtitles to him earlier. He looked dazed now, a bit lost.

"I'm not really hungry," he said to Louis.

"Are you sure?"

Now his father had to be hamming it up with the voice trembling. Was he trying to make him feel guilty for leaving?

"I have to feed the parrot," Kruger said.

"Right."

The parrot didn't need feeding. The parrot could survive for days on what was in his cage, and Louis knew it. Louis knew more about birds than Kruger did. Kruger had in fact acquired a parrot in part to have something to bond with his father over. Louis had been critical of the purchase, though. When Kruger had sent him a photo of his bird, he'd said that keeping birds at home was cruel, that birds were for the wild. Kruger drew the parallel for the first time between his father and his parrot, two prisoners who only had him to rely on for company. It was selfish of him to leave just because he'd decided he was done gathering material for the day. He could stay for soup and not look at it like work, couldn't he? Decide right now that even if something hilariously depressing happened during dinner, he wouldn't use it. Decide to simply live through soup night at the nursing home, with no ulterior motive. To simply have dinner with his dad.

The Metra sounded nice, though. It had to be fairly empty at this hour, from the suburbs into the city. Kruger could just look through the window for a while, try to not think about anything. He gestured for his father to conceal the gun under his belt a little better, and said his goodbyes.

18

IN SPITE OF THE SNOW, MANNY'S FLIGHT LANDED AHEAD OF SCHEDULE. He'd spent the last forty minutes in the air working, writing down memories of Brooklyn Hospital's pediatric ward, the long hours he'd spent there with Rachel, August, and all those other sick children he'd never asked about. What he had on paper so far wasn't funny, but it didn't matter. He just had to let it all out for now, how cold and afraid he'd been (why was it always so cold in hospitals?), how cowardly, how angry at Rachel, at times, for talking to other parents in the hallways, for letting their worry add to her own. Manny had never felt so selfish as when August was sick. Hospitals were places of high contamination, and the fact that the ailments August and other children suffered were mostly congenital malformations and noncontagious blood diseases was of no comfort to Manny at the time. He was afraid of another type of contamination, of his family's bad luck piled on by other families' worse luck. Snowballing. When he saw a deformed kid on the ward, he looked away, didn't even nod at the parents. He held his breath, too. He thought bad luck would travel like bad smells.

Manny had been so focused on remembering his son as a newborn that he experienced a moment of unreality when he turned his phone back on and saw a text message from all-grown August, sent an hour earlier.

I'll meet you at the Empty Bottle

Manny had almost forgotten about the Empty Bottle, or why he'd come to Chicago in the first place. He wanted to skip it now, skip

Dorothy's apartment, too, just check in at the airport's Hilton and write all night, like in the good old days. He knew he would have to ask August for permission to use his life story, but if he came to him with an idea of how the show would be structured, the beats, it would be a stronger case. His son would see the thought that had gone into it. He felt bad canceling on August, knew that Rachel would probably give him a hard time about it, but August would understand. He respected hard work. Manny was starting to type his excuse when his son's next message came:

I'm here

Manny didn't let this stop him. He could still tell him he wasn't feeling well and ask to meet tomorrow instead.

At the bar

came another message.

With your future students

Now it was trickier. Now third parties were involved. Parties Manny hadn't disappointed yet. August had likely told them he would be coming.

They're already asking for legal advice

Manny erased the message he'd been working on.

That's smart

he replied.

Smart kids. I'll be there in an hour

He put his phone back in his pocket and looked for directions to a cab. He made accidental eye contact with a woman who seemed to recognize him, and he pretended to need something from the Hudson News immediately to his right. The woman could've been a fan with no interest in his present troubles, but Manny didn't risk it. He'd been insulted on the street a dozen times since the stories had broken. Mostly about the proposals, only once about punching Lipschitz. Several news outlets had labeled him a predator after one of the three women maintained he'd offered marriage *before* they'd fucked. Manny was pretty sure he'd said it *after* sex, but he didn't feel like correcting the woman's story yet. If there ended up being a trial and the timing of the proposals became a pivotal detail, he would give his version, but now, in all honesty, he couldn't really see the difference it made. It wasn't like any of these women had been saving themselves and he'd ruined it.

Manny thought he could get something for August from Hudson News while he was there. He used to bring him a present from each tour stop back in the day. Toys at first, but then August had started asking for unique things, things that could only be found wherever Manny went. Manny had brought home local papers after that, the *Tampa Bay Times, The Bellingham Herald,* which August proceeded to read from front page to obituaries. Rachel had found it cute, how nerdy that was, and how close the boy wanted to be to his dad, going over the news of the towns Manny had been in on the day that he'd been there. Who passed on Legos to read about the weather in Raleigh? she'd marveled. *Last week*'s weather in Raleigh? What a quirky child they had! It had made Manny uneasy, though. August's interest in what had happened in those cities was the photo negative of what his had been, and he'd *been* there. On tour, he tended to forget where he was. He slept until noon and woke up sad most days not to be in his bed, with Rachel. He saw the long hours before a show as time to kill, not opportunities for discovery. Why was his son so interested in knowing where he'd been? People were the same everywhere. Manny had brought the newspapers as a joke, and his son hadn't gotten it.

There wasn't anything nice to bring back from the Hudson News, really. A model airplane could be funny, Manny thought, because it was the type of thing good dads bought for their sons in the movies, but perhaps he should steer away from self-deprecating joke gifts. Self-deprecation was just another way to talk about yourself, and he should be a good father tonight, not joke about all the times that he'd sucked. Tonight would be about August: August's life, August's internship, the trial August hoped to work on. Manny would listen and offer advice, if advice was requested.

People magazine had a starlet on its cover, one who'd been sentenced to hundreds of hours of community service after being caught shoplifting and who was now letting the world know how transformed she'd been by the experience. She'd served her sentence but was still volunteering at a homeless shelter in L.A. Manny wondered if he would have to do something like that, too. His agent had hinted at it, asking if there wasn't anything they could use to make him look like a good guy. Any volunteer work he did on the side? Of course not. He donated a lot of money to cancer research, though, he'd said. Over the years, he'd probably given a million dollars. He'd been proud to tell Michelle this. He'd never told anyone about it before, not even Rachel. He believed that charity wasn't something you advertised, that advertising it rendered it worthless. So he was ashamed to realize he'd expected praise from Michelle, when he'd told her. All she'd said, however, was it didn't really count, because all Manny had done was give money, and not time. Manny was afraid she'd suggest he visit cancer wards now, make the dying people laugh. He didn't want to see people with cancer.

Manny considered getting August a T-shirt from the Hudson News rack, but quickly realized he didn't know his size. He knew it wasn't a symptom of being a bad father not to know your son's size, but it still disturbed him to think that there'd been a time when he'd kept track of his baby boy's slightest variation in weight, when he'd learned to think in grams to better care for him, and to feel his stomach for signs of obstruction. For years, he'd kept track of the kid's temperature, of how much and when he'd last eaten, and now Manny had to think about it before he could remember August's age. The distance they kept as adults, though, was a positive thing. They were able to keep it because August was cured. It was proof that Manny's strategy of avoiding contact with other people's pain and hardship had paid off and kept theirs circumscribed, somewhere in the past, inside a black sphere, Manny pictured, getting smaller and smaller behind them as time went on. They'd made it. They'd avoided contamination.

He'd started giving money to cancer research when Rachel, during one of August's many hospital stays, had befriended a mother in pediatric oncology. Manny'd never met the woman himself. He'd refused to set foot on the cancer floor. He hadn't had much money at the time, but he'd begun making small donations to leading labs in cancer research, the Anderson Center, the NIH, Stanford. August's two following surgeries had gone splendidly. Even Rachel's friend's son had started doing better, or so Rachel reported. Manny had kept giving. As he gave more, his career took off, too. August began shitting on his own. Manny kept giving. The more he gave, the more famous he became, and if fame meant touring extensively, being less a part of his child's life, Manny reasoned it was a way to balance out the intrusiveness he'd been forced into at first, pulling the shit out of August several times a day. It was good to give August some space once he could do everything by himself. Manny cheated on Rachel one night in Ohio and made his first-ever five-figure donation the following day. He never gave less after that. When Rachel started talking about couples' therapy, he doubled his usual donation. The day their divorce was finalized was the day he gave the most. Since then, he'd kept the donations steady, the same amount twice a year. Maybe he hadn't given as much as he could have the last few years, and that's why life was catching up with him. He worried now that Lipschitz and the women's accusations would only be the beginning. The beginning of a long fall. He hadn't given anything to cancer research since it had all started. He'd felt the situation demanded something different, something drastic. Perhaps Michelle was right and he ought to forget about money, upgrade to time given to those who suffered. The problem was, no one wanted his time now. No one wanted Manny to spend it on them. Except maybe journalists. There was this journalist who kept asking him for quotes and corroborations. He could give her a few minutes, Manny thought. That would make her day. Maybe he could even tell her about what he was working on, a special about his son's illness . . . Is that how he would phrase it? He could pretend that he'd already been working on it the night he'd punched Lipschitz. Yes, that was a great idea, Manny thought as he handed the checkout guy a Take 5 and a Red Bull. He could tell the journalist how writing about the hardest four years of his life had made him vulnerable, his nerves so very *raw.* Journalists loved that word.

"You're Manny Reinhardt!" the checkout guy said. His name tag said "Severin." "*Fuck* these bitches, man!"

"Excuse me?" Manny said.

"Fuck *these* bitches!" Severin repeated.

The emphasis switch made Manny think he was talking about a group of girls near them, rude customers, perhaps.

"They're taking advantage of you," Severin added, grabbing the Take 5 and Red Bull from Manny's hands. "Clear as day. They're just climbers, everyone can see that."

Manny had only worried about being insulted so far, not offered support. He'd read a few people arguing under articles online that he wasn't a predator but just a sad guy trying to get laid, and weren't we all, and even though the comments had cheered him somewhat, he'd sensed that they came from men trying to defend themselves more than they were standing up for him. He'd come to terms with the idea that "sad guy trying to get laid" was probably the best characterization he could hope for these days, yet the interpretation that he was the real victim here disturbed him.

"They were using *you* for your con*nec*tions," Severin went on.

He had Manny's Take 5 in one hand, the can of Red Bull in the other, and with them he drew circles and lines in the air—circles for the people in the story he was telling himself, lines for what they'd wanted from one another. He said the word "bitches" a few more times, and then finally scanned the Take 5, but not the Red Bull. He would never scan the Red Bull, Manny realized, that second beep would never come and put an end to this.

"No one will ever trust any of these bitches," Severin said. "They'll never work in Hollywood, believe me. Maybe some lousy director will give one of them a role in a movie no one will see, but then, if anything, it will all be reality TV after that."

"I don't need the Red Bull, actually," Manny said.

"Are you sure?"

"Positive."

He didn't need the Take 5 either, in all honesty, but walking out on it would be a sign of weakness.

"How much do I owe you?"

Severin stared at him for a few seconds. Manny thought he was calculating his next move, thinking about what he could say to force an interaction worth transforming into an anecdote later. Manny knew one of two things could happen at this point. The man could either tell him a story or ask for one. It wasn't true that people were always asking comedians for a joke, but they did seem to at least want a *story* when they met one offstage, a snippet of what was on his mind. Manny was already thinking about what he could say—perhaps he should mention his son was waiting for him in the city, that's why he was in a hurry, and his son had been sick as a child, did Severin know that? But then he thought he saw Severin swallow back tears.

"Are you okay?" he asked.

Severin nodded.

"You remind me of my old man, is all," he said.

"Was your old man fat and Jewish?" Manny asked.

A joke, he thought, given Severin's being Black and skinny, but then he remembered adoption was a thing that people did.

"It's in the voice," Severin said.

The voice? Manny wanted to ask again if the dad had been fat and Jewish, but stopped himself.

"When I was a kid," Severin went on, "he could do all the voices. *Trading Places*—he could say all of Murphy's lines, and Aykroyd's lines, and even Jamie Lee Curtis's lines, in their own voices."

"Sounds like a great guy," Manny said.

"Your voice is very close to what his *real* voice was like, though."

But that wasn't it, that wasn't what Severin had wanted to delay Manny with. What Severin had wanted to delay Manny with was the following story: In middle school, he, Severin, had had a friend, Jimmy. He would hang out at Jimmy's every day after school. Jimmy was a huge Jim Carrey fan, and together they would watch *Dumb and Dumber* almost every afternoon, or *The Mask*, sometimes *Ace Ventura: Pet Detective*. This was the mid-nineties, Severin told Manny. Jim Carrey hadn't taken his *Truman Show/Man on the Moon* turn yet. Anyway. Jimmy knew a lot about Jim Carrey from interviews he'd read in movie magazines. He dreamed of a career in Hollywood and felt a kinship with Carrey. Not only had they both been named James, but Jim Carrey's father had been an accountant, just like Jimmy's, and Jim Carrey had grown up in the suburbs of Toronto, which was basically Canadian Chicago, Jimmy said, and so the Chicago suburb he and Severin were growing up in had to be similar to what Jim Carrey had had as a child, in terms of what was on sensory offer. Jimmy spent a lot of time talking about Jim. Whenever something didn't go the way he wanted (baseball practice, mostly), he drew parallels with Carrey's setbacks (his many rejections from *SNL*). Severin couldn't tell, though, how serious Jimmy was about becoming an actor, or a comic. There was never a mention of acting classes, let alone of writing sketches, of writing anything. It seemed Jimmy expected that wanting fame hard enough would lead it to his door.

"Your friend sounds like an idiot," Manny said to Severin, hoping to speed things up. People usually held you hostage with *their* life story, not an old friend's, so he assumed Jimmy was only a preamble to Severin's leading act. Wrong calculation on his part. Insulting Jimmy had the opposite effect: it sent Severin on a tangent of excuses for Jimmy's character, which included a tedious yet vague flashforward to Jimmy's time in high school, how he'd fallen in with the wrong crowd, a mention of a drug addiction that Jimmy couldn't have foreseen in middle school but was somehow supposed to absolve him from (or explain, in retrospect) all the stupid things he'd done or believed back when he hadn't even known about opiates. Manny didn't like that kind of thinking. Everyone was going to have some terrible thing happen to them at some point in life. Everyone, in the end, if you measured their worth against the amount that they'd suffered, could be absolved. Or partly absolved. That wasn't a good reason not to tell people when they were being assholes. Or else what? Would our only option be to love everyone in anticipation of the shit that was going to befall them? And how was a Hudson News guy able to go on and on about his childhood friend like this? Wasn't O'Hare supposed to be one of the busiest airports in the world? Where was everybody?

Severin got back on track with his Jimmy/Jim Carrey story, and Manny vowed not to interrupt him again.

Jimmy desperately wanted to be friends with Jim Carrey, Severin resumed. To the point that Severin could feel insulted, at times, seeing in Jimmy's desire an implication that he, Severin, wasn't a good enough friend, that only Jim Carrey could really understand what Jimmy went through. But then it was true, Severin admitted, that he didn't always quite get it, what Jimmy "went through." Jimmy mostly seemed angry that he had to go to school in the morning, and to believe there were countless better ways to spend his time and creative energy, though once again, Severin said, he'd never heard Jimmy say anything about writing, or seen him take any steps to put a show together. When Severin finally asked about it one day, whether Jimmy was writing anything, they had a disagreement on the meaning of inspiration. Jimmy said that Severin didn't understand the first thing about making art, that you couldn't just decide to write something great, force it into existence. One day, it just came to you. That was how art worked. When he said again that Severin didn't get it, but that Jim Carrey would, Severin suggested Jimmy write him a letter. It was public knowledge what agency Jim Carrey was with, he was pretty sure he'd seen a journalist mention it in one of the interviews: Jimmy could send a letter care of Jim's agent, become Jim Carrey's pen pal. Jimmy got to work almost immediately. He put Severin in charge of finding the interview in which Jim Carrey's agent was mentioned and calling 411 for an address. By the time he wrote down the Beverly Hills zip code on a Post-it and hung up with directory assistance, Severin assumed Jimmy would be done with his letter to Jim, but he was only getting started.

"I'd never seen him spend so much time on anything," Severin told Manny. "When I saw he was actually crumpling paper like in the movies, writing *drafts,* I thought it could take a while, and I might as well kill time writing my own letter to Jim Carrey."

Perhaps Manny could see where this was going, Severin said.

"Jim Carrey ended up responding to my fan letter, and not Jimmy's."

Severin received a personalized letter, warm and kind, written by hand—unmistakably Carrey's hand, according to Jimmy, who recognized the signature from several autographed photos he'd seen, and declared that the rest of the writing matched it.

"Wait, you showed your friend your letter from Carrey even though he didn't get one?" Manny said, breaking his rule not to interrupt again.

"I know," Severin said. "That was stupid. I was so sure his own letter was coming."

For a few days, they looked at Jim Carrey's letter together, alternating between casualness ("Jim wrote a letter, no big deal") and a verging-on-demented attention to detail that one might think was reserved for scripture analysis ("Why would Jim call the L.A. sun 'opaque'?"). Severin had mentioned loving dinosaurs in his letter, and Jim Carrey had drawn a string of them below his signature, though only of the herbivorous kind—a decision the two friends couldn't help but think deliberate and full of meaning. But what meaning exactly? The colors were beautiful.

The next couple of weeks had been the happiest of their lives so far. Full of promise and anticipation. Jimmy imagined what his own letter would contain. At that point, they still thought it had gotten lost, delayed in the mail, or that perhaps it was so long and intricate that Jim Carrey was still composing it. When a form response came, however (typed and not handwritten, "Your support means the world to me," etc.), that was the end of their friendship. Jimmy couldn't save face after that.

"We never really had a fight," Severin told Manny, "but I could tell Jimmy was mad I sent my own letter to Jim Carrey to begin with. And he was right to be. I loved Jim Carrey, but not as much as Jimmy did, and it wasn't worth losing a friend over."

"You couldn't have known what was going to happen," Manny said, but Severin wasn't listening.

"I should've never written this letter," he said. "It only brought me trouble."

For his story was not over yet.

It took his parents a little while to notice the rift with Jimmy. When his father did and asked what had happened, Severin considered lying—he thought his father would be disappointed in him for wasting time writing to celebrities, and even more so for caring about a response. But Severin couldn't lie to his father. He was the one person he could never lie to. What bothered Severin's father, though, when Severin told him the story, was not so much that his son had written to a celebrity but that the celebrity was Jim Carrey. "Why didn't you write to Eddie Murphy?" he said. "Did Jimmy make you write to Jim Carrey? Do you even *like* Jim Carrey?" After which Severin understood that he not only *did* like Jim Carrey, but in fact liked him a lot more than he did Eddie Murphy. He didn't tell his father that last part.

"I didn't want to hurt his feelings," he explained to Manny.

"Actually, I don't need the Take 5 either," Manny said, but Severin kept going.

"The day he found out about my letter to Jim Carrey," he said, "my dad asked me to write to Eddie Murphy."

When Eddie Murphy didn't respond to Severin's letter, his father encouraged him to write a second, then a third. The boy received the same form response every time.

"My father was confused," Severin said. "He didn't understand why Jim Carrey would answer and not Eddie. He kept calling him Eddie. Like, the more Eddie Murphy dissed us, the more my father talked about him like a friend who had to have his reasons."

"Eddie's a very busy man," Manny said.

"I told my father that!" Severin said. "I said, 'Eddie's busy! He gets hundreds of these letters, thousands, and I'm not that special.' My dad, though, he kept saying it was something else, like Eddie was *delib*erately not answering, like maybe he was teaching me a life lesson. Maybe my letters had to be better, maybe I had to put more work into them and *then* he would answer. Like Eddie was trying to show me that life wasn't easy for a Black kid and I had to work ten times harder than white people for anything, including a response from him. That's what my dad thought. He was convinced Jim Carrey only answered me out of pity, *because* I was Black. I told my father I never said I was Black in my letter to Jim Carrey, but he said I must have. He became a little crazy over the whole thing."

"I'm sorry to hear that," Manny said. He knew Eddie Murphy had not thought twice about Severin's letters—if he'd even seen them at all. Manny himself had answered little fan mail over the years, and there'd never been any rhyme or reason to which letters deserved a response and which didn't. He'd left smart and funny letters unanswered (letters that had actually pleased him, sometimes even moved him, let him believe for a second that his life and work were not entirely in vain) and spent hours crafting elaborate responses to idiots who'd just written to call him a turd.

"I'm sure Eddie wanted to write back and didn't get the time," he told Severin. "The best letters we get are often the hardest to respond to. We think our response would be more disappointing than not answering at all."

A lie. Manny had never thought that an absence of response could ruin someone's week, or year (or even more, it seemed, in Severin's case). He'd only ever imagined the positive, how a letter from him could make someone happy, for a minute or two.

"I don't really care that he didn't answer," Severin said. "I don't think my letters were that good, to be honest. My dad kind of fixated on it, though. I stopped writing after the third letter, and I thought he'd forgotten all about it, but when my mother died six years later, he said again that I should write to Eddie. I don't know what he expected from that. Like if he thought that the pain I was in over my mom would make me worthy of an answer this time. Anyway. Eddie didn't respond to that letter either."

Manny didn't say he was sorry this time. What kind of father asked his bereaved son to write to a celebrity?

"Your father sounds like an interesting guy," he said diplomatically. "When did he pass?"

Turned out the father was still alive, though perhaps not for much longer. The reason Severin had spoken about his voice in the past tense earlier was that the old man had had cancer in his jaw and had to have most of it removed. He couldn't speak anymore.

Hearing the word "cancer" annoyed Manny. He was okay thinking or talking about it himself, but when others did, he felt a breach open, he felt exposed.

"I'm sorry to hear about your father's illness," he said, after which a new customer came to his rescue, finally, entering Hudson News with purchasing needs, a deliberate approach to the energy drinks display. "I hope he gets better," Manny added, meaning it, too, feeling his own freedom within reach.

"I don't think he will," Severin said. He hadn't acknowledged the new customer's presence yet but did lower his voice for what came next. "I know you know Eddie," he said. "I was thinking maybe you could convince him to write back to us, you know, before my father dies. It would mean so much to him."

He didn't wait for Manny's response. He wrote his name and address on a piece of paper and gave it to him.

"I put down my email, too, if Eddie prefers that. An email would be fine, I think. Will you ask him?"

Manny knew he wouldn't. He didn't know Eddie that well. Why did people ever ask him anything?

"I'll see what I can do," he said.

Severin didn't thank him, just nodded. The new customer came to stand in line behind Manny, and Manny left the store without drink or food, and without turning around, either (an exit in side steps), for fear of being recognized by the man at his back, for fear of hearing more stories.

The cabdriver didn't recognize Manny, but quickly told him about his idea for a TV show anyway. A show about cabdrivers, and all the different kinds of people they met. Like no one else ever had this idea, Manny thought. He didn't want to be a dick, but it was hard not to judge everyone all the time. Here was the interesting show, to his mind: a show about a cabdriver with no curiosity for his customers whatsoever. Though maybe it was the same show, in the end, and Manny should relax. He'd chanced upon the best kind of driver. The cabdrivers who told you about how interesting their job was because they got to meet all sorts of people were the ones who never asked you a single question.

THE
EMPTY BOTTLE

—

19

ANDREA BOCELLI'S "CON TE PARTIRÒ" STARTED PLAYING ON THE speakers over the bar.

"Who put this on?" Dorothy asked the bartender.

"Is that the song from *The Sopranos*?" Ashbee said.

The bartender pointed at Phil, who, to Ashbee and Dorothy's annoyance, was finalizing his approach.

Since the day Dorothy had used it in workshop, Phil had been trying to make "Con Te Partirò" his class's anthem, or at least its private joke. He wanted the memory of what they'd endured that afternoon, trying to keep a straight face while listening to it, to unite them. It was starting to work. He made eye contact with Olivia when the first notes played, and she smiled at him. Dan did, too. He was bringing the group together! Phil knew the Second City troupe was gathering backstage for a preperformance ritual (holding hands, letting the energy flow), perhaps uttering a nondenominational prayer for the night to go well. He envied theater people their circles, but also knew better than to suggest his classmates start one. They weren't, in fact, a unified group of performers. They went onstage one at a time, killed or bombed alone, always. A circle would've sounded ridiculous to them. Each-in-their-corner preshow cohesion around "Con Te Partirò" was as good as it would get.

"I've created a monster," Dorothy said to him, gesturing at the speakers.

"Did you see Manny Reinhardt's son is at the bar?" Phil asked. "Is Manny on his way here for sure?"

"How do you know that's his son?" Dorothy asked after Phil

pointed out August. She hadn't seen a picture of him since he was born.

"Some girl from Second City," Phil said. "She said they went to college together."

"You're not supposed to fraternize with the enemy before battle," Ashbee said.

"I don't see Second City as the enemy," Phil said.

"Please," Ashbee said. "Please don't say we're all one big fucking family."

"I see Second City as delusional for believing anyone cares about improvisation as an art form," Phil said.

"That's the spirit," Ashbee said.

Was that punching up? Phil wondered. Making fun of improv? People liked stand-up better than improv these days, but Second City was, as an institution, a lot more famous than their MFA, so who was below whom tonight? Who was the underdog? He had to have been punching down, Phil thought, since Ashbee liked it. Ashbee preferred it when comedians punched down. He said punching down was funnier, because no one really knew the people who were up, but almost everybody had been a form of down at some point, and so punching down was in fact the most inclusive form of comedy, if you thought about it. Everyone could relate. You could get more specific, too, when punching down, whereas a lot of guessing went into imagining how the powerful lived, and guessing wasn't funny.

Phil's ears were pulsing. He hadn't slept much the night before, rehearsing his Aristotle bit until three. He shouldn't have taken that Adderall from the Second City girl in the bathroom. Maybe it was laced with something. Maybe it wasn't even Adderall.

"I feel like shit," he said to Ashbee. "I need water."

Dorothy handed him her untouched glass. She watched Phil down it in one go. "Con Te Partirò" ended.

"Remember when songs used to end in, like, a fade-out?" Phil said, giving the now empty glass back to Dorothy. "I liked that. Like 'Time of My Life,' it just fades out. It feels like the band is just leaving the room or something, or maybe like *you're* leaving but the party keeps going. Or like the song never ends, or just goes somewhere else."

"What do you mean, goes somewhere else?" Ashbee said. "Are you high?"

Phil knew his comment would've made more sense, poetically, if he hadn't taken "Time of My Life" as an example. "A Pair of Brown Eyes" would've been a better choice. "A Pair of Brown Eyes" faded out too, and it left you all sad and wanting to catch the very last of it and play it again.

"I'm just saying that 'Con Te Partirò' ends so dramatically, that high, sustained note, plus that last cello *ding,* like, full stop. I don't like that. It's so final."

"We'll pass on your note to Andrea Bocelli," Dorothy said.

"Shit. I didn't mean to insult Italian culture," Phil said, truly thinking he'd made a faux pas. "I'm so sorry. And I made fun of improv two minutes ago, when you're teaching improv this semester—"

"You're all good," Dorothy said. "I teach improv this semester because someone has to do it. We take turns. I don't like it any more than you do."

"You don't?"

"I mean, there's something essential to learn from improv," Dorothy said, "but once you've learned it, once you're not afraid of it anymore, you're supposed to move on to written things. At least *I* think so. It's like riding a bike. It's a good skill to have, and once you have it, you have it forever and all that, but it's a bit much to ask people to care, or to pay to watch you ride one onstage."

"Whereas stand-up comedians, we, what, drive cars? Parachute jump?"

"No," Dorothy said. "We just think onstage. Like adults."

"And improv, they're kind of like children," Phil said. "On their bicycles."

"Don't quote me on that."

The beating in his ears—he'd had to get very close to Dorothy to hear what she was saying.

"I see what you mean," he said. "There's something sort of obscene about improv, everyone searching while onstage. It's like they want their epiphanies to be public."

"Their *epiphanies*?" Dorothy said.

"While we keep ours private," Phil said. "Our writing epiphanies, I mean. Not, like, our life epiphanies."

"Our *life epiphanies*?"

"Did you have one, by the way? When you were stuck with Sword and you thought there was a shooter?"

He should've asked earlier, Phil realized, when they were all drinking at the Gage with Sword. Phil was taking this class with him about catharsis and epiphanies. What if Sword himself had had an epiphany in the last week of a semester in which he'd taught a class about it? How awesome would that be? Epiphany squared!

"I don't understand the concept of epiphany," Dorothy said.

"It's like when all of a sudden you see the world in a new light," Phil said.

"I know what it *means*. I'm just saying, I don't understand why people ever speak of it in positive terms. There's a crack in reality? Everything is different than you thought? That sounds terrifying to me. Epiphanies sound terrifying."

"Wordsworth called them 'spots of time,'" Phil said.

On some level, he already knew that this fact, years down the line, would be the only thing he remembered from Sword's class.

Dorothy agreed with herself, but also pretty much immediately with the opposite of what she'd just said. An epiphany would've been great, actually. Could she perhaps have a delayed one? Was it a sign of moral sickness that she hadn't had one in that room, where and when she'd thought her life might end? The one crazy step she'd taken since the shooting scare was deciding not to carry a purse everywhere any longer. Did that count? As an epiphany? What was she doing at the Empty Bottle anyway? She should be home, taking a bath, reconsidering her existence, trying to force an epiphany out of her brain. Her default appreciation of life was that nothing really mattered. Certainly, this "belief" could stand to be shaken up. Why wasn't it being shaken up? By the day's events? What was wrong with her? Though perhaps nothing was wrong with her. You couldn't change your worldview every time something scary happened. A good friend of hers from childhood, for instance, had had cancer a few years back, aggressive. She'd gone through hell and beat it, then proceeded to return to work at Merrill Lynch, a job she'd always hated and dreamed of leaving. If that friend hadn't taken surviving cancer as her sign to make drastic changes, if her worldview had come out of the experience unaltered, didn't it mean that epiphanies were for fiction and not real life?

Or maybe her friend had simply exhibited true strength of character, Dorothy thought. Maybe Dorothy herself was exhibiting strength of character by never having had an epiphany. Maybe epiphanies were for dumb people. Uncommitted people. Lazy people.

This circular thought (from epiphany being stupid to epiphany being what she needed back to epiphany being stupid) took all of a second for Dorothy to go around. Once again, it hadn't exactly been a thought, the words hadn't exactly *appeared* in her head, but she'd experienced a series of split-second flashes that had contained a sense of them. Her brain was so used to opposing any point of view it became aware of, for sport, that it did the same with Dorothy's own immediate opinions now, too. She was used to seeing these small debates hold themselves in her head, almost entirely in spite of her. That was what should be taught, she felt at times, in a stand-up MFA: how to disagree with anything anyone was saying, how to disagree with what you yourself were saying. The opposite of "Yes, and," in a way. How to hold one thing and its opposite to be true, by way of questioning everything all the time. To ask yourself so many questions you ended up believing in nothing. Questions were the primary tool of comedy. Comedy started when someone asked, "Have you noticed?" or "You know this feeling when . . . ?" or "What was God thinking?" A good comedian tended to cut out the actual question marks when he revised, to let the questions ask themselves more powerfully through the bit. But it always started with a question. When Chappelle opened his special talking about a friend who'd never considered suicide in spite of his terrible life situation, he didn't literally ask, "Why do some people kill themselves and others don't?" But really, he did. Questions were right at the root of comedy, as they were in many other disciplines, from philosophy to the hard sciences, except that in comedy you were never looking for the real answer, but for the *funniest* answer, and in order to find the funniest answer, you had to first go through all possible answers. It was exhausting but necessary. The inside of Dorothy's head was a relentless stream of questions—is this better than that, is that homage or plagiarism, is that funny or depressing, is it both, why do people jog, why is this person telling me this, why did my uncle kill himself and why, of all the methods at his disposal, did he go for the rope, how is it that some potatoes look like people, real people trying to tell you something, and other potatoes just look like potatoes, why have I never wanted to have children, what's my bit and what's me riffing on someone else's, what's mine and what do I own and how serious is this—it was all questions, all the time, and the volume of questions was nothing compared with the volume of possible answers, and the faucet only turned off when Dorothy fell asleep at night, although it had happened once or twice that it hadn't, that she'd kept asking and asking and asking in her dreams. Epiphanies couldn't happen in this context. The best you could hope for was a good punch line.

Phil was saying something now about Tobias Wolff, about the epiphany in "Bullet in the Brain" being his favorite of all the epiphanies he'd read in Sword's class, because it changed nothing in the protagonist's life, because the protagonist died as he was having it.

Dorothy nodded. She hadn't read "Bullet in the Brain," but what a great title, she thought. She was surprised Sword had allowed himself to teach a story with such a triggering title, but good for him. Maybe he was a good teacher. Didn't he teach film, though? She was curious about him, she realized, how he prepared his lectures, who his favorite students were, how he'd met his wife. There was so much they could've talked about in that conference room. Perhaps they'd wasted an opportunity to become great friends. Now that she knew they'd been in no danger, Dorothy was rewriting her time with Sword as a nice, cozy hour, to be cataloged next to other experiences she'd had of being pleasantly stuck (at home in a blackout, at summer camp in a big storm). She felt a strange nostalgia for it already. She texted him:

> one of my students is wondering if you had an
> epiphany today

and Sword right away replied:

> Phil?

Dorothy confirmed. She apologized for having been a pain in the ass in the conference room earlier. She wanted Sword to rewrite the afternoon in his head, too, to remember it as a wonderful time with her. He said he didn't recall her being a pain in the ass. He said he had a good time. As good as could be had under the circumstances.

> How's your wife doing? Was she happy to see you?

Sword texted back "Asleep," and Dorothy wondered whether that meant the wife had been asleep when he'd come home, or was sleeping now. She wanted to write "Wake her up!" and give marital advice, but she decided to hold off on that until she knew the wife a little better, until they were all friends. She wrote:

> You should come to dinner sometime

and then turned on her stool to try to get the bartender's attention. She locked eyes with a former undergraduate student of hers on the way—she taught freshmen every spring, Intro to Comedy, a class in which famous comedies were autopsied and as little time as possible was spent on the students' actual material. Two kinds of freshmen ever took that class: those who'd been told their whole life that they were funny, and those who had never made anyone laugh but hoped they could become a different person in college. Both categories

were beyond her reach. No one had ever had an epiphany in her Intro
to Comedy class, that was a certainty. Dorothy smiled at the girl (a
girl who'd been in the second category, she remembered, wanting to
be cured of her humorlessness), but the girl looked away, took her
beer from the bar, and went elsewhere with it, opening as she left a
clear line of sight to Olivia and her sister. They were both speaking
over each other, it seemed to Dorothy, fighting for Manny's son's attention. Olivia's twin had Olivia's dimples, Olivia's big eyes, Olivia's
round ears and slight overbite. The differences between them were
obvious, though, too—Olivia's wild eyebrows vs. her sister's plucked
ones, a ten-pound weight gap, Dorothy guessed. But the most strik-
ing contrast was in the girls' body language, the way they flirted with
August. A lot of hand gestures and hair movement on the twin's part
(was it Sally? Sadie?), a more relaxed posture for Olivia—one elbow
planted on the bar, the other arm only moving to bring up alcohol to
her lips. Dorothy started a new note. "Two kinds of people," she
typed. "People who, when they meet twins, focus on the similarities,
and people who focus on the differences." This would go nowhere
beyond note stage. She'd felt no excitement typing it. She'd just had
to do it. She'd also thought that Sword might respond to her invitation to dinner while she typed the note about twins, and that was
what typing notes was for, too, to kill time before real life happened.
After which real life quickly became material to take notes on again,
until a new flavor of real life came, and so on and etc., until you died.
She wondered what she would cook for them when they came, the
Swords, whether the wife ate meat.

When she looked up from her phone (no answer from Sword), the
twins were still talking to August, but August wasn't focused on them
anymore. He was looking straight at her, straight at Dorothy, and he
was smiling.

Olivia saw the smile and followed the look.

"You a fan of Dorothy's?" she asked August.

She thought calling a famous comedian by her first name made her look cool. She still didn't know August was August Reinhardt.

"Big fan," August said, turning back to the girls. He liked Olivia. No use in denying it. She didn't talk as much as her sister and seemed less interested in him overall, but he liked that about her—not because he thought she was playing hard to get and that was attractive (August hated that kind of mind game), but because he took Olivia's occasional and brief retreats from their conversation as signs of an intellectual complexity he found alluring. He liked seeing people's minds go elsewhere. He never felt threatened by it, or insulted. If anything, it was people who paid his presence and what he said too much attention that he found dubious. People like Sally. While Olivia was both there and not, perhaps tweaking in her head what she would say onstage, perhaps pondering the meaning of life, Sally had kept her focus on him and him alone, asked a thousand questions about his job, what had made August want to be a lawyer, if it was like with doctors, who always wanted to become doctors because someone they loved had gotten sick and died, and yes, was it the same for lawyers, like, had they all witnessed a primal injustice? August said no. He was interning still, but the plan was to go into corporate law, and he didn't recall an original corporate incident in childhood that could've given rise to his vocation.

Now Sally was asking what his favorite shows about lawyers were, his opinion on the way lawyers were portrayed in fiction. August said he didn't watch a lot of TV, but maybe *The Good Wife*? The answer surprised Sally. August didn't say that the only reason *The Good Wife* came to mind was that his mother had worked on the show. He repeated that he didn't watch much TV. Sally said she took issue, sometimes, with the amount that shows and books and movies focused on lawyers, and doctors, and cops, and journalists, as if other professions weren't interesting. It offended her that fiction treated "regular" office jobs as mere background noise in "regular" people's day-to-day, something of no relevance to the protagonist's life, or else a joke, or a soul-sucking machine. She herself worked for a company that studied real estate development feasibility, and she was happy there, her colleagues were wonderful, the work was stimulating, and she didn't appreciate it that people, when she told them what she did for a living, assumed that her job was boring, or that she couldn't really be passionate about it, as if only detectives and surgeons and good-hearted attorneys ever took their work home with them, or didn't count their hours. August said attorneys very much counted their hours, even the "good-hearted" ones, but he knew what Sally meant. "You know what I mean," Sally said, and she repeated the word "passionate," how lawyers were passionate, or depicted as such, in a way that real estate development feasibility teams never were. August pretended to see what Sally's issue was, but deep down agreed with those shows he didn't even watch. Wasn't it the case that most jobs were less interesting than doctor or lawyer or detective? These were jobs in which you got to see other people's lives from within, and the people in question had to tell you everything about themselves without you needing to give them anything back—anything personal, that is: just your expertise, a service. Being a lawyer was so much better than being a writer, too (the career his father had wanted for him), because you didn't have to try to make anything mean anything, you didn't need to transform what you were living or witnessing into anything bigger than it seemed, you only had to respond to a situation in the way that you'd been trained, and then move on.

"Dorothy's amazing," Olivia said to August, as if the previous few minutes of conversation between him and Sally hadn't happened. "But do you like Manny Reinhardt? I hear he might be coming tonight."

"I do," August said. "I do like him."

"He's the fucking best," Olivia said.

August had to say something now. Olivia loved his father's work, and he could see it coming that his father was going to like her, too, and even though she and Manny wouldn't fall in love or anything like that, the relationship they'd have would make it impossible for August to exist as a boyfriend. When it came to dating, or even just sex,

August didn't go for complicated. He'd had his heart broken once, in college, after a one-night stand he hadn't previously understood would be a one-night stand. He'd been in love with the girl for a while. Admired her. It was a girl he'd envisioned a future with. She had a boyfriend back home she hadn't told him about. They'd been friendly but not friends, and after the one night, they'd been nothing at all. August hadn't told anyone how painful this had been. He'd suffered in silence. That's why he didn't think his father had done anything wrong with the women he'd proposed to. They'd had a different understanding of where their relationship would lead, just like he, August, had had a different understanding of where his night with the girl in college would lead. These things happened. You got hurt. You got over it.

"Manny Reinhardt is my father, actually," he said to Olivia.

Olivia spit back into her glass the sip she'd just taken.

August thought perhaps it was cold of him to think that the women who'd accused his father of emotional misconduct should get over their heartbreak silently just because that's how he'd gotten over his at an even younger age. It was unfair how people who got over things always judged so harshly those who couldn't.

"You're his *son*?"

"The one and only," August said. "As far as I know."

"Jesus."

"Maybe women are going to come forward, though. Say he got them pregnant. Maybe I'm in for new siblings."

"Like with the prince of Monaco," Sally said.

"No one knows who that is," Olivia said.

"He gets demands for paternity tests from a hundred women a week," Sally explained. "He's fathered like nine illegitimate children already."

"How do you know this?"

"I read world news."

"Monaco isn't the world," Olivia said. She turned back to August. "How's your father holding up? Does he hate women now? Is he really coming tonight? What makes him laugh?"

August took a deep breath and answered: "Okay. No. Yes. Holocaust jokes."

"No, but, like, who are his favorite comedians? What are his favorite bits?"

"Your friend is coming over," Sally said to Olivia.

Artie had been looking at the twins flirt with August for a while, trying to decide whether or not to infiltrate the conversation and subtly let August know he had his eye on Olivia.

"Show starts in five," he announced.

He'd come from the side and was now standing between Olivia and August.

"I'm Artie," he said, extending a hand.

"August Reinhardt," August said.

"Of the Reinhardt family?"

"When will your father be here?" Olivia asked.

"I don't know, fifteen minutes? Half an hour?"

Olivia turned to Artie and put her hand on his forearm. Artie knew what she was going to ask. The way the battle worked was simple: three stand-ups would go onstage first and do five minutes each, then the whole Second City troupe would do a thirty-minute improv, after which the last three stand-ups would close the evening. It had been decided that the comedians would go up in alphabetical order, which meant Olivia would go third, and third meant Manny might miss her bit. She wanted Artie's later spot, she wanted to go as late as possible.

"That's two favors just for today," Artie said to her. "Two big fucking favors."

"I know," Olivia said. "I'll make it up to you."

Her hand was squeezing his arm now. Artie assumed she would let go, or at least loosen her grip the moment he agreed to switch spots with her, but her hand remained on his arm after he did, and if anything, it seemed to hold him tighter.

"You're the best," Olivia said, for the second time that day.

Artie stopped himself from looking around to make sure other people had heard her. Other people like August. He kept his cool, checked the time on his phone, and, just as he did, saw that Ethel was calling. She'd never called him before. He felt propelled down to a secret hole in the ground. Rather, he felt his body stay on the surface of the earth, for show, but his stomach and brain drop many feet below to a secret underground that had been there all along, a secret underground in which Mickey was dead. If Ethel was calling, it meant his brother was dead. But maybe he wasn't reading the name right? Maybe it was *Esther* and not Ethel? Did he know any Esthers?

"Ethel?" Olivia said, bending over Artie's lit-up phone. "Who's Ethel? Should I be jealous?"

"I have to take this," Artie said.

He stepped out of the bar and into the cold to pick up the phone. Ethel spoke before he could say hello.

"Your mother needs to stop calling my mother," she said.

"Is Mickey all right?"

"That's not why I'm calling."

"Is he with you? Put him on the phone."

"This group therapy thing you're doing"—that's what Ethel called the degree he was getting—"it's working. You're more assertive already."

"Put Mickey on the phone."

"I'm serious," Ethel said. "I was worried about you going to Chicago. Our little Artie trying to make it big-time in the big city, with his tiny little brain and his tiny little jokes."

She was teasing, Artie knew. She'd laughed at his jokes before.

"Tiny little brain," Ethel repeated. "It must feel even tinier in the big city."

"Stop saying 'big city,' " Artie said. "I used to go to New York, like, every other weekend. I know how big my brain is."

Ethel thought that was hilarious, though she merely said it ("That's hilarious") and didn't laugh.

"Seriously," she said. "Your mother needs to stop calling my mother. When your mother calls my mother, my mother calls me. I don't answer, but still. I'm going to have to at some point."

It was an odd thing to imagine, someone having power over Ethel, even just the power to annoy—Ethel having a mother of her own. To Artie, Ethel had always had the aura of a character in a novel, the kind that had secret control over the plot. No one told that person what to do.

"Why don't you answer her right now?" Artie asked. "Tell her you're with Mickey, and then they'll both stop calling."

"Mike is an adult," Ethel said. "Your mother shouldn't have had babies if she wasn't ready for them to have a life of their own. You should tell her that."

You tell her, Artie wanted to say to Ethel. *Mickey* tell her.

But again, Ethel wasn't someone you told what to do. The reason she had the aura of a character in a novel was that her grandfather and Philip Roth had gone to middle school together and remained good friends: Ethel had met Roth as a child once or twice, and Roth had commented on her wits, said he would put her in a novel one day. The fact that he hadn't, and would never, the fact that he'd probably never meant to, or that Ethel hadn't achieved much of note in her thirty-five years of life, or that Artie had only read two of Roth's twenty-eight novels and none of the short stories, were all irrelevant. Roth had been a giant in Artie's household, and the Roth connection had helped Artie's parents appreciate Ethel at first, in spite of the seven-year age gap with Mickey. If Philip Roth had seen something in her, certainly they could, too, Leonard and Leora. Also, Roth *might* have put parts of Ethel in a novel and no one had noticed. Ethel could've been the wind in the trees at Indian Hill, or a dimple on a kid's face in *Nemesis* (there was this thought that if Ethel was part of any of Roth's books, it would be *Nemesis,* since the protagonist bore Ethel's last name, and Roth had to have been thinking about her grandfather, who'd had polio as a child, when he was writing it). After Ethel had left Mickey for another guy, however, and broken his heart for the first time, Artie's mother had ceased imagining her in a Roth book. Her interest turned into hatred, a hatred she didn't believe could get any deeper, until Ethel *came back* to Mickey, then left him again, and came back again. No part of that evil girl could be in any one of Roth's *lines,* Artie's mother had decided after that. Or if she was, she'd said, if Ethel was in *Nemesis* at all, she was the polio epidemic itself. Artie's father had tried to calm her down, saying that Mickey would get over the girl eventually. "It takes a minute to recognize the right woman for you," he'd added, and his wife had fallen silent after that, silent for days, a silence Artie remembered trying to interpret at the time. Had his mother been angry because her husband failed to worry enough about their son? Or because he'd made love sound so trite, a mere arrangement of comfort, the "right woman" like the right shoe? It was after that remark about the right woman that his father's input had dried up considerably.

"Do you love Mickey?" Artie ended up asking Ethel on the phone. *That* was the kind of question you asked someone with a literary aura, someone who might or might not have been polio in *Nemesis.* It was snowing again, too. Light flurries of snow that invited confession.

"That's a real personal question," Ethel responded.

Was it? Artie wondered. Didn't it concern him, too? He told Ethel that he'd once heard Mickey say that there was no such thing as personal questions, only personal answers.

"That's a bit highfalutin," Ethel said, but then she thought about it for a second. "I guess he's right, though."

"So?" Artie asked again. "Do you love him?"

"That would be a personal answer," Ethel said.

The snow started coming down in larger flakes, and Artie watched as some of them fell directly into the trash can near him. Traveling all this way through the sky, to end up right inside that black hole, with the pizza crusts and the cold, bagged dog shit. His stomach turned.

"Do girls ever really love anyone?"

His question was so absurd Ethel couldn't wait to hear the reasoning behind it.

"I mean girls . . . ," Artie went on, "you're so ready to get hurt . . . it feels like you never go all in. You're always just waiting for the other shoe to drop. It's like it would be shameful to trust a man or some-thing."

"Listen to you, with your one-and-a-half-girlfriend experience," Ethel said.

"I've had four girlfriends already," Artie said.

"You're counting them. That's sweet."

She said the fact that he counted girlfriends was evidence that men were shit, and you couldn't fault women for being cautious. Artie wondered who *didn't* count their girlfriends. Or boyfriends. Didn't *she*? She'd always left Mickey for other men, and probably would again . . . didn't she even keep track of their names?

"Mickey never did anything to hurt you," he said.

"How would you know that?"

Ethel was right, Artie realized. He barely knew his brother at this point. The last thing they'd bonded over had been the Holocaust sur-vivors' holograms, two summers prior. He took the phone away from his ear to look at the time. The show had probably started by now. Dan had to be onstage. It would be Marianne after that, then him.

"I do love him," Ethel was saying when Artie put the phone back to his ear. "I do love your brother."

"Will you put him on?" Artie asked, and this time, Ethel did.

Mickey was high and spoke too slowly about Galileo. Artie hated Mickey on heroin, the gooeyness and elasticity of each word, his sen-tences like syrup through a sieve.

"I dreamed about Galileo," Mickey said—four words it took him twelve seconds to get out. "He was in his prison cell, but I wasn't in the dream at all, I was just watching."

"That's too bad," Artie said, as fast as possible, like it could get Mickey to pick up speed, like Mickey, wherever he was, could take a hint. "I'm sure you guys would've had an interesting conversation."

"But no," Mickey said. "You don't get it. I *wasn't* in the dream. I wasn't in my own dream. I couldn't do anything for Galileo."

Artie was relieved his brother was okay. Safe for now, at least, right this moment. But there was disappointment, too. He didn't want to explore the feeling, figure out what he would've preferred (his brother in the hospital? hit by a car? his brother dead?), but Mickey's sluggish pace invited frustrated visions.

"I get it," he said, to bat them away. "You weren't in your own dream. You couldn't do anything for Galileo. You left Galileo to rot in his cell, and that sucks."

"Does it happen to you?" Mickey asked. "To not be part of your dreams? To watch your own dreams like you're watching a movie?"

"I'm always in my dreams," Artie said. He was sure the fact made him uninteresting somehow.

"Then you could've saved Galileo," Mickey said.

Artie had to hang up. If he talked to his brother any longer, it would sink him, fuck up his rhythm onstage.

"I have to go," he said.

Mickey said goodbye, but forgot to hang up, and though Artie had been impatient just a second ago to get off the phone, this changed things. He couldn't resist listening to people who didn't know they were being listened to. He was the kind of person who went through the entirety of a three-minute-long pocket-dial voicemail, just in case.

The sound was clear in Artie's ear, though Ethel's voice reached him from a greater distance—she had to be a few feet away from Mickey and the phone, and it sounded like she was moving around, too, perhaps folding laundry, putting things in drawers. Artie imagined the phone gone dark next to Mickey on the couch, or on a coffee table, picking up on everything the couple said to each other and offering it to a third party, fully aware of what it was doing. It was so easy to think of phones as sentient entities, with a capacity for duplicity, for intention. He often wondered if cavemen had loaned thoughts and emotions to rocks, or the tools they built.

Ethel, eight hundred miles away, was telling Mickey that he'd confused Galileo and Giordano Bruno. "It's Giordano *Bruno* who would've needed saving," Artie overheard her say to his brother. "It's *Bruno* who got burned at the stake for his heliocentric theories. Galileo was just put under house arrest." Mickey said that house arrest wasn't a picnic either, but Ethel countered that Galileo had had a nice villa in Tuscany, not a crummy studio in Hoboken. After a few seconds, she added that the other part of Galileo's sentence had been to recite some psalms once a week, as penance, but that his daughter had taken care of that for him, so really, the guy had had a pretty nice end of life, all told, and wasn't it crazy that you could carry other people's spiritual duties for them? There was silence between them after that, the sound of plates clinking, and then an announcement, on Ethel's part, that stew was served. "Did you put turnips in?" Artie heard Mickey ask, all the way back in New Jersey. Ethel had. "And I made us a nice little cobbler, too," she said.

Artie hung up. The words "nice little cobbler" echoed in his head. How was the trash can not full of snow yet? He realized he'd never seen it, actually—a trash can full of snow. Snow accumulated on the rim, but never at the bottom, or all the way up.

He typed "trash can" and "snow" in his new note-taking app, which alerted him to the fact that he'd written a note about trash cans before, and others about snow, and did he want to merge them all together in a single document for ease of reference?

When he looked up from his phone, Kruger was there staring at him. Artie hadn't heard him come near—had a cab just dropped him off? Had he been walking and snow muted his footsteps? There were no footprints around him, in any direction.

"Dorothy has your phone," Artie said.

"I'm glad you're okay," Kruger said.

He'd found a note from Dorothy on his door, a piece of paper taped there, saying that all was well, to meet them at the Empty Bottle. He'd expected, therefore, to find Artie alive tonight, but some of the fondness he'd felt for the boy earlier, picturing his funeral, was carrying over. He was *glad* to see him alive, gladder than he'd been to see anyone else alive in a long time. Artie felt it, this odd warmth, emanating from his teacher. He assumed Kruger was drunk.

"Did I miss you up there?" Kruger asked. He seemed to care deeply. There was snow caught in his eyelashes, and it reminded Artie of ash building up at the tip of his brother's cigarettes, that texture, the frailty of it. How Mickey sometimes forgot he'd lit a cigarette already and got started on another, how it had happened that he'd left two or three smoking in different ashtrays, and Artie had to put them all out.

"We should go in," he said. "The show's probably getting started, and I'm up third."

"What are you going to go with?"

"I think my priest-at-confession bit," Artie said. He'd hesitated between that bit and another, but hearing Ethel talk about Galileo's daughter praying in her father's stead—he'd taken this as a sign.

"That's a good bit," Kruger said, even though he hadn't treated it kindly in workshop a few weeks back. Perhaps he hadn't meant it. Perhaps people only meant a small percentage of what they said. "You're gonna kill it."

Artie wasn't thinking about killing, really, or about going onstage at all. He was thinking about turnips, and nice little cobblers, and the snow on the trash can, and the snow on Kruger's lashes. What kind of cobbler was it that Ethel had made for Mickey? That's what he wanted to know. Was it peach? Blueberry? He regretted having hung up before he could find out. Surely, Mickey had asked Ethel what she'd put in the cobbler. There was a chance he was still asking her.

Marianne was onstage when Artie and Kruger walked in, doing her bit about puzzles—about once writing a letter to the puzzle company after she completed a fifteen-hundred-parter and realized a piece was missing. The bit could've worked, but Marianne always wanted things to mean other things—she wanted everything to mean at least three different things—and it was confusing. The puzzle couldn't just be a landscape: it had to be a reproduction of Picasso's *Guernica*. The missing piece couldn't be a regular piece: it had to be a "double wings," etc., etc. It was a lot to ask an audience to keep track of and care about. Marianne understood this now. No one was laughing. She said good night and called Artie to the stage.

Artie climbed the steps there, high-fived Marianne, and considered pratfalling to get things started. He'd never quite settled on an entrance. Several times a week, he went to open mics around town to work on options, but it always took him half his stage time to get comfortable, to get the audience to like or just pay attention to him. There had to be opening words that made people listen right away.

He didn't pratfall. He stood straight behind the microphone and said:

"I don't feel like joking tonight."

It felt cheap, and not many people laughed, and the few scattered laughs were quick to die, but still. The room got quieter and more receptive than any he'd performed for before. This was his biggest crowd ever—two hundred people, maybe more, while his previous record verged on thirty. Silence wasn't an absolute notion, Artie realized. Two hundred silent people were more silent than two silent people.

"A few hours ago, I thought I was going to die," he said. "I was in the bathroom, at school, and the lady in the next stall tells me there's a shooter in the building. *She*'s in the men's room, by the way, so don't give me shit."

Artie knew it wasn't a good idea to improvise about something that had just happened. Olivia could do it. Jo. But not him. For whose benefit was he even trying? And anyway, wasn't the idea behind a battle with Second City to prove that stand-up was the higher form of comedy? That comedy was in the writing, the perfectly picked word, the revised and rehearsed to death?

"She's hiding from the shooter," Artie went on, "she's crying and all, and I have this protective layer of never fully believing life is real, so I'm fine, but still, I'm not a dick, I try to comfort her. She thinks this is it. She thinks we're going to die together, so she wants us to mean something to each other, she wants to trade life stories before it all ends, fears and regrets and all that, and you know what she tells me? She tells me about the *novel* she's writing. That's what's on her mind."

Why? Why was he doing this, why was he telling the audience about his half hour with author Vivian Reeve instead of launching into his bit about confession? Artie would ask himself this later. The energy of improv didn't allow for big questions, same as when you tripped off a cliff (one could assume), you didn't ask yourself *Why am I falling?* but rather tried to look for a branch or something to hold on to.

"What really bums her out is she won't be able to finish writing her *novel*. Isn't that funny? That, in the face of death, she would be bummed about *that*? I can tell that you don't find it funny. I can tell because you're not laughing. But think about it for a second. How sad it is. If you think about how sad it is, it becomes funny."

Manny Reinhardt walked into the bar as Artie said the words "you're not laughing." Artie was probably the first to notice him—his eyes kept track of the door's every swing when he was onstage, who was leaving, who looked at those who left with envy. He considered saying something about Manny's entrance, but improvising within the improv, that would be ruled a suicide, he thought, and understanding this brought him back to his senses. He had to get started on his actual bit, the one he'd performed a dozen times. It wasn't great (the ending, in particular, sucked), but it was something that existed already, he knew what was in it. Some people thrived on the mystery, the process of discovery, but Artie wasn't good at not knowing what lay ahead. He in fact sometimes thought it was because of how bad he was at dealing with the unknown that he wrote jokes and went onstage with them. He needed to know there could be five minutes here and there, short moments in his life he had control over. He needed minutes when he didn't have to wonder what to say (it was already written!), or whether his parents were happy, what would happen to Mickey in the long run, and how did he like the cobbler.

"Anyway," he said. "I was walking the other day, not far from here actually, and I passed by a church, and you know those big scoreboard-looking things they have outside, where they LED-display quotes from God? Like 'God says: I'll be back in a minute'? Well, they didn't have a message from God on this one, or maybe it was straight from him actually, I don't know, like a memo he sent, but in any case, it was purely informational. It said: 'Confessions: Half an Hour Before Mass.'"

This felt better to Artie. He could see the sentences lined up in his mind's eye, like items on a conveyor belt at the supermarket—the milk first, the coffee, the canned stuff, then, far away in the distance, the more fragile things, the fruit and the eggs, to handle with care at the end. All he had to do was scan everything.

"I'm not Catholic, so I was a little surprised. I thought confessions were for whenever you needed them, that there was always someone on duty in there ready to take yours, like night watchmen at Holiday Inns. But *half an hour before Mass*? Half an hour before show-time? For the *whole* congregation? That feels a bit short to me."

He knew better than to use the conveyor belt analogy with other comics. You always heard artists in interviews say that breakthroughs happened when you stepped out of your comfort zone, but Artie liked comfort, comfort allowed him to project confidence, and positivity, and to look at the audience, see that Olivia, who still hadn't noticed Manny Reinhardt, was scribbling something on a loose sheet of paper at the bar, that Phil was gulping water next to her, that Sally smiled encouragingly. Reinhardt, to Artie's surprise, hadn't made his way through the room to meet his son, or anyone else. He stood by the door, listening.

"Also: *Right* before Mass? So that everyone can see if you're going in or not? If you go in, there's gossip, people start betting on what you're confessing to, and if you *don't* go, they notice, too, like 'Fucking Cindy, thinks she's so perfect.'"

Artie's bit went on to imagine how some priests' association had come up with the thirty-minutes-before-Mass rule. The priests were sick of taking confession, it turned out. Really, they thought they should get paid to do this, same as shrinks. Also, they were judging the shit out of everyone who came in, according to Artie. He gave examples. He got laughs. Manny Reinhardt, at the back of the room, kept his eyes on him the whole time. What Artie first took as politeness quickly started irritating him. Why wasn't Manny making a beeline for the bar, why was he *staring*? This wasn't ballet, he wouldn't miss a tiny little wrist gesture if he made eye contact with his son for a second . . . couldn't he just look away? The end of the bit was nearing (the eggs, the delicate fruit), and Artie didn't want too much attention paid to it. He hated that a bit could be judged on the strength of its landing alone, that comedy still valued the destination more than the journey, that his bit's weak ending could get the audience to reassess the quality of its parts. He remembered the ending of so few things himself, books, movies—even his favorite ones. Mickey had always placed a lot of weight on last scenes, last shots, last sentences, but to Artie, these had never been more than suggestions, leaving him free to imagine what happened when Private Ryan came home, or after Zooey left the apartment, or how Natalie Portman fared at boarding school after Jean Reno died. He'd always kept his favorite stories alive beyond the credits.

Yet wrapping things up wasn't optional, and Artie had a placeholder ending for now, in which he wondered to his audience what would happen if he were to show up to confession before Mass and take up the whole thirty minutes to confess to something elaborate in painful detail. Would he get kicked out? Could the church kick him out? He imagined a priest giving him feedback on his confession, calling him boring, his story too convoluted. Priests too, no matter how much they read the Bible, had to have opinions on storytelling shaped by TV, no patience anymore for certain digressions. Priests too demanded a quicker pace. The bit ended on the priest recommending Artie spend more time on Twitter, condensing his thoughts and emotions to 280 characters or less. The audience liked it fine, but as he went offstage, it dawned on Artie what he needed to do. If he wanted a better ending, he had to actually try it. Go to confession himself. See what happened. Research wasn't typically his method (he preferred making things up), but he'd been thinking about this bit for months now, and the last move kept eluding him. There was something he was failing to imagine. Artie knew that the something in question could be anything—a detail in the woodwork in the confession booth, a flimsy partition, a priest with a lisp—but part of him also thought the spiritual experience itself could unlock the bit, give him a new understanding of what it was he'd been looking for. He would go tomorrow, he decided. Was there Mass on Thursdays? Certainly, he could find something to confess to.

"That was good," Dorothy told him. "You were good."

She'd stayed stage right his whole bit, like a boxing coach.

"Reinhardt is here," Artie said.

Manny, his son, and Olivia were heading backstage when Dorothy spotted them.

"Come with me," she said to Artie. "I'll introduce you."

Manny was already making Olivia laugh when Artie and Dorothy walked in, slumped in a couch, asking about her GPA. Was she getting straight A's in her comedy classes so far? That was how you told a good comedian from a hack nowadays, wasn't it?

"Leave the girl alone," Dorothy said, even though (or perhaps because) that was the last thing Olivia wanted.

Manny jumped up to give Dorothy a hug.

"All right, all right," Dorothy said, patting Manny's back. "It's nice to see you, too."

She didn't mind the hug, was in fact happy the hug was happening in front of her students, but she knew that cutting it short was her best look.

"This is Artie," she said.

"You have a good presence," Manny said.

Kruger joined them in the greenroom then, and for nearly a minute, he pretended not to notice Manny. He focused on Artie, giving him his most elaborate critique to date. He could tell Artie had compressed the bit a lot already, Kruger said, sharp edits had been made, great edits, but his description of the church's billboard didn't quite hit yet, and there were still many extra syllables to cut here and there.

Dorothy understood that Kruger was marking his territory, showing Manny who was boss here. He must've thought he was being subtle, but he was an actor, in the end, and actors, even the most talented ones on film, tended to overdo real life. Right this moment, for example, by talking to Artie and not acknowledging Manny's presence, Kruger was performing "secret animosity," but performing "secret animosity" meant he had to *hint* at animosity, and automatically lose the "secret" half of the prompt. He was showing his hand, when a nonactor would've kept it better hidden.

"Where were you all afternoon?" Dorothy asked him. "Manny's here."

Kruger ignored her question and went to shake Manny's hand. He told him how great it was to have him on board. The students were huge fans, he said. Every word out of his mouth sounded false. Manny, to Dorothy's annoyance, entered his game. He said the honor was all his, even though Kruger hadn't spoken of honor.

"Are you good friends with our dean?" Kruger asked. "He defended your hire tooth and nail."

Kruger knew he shouldn't have said anything about the hiring process, especially in front of students, but it bothered him to see Manny so comfortable already, so at ease around Artie and Olivia.

"I don't know any deans," Manny said. "I made it this far without understanding what it is a dean does, actually. At this point, I'm trying to see if I can get away with never having to find out."

"I have a similar plan with the blockchain," Dorothy said, determined to move the conversation away from teaching and academia.

"You must be Manny's son," she said to August. They shook hands. "I hear you're a lawyer."

"Still just an intern."

"He's being modest," Manny said. "He's working on this big trial opening tomorrow."

He wanted to keep sparring with Kruger, but that was impossible now that Dorothy had made August the center of attention. He couldn't take focus away from his own son.

"You're working on the Delgado trial?" Kruger asked.

"I actually won't be in court," August said. "They didn't pick me to assist."

"What happened?" Manny said. "I thought it was a done deal."

"They took Laura," August explained. "I'll help with the trial, but from the office. I'll still learn a lot."

Manny's first impulse was to ask whose dick this Laura had sucked to get the job. He refrained, and said instead that he was sorry, that it was all his fault.

"They didn't want the name Reinhardt near the case," he said to August. "I made our name radioactive."

"It had nothing to do with you," August said. "Laura is very good."

No one in the room quite understood what it was Laura had won and August lost, but his dignity in the face of it all impressed them deeply. It wasn't tainted, it wasn't false, and they all—Dorothy, Artie, Manny, Kruger, and Olivia—wondered if they'd seen such a thing before: a person defeated, not blaming anyone for their failure. A person failing without scapegoats.

But August had always been like that. He'd always refused to blame others for his mistakes, even as a child. Maybe it was because he didn't have siblings, Manny thought—though a different child might've blamed his parents for not having given him one. August wasn't someone who blamed himself much either, only in rare situations where he was truly at fault, situations he was able to recognize, analyze, and move on from. He didn't mull over small slights and losses, he *couldn't* have been a writer, Manny realized in that moment, or a comedian, or any type of artist. Comedians didn't know their place like that. Half the job was bouncing between self-hatred and megalomania at absurd speeds, ignoring at all costs the possibility that you could ever belong to the stodgy middle.

It was beautiful to see, though, this strength. A man knowing his worth. Manny was proud of August. But unadulterated feelings were hard for him to experience, and his pride came with a hint of irritation at how his son's perfection was making his own faults more salient. August would never sleep with the wrong woman, Manny thought. It was conceivable he'd never hurt anyone.

The room was quiet for a beat, in awe of August's graceful attitude ("They took Laura"/"Laura is very good"), but then a burst of muted laughter filtered through the door, and the reminder that comedy was unfolding in the next room, even in its diluted form of improv, made everyone uncomfortable. It was true what they said, that laughter was incompatible with nobility. Manny said:

"Fuck Laura."

August forced a smile to please his father.

"Fuck all Lauras," Olivia added.

"Except Laura Dern," Artie said.

Dorothy understood why the kids would riff with Manny, but it pained her to see August have to take his father and two strangers trivializing his world, reducing days and weeks of work (not against Laura, in all likelihood, but *alongside* Laura) to those three syllables: "Fuck Laura." She looked at him, at August. Maybe he did look a bit like young Manny, she thought, if young Manny had swum a mile a day every day of his life.

"Do you swim?" she asked him.

"Are you flirting with my son?"

"Every morning," August said.

The laughter reaching them from behind the door sounded canned. Recorded years ago. Dorothy found it hard to believe that it was coming from actual people, and a sense memory arose, from childhood, of staying in during recess, reading in hallways or writing riddles on the bathroom walls. There, too, she'd heard muffled laughter, and screams, the sounds of children having fun in the schoolyard. There, too, the sounds had felt disembodied, and already reaching her from a distant past, or somewhere else she couldn't go.

Her brain sent her a specific image from hours earlier, an image of Sword's hand the moment he'd locked them in. The minuscule door lock. Her mind was sorting through all of the day's stimuli without her having a say in editing them, Dorothy realized, discarding useless ones forever, preparing others to settle in and sediment.

She wanted to check if Sword had answered. She had this urge to know how he was doing, and his wife. She really wanted them all to be friends now. She tended to get along with depressive people. She felt her pocket for her phone and remembered she still had Kruger's. Handing it back to him triggered a chain reaction—Kruger checking his email got Manny to google himself, which cued Olivia to browse images of gelato stores online for the bit she was working on. Seeing all the comedians in the room tapping their screens, Artie became worried he'd missed something. He unlocked his own phone, hoping to catch by osmosis the smatterings of everyone else's inspiration. Nothing came. He looked up Catholic Mass schedules near him.

Kruger had to read his agent's email several times, not that it contained unbelievable information, but Michelle was rescheduling his meeting with Paramount, and the name suddenly seemed so absurd to him that despite having seen it top mountains onscreen for decades, he was unsure of exactly what it referred to, or how to pronounce it. *Paramount.* Why had he asked Manny about a potential friendship with the dean? He knew better than to ask questions to people he feared or respected (his father, better comedians than him). You could say more with a question you asked than the other guy with the answer he gave, Kruger knew that, had always known that, yet he'd gone for it, he'd shown Manny the truth of his petty thoughts, and gotten nothing in return. Worse than that: Manny's answer had made him look ridiculous for caring about deans in the first place, for forgetting that comedians shouldn't care at all about deans. He'd made a mistake. You only asked questions to people who couldn't hurt you with their answers. That's why the internet was so powerful. Or strangers, people you knew you'd never see again. On the Metra, for example, he could've asked Veronica about his father. Veronica knew something he didn't. People talked in Naperville. He could've used her as a search engine: "What did that guy really say to my dad at the Glass Eye?" She would've told him. She didn't know him well enough to lie to him. He looked for her on Instagram, Veronica Tuft, perfect, one of those names you could only spell one way. He composed a message, polite, but empty of small talk, containing only the question he wanted her to answer.

Jo half opened the door seconds after he sent it and poked her head in.

"Fantastic," she said. "Everyone and his phone is here."

"We're hiding from improv," Artie said.

"Well, they're almost done," Jo said. "I'll be onstage in five minutes, if anyone here likes laughing."

Her head went back into the other room, bringing the word "jack-in-the-box" to Kruger's mind. Something fighting to get out, something constantly being compressed back in. Forces opposing, creating comedy. That was in Bergson, too, if he remembered correctly. Was it today that he'd talked about Bergson in class? *What a pretentious fuck,* Kruger thought. Of himself, not Bergson. His students had to make fun of him. He'd quoted other philosophers in workshop, too—Kant about laughter ("the sudden transformation of a heightened expectation into nothing"), Herbert Spencer ("an effort which suddenly encounters a void"). They hadn't liked these quotes about nothingness and void, they'd found the quotes depressing, but void was at the center of any comedian's career, Kruger had insisted—the blank page, the doubt once it was filled, the silence when a joke crashed, the abyss you faced onstage, the emptiness you felt afterward. They had to be ready for it all. He hadn't mentioned the postmortem oblivion, though. He assumed they knew about that, how comedians almost never reached posterity, how quickly the material aged, and the delivery, how a comedian dead twenty years might as well have lived in the Middle Ages, might as well have been one of those court jesters about whom the only thing we remembered was the funny hats.

Back at the bar, Olivia stayed close to Manny to gather last-minute intel on what made him laugh. Just like his son had an hour earlier, Manny took a money clip from his pocket and got the bartender's attention right away. No one in the audience seemed to have noticed him yet, the room was dark, only those with their faces toward the bar were identifiable, their features lit by the Christmas lights running along the liquor shelf. Manny ordered drinks for the group.

"Is that your twin over there?" he asked Olivia. Sally was still where she'd left her, a couple of stools down from them.

"Good eye," Olivia said.

"She's your twin," Manny said. "I have eyes that function."

He asked if they should buy her a drink, too.

"She doesn't drink much. I do the drinking for the both of us."

Go home and kill yourself, Olivia thought. *"I do the drinking for the both of us" . . . are you fucking serious?*

Still, Manny had the courtesy to smile.

The bartender brought all the drinks, and while Manny distributed them, Olivia drank half her pint in one gulp. Where were all the smart things she'd prepared for the day she met Manny Reinhardt? She'd always imagined he would take her under his wing if they met, immediately see something in her no one else ever had, become her mentor, her friend, like in a movie, but it felt to her now like the cameras were rolling and she'd forgotten to write the script.

Jo went up onstage, and Olivia thought finally she could stop trying to figure out the right thing to say, focus on Jo's bit. Except a new type of dread came over her as Jo started talking to the crowd. What if Manny didn't find Jo funny? Would Olivia have the guts to laugh anyway, or would she just go along with the man's judgment? What kind of friend was she?

"Isn't it funny to think that we're all going to die?" Jo's bit opened. "Everyone in this room? Every single one of you?" The comedy was in the pauses, of course, the intensity with which she looked at the audience, singling out a few members. "*You*'re going to die," she said to one. "And you, and you." People were laughing. Manny, too. Olivia relaxed for a second, but she knew Jo wouldn't get satisfaction from plain, hearty laughter: she'd need to wring it out before she could go on, she'd need to hear it die. Where other comics would have pointed at three audience members, bagged the laughs, and ridden on to the next beat, Jo was going to single out way too many, confuse everyone into silence, make them so uncomfortable they had to laugh again. Jo could potentially say "and you, and you, and you" to the entire room, Olivia knew, with long silences in between. Have that be her five minutes onstage. Jo had that kind of confidence. She stopped after the nineteenth audience member, though, once laughter had waned and come back to life. "You are going to die, too," she said to him. And then: "Shit! I forgot the trigger warning. Trigger warning: to-night, I will be doing some crowd work about death." People laughed some more, and Jo pretended to be surprised.

Olivia had never heard her do crowd work about death before. Perhaps it was something she'd just come up with, and this gave her courage. Maybe tonight was the night they all went onstage with what they'd just been thinking about the last couple of hours.

"Everyone in this room, no matter how healthy or careful, will die," Jo repeated. "Isn't that just wild to think about? Really, take a moment to think about it. *Every*one."

In the few seconds Jo left the audience to think about it, Olivia realized the true wild thing wasn't so much to picture everyone around her dead, but to imagine that all of them, now so happy, so drunk, so full of laughter, would be asleep in a few hours. That's the image that appeared in her head: everyone asleep. It was a good image, more potential for comedy than the whole room at the morgue, she thought. Not that death couldn't be funny, but sleep seemed to her an even more vulnerable state, in a way, and exploiting vulnerability was al-ways funnier than poking at fears. How strange was it that people fell asleep every night? When you thought about it? Some people even fell asleep next to other sleeping people! How insane! She might write about this, she thought. Imagining a whole room asleep. Although Jo might consider it too close to her own bit. Would it be? Having ideas while listening to other people wasn't the same as stealing.

"Don't you wish," Jo was saying onstage, "that we could all know in advance how and when we were going to die? A little flash-forward, a quick movie of our death? Not just for ourselves, to be done with the wondering, but also for everyone else? Like when we meet someone, when we shake their hand, for example, we get to see how they will die? That would be valuable information, I think. That would help us get a sense of the person. Not only because we would know that the person would die choking on a doughnut, but also because we would know that she knew it too, and had to live with it. It's so hard meeting new people. Don't you think? And being alive, in general. All we can do is imagine things." She picked a guy in the first row and asked, "You, for example, how do you imagine you will die?"

"Car crash!" the guy said, without hesitation. He sounded psyched about it.

"Do you think the car crash will be your fault, or someone else's?"

"Probably mine," he admitted.

Jo picked others in the crowd to chat about how they expected death to find them, and they all went along with it. The mood turned to that of a *Little Big Shots* episode, Jo as good-humored Steve Harvey, the audience as the excited children eager to talk, and everyone was jolly by the time she said good night and called Olivia onstage.

As she passed Sally's stool on her way there, Olivia tried to avoid looking at her. There was nothing sadder than your twin's encouraging smile, she thought, nothing more meaningless. Sally actually stopped her, though, grabbed her forearm and forced her to look. Olivia turned around, heard her twin say "You're the best!" but focused her attention on Sally's hair rather than her face. Olivia had found her first white hair just before Thanksgiving, and she'd wondered then if Sally had, too. She couldn't bring herself to ask. In the bathroom earlier, she'd plucked out two new ones. She didn't know what she wanted to see in Sally's hair, if spotting white there as well would make her feel better or worse. She didn't want either of them to grow older.

Olivia knew she was a bad sister for telling Sally not to press charges against Jarrett, but also that life was short and she could die any second, or have her whole head of hair turn white overnight, and she didn't want to think about Jarrett in the time that was left, and wasn't that something to respect as well? She turned back toward the stage and kept convincing herself that she wasn't a horrible person.

If it was the kind of case where she had to testify, she would do it. She would do everything she could do to help. She remembered the day Sally had first told their mother about Jarrett, she could describe it to the court. Sally was fourteen and talking about things that had happened seven, eight years prior, and their mother hadn't believed her. She'd thought the girl had wanted to divert attention from her poor report card. "What about you, Oli?" she'd asked. Olivia's report card had come in spotless. "Did Jarrett make you do things, too?" The problem was that Olivia had lied to her mother that day, and her sister, she'd said, "No, never," and if she told a jury now that she'd lied that day, would they believe another word she said? She'd trained herself to forget as much as possible, but some details had stuck, she could go into those. Jarrett had asked her to kiss it once, but mostly he'd just wanted her to touch it (she hated herself for thinking the "just," for always thinking it could've been worse, but she did think it, and it did help). She remembered the exact shade of pink and how soft it had been, and warm, too, like a gumball from the gumball machine by the newsstand her mother worked at, the one that was always in the sun in the afternoon. It was all true, but it would sound made up, Olivia thought. To her, almost everything did.

It wasn't a problem for her to have this much on her mind as she made her way to the stage. She knew it would all disappear the moment she started speaking into the microphone. It was almost a game at this point, testing how many unrelated-to-comedy thoughts she could hold in her head up to the last second—the more there were, the greater the relief would be at seeing them fly away with her first line, like a flock of scared-off birds after a gunshot. That's what Olivia had pictured her first few times onstage, a little explosion and then the birds, but now it was just a feeling, a great emptiness and then a warmth. If she'd had to describe it, she would've mentioned a beam, all her thoughts and energy gathering into a dense beam trained on the material, its delivery, the crowd's reactions to it, not on her graying hair or the lie she'd told all those years ago. She couldn't do anything about the lie now, but she'd read an article in *Scientific American* according to which white hair could sometimes go back to its original color, and that had given her hope. Jarrett had dyed his hair, she remembered. She'd seen the bottles in the bathroom, with the generic male model. Whenever she thought of Jarrett now (when she couldn't help it), it was in fact the do-it-yourself hair dye model's face that came to mind, and she liked to think she'd forgotten Jarrett's features entirely, that she might not recognize him if he walked into the bar, but of course she would.

If she ever admitted to having lied that day, people would ask why, and she'd have to lie again, say that she'd been afraid Jarrett would get back at her. But she hadn't been afraid at the time. When Jarrett had thanked her a few days later on the couch (the couch where everything else had happened, but on which that day he'd just said, "Thank you for sticking with me"), she'd had the thought that she could kill him—she had the strength by then, and he didn't expect it in that moment. So no, she wasn't afraid of him. She was angry that he'd made her life a cliché, cute little girls growing up poor but happy with their hardworking single mother until molester stepdad came along. She wanted people to never reduce her to this. But anger or pride hadn't been the reason for the lie, either. Olivia didn't like remembering how easy it had been to say it, "No, Jarrett never did anything to me." It had rolled off her tongue. It was instinct. Not instinct to protect him, or to protect herself, but to be believed. A storytelling instinct. She'd sensed that in that moment it was the truth that would've sounded like a lie, like she was just repeating Sally's words to get some attention herself, so she'd gone for the other thing. And though she'd always encouraged her mother to believe Sally, to kick Jarrett out (which the mother had ended up doing, months later), Olivia knew she'd committed to her own role so fully no one would buy it if she told the truth now. After all these years, she wasn't even sure she could act it convincingly herself.

She took the microphone off the stand.

"Has anyone been to a Holocaust museum lately?" she asked the audience.

The audience laughed, more than encouragingly—they were enjoying the bit already. Olivia berated herself, though, for starting with a question. *Next time,* she thought, *no question. Next time, start in the museum.*

"I try to go to the Holocaust museum once a year," she said, "around Thanksgiving. For emotional prep before I go see the family. Not that we're Jewish or anything. But the amount my mother and her sisters complain, you'd think maybe there was a mix-up at birth. Like, maybe my grandmother knew her daughters would be stupid, so every time she had one, she swapped it for a Jewish baby at the hospital. It had to be easy back then, don't you think? With everyone smoking in the hallways, there must've been a perpetual cloud in there—you could probably just smother patients in their sleep and steal babies and no one saw anything. You know, these hospital nurseries, by the way, with all the babies in their little bins, all lined up like that, it always makes me think of a gelato shop. And the new parents behind the window, looking at all the flavors . . . like they're actually deciding which one to get."

Olivia thought she could go there instead of where she was headed, keep digging at the newborn/gelato bin thing. The audience was liking it. But she couldn't just digress, this wasn't her show, she didn't have an hour, she only had five minutes, and she'd probably used up one already, maybe more.

"I love it when there's kids at the Holocaust museum. It's always nice to see families there, little children seeing this stuff for the first time, their parents explaining the shoes and the tattoos. The soap is more for teenagers, I think. No? When were you guys told about the soap? The Nazis making soap out of people?"

She never really waited for audience answers.

"I was told about the soap in eighth grade," she said. "I didn't get it. Did you guys get it? I really didn't. I remember everyone in my class nodded like they understood how you made one out of the other, but I truly couldn't see it, I felt like a fucking idiot. In retrospect, I think mine was the appropriate reaction. Like everyone in my class was a psychopath for understanding the process of making soap out of people. Like that made total sense, it was a thought they'd all had. But whatever, I like the Holocaust museum. Clear distinction between good and evil, that's relaxing. Helps to get perspective on your own problems. Also, I know the museum by now, I have a routine. But I get there last month, and they changed everything. They have this new feature now, they have a Holocaust survivor hologram, you heard of this? It's amazing, they film a Holocaust survivor for hours and they ask him everything about his experience, and out of the footage, they make a hologram that can answer any question anyone may ever have about the guy's life. It's a bit creepy, but I mean, maybe it's a good idea, because we had a real live Holocaust survivor visit my class back in the day, still eighth grade, and we were too fucking terrified to ask her anything. We didn't want her to relive the camps, even though that's exactly what she was there to do, to tell us how horrible it was, but whatever. We basically just asked about the tattoo, and the sleeping conditions. Some girl asked how much weight she'd lost. Stuff like that. But last month, I ended up alone in the room with the hologram at the Holocaust museum, and I let it all out. And I mean all of it. Like, I started with questions about the war, but then the guy was so nice and smart, and he seemed to really have his shit together, so I figured it wouldn't hurt to ask for life advice."

Olivia wasn't stealing, to her mind. Artie's idea had been to discuss *pop culture* with a Holocaust survivor's hologram. She'd been the one to take it further and imagine the hologram as a life coach.

"I asked about a guy, and after hearing the whole story, which I'll spare you, the Holocaust survivor said, 'This idiot doesn't deserve you.' Can you believe it? I'm sure grandfathers say stuff like that to their granddaughters all the time, but for me it was a first. I told him, 'You're like the grandfather I never had,' and I was getting pretty emotional, but the hologram said, 'Four children, fifteen grandchildren, and six great-grandchildren so far!' And then there was this awkward silence, like he knew he'd bugged, but we both decided to just ignore it. I could've cried, guys. I wanted to take him home. I think I've always wanted a Jewish family. And I've also always wanted a family you can turn on and off, so the hologram man really fit the bill. Full of wisdom and super knowledgeable, but only talks to you if you talk to him first. You're right, maybe I was falling in love a little.

He was pretty funny, too, like I asked what it felt like to be made into a hologram, and he said, 'Better than Auschwitz.' Isn't that something? I think maybe we were flirting. The problem is, a family came into the room after that, and it kind of ruined the mood. They had a kid, and he completely stole my survivor's attention, he started using him to help with his World War II homework, stupid questions about Nazis, and forgiveness, and the father was filming it all, to make memories. I tried to make eye contact with my survivor so that we could joke about the family later, but he didn't look back. Very professional. At some point, the kid ran out of questions and the mother went for it, she asked the hologram about the future, did he see similarities between 1939 Germany and today's America, and I couldn't help it, I said to her, 'He's not a fucking Magic 8 Ball,' even though I'd kind of just used him like one. After everything we'd shared, I thought the hologram would side with me, but all he said was 'One at a time, please,' because I'd interrupted the lady and he'd bugged again. I felt betrayed, I'm not going to lie. I made a note in the guest book that I hope they start selling these holograms at the gift shop soon so we can all go home with our own Holocaust survivor. I think it works better as an exclusive relationship."

Olivia wrapped it up nicely, she thought, imagining a hologram in every household waiting for the kids to come home and chat about their day, but all in all, as she left the stage, she felt the bit had been too baggy in the middle. She had a lot of cutting to do.

She assumed Artie would want to talk to her right away, but she didn't see him at the bar. Perhaps he knew she always went for a cigarette after a performance and was already waiting for her outside.

Phil was the first to say "Good job," and also the last for a while. His eyes rolled back in their sockets as he finished saying it, and his body went limp. Olivia tried to catch him as he fell, but the side of his head still hit the bar on the way down.

"What the fuck?" she heard someone say.

"Is this a joke?"

She had her arms in Phil's armpits and everyone made space around them as she laid him on his back.

"He's having a seizure," Olivia said.

"He took some Adderall earlier," someone from Second City said.

"Is there a doctor in here?" Dorothy asked, but why would there have been a doctor at the Empty Bottle on amateur comedy night? She took her phone out to call 911 and looked around for her purse— a stupid reflex, she thought. What would she have found in there anyway? Tissues? She could've *wiped* Phil's forehead?

"My girlfriend's a doctor!" some drunk guy said. "She's smoking outside, I'll go get her."

Olivia was kneeling by Phil's side. She'd tilted his head back so that he wouldn't choke on his tongue, but beyond that, she had no idea what to do. She thought it might be important for Phil to know exactly how long his seizure had lasted, so she started the stopwatch on her phone.

The girl who'd given Phil the Adderall said it wasn't her fault.

"He told me he'd taken it before," she said, and then she started crying and saying it was horrible, all of this happening on his birthday.

"Phil's birthday is in May," Olivia said.

"He said it was today," the girl insisted, like it mattered. She looked like no one had ever lied to her before.

"Maybe he has epilepsy," Sally said, and this somehow irritated Olivia more than anything else her sister had said so far. Why did she always have to say out loud what everyone else was thinking? What was the social function behind such behavior? It wasn't just Sally, though, Olivia knew. Everyone talked too much. She was so used to editing sentences, combining three words into one, cutting adverbs, that she'd started doing it to people's speech in her head now, too, noticing where they could've sharpened an anecdote, or not spoken at all. She tried to focus on Phil. She grabbed his hand. It was cold, but the fingers wrapped around her palm immediately and squeezed so hard she thought her hand might break.

The drunk guy came back with his doctor girlfriend. She was drunk, too. Artie was behind them—so he had been outside, Olivia thought, waiting for her. She expected the drunk doctor to congratulate her on positioning Phil right, but the doctor made adjustments instead, turned Phil on his side, took the glasses off his face. Olivia thought she should've thought of that, the glasses.

Phil regained consciousness. His grip on Olivia's hand relaxed, but he didn't let go.

"Sir, do you know where you are?" the drunk doctor asked. She looked nauseous, worse off than Phil, in many ways.

"He hit his head on the bar," Olivia said.

"How hard?"

"Pretty hard."

Phil ended up saying he knew where he was, and that it was his birthday. The doctor asked if he'd taken anything to celebrate.

"It's not his birthday," Olivia said again, which, combined with the fact that she was holding Phil's hand, got the drunk doctor thinking they were a couple.

"Has your boyfriend taken any drugs tonight?"

"Only Adderall, sounds like. And a beer or two," Olivia said. She didn't see the point in correcting the boyfriend/girlfriend assumption. It wouldn't even be funny. "He had a bourbon earlier, too," she recalled.

"I wanted tequila, though," Phil said. And: "She's not my girlfriend."

It made the girl who'd given him Adderall laugh.

Phil told the doctor that he had seizures about twice a year, and it was nothing. The drunk doctor said someone should take him home, make sure he didn't fall asleep for a few hours, in case he had a concussion.

Olivia thought she could've told Phil that, about the concussion. She'd seen the medical shows, and that Altman movie with the kid. It was such a cliché line—"Don't let him fall asleep!"—she wondered if the doctor was a real doctor.

"Make sure to drink lots of fluids," the drunk doctor told Phil. "Your friends will watch over you."

"What fluids?" Dan asked.

"What friends?" Jo said.

Sally looked at Olivia. Was it okay to resume making fun of Phil so soon? Olivia had once explained to her that there was no such thing as too soon in comedy, only not funny enough.

"We'll take him home," Olivia said.

"You know where he lives?" Dan asked.

"He lives with his aunt on Kedzie."

"Wait, are you guys *actually* dating?"

"How do you know his birthday *and* where he lives?" Jo asked. "Do you listen when he talks?"

"You know I can hear you, right?" Phil said. He was sitting up now.

"Marianne did our birth chart our first week here," Olivia said. "I remember everyone's birthday."

"Why?"

"What do you mean, why? I remember them, that's all."

"What's my birthday?" Dan asked, and then Marianne, and then Jo. Olivia remembered all of them.

"What a useless skill," Jo said.

They all looked sad for Olivia, that she was wasting brain space on this.

The bartender had turned on the lights after Phil's fall, and the audience had a collective deer-in-the-headlights glow, everyone's face too bright, everyone a bit regretful of their last few decisions. The drunk doctor's drunk boyfriend was the first to notice Manny. He asked him for a photo with Phil in the background. "The guy who fished out," he called him. Manny refused.

"The kid had a fucking seizure," he said. "How about we leave him alone for a minute?"

Phil, though, who'd overheard the whole thing, said it was fine.

"I don't mind being in the picture."

Manny searched for Dorothy's eyes. What was the protocol here? He was living his first moments as a teacher. Did you go with what the student wanted? Did you deny him in order to preserve his dignity? Wasn't Phil's dignity Phil's to do with as he pleased? Dorothy looked back at Manny and shrugged.

Phil hammed it up for the camera. Still sitting, he tilted his head to the side, closed his eyes, let his mouth hang half-open. The drunk doctor took the photo, and then traded places with her boyfriend so she, too, could have her future phone memory with Manny and the epileptic.

"Do you want me to lie back down?" Phil asked, in between shots. Another thing he'd learned from Sword's class on epiphany was proper usage of "lay" vs. "lie."

"That would be great!"

Six photos were taken in total, Phil adjusting his position slightly for each. Manny didn't smile in any.

Olivia went for a cigarette. She expected Artie would be there on the sidewalk—she'd seen him go out again. She wasn't eager to talk to him about her bit, but she knew it was big of him not to bring it up in front of the others, to give her a chance to explain herself. *What a great guy,* she thought, and it irritated her that great guys irritated her.

"That was crazy in there," Artie said when he saw her. "Did you know Phil had epilepsy?"

Olivia would've preferred he rip off the Band-Aid, accuse her right away of stealing his material, so she could start her defense—it wasn't stealing if Artie's bit only existed as an idea in his head, ideas weren't anything until you shaped them and brought them to the stage, etc.—but she had to follow his lead. She would look guilty if she didn't. She had to act surprised when he mentioned it.

"He just fell," she said. "Scared the shit out of me."

"You looked like you knew what to do."

Olivia said she'd watched every medical show in existence since she was a child, a habit that, according to her calculations, equated to all of med school plus a first year of residency in an understaffed hospital. She was pretty sure she could intubate someone if she had to.

"Did you ever want to be a doctor?" Artie asked.

The small talk was killing her.

"You're really not going to say anything about my bit?"

Artie said he would if she gave him a cigarette. Olivia handed him one, and her lighter.

"I thought you were anti," she said.

"I don't like the smell," Artie said. The clicking of the lighter, though, the fizzling of the cherry, the peace of the first inhale—he understood why people lit cigarettes all day. "But if I'm smoking, I don't smell it anymore. Isn't that weird? Is it that I can't smell it, you think, or just that it stops bothering me?"

It was Mickey who'd taught him the trick, that summer Artie hung out with him and his friends in Parker's garage. Artie'd never said it outright, that the cigarette smell bothered him, but Mickey had come to him and said, "If you smoke one, you'll stop smelling it" before putting a lit cigarette in Artie's mouth. The smell had disappeared instantly. How amazing it would be if more things in life worked that way, Artie had thought back then. If the things that bothered you stopped bothering you the moment you started partaking. Perhaps it was how life worked already, though, and he hadn't noticed. He hadn't been as diligent a note taker at the time, and that thought had been lost.

"Weren't we going to talk about my bit?" Olivia said.

Artie was smoking annoyingly, like actors in the movies. Hollywood, she thought, seemed to have agreed that people couldn't smoke and talk at the same time, that smoking was mostly for pauses and contemplation.

"Your bit was good," Artie said. "It needs work, but I like what you did with the children."

"The children?"

"The children going to the Holocaust museum for the first time," Artie said. "It's funny."

The critiques could get elaborate in workshop, especially with Marianne, who liked to sprinkle theory over everything, but really, it always came down to that: funny or not.

"The soap thing, though," Artie added, "I don't know if you know it, but it's a legend. Nazis never made soap out of people."

"What?"

"But maybe it doesn't matter. For your bit, I mean. It's still part of the collective imagination. They *did* tell us about it in school, so I think it's fine if you keep it."

Olivia couldn't decide if she believed Artie about the soap, but more confusing was his calling the bit hers. Could it be that she hadn't actually stolen anything?

"The lampshades made out of skin, though," Artie said. "I think that was real."

Olivia watched him smoke cinematically for a minute, long inhales and long exhales, like yoga.

"Why are you telling me all this?" she ended up asking. "Why are you telling me anything that could make the bit better?"

"I don't think it'll make the bit *better.* I just thought you might want to know about the soap."

"You're not mad I took your hologram thing?"

Artie didn't know whether he was mad or not. His immediate reaction to hearing Olivia onstage had been anger, but anger at himself, for telling her about the Holocaust survivor hologram in the first place. You weren't supposed to talk about work in progress. Relief had followed quickly, though, a type of relief he was still trying to interpret—was it relief that he would no longer have to work on the bit himself? Now that Olivia had very publicly planted her flag in it? Relief that she liked him enough to steal from him? Liking someone's ideas wasn't the same as liking that person, he knew that, but still. It had to be, to some extent. What Artie knew was that she'd done the stealing in front of him, and that had to mean something. She had to know he'd have time-stamped notes on his phone, his computer, drafts of jokes about his own visit to the Holocaust museum that proved the bit was his. Unfinished, sure, but his. In essence, his. She had to know this, and yet she'd gone for it, she'd risked the consequences of having him expose her as a thief, of owing him one if he didn't, of having him hold this over her head for the rest of her career. It was almost a proof of love, if you thought about it, Olivia stealing from him. She'd tied her fate to his. It was nice to think about it that way.

"You can have it," he said to her. "You can have the bit."

Olivia asked what he wanted in exchange.

"Just do something great with it," Artie said.

"I can trade you some jokes. I have a lot of molestation material I'm not using."

"I don't think my mother would allow it. Wasn't sexual abuse on the 'Do Not Joke About' list?"

"I think it was," Olivia said. "But I give you my blessing." She put her cigarette out in the snow and glanced at Artie, who was halfway through his. The slow, lengthy puffs had been unnerving at first, but they were becoming hypnotizing now. Also, Olivia had noticed, Artie didn't look at her as much when he smoked. "You can tell your mother you have the blessing of an actual victim," she said.

Her heart raced as she said "victim," and it started beating even faster in the silence that followed. Olivia was using the word in connection with herself for the first time. It hadn't been as hard to say as she'd imagined, but still, she wanted to take it back. She'd thrown it like a top, though, the kind you launch with a thin rope: all she could do now was watch it spin and spin between them.

"I'm sorry," she said to Artie. "Pretend I didn't say anything."

If Artie really liked her, she thought, he would ignore what she'd set in motion, help her make the word "victim" disappear.

"Deal," Artie said after his longest exhale yet. "You take the Holocaust jokes, I take molestation."

They shook on it. The word was gone. Artie buried it even deeper.

"I was surprised you went for it," he said. "I assumed you'd want to show Reinhardt a tried-and-true bit. You kind of rushed into this one."

"I know," Olivia said. She was still shaky from her admission, but a good enough actress to play her regular self and hide it for a minute. "But I thought it was better to introduce myself to Reinhardt with something that needed work. Something with potential, like strong beats and all, but a lot of room for improvement. It's better down the line if he feels like he *shaped* me or whatever. No teacher wants a fully formed student. There's no credit to take from that."

"You're fucking evil," Artie said.

As far as descriptors for herself went, "evil" was a word Olivia liked better. She smiled as she lit her next cigarette—no small feat, doing both at once—and they resumed talking about Phil. Joking about him. They thought it would be funny if a rumor started that Phil had uttered racist slurs during his seizure. They both honed their physical comedy skills with epileptic episode impressions. Ventured the possibility that the universe was against Phil ever performing again.

"The fake campus shooting right before he's up for workshop, the seizure right before he goes onstage . . . I think the world is trying to tell him something," Olivia said.

Artie agreed, but really, he thought the world might've been trying to tell *him* something, too. It wasn't normal that he just gave bits away. Or that he hadn't feared for his life earlier, in the bathroom, with Vivian. She'd cried the entire time. He'd almost been bored.

"People react to similar experiences in different ways," Olivia said. "Like you and your brother. You had the same childhood, wouldn't you say? Pretty much? And he's out there getting high, while you don't even know how to smoke a cigarette."

She was talking about herself, Artie thought. Herself and Sally. Maybe she always was.

"Vivian is going to write a memoir about today," he said. "I can feel it. Her near-death experience in the men's room. And I still haven't thought of a single joke to make about the whole thing."

"Now *that*'s more of a problem," Olivia said.

She offered to help. They riffed for a minute about gun control and the memoir trend. They joked about Vivian herself. A novelist had to be the worst kind of person to be near in a catastrophe, Olivia said. Maybe that could be his angle. Had Vivian been narrating at all? In the men's bathroom?

"She kept weeping and saying she'd never finish her book," Artie said. "That's it."

Olivia shook her head slowly, like she was hearing about an accident that could've been prevented.

"It has to suck," she said, "going through life thinking that what you do matters at all."

Meanwhile, debate was raging at the bar about whether or not to resume the comedy battle. The Second City girl who'd given Phil the Adderall actually said the words "the show must go on."

"People came here to see us."

"It's not like they paid money," Jo said.

" 'Show must go on' applies to all shows. It's not only for paying customers."

"Stop saying 'show must go on.' "

Phil said he didn't think he could go up onstage.

"I feel a little woozy."

"You told the doctor you were fine," the Adderall girl said. "You said this happened to you all the time."

"That's not what I said. I said twice a year."

"If you don't go, we win by forfeit," the girl declared.

"Fine by me," Phil said.

Dorothy said, "No fucking way are we losing to improv," but Dan presented her with the evidence: their audience had moved on.

"Look around," he said, and Dorothy did. People were asking Kruger for selfies now, too, fighting to buy Manny a drink. "I think they're over us."

Dorothy didn't know what to think of the treatment Manny was getting. She'd expected a milder welcome—hardcore fans trying to get a joke out of him, sure, but perhaps a more confrontational part of the crowd, too, or at least some hesitation to be seen with him on social media just yet.

"They're not over Manny," she told Dan.

She should've been glad about it. Why wasn't she glad? Wasn't it what she wanted, her friend being given the benefit of the doubt? Except Manny was being given more than the benefit of the doubt, Dorothy thought. It was unrestrained support that people were showing, the men and the women. They were on his side. She was

too, granted, but she hadn't needed to trash or ridicule Lipschitz and
the proposed-to women to get there, the way she was hearing strangers do now, left and right. "All wannabees," people kept saying to
Manny, Lipschitz "a jealous ass with no talent," the women "attention
whores," all three of them (even the one who'd stayed anonymous).
Dorothy didn't like it when idiots wound up on her side. To have stupid enemies was bad enough, but stupid allies were humiliating. She
supported Manny because she knew him, and for old times' sake, for
all those nights he'd told off assholes who wouldn't take her seriously, the club owners who wouldn't pay her as much as him, and for
that one day he'd come to repair a broken pipe in her kitchen when
she didn't have the money for a plumber. But all these people, what,
they did it because Manny was famous? Because Manny was funny?
Who was asking them to take sides at all?

"He tends to get away with things," August said into Dorothy's ear.
"It's better to just be happy for him."

Why was he telling her this?

"Do I look angry?" she asked August.

"A little bit," he said.

Dorothy saw Artie and Olivia come back from their cigarette
break. She watched them pause to take stock of the room, the small
gatherings around Manny and Kruger, Ashbee deep in conversation
with a woman near the stage. She was surprised to see them walk
toward her, and Phil, and Jo, and August, and Dan, that they wouldn't
try joining the more exciting crowds.

Olivia asked Phil how he was feeling, and Phil said it was nice of
her to ask, that she was nice, to which Olivia replied that there was a
difference between being nice to someone and not wanting that person to *die,* but Phil disagreed. That's all that being nice was, he said:
making sure that people were not dead. Jo said that was a low bar, and
was Phil not loved as a child? Which got Olivia thinking about Sally.

"Where's Sally?" she asked.

"Bathroom, I think."

"Again?"

"Maybe she has her period, too," Jo said. "Don't you keep track of everyone's cycle? I wouldn't be surprised, after the birthday revelation."

Olivia said it was sad that just because she'd known Phil's birthday, the drunk doctor had assumed she was his girlfriend. Jo said everything that related to Phil was sad, and could they talk about something else?

For a second, Olivia pictured Sally dead in the bathroom, or worse, crying.

"We have to figure out what to do with him for the next three hours," she said, getting rid of the image.

Three hours was the amount of time the drunk doctor had told them to keep watch over Phil. Olivia was taking the mission seriously.

"I'm fine," Phil said. "Really. I barely hit my head."

"There's a lot of empty space in there, though," Jo said. "Your brain probably bounced on the side of your skull and cracked. It's probably leaking now."

"I'm just tired," Phil said. "I just want to go to bed."

He yawned to illustrate his point, and that got Marianne to yawn, and the few members of Second City that had gathered around them to yawn.

"What's with the yawning?" Olivia said. "What's wrong with you people? It's not even midnight and you're already talking about bedtime. This is a night job."

"You'll die if you go to bed," Jo said. "You'll slip into a coma and die."

It sounded like a curse, addressed not only to Phil but to everyone around her.

Marianne said she'd gotten up early, and that as far as she was concerned, the evening was over: She'd done her time onstage. Second City had won the comedy battle.

"You *did your time*?" Olivia said. "Sorry, is there a clock we had to punch and no one told me?"

"I resent the idea that because we're artists, we should be stage-ready at all times," Marianne said. "Part of the job is knowing your limits and when the work is done."

Jo said no one here had called Marianne an artist.

Olivia said they weren't exactly running marathons here. "I think we can all do two bits in the same night."

Dorothy agreed with her, of course: There was a microphone, an audience, and a roomful of comedians. Surely, they could find a way to kill a little time while Phil recovered. Part of her job as a teacher, however, was to let her students figure out what they stood for, without taking sides. That's what she would tell Manny later, when they were alone, if he wanted to speak ill of Lipschitz or the women. She'd say, "I'm not taking sides. I'm a sage now. I see everyone's arguments and I don't judge." If pressed to form an opinion, she'd focus on the words the media was using: "emotional misconduct." What a joke, she'd tell Manny, like that wasn't and hadn't always been what life was, a long stream of emotional misconduct, like it wasn't just people misunderstanding and hurting and lying to one another constantly. She could get behind emotional "abuse," but where did "misconduct" start? It sounded so silly she believed the notion had been coined by a cynic who'd wanted to ridicule it and its future users. The number of people she could've sued for emotional misconduct, Dorothy thought, and it must've made her smile, because August asked her what was so funny. She pretended not to hear him. What right did the kid have to know what was making her smile? She took her phone out to shield herself from more questions. Sword had responded, finally, to her text about having dinner with her. She'd thought it pretty clear that her invitation had included Sword's wife, but Sword was saying he couldn't have dinner with Dorothy. He was very sorry if he'd given her the wrong impression, but he wasn't available, his marriage was central to his life, etc. He'd said this already, Dorothy thought, about loving his wife. He'd said it just a few hours earlier. Did he think she'd forgotten? Or had he forgotten himself that he'd said it? It irritated her when people told her things twice. She always took it as an insult, either to her capacity to listen and remember simple information or to her general presence, her aura, which had to be pretty dim if Sword was able to talk to her on autopilot and forget what he'd confided to her.

Also, she'd been joking before, about being willing to sleep with him after the death scare. Did people not understand her jokes anymore? Maybe Sword felt she was harassing him now. How ridiculous, she thought, to assume she'd wanted romance. Wasn't it obvious that she was out of the game? When she'd heard Manny's accusers called "attention whores" a few minutes back, Dorothy had gone through a familiar taxonomy in her head, a taxonomy of whores, according to both men and women: if a woman did the seducing, she was a whore, if she was sensitive to a man's charms, she was a whore, if she was seduced and felt taken advantage of, she was a neurotic whore, if she got hurt and told people about it, she was an attention whore, and if she didn't respond to a man's advances, she was a frigid whore. Dorothy was content not to fit anywhere on the list anymore. Perhaps she could've been considered the frigid whore type a few years ago, but since no one ever thought of hitting on her now, and unless there was a category beyond frigid that she'd never heard of, that men never even approached (the saintly whore?), she'd managed to exit the wheel of whores entirely, and what an amazing feat that was—like those truly enlightened Buddhists who exit the wheel of life and suffering. Dorothy was aware that people would have to act shocked if they knew how many times she'd thought the word "whore" in the last few seconds, and that society wasn't supposed to think like that anymore, but she wasn't society, and she wasn't an exception to it either. It was good to want to change the way people perceived women, of course, but delusional to believe that it could happen overnight, or over a decade, or over two, and pretending that it could, or pretending that you knew what society thought, or what *anyone* thought, for that matter, was ludicrous and borderline fascistic. The collective imagination had fashioned a wheel of whores long ago. You couldn't just erase that construction with a handful of op-eds. There was a wheel, and Dorothy had just been thrown back on it. Sword had made that decision for her, mistaking her for a woman still interested in sex and flirting, a whore of some kind, then, though Dorothy won-dered what kind exactly? A sad whore, probably—she'd just been re-jected, after all, without even having asked for anything. It was useless to work on the way people perceived you, Dorothy thought. You couldn't expect anyone to see you the way you wanted them to. The world wasn't a place that mirrored the way you viewed yourself. What you projected was always misunderstood, was always leading to some sort of emotional misconduct. Could she sue Sword for not wanting to be her friend?

She was getting worked up. She hadn't been this angry in a while. She remembered how nice it was to go onstage angry. The worst per-formances of her career she'd given happy. You couldn't go onstage happy. Happy meant limp, it meant blurry. Comedy was tension, high def, walking the tightrope of pretending a joke you'd spent hours shaping was just occurring to you for the very first time. Her anger erased all the worries she'd been waking up to since Kiki'd started scheduling the new tour, about how she should present, whether she should paint her nails, wear a dress, how she would be categorized (a female comic, a veteran comic, a niche comic, a comic's comic—each option equally bad), if anyone would laugh. Instead of imagining how the new jokes would be received, Dorothy could get behind the mi-crophone right now and see for herself.

She looked at Marianne, who wanted to go home.

"What's this about Second City winning the battle?" she said to her. "I think the rules are Second City and six *members* of the Stand-Up MFA have to go onstage to fight it out. Six *members*, not students."

Dorothy was making this up. She wasn't sure what the rules were, or whether anyone had ever bothered to write them down. She wasn't sure why she'd felt the need to invent one, either: nobody would've stopped her if she'd gone up onstage without an explanation. But the kids believed her rule. More than that, they got excited about it. It meant that a teacher could go onstage instead of Phil! The kids *wanted* to see their teachers perform, Dorothy realized, they wanted to see *her,* to see experience up there, and how moving was that? The an-swer was "very." It was very moving. Until the decision was made, at some yet-unregistered-by-science speed, that the person who should go onstage as Phil's replacement was Manny.

"It makes the most sense," Olivia said, though she didn't explain in what way.

"Go big or go home," Phil said.

"What makes the most sense?" asked Sally, who'd missed everything while in the bathroom. Olivia thought her twin would always be cursed with bad timing. Just a minute ago, she would've been happy to see her.

"If Manny goes onstage, we'll accept a draw," the girl who'd given Phil the Adderall said.

"Fuck a draw," Olivia said. "This ain't team bingo."

Dorothy said that Manny might not want to go up.

"I think his agent told him to lay low for a while."

"*Lie* low," Phil said. "I think."

"Agents don't know shit," Olivia said, though she was actively looking for one. Turning to August, she asked: "What does his *lawyer* say?"

August said he wasn't his father's lawyer. He didn't say "father," though, but "Manny."

"Manny will do whatever Manny wants."

What Manny wanted was to get away from the fans around him. If Dorothy was uncomfortable seeing the support people gave him, he found it near unbearable. "These chicks have no case against you," "bloodsucking attention whores" . . . the more they spoke, the more Manny wanted to give each woman a call, propose marriage, this time for real. That would be the best ending to the story, he thought, if one of them accepted and they actually got married and lived happily ever after. Hilarious. Couple of babies. Ready-made bits about raising toddlers in your fifties, teenagers in your sixties, living with a younger woman. He could write the stuff in his sleep and roll it out until he died.

It was a relief when Olivia came over to ask, "Would you go onstage to help us win?" He would, Manny said, gladly, and then, to himself: *Anything to get away from these idiots.* He hadn't expected much from his fans, historically (when hoping for success, no one ever spent time imagining the audience that would come with it), and yet they'd still managed to disappoint—to sadden him, more exactly. He did all this so *these* guys would laugh? He'd turned the question over in his head for decades now, how it could be that nothing felt better than a crowd laughing, and little worse, an hour later, than individuals from that very group telling him what it was he'd said that made them laugh. It always sounded so small, what he'd written, when a fan repeated it. That's why he'd wanted for his son to be a novelist. Novelists could go their whole career without meeting a reader. Even more prodigious: a novelist without readers could still be a novelist. Was that right? Manny wondered as he followed Olivia through the crowd and to the stage. Did he really believe that? Maybe it was just one of those lines that sounded good in his head. He'd fantasized about anonymity earlier that day, but the truth was, if Manny had been turned back into a nobody all of a sudden, he would've done everything in his power to become famous again, started over— the local open mics, the birthday parties—done anything to climb those five steps to the stage and forget he was the same as everybody else. He watched Olivia take them now, those steps, and even though he would be where she stood in a second, he envied her, he couldn't wait, he wanted to be up there this very instant. A minute ago, he hadn't been thinking about performing, but now that it had been decided, the impatience was so sharp it was turning into loneliness. He was defiant, too, and slightly paranoid, the way he used to feel when he'd started stand-up, like it was gym class in high school and everyone was pointing at him. He was nothing offstage, but in a minute, he'd show everyone what he was made of. He was a plane waiting for authorization to take off, clunky on the runway, boorish and loud before it was finally airborne, rising and rising, leaving everyone small on the ground. Olivia hadn't even started speaking before the audience understood what was happening—Manny Reinhardt was going to go up for an impromptu set, and in the midst of a sex scandal, at that! How lucky they all were! And how fucking stupid to feel so lucky, Manny thought. The one good thing about being Manny Reinhardt was he'd never be stuck below stage level having to look up at Manny Reinhardt.

He half listened to Olivia say something about a special guest, a new recruit in the MFA program. He was only waiting to hear his name so he could join her onstage. It had never felt particularly meaningful, his name, or like it even belonged to him, but he recognized it from years of people using it as a starting pistol in a race, agreeing that those sounds it made would get him going. Olivia said the name. Manny went up. He pretended to be disoriented by the welcoming applause.

"Not sure what I'm doing here," he said. "Sorry. I just go where I'm told now. I just go where women tell me."

It wasn't very funny, but people laughed. Would they laugh at anything he said? Manny'd wondered about that before, whether he'd reached such a level of fame that people would pay to hear him say strings of random words. He'd done shows on autopilot before, and audiences hadn't seemed to notice.

"It's safer that way," he added.

His eyes met Dorothy's in the audience. A brutal sadness washed over him. She hadn't gotten fat, or too wrinkly, she hadn't done anything stupid with her hair, but she'd aged, undeniably, and though he'd had an hour to take this in already, it hit Manny with blunt force only now that he was looking down at her, the irreversibility of it, how young Dorothy would never spring back out from under older Dorothy. It was silly to be so hurt by such a naïve realization, that time passed, that people changed forever, but hurt Manny was, overwhelmed by hurt even. What was the point of all this? Of writing, of going onstage, of art, of fucking? Wasn't it to make time disappear? Time wasn't disappearing, Manny thought. He was failing. Why had he wanted so bad to be onstage a minute ago? He wasn't in any state to do this. He was sinking. He looked at August, hoping it would help, but August was miles away down there in the pit.

"My son is here in the audience tonight," he said into the micro-phone, and then repeated the words "my son."

"Fun fact about my son: he never once shat himself.

"He was born with this condition wherein the shit stays in the body. His mother and I literally had to pull it out of him every day. Several times a day. There was a lack of nerves in his asshole, basi-cally. Little guy couldn't push it all the way out. His shit went up to a certain point, like inches shy of the finish line, and then it got cold feet, like, *I can't do it, I'll stay right here until someone comes for me*.

"We had to use these tubes. Every week I went to Duane Reade to buy like fifty of them. And I pumped and I pumped."

There was Manny's answer: no one was laughing. No one looked impatient, though, either, or confused: they trusted this would get somewhere. Manny had earned that kind of trust over the years. Had he been in a better mood, he would've stopped for a moment and taken it in, reveled in this achievement.

"It's fine that you're not laughing," he said instead. "It's fine. You know who else didn't laugh? Jesus. Jesus never laughed. In fact, there's debate, too, about whether Jesus ever took a shit or not. I know this from everything I read about shitting when my son was a baby. *Excreting*, sorry. I read that the *nourishment within Jesus was never corrupted*. How about that? I told my wife when I found out: 'Honey, major thing in common between our son and Jesus Christ!' I thought she would find it funny, or, I don't know, interesting, that our son was like Jesus in some weird way, but all she said was 'Oh yeah? What about farting? Did Jesus Christ ever fart?' Because our son couldn't fart, either. She was so fucking angry. I don't know if she was trying to tell me I was a jerk for joking about our son's condition or if she was saying, 'Fuck Jesus, my baby is a better Messiah, my baby can't even *fart*!' I still don't know. To this day. She kind of scared me in that moment."

Manny looked down at his feet. They didn't quite seem to belong to him.

"I miss my wife," he said, still looking down, and that got him his first real laugh of the evening. Finally, the audience thought, mention of a wife (which they knew, from previous bits, to be an ex-wife), Manny going for more traditional jokes, men and women, the misunderstandings between them.

"I miss my son too, actually," Manny said, burying right away all hope for lighter material. "I miss my son even though he's right here." He looked at August again, but only for a split second.

"I still have nightmares about the hospital. We went there all the time, when he had fevers, when he threw up, when the shit didn't come out right, or there wasn't enough of it . . . we were constantly afraid of obstruction, of infection. And every time we went, I felt like we were flipping a coin. I felt like it was a hospital, so someone *had* to die, like each ward had a certain number of deaths to give per week, and if someone *had* to die, it was going to be between my kid and another kid, and so I tried not to look at the other kids, but whenever I did, because sometimes it's hard not to look, especially when a kid is deformed, or there are limbs missing, or she looks like your grandma, I thought, *I hope you die and not my kid.* I wished for so many children to die, guys. That's why I don't believe in God. I should've been struck by lightning *in my own home,* I wished death on so many children. *Sick* children. Children who were afraid already, who kept pretending they weren't just so their parents would stop crying for a second and they could live their last moments in peace."

There was confusion in the audience, even among those who'd started laughing at the last few lines. What was Manny doing, talking about sick children? No one had expected him to address the accusations onstage, but wasn't it worse to admit that you'd wished sick children dead? Worse than hitting someone, worse than taking advantage of young, innocent women? Did they really have to think about this now?

"I don't know if any of those kids died," Manny went on. "I assume a few of them did. Not because of me, but just . . . some of them were in real bad shape. My wife, she was the opposite of me, though. The second we were in the hospital, she thought nothing bad could happen, that all we had to do was stick together, all the parents and all the children and all the doctors, like we were a team, like there was some kind of 'if one gets better, we all get better' type deal. I could've strangled her."

The little encouragement the crowd had given him before stopped dead at the word "strangled."

"I sense a mood switch," Manny said. "The mood shifted here. I talked about hoping for children's deaths and you were all on board with it, but now I say the words 'strangle my wife' and you all get nervous. What's up with that? I never strangled my wife. She can confirm that. I never even *wanted* to strangle her. It was just a way of speaking. It's just words, guys. I admire my wife. I mean, ex-wife, yes, but who cares, I admire the *person,* I didn't admire her because she was my wife, I didn't stop admiring her when she left me. Right, Dorothy? Remember how much I loved Rachel? I couldn't shut up about her after we met."

Dorothy panicked when she heard her name. She went through different options in her head: Play Manny's game, respond to him honestly ("Yes, you loved your wife, yes, it was annoying how much you talked about her")? Or make a joke about how drunk he was? Manny was off his orbit, that much was clear, but Dorothy couldn't tell how controlled the new trajectory was, if she should help him keep climbing or try to mitigate an unavoidable crash. Manny decided for her by forgetting he'd just asked for her opinion.

"But if you say you admire your wife," he went on, "then who the fuck is going to laugh? Hmm? I never wished her harm. Even in the middle of the divorce. I never even raised my voice to her. Not once. I see you don't believe me. We can call her right now if you don't believe me, we'll ask her. I'll put her on speaker."

Manny took out his phone and dialed Rachel. The crash was imminent, Dorothy understood, but the rest of the crowd still seemed to think this could go somewhere.

"It's ringing," Manny said, even though the audience could hear the ringing for themselves, amplified by the microphone.

He didn't *look* drunk, Dorothy thought, but he had to be. You had to be drunk to call your ex-wife onstage.

The call went to voicemail: "Hi, you've reached Rachel, I can't come to the phone right now—" How many times had Manny told her to change that message? "I can't come to the phone," how ridiculous, the phone was *on* her person, everyone's phone was *on* their person now, what was this nonsense about not being able to *come* to it? Manny considered leaving Rachel a message along those lines, for the audience to appreciate, but the beep came and he didn't have it in him to speak after it. He hung up and looked at his reflection in the black screen of his phone. Was he alive right now? Was that his face?

"What boring times we live in," he said. He didn't speak the sentence directly into the microphone, but it was a small room, and a quiet one now, too—everybody could hear him. "The phones," he said, "the surveillance, everyone reachable all the time, everyone's opinions uploaded all the time. We're all becoming fucking machines."

He sighed, disappointed at his own tangent. Ex-wives and tech—could he have picked more cliché topics?

"It used to be scary, being hooked to machines. Like in the hospital, the feeding tubes, the breathing tubes, the shitting tubes. But at least it was temporary. There was hope to get off them. Now we've become the machines ourselves, and we don't even mind, we like it. It's even worse than that, actually, we haven't become machines, the machines have become us. I see some of you are filming this right now. Your machine is seeing me onstage right now and you aren't. Your machine will store something for you that you haven't even seen for yourself. The machine is more engaged than you are. I'm talking to you, and you're not even moving, you're just looking at your machine to make sure the image doesn't shake."

A handful of people had indeed been filming Manny's meltdown. Dorothy was trying to keep track of them, and Ashbee was, too, already wondering how much money he would have to offer to delete the videos, if it came to that.

"Fucking machines, all of you," Manny said. "Except my son, of course. My son is perfect. He even shits on his own now. He had a few surgeries. At four months old, at one year old, at two. He had a colostomy bag for a while. A colostomy bag, for those of you who don't know, is kind of like the ancestor of social media. We could see his shit in real time. But then they fixed him, he grew up, and I assume everything's in order down there for him. I can't really ask. That's the thing about children—they're born, you pull the shit out of them, you take them to the hospital in the middle of the night, they piss in your mouth, they tell you everything they know, and then at some point they decide nothing concerns you. For a few years, you pretend what they say is interesting even though it's not, and then one day, probably right when they start shaping their first original thought, they decide to keep it to themselves. Have you ever wondered about that, by the way? About the first thing your kid decides *not* to tell you? I suspect it's the first truly interesting thing that happens to them. And of course, they're idiots, so they forget about it themselves. The first thing they decide to lock up in their heads, they forget. It's lost for everyone and forever. How sad is that?"

It was sad enough that Manny started crying. Nothing, in that moment, had ever seemed sadder to him. He cried for a solid thirty seconds, and then got it together enough to wonder how to exit the stage. To say good night or to just leave without another word. He left without another word.

The people who'd been filming kept filming for a minute, in case Manny came back. One camera stayed trained on the door he'd disappeared through, but all it caught was Dorothy pushing it herself to meet Manny backstage.

Kruger and Ashbee looked at each other from across the room and shrugged. They would let Dorothy deal with it.

"Dude went full Jonathan Winters up there," Kruger heard Jo say. It pleased him to hear that name, that young comedians still knew it.

"Who's Jonathan Winters?" Sally asked.

"I think he was faking it," Phil said.

August explained to Sally that Jonathan Winters was a comedian who had once had a breakdown onstage, crying about how much he missed his wife and kids while on tour, showing the audience pictures of them.

"That's so sweet," Sally said.

Kruger was amazed at August's calm. The kid didn't seem upset that his bowel movements had been talked about in front of strangers for the last five minutes. If Kruger's own father had done that to him . . . well, at least Louis, for all his faults, would never do such a thing, Kruger thought. He wouldn't go onstage to begin with, but even if he did, even if someone forced him to tell a joke, his idea of one still started like this: "A man walks into a bar"—not "I walked into a bar," not "My son walked into a bar." Kruger checked his phone and saw that Veronica Tuft had responded to his message a little earlier, just past midnight. Maybe her baby was a bad sleeper, Kruger thought. He imagined her typing her reply while the child sucked on her tit. Veronica's message said she hadn't been at the Glass Eye the night Louis had fired his gun, but what she'd heard was that people there had been making fun of *Kruger*, not Kruger's mother. They'd been quoting and/or playing clips from an interview Kruger had given on Conan while promoting *The Widow's Comedy Club*, and having a laugh. "I don't think they knew your father was present at the bar," Veronica's message said. Kruger tried to remember what he'd said on Conan that was so stupid. He should've been relieved that it wasn't his mother who'd been made fun of by strangers at the Glass Eye, but really, he was annoyed it had been him. People always thought they'd give the perfect interview if they became famous, he knew, but he would've loved to see the man his father had shot give it a try. See what great lines he came up with. Veronica's message went on to say that the man in question had either quoted or played the part of the interview in which Kruger told Conan that Meryl Streep was like the mother he wished he'd had. That, apparently, had caused Louis to take his gun out, though it was hard to say for sure. "Maybe it was an accumulation of things," Veronica suggested. After seeing Kruger on the train, she'd watched the interview again. She was attaching a link to it, for Kruger's reference. She'd been surprised earlier on the Metra to hear him say that Louis had been defending his wife's honor (to her mind, this whole time, Louis had shot in defense of Kruger's), but maybe he was right. "Maybe he was defending your mother!" the message said. "It's a nice way to look at it!"

It wasn't a nice way to look at it, Kruger thought. His father had indeed defended his wife's honor. Kruger's mother had indeed been insulted. What was news to him was that he'd been the one doing the insulting. He didn't need to click on the link. He remembered giving the interview. He remembered thinking as he said the words "Meryl is the mother I wish I'd had" that it wasn't right, that he shouldn't have said it. Not because it would sadden his father, or make him angry (he didn't think Louis would ever know about the interview), but because Meryl might see it and be annoyed. He didn't even know what he'd meant by it.

"Should we go check on him?" Olivia said, regarding Manny.

"He was faking," Phil repeated. "I'm sure he's fine."

Kruger turned to August. August would know if his dad had been faking. All the kid said was it was late and he should go to bed.

"Big day tomorrow," he said.

"That trial?" Olivia asked. "I thought you weren't even going to court."

"I have to stay on top of it. In case they need me."

"You mean like an understudy," Olivia said. "You're hoping some-one fucks up and you can step in?"

August neither confirmed nor denied the assumption. He'd never been more interesting to Olivia.

"I don't get why this trial is such a big deal," Artie said. "Isn't it just another Ponzi scheme? Some rich guy fucked some people over?"

"It's the way he did it that is fascinating," August said. "Very ele-gant. There's a strong case to be made that it wasn't entirely illegal, either."

He really seemed unbothered that his anus had been talked about publicly, or that his father had left the stage in tears.

"I could tell you all about the financial details," he went on, "but I think they only interest me, and perhaps ten other people. What makes the trial juicy to everyone else is the family stuff. How a man can scam his own wife and children. His aging parents, too. The betrayal and all that."

"Didn't the daughter kill herself?" Kruger asked, closing Veronica's message on his screen, deciding never to look at it again.

"She jumped in front of a train, yes."

"Because of her father's scheme?" Artie said.

"Well, that's a question people have. Was the daughter's suicide connected to her father's activities, or was she unstable for other reasons."

"That's not what her father's on trial for, though."

"Correct. I'm just answering your question, Arthur, about what makes the case interesting to people. What makes it interesting to people is that they think there's another case behind it, a fucked-up family to scrutinize, something that's more real than just money moving between accounts, and that they're the only ones to see it."

Artie couldn't tell what was more condescending: August calling him Arthur, or August explaining to him (a performer, someone who was supposed to know) what stories people found compelling.

"No one calls me Arthur," he said, though that wasn't true. Mickey called him Arthur sometimes.

"Do *you* care about the daughter's suicide?" Sally asked August. "Why she did it?"

August said it wasn't his job to do so, no.

"I didn't ask what your job description was," Sally said. "I asked if *you* cared that the guy you're defending might've pushed his daughter to suicide."

"Leave him alone," Olivia said. "Not everyone has to be full of feelings all the time."

"Fuck you, Oli," Sally said.

It came out so naturally, so simply, no one but Olivia could've known it was a first: her twin saying those words to her. "Fuck you." Olivia heard those words every day from others—most of her acquaintances said them all the time—and in movies, and in shows.

She said them herself more often than she should have, too. If asked about it a minute ago, she might've defined herself as impervious to the words "Fuck you," "Fuck off," "Go fuck yourself," but now that they were coming from Sally, they stung, and Olivia was relieved to find out that they did, that it made a difference who said them, that Sally could hurt her by saying them. She didn't think Sally realized the power her words had had. Sally wasn't very quick to notice things. It had in fact always been the main difference between her and Olivia: Olivia noticing things just a touch ahead of Sally, a short but constant delay between them that was at the root of much of Olivia's aggravation and impatience with the world. In this moment, though, Olivia was grateful for what she'd privately dubbed Sally's extra beat. Had Sally understood that she'd surprised and unsettled her, she might've apologized for saying "Fuck you," she might've taken the words back, and Olivia didn't want her to. The surest way for Sally not to take back what she'd said was for Olivia to act as if she hadn't heard it.

"Let's go check on Manny," she repeated, and this time, they went.

Ashbee joined them on their way backstage.

"What if Manny's still crying?" Phil asked. "What's the plan?"

"I thought you thought he was faking," Olivia said. "Why would he be crying now?"

Ashbee said the plan was one of them should open the door an inch and see what the scene was like. If Manny was still crying: retreat quietly. If he wasn't: go in and pretend that what had happened onstage had never happened. What else could they do?

Artie volunteered to be their scout. When he peeked inside the room, Manny was bent over laughing. Dorothy was in the middle of a story, something about their youth, Artie gathered, the New York scene. Manny was laughing so hard Dorothy had to wait for him to recover before she could go on. When he started straightening up, Dorothy said, "Remember that guy Scooch?" and Manny started laughing again, even louder than before, even more bent. Artie's impulse was to shut the door and leave them alone, but Kruger, who'd heard the laughs, pushed it open and went in.

"What's so funny?" he asked.

He'd meant for it to be friendly, but it came out aggressive, like most of what he'd said to Manny so far.

"We were discussing your career," Manny said.

"Which part?"

"The overall arc," Manny said. "The absurdity of it."

Everyone in the room, students and teachers, wondered how seriously to take the passive-aggressive banter between them. Was it all in good fun? Or did Kruger and Manny really hate each other? If it kept rising, someone would have to address it. That was part of comedy: you didn't let a tension go unpoked too long. You put your foot in it, you made it worse if you had to, but you didn't save it for later. Who should do the addressing, though, was an equation still to be solved.

"We were just reminiscing," Dorothy said. "New York, the nineties."

"*I* remember Scooch," Ashbee said, but this time, Manny didn't laugh. His focus was still on Kruger.

"Did you already have that stick up your ass in the nineties?" he asked him, and Kruger said that he did.

"I was born with it," he explained.

"And you never considered taking it out? See what happens?"

Kruger, instead of firing back, paused to consider Manny's question.

"If I take it out," he said after a moment, "I say stupid shit."

"That's the whole concept of our profession," Manny said.

"Stupid shit like what?" Olivia asked.

"Stupid shit like Meryl Streep is the mother I wish I'd had," Kruger said.

"Jesus," Manny said.

"That's really stupid," Olivia said.

"I said that in an interview. My father's pretty sore about it."

"And your mother?"

"She died many years ago."

"Well, at least there's that," Manny said.

He was drinking water now, from a plastic bottle. The bottle looked small in his hand. Kruger wondered if he'd ever held a gun, who in the room ever had.

"How do you plan to make peace with your old man?"

It surprised Kruger that Manny would want to know. Maybe he was setting up a joke.

"I bought him a gun today," Kruger said. "He seemed happy about that."

"Your father was angry at you, and so you bought him a gun?"

Kruger hadn't thought of the act as stupid before Manny said this. Careless, yes. Selfish, perhaps (or perhaps generous?), overly dramatic, potentially disastrous, potentially rich (a source of material), but not plain *stupid*. That's why he usually kept the details of his life to himself, he thought. If he kept the details of his life to himself, he could arrange them into intricate structures and believe they made him complicated and interesting. Once you gave other people two or three elements to put together about you, though, their impulse was to distill and simplify, summarize into short, blunt sentences, a series of choices that you'd previously thought made your existence an impenetrable mystery.

"He's not even allowed to have one," Kruger said. "He shot a guy last summer."

The rationale behind admitting to this was Kruger thought Manny and the others would find it funny. But no one found it funny. Instant cold filled the room instead, as if an actual gun had been produced. Which brought Kruger to the decision of telling the whole story. The whole story would give perspective.

And so he told them about the Glass Eye, the family heirloom M1917 the police had confiscated, the girl reading Joan Didion on the Metra, the shooting lesson in the woods, Tony, his realization that he didn't personally know any Tonys, the words "negligent discharge," the emotional subtitles at the old folks' home, his father hurting his wrist trying to pry a newspaper out of his hands, his father pretending it didn't hurt. He'd never talked so much about himself. There were probably rules he was breaking, talking about himself so much in front of his students, but he wouldn't remain a teacher for long. He might not even finish the school year. Teaching had been his attempt to be closer to his father, both physically (moving all the way back to Chicago) and in spirit. But he didn't like it. He had nothing to teach anyone, and even his father knew it.

At some point in Kruger's story, the bartender came in to announce five minutes to last call. Beside him was the girl who'd given Phil Adderall, eager to share information of her own: the audience had spoken, and Second City had won the night's comedy battle. As per the rules, she reminded everyone, the losers now had to buy the winners a round. It was obvious she expected the stand-ups to express outrage, or at the very least disappointment, but no one paid her much attention. It wasn't clear what got them all to treat her news as irrelevant, but they simply nodded and turned back to Kruger after she spoke, to hear the rest of his story. It might've been a silent but collective decision not to give her the satisfaction, or it might've been that everyone in the room was in fact interested in what Kruger was saying. Either way, no one fought the girl on the night's results. Manny simply took out a credit card and told the bartender to put the round on his tab. The bartender asked how many drinks he was putting on the tab, how many people Manny was buying for, and Manny said it didn't matter, to put it all on his tab, everyone's next drink. "You mean, everyone in the bar?" the bartender asked, and the fact that Manny simply said "Yes," and nothing like a pro forma "No, I mean everyone in the next bar over, you idiot," was confirmation that he wanted the matter resolved quickly so that Kruger could go on.

Which Kruger did, once the bartender and Second City girl left the room. He told Manny and the others about buying the gun in the woods, about how his father had asked him to stay for soup, and about how the whole time he was there, he'd believed that Artie was dead.

"Sounds like you had the shittiest day of us all," Manny said after Kruger was done talking.

"I don't know," Kruger said. "Phil here had a seizure before stage time."

"Right."

"That was pretty bad," Olivia agreed, and then she turned to Phil. "You said some fucked-up shit while you were out, too."

"Wait, what? What did I say?"

"Pretty offensive stuff."

Dorothy, who'd always wanted to witness the moment a rumor was born, still nipped that one in the bud.

"You didn't say a thing," she told Phil.

The story of Kruger's day had moved her, and she wasn't ready to see focus shifted away from it just yet. It was the part about the old men watching emotionally subtitled TV that was sticking with her. She wasn't picturing it the way it had happened (men too lazy to figure out how to turn the captions off), but imagining the old men as lost instead, so removed from the world (like an untouched civilization, or an alien one) that they needed the descriptions to make sense of human feelings. She wanted to ask Kruger what show they'd been watching, but Kruger spoke first, still contradicting Manny's pronouncement that he, Kruger, had had the worst day of the group.

"You cried onstage," he said to Manny. "There might be videos of you crying circulating online as we speak. Artie had to shelter in place in the bathroom, thinking he might die. Dorothy was stuck even longer. With her *superior.* Most everyone in this room lost to an improv team at a school talent show. Your son just—"

"I see your point," Manny said. "It's not a contest."

"That's *not* my point," Kruger said. "Maybe it *is* a contest, I don't know. I don't make the rules. All I'm saying is, if it *is* a contest, I'm not winning it."

Dorothy wondered why it was so important to Kruger not to have had the worst day. Most comedians would've jumped on the title, worn it like a crown, falsely equating worst day with best story to tell, best potential bit. Kruger hadn't tried to make his account funny, though, Dorothy realized. She hadn't laughed once listening to it.

"Let's vote on whose day was shittiest," Jo offered, to settle the matter. "I personally think Ben's day wasn't so bad, because even though it sounds like he's kind of a disappointment to his father, first of all, who in this room isn't? And second of all, he knew this before going to visit him today."

"Thank you, Johanna," Kruger said.

"My son is not a disappointment," Manny said.

Jo ignored them both.

"As far as today goes," she said, "I think Phil wins worst day."

"Let me guess," Phil said, trying to disarm whatever comment Jo was preparing. "I had the worst day because I'm unfunny and it sucks to go through life being me?"

"No," Jo said. "You had the worst day because you didn't get to go onstage."

"I vote Ashbee," Dorothy said. "Tell them about your date, Ash."

Ashbee told them about his date, which got Dorothy to talk about Sword misinterpreting a friendly text she'd sent as a romantic proposition, which got others to inflate various aspects of the last eighteen hours in their lives in order to sound like bigger failures than the previous speakers. Manny mentioned his fear that crying onstage meant he had brain cancer.

"I don't think that's a symptom," Olivia said.

She wasn't liking the game very much, of making your day sound like the worst ever. She didn't want to talk about her day. She could tell that Artie didn't either.

"Where should we go next?" she said, hoping that a change of location would prompt a change of topic. "They're going to kick us out of here soon."

"There's a place open all night like six blocks away."

"Do they have milkshakes?"

"Why would we go anywhere else?" Marianne said.

"We have to monitor Phil for another hour," Olivia said.

"We don't *all* have to."

"I'm fine, guys," Phil said. "Really, I feel great."

"People always feel great just before they die," Olivia said.

Manny said that was reassuring. It meant he wasn't dying just yet.

"I enjoyed your bit, by the way," he added, to Olivia.

He said it needed sharpening, but the beats were all there, and the premise was killer.

"I agree," Artie said.

Olivia looked for a hint of sarcasm in his voice, of bitterness, but Artie was his usual earnest self—a little too encouraging, a little dull. She'd have to teach him, if they were to be friends their whole lives, to become harder to read.

Manny was starving, he said, and if they had to keep an eye on Phil all night, they had to go do that somewhere that had burgers. Everyone was in favor, even Marianne, now that it was Reinhardt suggesting it. Only August tried to excuse himself—early day tomorrow, he said, once again.

"I think you should come with us," Manny said to his son. "I think you should stay up all night."

He was serious—a father giving advice, not a drunkard encouraging his teetotaler friend to live a little. August noticed, of course. It had been years since his father had last pretended to give him advice.

"I'll call a cab," he said. "I need to sleep if I want to be any use at work."

He already had his phone out.

"You need to *sleep*?" Manny said. "Do you think your client is *sleeping* right now? The night before his trial opens?"

"How is that relevant?" August asked.

"What you need to do is feel what he feels," Manny said. "Go to work red eyed and unshaven tomorrow. Commit to the case. They'll respect you for that."

"I *am* committed," August said.

"Commit on a personal level," Manny said. "Show a little empathy for your client."

"Isn't the guy a real bastard, though?" Jo asked.

"That's not what being a lawyer is," August said to his father.

Would his dad never understand what he did for a living? Did it matter? August didn't think *he* understood what his father did for a living. He'd learned early on not to ask about it, that Manny hated explaining how jokes came to him, how he recognized a good one, and so on. He'd heard his father complain about journalists since he could remember, journalists and their stupid questions. He'd heard this so often, in fact, that he remembered his surprise at being told, in grammar school, that there was no such thing as a stupid question— he'd been convinced by then that all questions were stupid, that there was in fact nothing *but* stupid questions. With time, he'd understood that reality lay somewhere in between what school and Dad said, that life presented a mix of both good and stupid questions. Still, he'd never dared ask his father anything about his job, why it was that he kept on doing it if he was never satisfied, if it made him so sad, too, sometimes (for he remembered his father sad a lot, growing up, the crying a recent development, yes, but not such an unforeseeable one). He'd preferred to make his own assumptions back then. That's what all families did, wasn't it? Assume things about one another. You only asked questions to people you didn't know that well, or people you could cut out of your life if necessary. That was why his father never asked if August found him funny (August did). That was why August wouldn't ask his father about the crying onstage. He would let him say whatever he needed to say about it in the future, whatever he needed to tell himself—that it was nothing, that the crying was fake, that it was a revelation, the turning point of his career. It wasn't that August didn't want to know what his father thought, but that asking was too risky. Perhaps his students would dare. August hoped Manny wouldn't find their questions stupid.

"I guess I could eat a burger," August ended up telling Manny. Some battles were worth losing.

Kruger still hadn't eaten anything all day, but the hunger he'd felt at Sunset Hill had vanished entirely. He wanted to go home now. Sit with his bird, doze off in front of a movie, not think about his father sleeping with his new gun under his pillow. He wanted to go home, talk to his bird, tell him about his day, ask him what movie they should watch. He liked telling the bird about his days—the bird was a great listener. Kruger had assumed every one of the bird's days looked like the previous, but it struck him now, as he put his coat on, that the bird had to have bad days, too, that he'd perhaps just today had a horrible one. Maybe another bird had crashed against the window, maybe fire alarms had gone off in the building, maybe an insect in the corner of the kitchen had moved at exactly the wrong speed. Maybe the bird had had a stream of terrible days, actually, and no one to joke about it with afterward. The thought made Kruger want to stay out a little longer.

As he followed his students out of the room, he heard Dorothy, behind his back, ask Manny where his stuff was. Hadn't he come to Chicago with a backpack, a small suitcase? Manny said he hadn't. Manny had come to Chicago empty-handed.

20

ON THEIR WAY TO THE DINER, DOROTHY WANTED TO TALK ABOUT SNOW, tell everyone how her mother hadn't seen snow before the age of thirty-six, when she'd gone to Colorado for a friend's wedding. She'd found snow so beautiful she'd filled a glass bottle with it to bring home to her daughter. Dorothy remembered her mother coming home with the bottle, a green-tinted Coke one with a metal screw cap. "Didn't you know it would melt?" she'd asked. Her mother had known, of course. It had melted instantly. She'd just thought that putting it in the freezer would make it turn to snow again. Dorothy, who'd been ten years old then, had wondered whether her mother was mentally impaired. Still, part of her had hoped for the transformation to occur in the freezer. When she'd finally seen snow for herself, years later (her first winter in New York), she'd been excited and moved, yes, but unable to decide whether it was truly the first snow she was seeing, or if the water in the Coke bottle had counted for something.

Snow was falling lightly on them now, and Dorothy was about to tell this story to the group when Manny spoke first.

"What was it you wanted to tell me about Scooch?" he asked her.

"What?"

"Earlier, backstage. You asked if I remembered Scooch."

"Right," Dorothy said.

That guy Scooch, from their New York days. His last name had been so confusing (Skuzheskowski?) and he'd been so used to hearing people mispronounce it that he'd forgotten how to say it himself, where the stresses fell. Scooch was what everyone had agreed to call him after a while.

"I didn't really have anything to say about him," Dorothy said. "I'd completely forgotten about him, to be honest. But when I was back there with you, trying to cheer you up, I remembered him all at once. Out of nowhere. The whole person. Scooch. I don't know. Just the fact of his existence was funny to me."

"How could you forget about Scooch?" Manny asked. "You put him in a bit back then."

"I did?"

It had amazed her earlier to remember Scooch so vividly, after years spent not thinking about him. How extraordinary the human brain was! But now, what, there were whole bits she'd forgotten? That she'd written herself?

"Randy Scooch," Manny said. "That was a good bit."

"His name wasn't Randy," Dorothy said. "His name was Perry."

"I know. But in your bit, he was Randy."

She'd had entire conversations with Scooch, followed by thoughts about Scooch, sentences written with Scooch in mind. Why wasn't any of this readily available? The memories there for her to peruse? The bit kept almost appearing, in spots of color, a spotlight shining on it for split seconds at a time before plunging it back in darkness.

"Why would I have called him Randy if his name was Perry?"

"How the hell would I know *that*?" Manny said.

They made it to the place, and talked about other things. Mainly, while they waited for their food, they talked about Severin. Manny told everyone about his conversation with Severin at O'Hare's Hudson News, and they all felt bad for the guy. For years, a boy had waited for a letter from Eddie Murphy. Then he'd become a man and stopped waiting. Now that he'd just met Manny, he would start waiting again.

"Maybe we should write to him," Phil said.

"And pretend we're Eddie Murphy?"

"Of course not. Just write and say that, you know, we feel for him."

"What good would that do?"

Olivia asked if anyone at the table had ever written fan mail. Only Manny, Ashbee, and Dorothy had, though Kruger had thought about it.

"I guess it's a generational thing," Manny said. "I bet you guys have never even licked a stamp in your life."

Olivia recalled all the stamps she'd gone through in college to post her specs to Hollywood. She'd been sending fan mail then, in a way.

"Stamps are self-stick now," she said.

"Every day, in every way, the world gets better and better," Manny said.

The food arrived as he said it, and they laughed at how big it all was, the buns like Frisbees, the onion rings like handcuffs. Where did anyone find such big onions? America was so easy to make fun of, Marianne said, and everyone ignored her because it was true. Once they were done eating, it would look like they hadn't eaten anything at all. And perhaps that was the idea behind the big portions, to make people feel like they were just getting started, like there would always be more waiting for them.

"Maybe Phil's right, though," Manny said, not aware of how long it had been since Phil had heard someone say these words. "Maybe we should write this guy a letter."

He asked the kids if they had paper, or just their stupid phones. They needed paper for this. Only Marianne had paper. She handed everyone sheets. Dorothy asked a waiter for pens.

"This is my first assignment to you, as your teacher," Manny announced. "According to everything I've told you about Severin, write the man a letter that will make him happy."

"Happy?" Marianne said, like she'd never heard the word.

"We don't really know anything about him other than he works at Hudson News and his dad is dying," Dan said.

Olivia and Artie were already writing.

"Does it have to be funny?" Phil asked.

"You have an hour," Manny said.

They all focused on the task at hand, unperturbed by the ambient noise, the all-night crowd. At some point, the waiter who'd given them pens came to clear their near-full plates, but he didn't dare ask if they wanted anything else.

They wrote in silence for the prescribed hour. Manny, Kruger, Ashbee, and Dorothy wrote their own letters, too. Even August and Sally gave it a shot. Jo made herself laugh on several occasions. They all assumed there would be a communal reading of the letters at the end, that judgment would be passed on their quality, and that perhaps the best one would be sent to Severin. But they wouldn't send any letters. In fact, no note any of them had taken all day would result in anything of importance. Manny, once time was up, simply asked everyone to fold the letter they'd written and keep it for themselves.

"What are we supposed to learn from this?" Phil asked. "If we don't share our work?"

Dan said they were supposed to learn that 99 percent of what they wrote was garbage and no one cared.

"That is *not* the lesson I want you to take away from this," Manny said, but he didn't explain what the intended lesson had been.

Artie didn't much care what the intended lesson had been. He'd written to Severin as if they were friends, he'd asked about cobblers, what kind of cobbler he liked best, as if Severin would answer and Artie would write back, and so on and so forth, but finding out that it wouldn't happen like that was no great disappointment—it was just another nice thing he'd believed in for a moment.

"I think you should give us feedback on our letters," Phil told Manny.

Manny said that he might, at some point, that maybe he would keep it for class, that maybe his class would be called Letters to Severin.

"I think I'm going to confession after this," Artie announced. "Anyone want to join me?"

"I'll come with you," Olivia said.

"Wait, is 'confession' code for something?" Phil asked.

"It's just research," Artie said. "For my bit."

Jo asked if Artie was going to confess to a real thing or a fake thing, and Artie said he didn't know yet.

"I bet you've never done anything out of line in your life anyway," Jo said, and she was right, Artie thought. Why did he always feel like he had?

Jo told him he should record the confession on his phone so he could focus on being in the moment rather than worry about getting the wording right if the priest said anything funny.

"Are you allowed to record confession?" Artie asked.

"I don't think it's ethical," Marianne said. "Or even legal."

"I record pretty much everything people tell me," Jo said.

She said Andy Kaufman used to record people all the time, too.

"Are you recording us right now?"

"I don't record *you* guys. I meant real people. People who are real. Like my florist, or the person who waxes my legs."

"You buy flowers?" Olivia said.

"All the time."

"I've never seen you buy flowers. There are never any flowers in your apartment."

"Well, I don't buy them for *myself*," Jo said.

A rat the color of rust dashed out from under their table before anyone could ask Jo who she bought flowers for. How long had it been there? Had the rat been sleeping at their feet the whole time? If so, what had it seen, or heard, that suddenly made it want to run away? Some customers started screaming in the rat's wake, but Olivia felt compelled to follow it, to take its picture. She unlocked her phone to set up her camera, but was confused by the screen she saw, disoriented by all the numbers there, spinning in a straight line at different speeds, some faster than her eyes could make out, others more slowly, like worry beads, thumbed by an invisible hand. She remembered then what the stopwatch was recording—the seconds, the minutes, and now the hours since Phil's seizure. She watched the numbers add up for a second too long, registering a chunk of time no one in the world would ever get back. By the time she hit the stop button, the rat was gone.

ACKNOWLEDGMENTS

THANK YOU, JACKIE KO. I CAN'T CONVEY HERE HOW MUCH IT MEANS to me to have you in my corner.

Thank you, Caitlin McKenna, for believing in this novel.

Thank you, Luke Brown, for giving it a home in the U.K.

Thank you, Amy Schroeder and Evan Camfield—your careful edits made the book better.

Thank you, Adam Novy and Jesse Ball, for not asking questions.

Thank you, Chloé Acher, for letting me work at your place that winter.

Thank you, families Bordas, Cordoba, Freliez, Segura, and Levin.

And thank you, Adam, for everything.

CREDITS

THE SIDE-BY-SIDE IMAGES ON PAGE 55 OF ELÍAS GARCÍA MARTÍNEZ'S fresco *Ecce Homo* and its restoration by Cecilia Giménez are taken from Wikipedia.

All photographs of Brad Pitt on page 60 are stills from Joel and Ethan Coen's *Burn After Reading*.

The quote on page 96 is from the unpublished essay "Drinking Ranch and Getting Paid to Look at Others Drinking Ranch" and is used by permission of the author, Adam Novy.

The photograph on page 170 was taken by the author, Camille Bordas.

The photograph on page 214, *Park Trash Can in the Snow, Evergreen Park, Monroeville, PA*, is used by permission of the photographer, Roy Winkelman.

ABOUT THE AUTHOR

CAMILLE BORDAS is the author of three prizewinning novels. The most recent, *How to Behave in a Crowd,* was the first she wrote in English. The earlier two, *Partie Commune* and *Les Treize Desserts,* were written in her native French. Her fiction has appeared in *The New Yorker, Harper's Magazine,* and *The Paris Review.* Born in France, raised in Mexico City and Paris, she currently lives in Chicago.